"Elizabeth Musser steals our hearts ~~and car~~ries us to the edge of our soul, *The Pr~~omised Land~~* pilgrims whose lives intersect on the fa~~med~~ Camino, asking the important questions: When do we let go of our best-laid plans to discover a bigger and richer life? Who do we become when everything has been taken away? With a dash of mystery and tremendous depth, Musser fills the lush landscape of *The Promised Land* with vivid characters and masterful storytelling."

—Patti Callahan, *New York Times* bestselling author
of *Becoming Mrs. Lewis*

"Elizabeth Musser's novel *The Promised Land* transported me on two very memorable journeys. First, I savored the sights, smells, and tastes of France as I hiked the Camino with her unique characters. Second, was the touching journey of spiritual transformation these three pilgrims uncovered on their trek. So satisfying!"

—Lynn Austin, bestselling author of *If I Were You*

"*The Promised Land* is a captivating tale of pilgrimage not only along the rigorous way of the Camino but also through an equally rigorous exploration of the soul. Through the journeys of three broken and wounded pilgrims, Elizabeth Musser expertly navigates the complex landscape of captivity and loss, while pointing the way to redemption and hope."

—Sharon Garlough Brown, author of the SENSIBLE SHOES series

"What an intriguing journey Elizabeth Musser has taken us on in *The Promised Land*! She painted, with words, such evocative images, tastes, smells, and sounds that I felt as if I'd walked my own Camino pilgrimage along with Abbie, Bobby, and Caro. This engrossing, beautiful story kept me guessing through smiles and tears and did not disappoint in the end."

Deborah Raney, author of THE CHANDLER SISTERS series

Books by Elizabeth Musser

The Promised Land

When I Close My Eyes

The Swan House

The Dwelling Place

Searching for Eternity

The Sweetest Thing

Two Crosses

Two Testaments

Two Destinies

Words Unspoken

The Long Highway Home

NOVELLAS

Waiting for Peter

Love Beyond Limits from *Among the Fair Magnolias* novella collection

THE PROMISED LAND

ELIZABETH
MUSSER

BETHANYHOUSE
a division of Baker Publishing Group
Minneapolis, Minnesota

Published by Bethany House Publishers
11400 Hampshire Avenue South
Bloomington, Minnesota 55438
www.bethanyhouse.com

Bethany House Publishers is a division of
Baker Publishing Group, Grand Rapids, Michigan

Printed in the United States of America

Library of Congress Cataloging-in-Publication Data
Names: Musser, Elizabeth, author.
Title: The promised land / Elizabeth Musser.
Description: Minneapolis, Minnesota : Bethany House, [2020]
Identifiers: LCCN 2020029196 | ISBN 9780764234453 (trade paper) | ISBN
    9780764237850 (casebound) | ISBN 9781493428250 (ebook)
Subjects: GSAFD: Christian fiction.
Classification: LCC PS3563.U839 P76 2020 | DDC 813/.54—dc23
LC record available at https://lccn.loc.gov/2020029196

Scripture quotations from Psalm 121, 122, 126, 127, 131 are from the New American Standard Bible® (NASB), copyright © 1960, 1962, 1963, 1968, 1971, 1972, 1973, 1975, 1977, 1995 by The Lockman Foundation. Used by permission. www.Lockman.org

Scripture quotations from 1 John are taken from THE MESSAGE, copyright © 1993, 2002, 2018 by Eugene H. Peterson. Used by permission of NavPress. All rights reserved. Represented by Tyndale House Publishers, Inc.

Scripture quotations from Psalm 123, 124, 125, 129, 130; Luke 19; and 3 John are from THE HOLY BIBLE, NEW INTERNATIONAL VERSION®, NIV® Copyright © 1973, 1978, 1984, 2011 by Biblica, Inc.® Used by permission. All rights reserved worldwide.

Cover design by Susan Zucker

Author is represented by MacGregor Literary Agency

20 21 22 23 24 25 26   7 6 5 4 3 2 1

The Promised Land is dedicated
to three of my favorite females:

My beautiful daughter-in-law, Lacy Elizabeth Musser, you are the answer to every prayer I have prayed for my son since he was born. You are courageous and kind, hardworking and practical, godly and generous, as well as the best mother possible to my grandchildren.

Nadja'Lyn Alexandra Musser, my first granddaughter, you are the surprise that God delivered to our family in the most wonderful way. You bring joy, laughter, and love everywhere you go, Naj, and especially to your Mamie, who loves you so much.

Lena Sky Musser, my infant granddaughter, your birth in the middle of a pandemic and on the very day that my mother (your great-grandmother) graduated to heaven a few years earlier, gave us life after death, joy after grieving, spring after winter, hope in the midst of uncertainty. I already love you so much and can't wait to hold you in my arms.

CHAPTER

1

ABBIE

April 5, 2018

I have spent twenty years carefully stitching my family's life together, so when it suddenly starts to unravel I find myself in a tangled knot of anxiety.

My son Bobby is wolfing down a peanut butter and jelly sandwich in our kitchen. He says, "Mom, I have something to tell you."

Bobby is a good kid, so I don't think I'm going to hear about drugs or a pregnant girlfriend. But I don't expect this.

"I'm thinking of doing a gap year."

"A what?"

"You know, taking a year off between high school and college."

"To do what?"

"To see the world. Stephen talks about how great his gap year was, and it's made me think about it."

Stephen Lefort is Bobby's boss at the newspaper, where he's doing an internship in graphic design.

I'm speechless. I've always been accused of being a perfectionist, and I don't deny it. But is it perfectionism to want my son to do the next logical thing: go to college? After we've paid for his private high school education and he's gotten stellar marks on his SATs and has already been accepted to three outstanding schools?

A sharp piece of fear lodges itself in the back of my throat. To be honest, I have sensed Bobby leaving us little by little. Over the past year or two, his great big, generous, creative heart has meandered from school and sports and girls to something more ethereal.

Bill hasn't been concerned. Bill is never concerned.

"I thought I'd backpack around Europe, you know, seeing all the museums, like Swannee did. I'd like to spend some time in Paris hanging out with her artist friend, Jean-Paul." He's blushing under his bushy bangs. "Stuff like that."

I try to swallow down my fear. "I don't think going to Paris right now is the best idea, with secret hubs of terrorists all over Europe."

"But wouldn't it rock for me to do Europe the way Swannee did?"

Swannee is my mother, and she met Jean-Paul as a teenager, when Paris was under siege during the spring of 1968. She is an artist, and her sketches from that time are filled with riot police, burned-out cars, and chaos.

"That was a very confusing and messy time, Bobby."

"I know. How cool is it that Swannee was part of it?" His warm brown eyes are lit up like the Eiffel Tower at night. "And I could visit all those amazing museums like Great-grandmom Sheila did on *her* trip to Europe. I'll make it a family tradition!"

The jagged fear slips down my throat and into my stomach. "Bobby! Your great-grandmother died in a plane crash because of that trip!"

He talks over my outburst. "And I *have* to go to Vienna. You know it's always been my dream to see the paintings in the Kunsthistorisches Museum."

No, I do not know this. Although my mother probably does. It's the kind of thing he'd discuss with her.

"And I wouldn't just be soaking up art, Mom. Stephen says I can do some reporting for the *Press*. He knows people outside of Vienna I can stay with, and I can even help out missionaries who work with refugees at a ministry center there."

His beautiful, boyish face is alight with passion and enthusiasm. He's the spitting image of a younger Bill, thick, unruly reddish-brown hair falling in his eyes, which are the softest brown, light, gentle. He's tall like his father too, almost six foot one, and lanky, and the peach fuzz above his upper lip has recently turned to sandpaper scruff.

I look for a way to escape from the kitchen, but Bobby is standing in front of the only door. The words parade before me like howling ghosts: *riot police*, *insurrection*, *plane crash*, *refugees*. I paste a smile on my face and whisper, "Wow. It sounds like this is something you've been thinking about for a while."

When I tell Bill about our conversation that evening, he shrugs. "We have to let him go, Abbs. Bobby's an old soul. He won't get into trouble. Now, if it were Jason wanting to hop on a plane, I'd be concerned. But he'll have enough rules to break at boarding school to keep him busy. I fully expect him to be expelled before Christmas."

I do not find that remark humorous. Both boys are leaving us at the same time. And neither in the way I'd planned for them to leave. I close my eyes and see sixteen-year-old

Jason, all blue-eyed, blond-haired charm, saying, "It's got an awesome football team, Mom—you heard what the recruiter said. They need me." He'd winked and grinned, knowing full well that the dimple in his right cheek would melt my alarmed heart.

"Bobby will be fine," Bill says. "He's been taking care of all of us for a long time."

"Oh, Bill. That's the problem. He wants to take care of everyone he meets. He'll give all his money away to a homeless man or some struggling artist. He doesn't know how to make a train reservation or find a hotel. He's never had to—"

Bill holds up a hand to stop my diatribe. "That's exactly why we need to let him go, Abbs. He'll learn. Without us."

Three months later we're standing in the rotunda at the Atlanta History Center, all of the Middleton-Bartholomew clan, listening to Swannee.

"It was quite a feat to move this baby," she says.

"This baby" is the *Cyclorama*, a circular painting that is longer than a football field, weighs six tons, and is as tall as a four-story building. When we were kids, our folks would take my sisters and me down to Grant Park to the zoo and then into the old brick building that housed the *Cyclorama* for a hundred years. We'd walk around the circular room and stare at the painting of the Battle of Atlanta as Mama narrated history. "Eighteen sixty-four was a turning point in the Civil War. . . . The painting was originally intended for Northern audiences. . . . See the face of Clark Gable on that soldier?"

I was both fascinated and repulsed by the painted gore of bloody soldiers and dead horses.

Now the huge historic painting has been painstakingly moved to its new home in Buckhead. Both Mama and Daddy were consultants for this project—Mama because she is *the* Mary Swan Middleton, beloved native Atlanta artist, and Daddy because he's been a part of Atlanta's city planning for over four decades.

We're all here for this behind-the-scenes preview: Mama and Daddy; Nan, Ellie, and I; and our husbands and our children. Mama moves with grace, her white hair catching the light, as she describes the effort that went into the move.

Bobby is watching his grandmother with rapt adoration. As a child, he loved to go to her house and sit and watch her paint. He's followed her to a bunch of exhibits, carried her paintings, and helped her install them in homes around Buckhead. He breathes in the paint and turpentine and stories, and then he comes home to paint for himself.

Me, I can't paint anything but the walls of my house.

My father, sitting in his wheelchair to my right, speaks to me, and I turn to him. "Mighty fine to be here with you, Abbie. I remember going with you and your mom and your sisters to see it way back when."

It's the exact same comment he has already made twice in the past twenty minutes. I feel that same slice of fear, almost dread. For all intents and purposes Daddy is legally blind, but he insisted on coming with us to see the *Cyclorama*, and there's nothing Mama and my sisters and I wouldn't do for him. We are desperately trying to keep him healthy and fight off every demon, every type of disease or depression that could grab at him. But of course, we're failing.

Bill is standing on my other side, and I find his hand and hold it tight. Thank heavens he's steady amid all the change. My eyes dart from Daddy to Bobby to Jason, and I say in my head, *I can't lose all three of them at once, Lord. Not now. Not yet.*

We're lying in bed reading a week later, Bill and I, the gulf between us as wide as the Chattahoochee River that rushes through Atlanta, heading south. He closes his book. "I need a break, Abbie," he says.

"Yeah, I know," I concur. "It's been exhausting, but things'll slow down once we've moved into the loft."

"That's not what I mean."

A tingle runs down my spine. "What *do* you mean?"

"I've taken a consulting project in Chicago for three months."

Bill has always traveled a bit for work . . . but three months? Not a word comes out of my parched throat for several seconds, then I blurt, "But Bobby's leaving on Monday!"

Bill rolls over on his side so that he's facing me. "Yes, but it's not as though he's going to college and needs us to unpack his bags or fix up a dorm room. He's packing a backpack and flying to Europe! Jason leaves for boarding school on Tuesday. I'll be here to get the boys off and the house unpacked."

The expression in his eyes is cold, almost angry. "Why did you agree to this move if you aren't going to be around for three months?" I whisper.

He's lying on his back now, the gray in his hair picking up the light from his bedside lamp. He's wearing the ratty orange T-shirt that I've begged him to toss out for years. He finally conceded to making it part of his pajama wardrobe. The faded shirt has a rip in one sleeve where his tanned and toned shoulder shows through. He still smells like laughter and games, but his eyes are closed, and his mouth is turned down in a deep frown.

Finally he says, "I didn't agree, Abbie. You begged and begged and begged, and then you decided." His voice sounds hard, exasperated. And weary.

I'm trying to swallow, but all I get is a suffocating dryness.

We've lived in the Grant Park neighborhood of Atlanta for eighteen years. But this new place, a loft on Atlanta's trendy Beltline, well, it's airy with a view to take your breath away. And Daddy helped design it. Bill and I agreed it was a wise move. We agreed. . . .

"I just can't deal with your need to control everything anymore, Abbs. I just . . . need a break."

He rolls back over on his side, away from me, and I know that everything really is unraveling.

The boxes are ready to be loaded into the moving van, and I'm sitting in our big old empty house, sprawled on the tile floor beside Poncie, our spaniel mutt, who begs me with her eyes to explain what has just happened. "We're moving, gal. I've told you that before."

She's slithered from room to room for weeks now, her golden eyes sad and confused, as if I am betraying her right in front of her little wet nose. How dare I pack up every last item in the house?

Billy Joel plays from my iPhone. I take a long gulp of water and stroke Poncie's soft, fluffy coat. Billy's crooning about his dream. He just wants to be alone in his home with the person he loves.

I get a catch in my throat, and suddenly I'm weeping. Poncie snuggles closer to me, head in my lap, and I stroke and weep, stroke and weep as Billy sings the tale of my life.

I feel his longing.

It's my longing too.

If only.

How can everything be going so wrong?

I need a break, Abbie.

Every box is labeled with a number, and it's all gridded onto an Excel sheet so that the movers can lift the boxes out of the truck and take them to the exact room in the new place. I have it all planned perfectly, to the last detail.

Except . . .

I need a break.

BOBBY

Mom worries a lot. Like, all the time. So I feel a little guilty leaving her. Especially now, with everything up in the air. Mom hates to leave things "up in the air." To her credit, she didn't "fly off the handle"—another of her pet expressions—when I told her I wanted to take a gap year, but it was clear she didn't approve.

I've done okay in school—good grades and all—plus all the extracurricular junk required to make me a "good candidate" for an Ivy League. Mom again. I guess I checked all the right boxes because I got into one. But I don't want to go to an Ivy League. All I want is to paint, like my grandmom, Swannee. She's had an awesome career.

From the time I was little, she took me to places like the High Museum and the Atlanta Symphony, and that was okay with my mother because it was "culture." But when Swannee heard about my gap year and offered to pay for a four-month class with Jean-Paul, Mom did that lip-quiver thing that means she's desperately fighting the urge to say something she knows she'll regret. The thought of my not heading off to college in the fall is about killing her.

Fortunately Dad is okay with the gap year idea. He's a wealth management consultant, helping really rich people get even richer. I guess he's done a good job of it for us too, because we aren't exactly hurting for money. He even said he'd cover my gap-year expenses, right in front of Mom, and winked at me.

It was our friend Stephen who first put the gap year idea in my head. He grew up all over the world and said lots of kids in the UK and Europe take a year between high school and university to travel or work or gain new experiences.

Stephen and Tracie Lefort go to my church. He runs an online paper, *The Peachtree Press*, and for the last two summers I've done an internship there, mainly in photography and graphic design.

During the first weeks of my gap year I'll be staying near Vienna, where I can spend hours and days wandering around the Kunsthistorisches Museum. I'll also be helping at a refugee center called the Oasis. Stephen goes there pretty often and thinks I'd like it. And then before I take that art class in Paris with Swannee's artist friend, I'm thinking about walking the Camino—from Le Puy in southern France to the Spanish border. A sort of pilgrimage. That was Stephen's idea too.

When I tell him a few days before I leave that I'm seriously considering the pilgrimage, he says, "Caroline's supposed to be walking the Camino too, later this fall. I've asked her to take photos and write up some articles."

Caroline is Stephen's younger sister. She's a photographer and has worked for him off and on. Stephen's always worrying about her. He doesn't exactly say that, but he says things like "She's a free spirit" and "She's had a rough time. I'm trying to help her get her feet back on the ground."

"Does that mean you don't want me to send you photos and articles?" I ask.

"Of course not. You probably won't be doing the same route anyway. But could you check in with her in a week or so? Let her know which part you'll be walking, and the dates? It'd be great if I could do a series of articles about the Camino in the paper from when you start in August until the end of the season in October."

Stephen tends to throw out ideas on the spur of the moment, and I'm supposed to catch them and make them a reality. "Sure, boss. Give me her number and I'll text her."

"Thanks. You know she's a bit hard to pin down, but if y'all can keep each other apprised of your plans, that'd be great."

Dad and I don't say much on the way to the airport. We had *that* talk last night standing in the middle of this huge loft on the Beltline—our new home—about him taking on a three-month project in Chicago.

"Cool. Is Mom going with you?" I asked. He's had extended trips before, though never that long, and Mom has usually figured out a way to join him.

"No," Dad said, and his shoulders slumped a tiny bit. He brushed my hair off my forehead like he used to do when I was a little kid. "No, I'm going alone. I'm taking a bit of a breather for a few months."

"A breather?" I narrowed my eyes. "From marriage?"

When he nodded, I felt my stomach drop. "Are you . . . are you getting a divorce?"

"No, Bobby. No. I don't think so. I just need to get away for a while."

I understand, if I'm honest. Look at me, flying away. Far away from my dear but controlling mother.

17

"Do you . . ." I struggled to get the words out. "Do you have someone else?"

He drew me into an embrace. I thought he might be crying. Whether he was or not, he didn't answer my question.

In a way, I am furious with Dad for leaving right now. Jason and I are finally getting some freedom from Mom—but we love her. We don't want her to "go off the deep end"—yet another of her favorite expressions—if Dad leaves too. Plus, I still don't understand why they decided to sell our house so quickly. I like that house.

Poor Mom. It's not like she handles change well.

Before he hugs me good-bye at the international terminal, Dad says, "I think your mom needs a break from all of us, Bobby, whether she knows it or not. Keep her in your prayers, son. But you go discover Europe. It's not up to you to solve our problems."

Jason texts me while I'm standing in the security line, saying the same thing he's told me out loud a dozen times. *You're so lucky to be going far away.*

Your school isn't bad either.

I know. Then *What should we do? About Mom. She's going to go off the deep end.*

I smile.

No idea. I guess we just have to trust Dad.

I used to wander out onto Swannee's sun porch as a little boy and sit for hours watching her paint. She noticed my passion first, before my parents or teachers. She bought me my first sketch pads, my first colored pencils, and then the watercolors, little tabs of pastels that I rubbed my wet paintbrush against before brushing it on the white page. I thought it was pretty cool, watching the colors bleed into each other and making the white page look alive.

By the time I was eight or nine I graduated to acrylics and oils.

In high school I took AP art history. Mom was chagrined; Swannee, thrilled. She'd support my artistic endeavors to Hogwarts and back.

The first time I allowed myself to see that my grandmother was aging was about a year ago. I never told anyone, but that was the incident that made me seriously think about a gap year. I wanted to go to Europe while Swannee could still be my guide. Not physically, but mentally, spiritually, emotionally.

We had our canvases on the sun porch, painting a still life she had set up. We'd done this a dozen times throughout the years, but Swannee felt it important for me to go back to the basics and also see my improvement.

We didn't talk much; when we paint, we're both very intent on our work. But at one point she asked me a question, and I glanced over at her. While I answered, she sat with her paintbrush poised in her right hand. The brush shook, very subtly. It was moving because Swannee's hand was shaking.

It wasn't a big deal except for one thing. The still life she painted wasn't quite as brilliant and detailed as usual. It was as if I were watching Swannee age on the canvas. Her strokes not as swift and sure.

And it broke my heart.

I decided then and there I was going to Europe. Not that I thought she was dying or anything. But something deep within me urged me to go. So while Stephen gets the credit, or the blame, for planting the seed, deep down the gap year is for my grandmother—to find the inspiration she found and wrap it up in my imagination and bring it back for her to see and touch and feel.

A few weeks before my flight, Swannee and I were sitting out on her sun porch drinking extra sugary iced tea when her cell phone pinged with a message. "Oh! Would you look at this!" she said, obviously surprised. Then, "How nice. How lovely."

"What?"

"Oh, just that one of my paintings will be on display." And she let me read the email.

Dear Ms. Middleton, It is our pleasure to inform you that your painting, The Swan House, *has been purchased by the Cottet family and will be on permanent display in what critics call one of the loveliest small museums in Paris. . . .*

"On display *in Paris*! That's awesome, Swannee! You have to go see it!"

She tried to make light of the good news. "Oh, no, honey. It's not that big a deal."

But I could tell it was. To her. I think she would have actually considered making a trip to Paris if my grandfather's sight hadn't diminished even further.

"I've had such wonderful opportunities to travel and see the finest art. But I need to stay put now."

My grandparents are absolutely devoted to each other, which usually pleases me. But I hated for Swannee to miss this honor, one she'd dreamed of for so long. I understood. That longing of an artist to be recognized, not necessarily famous, but to know that what she'd devoted her life to, her vocation, somehow mattered to others as well.

So I wasn't surprised when she asked me, "Do you think you could try to visit the museum? I could get you a private viewing. But of course, only if you have time."

It amazed me how an artist as accomplished and appreciated as my grandmother could still lack self-confidence.

"I'd love to do that!" I said.

"Well, I'm sure Jean-Paul would be delighted to accompany

you and show you around," she said, then lowered her voice. "My last prayer for my art . . . I've always longed for at least one of my paintings to be hanging in a museum in Paris. So many of my adventures began there, and now they will continue to live on."

"I'm so glad it's *The Swan House*," I said, for this was her legacy, and she'd painted the Italian manor house in Atlanta many times. I scooted next to Swannee on her wicker couch. "Speaking of Jean-Paul and Paris, look at what I've uploaded to my phone."

I started swiping through photos I'd scanned from my grandmother's sketch pad—the sketch pad of her trip to Europe with her best friend, Rachel Abrams, in 1968. When I got to a sketch of a young teen sitting on a bench with Notre Dame in the background, I passed the phone to Swannee.

She held it close, chuckling, "There he is. Jean-Paul Dumontel."

For many years, Jean-Paul had come to Atlanta to visit my grandmom. I met him once when I was about nine or ten. At the time of this sketch he was a shy thirteen-year-old, traipsing around Paris with Swannee during the May '68 revolution. I think Swannee was just out of college, and she and Jean-Paul had bonded over their mutual love for art. In fact, they'd both dreamed of becoming artists.

And of course, they both *had* become artists and both quite successful. Jean-Paul had gifted one of his paintings to Swannee, and it now hung in my grandparents' home. He had always felt close to her—sending her marble from Italy and fabric from Provence and bottles of fine red wine from his favorite French vineyards—all because she'd practically saved his and his brother's lives during the riots of 1968.

Now I was going to follow in their footsteps—but those were two awfully big pairs of shoes to fill.

I set down the phone and asked, "Swannee, what if I go to Europe and take the art class and find out I'm no good?"

"Well, we know that's not true, Bobby. But if you aren't good *enough* or you lose interest, then you'll find another path. You'll go to school and try something else."

"And what if I go away and find my calling and never go to college? That would break Mom's heart. Dad would be annoyed too."

Swannee set down her Georgia Tech Yellow Jackets plastic tumbler and spoke slowly—she was never in a hurry these days. "We trust the Spirit to guide us. You must find your path and trust that our God is big enough and wise enough to get the people you love to listen."

My grandmother is a very spiritual person.

"I know one thing, Bobby. You must not be crushed under expectations. It will dry up your creativity. Take this chance, Bobby. Fly."

And so, I'm flying.

ABBIE

I watch him go, and a little bit of my heart flies out the window with him. It feels like a gradual death, like God is prying open my clenched fists and forcing me to wave good-bye without running after this boy-man.

But Bobby dreams in living color, and he paints his dreams on canvases with an understanding that seems precocious. And so my stomach lurches and I uncoil my fists, and I will myself not to cry as I watch him walk out the door. He turns and gives me a lopsided grin, then drops his bags and comes back to embrace me, as he did when he was a child.

I let the tears fall.

His father is taking him to the airport. Then what?

At least Bobby is starting his gap year in a place that seems safe. I try not to dwell on the term *refugee center*, but more on the fact that this is a place Stephen knows well, and I trust Stephen. He's helped us through one major family crisis already.

I scroll through my email on my phone until I get to a folder marked Travel. I stare absently at the list of emails confirming the flight I've booked, mine and Bill's, to France after the surprise party I'm planning for October. He's always wanted to go to La Rochelle, an idyllic spot on the west coast where one of his Huguenot ancestors finished his life at the end of the sixteenth century. For his fiftieth birthday, by golly, I am determined to make that dream come true.

I need a break, Abbs.

At least I hope I will still get to make that dream come true.

Two days after Bobby has literally flown the coop, one day after we've left Jason at football camp, I watch Bill pack his bags, the ones he just unpacked in the loft the week before, the ones I had packed at first for the move, every shirt pressed, every sock with its match. I feel the color drain from my face. He is resolute, determined, moving on autopilot.

"Can we talk?" It's the same question I've asked since he told me he was leaving.

He doesn't answer, just keeps packing.

Finally I step in front of him. "I want to talk about it, Bill. I need to. Please give me that."

He ignores me, almost. I do not know this person who has suddenly inhabited my laid-back, fun-loving husband. "We've talked for twenty years, Abbs. I have nothing left to say."

I feel myself shaking. I need something to do, something to arrange or pack or organize.

But he closes the suitcase, turns, and glances briefly out the floor-to-ceiling windows of the brick loft, located in an old steel mill refurbished to be stylish condominiums. The view is breathtaking, with the Atlanta skyline in the distance and Piedmont Park in the foreground, but he doesn't seem to notice any of it.

"Will you call me?"

He pauses, shoulders slumped. Then he turns, and with a weariness that sends a shudder through me says, "Just give me some space, Abbs. I need some space."

So they've all left, Bill and Bobby and Jason, and here I sit in this loft. I have plenty of "space."

I can walk to the Piedmont Driving Club, where I play tennis twice a week, and then meander next door to the Botanical Gardens, where I volunteer. Or I can take the Beltline path in the opposite direction and in just a few short minutes be at the trendy Ponce City Market.

Perfect location, perfect direction, with the sunlight seeping through the windows in the morning. The sunset off the back of the loft will be fiery red.

It is all perfect, just as I wanted it to be. Horribly, horribly perfect.

I force myself to go to my parents' house on Sunday for the big Bartholomew-Middleton monthly gathering.

"Hey, sis!" Ellie calls out. "How are you doing with the move?"

I press my lips into a tight smile. "Okay. A bit overwhelmed, but okay."

"Where's Bill?"

"He's still in Chicago."

"Bummer. He doesn't usually have to stay over the weekend."

"Some crazy emergency," I lie.

Ellie gets a twinkle in her eyes as she cradles baby number six, Abigail, named after me. "You sure you're not pregnant? You look pretty thin and worn out."

I'm tempted to tell her about that river running down the middle of our bed. Instead I chuckle and say, "I'm sure. Thank the Lord." An empty nester—sons *and* husband all gone at once—and pregnant at forty-four? No, thank you.

I take little Gail in my arms and coo down at her. She stares back, huge gray eyes in that tiny cream face. "She's so lovely," I choke out.

And she is. My eyes water, and I let the tears spill. Yes, for the joy of holding this tiny new human. And yes, for the absolute devastation I feel when I think of my life.

The next morning I'm sitting on the tiled floor in the middle of the den area, surrounded by neatly labeled boxes. I have yet to lift a lid on any of them. I pull myself up and walk zombie-like into every room, cursing those boxes, so perfectly packed, telling me exactly what I need to know. I could put this place together alone, simple.

But I have absolutely no desire.

Bill has been gone for five days. No calls, no texts, no emails. No jovial voice teasing me over the distance. No one saying, "Hey, Abbs of the perfect abs, wanna meet me at the club for a workout before dinner?" No laughter, big and boisterous, coming across the line or in the door.

At least Bobby has texted. Six words. *Doing awesome in Vienna. Vienna, Mom!*

Jason is settled in his dorm, his head, I presume, tucked into a helmet at football practice.

Alone. I feel abandoned.

I open just one box, the one marked *Cross-stitch Project*. I carefully lift out a canvas, eighteen inches by two feet. *William Edward Jowett* is stitched in white across the bottom against a background of royal blue. Above his name I've stitched a beautiful oak tree with fifty green-leafed limbs, and beside the limbs are tiny replicas of all the things my husband loves: cars and computers and sports and family. I've almost completed the project, just a month left of stitching when I've been working on it for two years. Another surprise for Bill's fiftieth birthday.

Bill loves history; he's traced his family back to the Huguenots in sixteenth-century France. The story of his ancestor who fled France and landed on the shores of Florida fascinates Bill. I'd planned to visit Fort Caroline next week to take photos of the Huguenot insignia on the fort and work it into the canvas.

But will Bill even be here for his birthday, three months from now?

A knock at the door. My heart races. Maybe it's Bill. He'll wrap me in his big strong arms and say, "Hey, Abbs. It's okay. I'm sorry."

But it's my sister.

Nan steps inside and takes in my surroundings. I can tell she's trying very hard to hide her shock at the boxes, the same boxes sitting in the same position as when she stopped by a week ago.

"Hey, need some help unpacking?"

I shrug.

"Ellie's right, you did look pretty awful yesterday. I know it's a rough time with both boys gone at once. And I'm sorry Bill had an extended leave. Horrible timing."

You said it, sis.

"You want a bottle of water?" I manage. "I have stocked the fridge."

"Sure."

I retrieve a LaCroix from the refrigerator. "It's been harder than I imagined. I tried to plan it all out, but you just never know."

Nan gives me a hug. "Abbie, you did it all perfectly. But even you need a break."

I need a break. Give me a break.

I can't stop the river of tears. I cover my face with my hands and swipe at them, to no avail. Finally I turn to a startled Nan and blurt out, "Bill's left me."

"What?"

"He told me just before we moved. Said he had a contract in Chicago for three months. He helped me get all our stuff moved in and get the boys off and then he left."

A dozen different expressions parade across Nan's face. First a tiny smile, like she thinks I'm joking, then a wrinkled brow because I'm obviously not. Then disbelief. Finally, she simply looks stunned. "Wow, Abbie. That's crazy. I don't even know what to say."

"Yeah, me either. But he knew what to say, all right. He said he needs a break from my control. I've driven him crazy, Nan. I've literally driven him crazy, and now he's gone."

We sit in silence for a while. No way Nan can protest that I'm not a control freak. I've driven my whole family a little cuckoo for a long, long time. And now I've driven my three favorite people away.

"What should I do?"

Before she can answer I say, "I've texted him twenty times. Nothing. No answer to my calls. I wrote and apologized for everything. Maybe I should fly to Chicago."

Nan reaches over and touches my hand. "Maybe you shouldn't do anything right now." She meets my eyes; hers, chocolate brown, filled with that absolute *knowing* of devastation. Oh yeah, Nan knows all about loss.

"Don't do anything except what he asked. Give him a break."

This causes a flood of more tears, and Nan pulls me close.

"The boys don't know," I volunteer eventually. "They think he's just on an extended project. I couldn't bear for them to know the truth."

CHAPTER

3

BOBBY

My first days in Vienna unroll before me like the video for a study-abroad program we saw in art history. Everything is awesome and beautiful. Really, really amazing. On my second day in Vienna, with three other young adults who are helping at the Oasis, I tour St. Stephen's Cathedral, the Vienna State Opera House, and the Hofburg Palace. That evening we take an audio tour of Schönbrunn Palace, exploring its ornate staterooms and guest apartments, and then attend a classical concert outside in the gardens, entranced by the music of Strauss and Mozart. And being part of *this*. Europe. Afterward we march arm in arm along the cobbled streets, drunk on the beauty and the history and the taste of freedom.

But when we get to the Kunsthistorisches Museum the next day, I beg to be left alone. For hours I wander from gallery to gallery. First I view an exhibit on loan from the Hermitage Museum in St. Petersburg, where paintings from that museum and the Kunsthistorisches are paired, works by Botticelli, Tintoretto,

Rembrandt, and van Dyck. Next I stand openmouthed in front of paintings I studied in art history.

I take out my phone and text Swannee everything she already knows. *I'm here in one of the largest museums in the world. It's awesome! I smile every time I walk into a new room and see paintings I studied, hanging there like a bunch of old friends.*

I snap photos of my favorites and send them to her, because I want my grandmom to see it all, to somehow be here beside me: Vermeer, Gainsborough, Rubens, Caravaggio, Raphael, Tintoretto, Rembrandt, Poussin . . .

I take a selfie in front of Caravaggio's *David with the Head of Goliath* and send that too. Swannee explained this painting to me years ago, telling me that Caravaggio did three paintings of the same theme.

"The one in Vienna shows David more triumphant. Do you see the difference from this one, which is at the Borghese in Rome?"

We were looking at the paintings in her coffee table book, *Italian Artists of the Baroque Period*. I flipped back and forth between the two pages.

"David looks proud in this one and sad in the other," I ventured.

"Exactly! In the Borghese one, Caravaggio painted his self-portrait in the head of Goliath."

"That's gross!" Both the idea and the depiction of the head, blood gushing from cut veins as the head hangs from David's outstretched arm, disgusted me.

"True. Art historians believe this is perhaps Caravaggio's plea for forgiveness from the Pope for his licentious ways."

Swannee often painted symbolism in her works, and she wanted me to see how the greats did it too.

While I'm still sitting on a bench, staring at this dark and gruesome painting and recalling our conversation, Swannee texts me back.

Oh, Bobby, dear child. How wonderful for you. And for me! Thank you.

I come back from the museum completely exhausted—an emotional and creative exhaustion, the kind that inspires and motivates and tears at the soul. I set my alarm to wake me in an hour, in time to get ready for a kids' program we're putting on at the Oasis. Then I fall asleep with the late July sun spilling across my cot, dreaming of light and shadow and truth.

The first time I see her, she is singing for a group of children who are packed inside the main room of the Oasis. She radiates warmth and conviction . . . and mystery. She's singing in a language I don't recognize at all—certainly not French or Spanish or German—her voice mellow and deep and soothing, and her dark eyes shining with a combination of innocence and wisdom.

The children are mesmerized, and so am I. I'm supposed to be pouring a jug of watered-down fruit juice into small plastic glasses, to be served with snacks after the singing and games, but I keep looking up so as not to miss a moment of the girl's singing—and consequently I spill juice all over the table.

After the service, I find her in a group of young people of different nationalities. They are talking in German, of which I know not a word, but Werner is with them, and he and I have been traipsing around Vienna together for two days. He motions to me and switches to English. "Hey, everyone, this is Bobby."

The five teens smile and nod, and a few murmur, "Welcome" with strong accents.

Mom says I have a terrible habit of saying the first thing that comes to mind, which is what I do immediately when I find myself standing beside the mysterious girl.

"Do you believe in fate?"

She smiles a little, a question creasing her brow. "I believe in *faith*," she says slowly, in an English that sounds exotic to me.

"Yeah, I know that. But fate, like you were supposed to meet someone. Like it was just in the stars."

"In the stars?" She looks confused.

"Meant to be," I explain.

She smiles at me, parting her lips just slightly. "If you'd lived the life I have, I think you wouldn't call it fate. You would call it providence." Then she makes a sound like water just beginning to boil, soft and full and promising heat. Her laugh.

"Where are you from?" I ask.

"Many places."

"Do you always speak in riddles?"

"I always tell the truth."

"What's your name?" I try again. "I'm Bobby," I add quickly.

"Rasa," she whispers, and it sounds like the wind through the chimes in my grandmother's garden. "Are you a new volunteer? That is why you came, right? To help." She nods toward the children sitting at tables, drinking the watered-down juice and munching on cookies.

"Yes. Yes, of course. To both questions."

Tiny lines crinkle beside her dark eyes, and her whole face begins to smile. "Great. It's nice to meet you, Bobby."

"Will you be here next week for the kids' club?" I ask her after the children have left.

"No, I'm going home on Thursday."

My stomach drops. "Home?"

"Yes, back to Linz. It's several hours' drive from Vienna. My father works in the church there. The Iranian church," she emphasizes—proudly, I think. "I help lead worship." She is wiping off the tables, collecting the crayons. "But perhaps you could come to Linz someday and help at the House of Hope."

"House of Hope?"

"It is like this. Another place for refugees to come, to play games and learn of Isa. And feel at home."

Who's Isa? I wonder. "Well, maybe." After all, my schedule is wonderfully flexible.

"Maybe, then." She nods. "Maybe I will see you again, Bobby."

She tosses her mane of thick black hair over her shoulder, glances back at me, and is gone.

ABBIE

I make the decision hastily. *"Sometimes you must throw caution to the wind,"* Daddy used to say to his girls. Especially to me, the careful planner.

Poncie sits beside me in the Mercedes. I have brought one small suitcase and my cross-stitch box and my wounded heart. I am going south, to Fort Caroline in Florida, to stand where Bill's ancestor landed. Bill will see my love for him when I stitch it into the canvas. Of course, I don't have to go there to find the emblem; everything is available on the Internet. But I am going there to feel what Bill felt.

I don't tell anyone, but I plan to be away three days. Three days to figure out how to get my husband back.

Perspiring in the humid July heat, I sit on a bench by the St. Johns River in Florida. The stone monument nearby commemorates the first landing of French Protestants on American soil.

I am surrounded by the tangled limbs of the river oaks with Spanish moss hanging like so many old men's beards, scruffy and strangely beautiful. I exhale. I am here, in the place that inspired Bill to first open his heart to me so many years ago.

A fishing boat sails slowly in the distance, tracing a path in the turquoise water. Across the way are a few homes, pastel, with a view of the water. But I wonder what was there in 1562 when the brave navigator Jean Ribault planted his stone column in the soil of what he called La Florida. Not *planted*, I correct myself. Erected. Did the thick breeze twist the moss in eerie shadows, warning of impending doom? Did the sulfur smell intoxicate or repel?

I walk to the plaque marked *New France* and read about Ribault and René de Laudonnière, his second-in-command. Laudonnière was Bill's ancestor, and the reason I am here.

Ribault named the waters the River of May because his ship entered its mouth on May 1. There the men landed and gave thanks to God for a safe voyage—the first people seeking religious freedom to come to what is now the United States.

I make my way to the fort a half mile away. Not the real fort, but a replica built in the 1950s to simulate what these brave settlers built. A tiny triangle of land for three hundred Huguenots.

Above the thick wooden doors is the French royal coat of arms, the same one that adorns the pillar by the St. Johns. This one is royal blue and embedded with three fleurs-de-lis, the emblem I want to stitch on Bill's canvas beside the one I'm stitching of the Huguenot cross. But the scene this fort depicts is cruel. A massacre. The Spanish leader Menendez slaughtered the Huguenots, who huddled inside begging for mercy. Or did they beg? Perhaps they died bravely, quietly. They had fled the horrors of persecution in France only to be massacred in this new land.

The day is perfect, the sky a cobalt blue, the sun fierce, the wind balmy, the sound of the wide river in the background. Why am I here, really? At first it was all about research for Bill's birthday present. But now I am looking for something more—I am desperate to figure out how to get him back.

In the center of the fort is a plaque listing the names of those who came. I suck in air when I read *René de Laudonnière*. Bill made the trek here during graduate school as a sort of pilgrimage, to pay respects to these people who refused to recant despite knowing their refusal meant certain death. He said he wanted to find the *why* behind the faith of these Huguenots that had seeped into his blood, his heritage.

I was in my junior year at the university, and he was completing his MBA, and we'd been dating for six months. The day after he returned from his trip we'd arranged to meet at a park near campus. Bill came directly from a five-mile run, wearing a gray T-shirt and dark blue gym shorts, his thick reddish-brown hair dripping perspiration. Back then, I didn't care what he smelled like or what he wore; I just wanted to be with him. And we'd been apart for a whole week.

"So, tell me about Fort Caroline."

"My dad always reminded us that 'God has no grandchildren,'" he began. "But being there at Fort Caroline, I could almost feel my ancestors' determination and faith. I felt proud of them. And thankful to be a descendant who shares the faith they lived and died for."

He took my breath away with that statement. I felt I was peeking into something deeper in his soul than he had shared with me up to that point.

"My ancestor wasn't slaughtered," he told me as we sat on a blanket and munched on grapes and drank Coke. "He was one of the few to survive. Three hundred massacred in the cruelest of ways, and he survived." Bill's face went ashen, and he had a hard time saying the next words. "He survived the Fort Caroline Massacre and then, almost ten years later, he survived the St. Bartholomew's Day Massacre in France, and he ended up in La Rochelle fifty years before the siege."

I drive to what's called the Huguenot Beach, several miles past the fort, and stare at the wide, flat, sandy surface stretched out before and behind me. I see the vestiges of Hurricane Irma all around. The cement walkway is broken and uprooted and tumbling toward the water, the majestic palms and Spanish oaks uprooted. Beat down, like poor Ribault's ships.

Four hundred and fifty years after Fort Caroline, nature is still wreaking havoc here. Perhaps we predict its force and timing more accurately, but no one can stop the impending storm. No one but God.

I return to the entrance to the beach and read the words on the green wrought iron plaque.

The First Protestant prayer on American soil, offered by Jean Ribault; the first settlement of men and women seeking religious freedom; the first Colonial Thanksgiving, celebrated June 30, 1564; the first known commerce; the first artist of North America, Jacques le Moyne, who documented native Timucuan life; the first recorded birth of a European child in the Continental United States; the first international port of trade. And, with the Spanish attack on the colonists, the first battle between European forces on soil that later became the United States.

And as I'm reading, I think of my own list of firsts: the first time we met, the first time we kissed, the first time I realized I didn't ever want to live without him, the first time Bill said he loved me, the first time we stayed up all night long, the first time we cried together, the first time we made love . . .

Bill's ancestors bent down and worshiped on this shore.

I kneel down and pray, "Help me get him back, Lord. Please."

CHAPTER
4

BOBBY

I've worked beside Rasa for three days, three pretty sweet days. I have to see her one more time before she leaves for Linz. At seven forty-five I wait for her outside the guesthouse in the town of Baden, where she's staying with the other volunteers. She looks surprised at first, then smiles.

"Could we take a walk in the park here? Just for a few minutes?"

We climb the stone steps past urns filled with fancy displays of flowers, like the ones Mom fixes at her garden club and posts on Instagram.

"I like the name Bobby," she says as we wind around the little paths in the park. The sun is peeking through the trees, drying the dew on the grass. "Did I tell you about the other Bobbie in my life?"

My face falls. "No." I feel deeply disappointed.

"She taught me so many things of faith. She lived brightly. She was contagious."

"Oh." I am relieved, but I can't think of anything else to say.

"She died a few years ago. Cancer."

Rasa's eyes are black pools, inviting me to swim into her story. "I miss her every day."

"I'm sorry." We walk to a little overlook that gives a view of the vineyards below.

Rasa moves like a ballerina or a princess. She's so graceful. "Yes, grief is so odd. It catches me at times when I expect the least of it."

Her minor faults in English make me smile to myself. "How did you meet Bobbie?" I venture, because she seems to want to continue the conversation.

"I was just a little girl. My father was a professor in Iran, loved by his students. But he had to flee." She turns her face downward. "Because of me. Because of a New Testament."

"Were you Muslims? And not allowed to have Bibles?"

"Exactly. My Christian Armenian neighbor gave it to me. The secret police questioned my father. They would have murdered him. So he fled, and my mother and grandmother and I hid. My little brother, Omid, was born while we were in hiding." She gets tears in her eyes. "It was such a hard journey, but of course Isa was with us. Always Isa with us."

"Who is Isa?"

She jerks her head up, shocked. "You don't know Isa?"

I shake my head a bit warily. "Nooo, I don't think I've met him. Or is Isa a woman?"

She laughs, and it sounds like soft music. "Oh, I am sorry! I forget. You call Him Jesus."

"Jesus!" I let out a breath and dissolve into laughter too. "Oh, yes. I do know Jesus." I blush. "I mean, I know about Jesus."

"And Jesus sent us Bobbie. My other Bobbie." Her eyes are dancing now as she looks at me and touches my hand.

I feel something like an electric shock and try to recover, stumbling over my words. "Was she, what was she like?"

"Wonderful! And brave. She's the one who rescued us— she came to Iran with a truck filled with chickens and hid us underneath them." Her eyes crinkle with the memory, and she holds her nose. "A terrible smell!"

I laugh, and then suddenly realize that this sounds familiar. "I think I've heard this story. From Stephen. Could that be?"

"Yes, yes, of course! Stephen was part of the rescue too. Bobbie was Tracie's aunt."

"Did I tell you that I work for Stephen?"

"Three times now," she teases.

We've wound our way out of the park and are standing on a cobbled street. She glances at her phone. "I should be getting back. My train leaves in a little over an hour."

"Could I get you something to drink? Coffee or tea? Just for a few minutes."

Rasa furrows her brow and then nods acquiescence. We take a seat at the sidewalk café, where she orders mint tea and I get an espresso. The August sun is rising, chasing shadows across the cobblestones, and I lean back in the chair.

"Bobbie rescued us, and we were reunited with Baba—my father—in Vienna. And Bobbie and Amir took such good care of us."

I had met Amir at the Oasis a few nights earlier. "I remember now that Bobbie passed away. A few years ago."

"Yes. She was only forty-five. But she faced her cancer bravely, and she had those sweet years with Amir."

"Stephen and Tracie were heartbroken when she died."

"Yes. We all were." Rasa's face is drawn, but then I see the trace of a smile. "But she got her wish. She got to meet Stephen and Tracie's children. Barbara Hope, her namesake, was born only two months before Bobbie graduated to her heavenly home."

Rasa is telling this story as if it were found in the Bible. "Tracie flew over from Atlanta with the baby so that Bobbie could meet her."

"And Amir has stayed here?"

"He travels the world sharing about Isa." Rasa breathes in and closes her eyes, and her black lashes fall thick against her olive skin. "I would marry Amir if he were only twenty years younger."

I feel the heat creeping across my cheeks. After an awkward silence, on my part anyway, I say, "Have you heard of the Camino? I'm thinking of walking it."

"Yes, of course. It's a pilgrimage in Spain and France." She takes a sip of tea. "Muslims make pilgrimages too. To Mecca. When I was quite young I dreamed of going there. But then Isa found me, and He and I began our pilgrimage together. It is much better." Her face darkens. "But it began as a very hard pilgrimage of escape. Along the Refugee Highway. Have you heard of it?"

I nod. "A little. From Stephen and Tracie."

"But the Camino, it is a spiritual pilgrimage. Not like a refugee walking to freedom." Her black eyes are intense, a whole world of life hiding within them. "I think it is a good thing for you to do, Bobby."

"Why don't you come?" I say, too enthusiastically, leaning across the table.

She sits back, eyeing me with amusement. "Just like that? You meet me and ask to take me to an adventure with you? Alone?"

"We wouldn't be alone; there are hundreds of pilgrims walking the Camino in August. We'd stay in hostels and *auberges* with others."

"You are a very strange boy, Bobby. You go too forward. My parents would not approve of me taking a pilgrimage alone with an American boy, even if there were hundreds of other pilgrims around."

I know she's right, but I'm not one to give up that easily. I haven't felt like this in so long.

ABBIE

I stretch out on the chaise lounge on the porch, Poncie at my side, and stare at a lone palm tree and the pristine beach beyond. While doing my Huguenot research I'm staying at the condo of Mama's friend Rachel in Ponte Vedra.

"You aren't one to drop everything and drive south," Rachel had said when I'd called a few days earlier, desperate to do something but trying to mask my rising panic.

"I'll explain later," I answered, and that sealed it.

The Atlantic's waves rush and crash on the sand. I give Poncie's tummy a scratch and look down at my phone, where a ping has alerted me to a message.

Bobby's text makes me smile. *A week in wonderland and not a terrorist in sight, Mom!*

Very funny.

I know the texts he sends to Mama are longer and detailed, but I'm not jealous. I'm thankful they relate so well. But still, when she calls a little while later to talk, I get an empty feeling in my stomach.

"He is experiencing everything as it should be," she says. I hear relief in her voice. "None of the bedlam Rachel and I walked into."

"And no terrorists either."

"What?"

I read Mama Bobby's most recent text and she laughs. "Love it! Oh, Abbie, I know this is hard for you, dear, but I hope you can let him enjoy it. You made a sacrifice, letting him go. He'll always be grateful."

Hard. Yep. I swallow back a knot of regret. I haven't told Mama yet about Bill leaving.

Bobby, Jason, Bill. I miss them all, and the missing is a physical ache. I don't want the boys to need me, not really. And yet . . . maybe I wish they did, just a little? And Bill? For twenty years, he's needed me to care for him. Or so I thought. And suddenly my days are completely empty of responsibility to my family.

I take out the cross-stitch pattern and continue to graph the Huguenot cross onto it. Then I will finish graphing the French royal coat of arms and choose the colored threads. And once I get back home—my new home, which feels nothing like home—with nothing else to do, I'll put on an old DVD of family videos and stitch and watch, stitch and watch.

"Hey, Mom!"

I smile at the sound of Bobby's voice. Has it dropped another octave in the ten days he's been gone?

"Hey, sweetie."

He jabbers on about his time in Vienna. Then he stops abruptly and asks, "How are you?"

"Doing good," I lie. "I'm down at Rachel's place in Ponte Vedra."

"Oh, that's cool."

"Yes. I went to visit Fort Caroline and the Huguenot Beach—you know, all those places your dad is always talking about. It's inspiring me to put the finishing touches on the cross-stitch."

The boys know all about my gift—they've watched me stitch it for months.

"I'm glad you're getting away, Mom. It's not good for you to be in the new place alone."

"Well, I'm heading back to the loft tomorrow. I want to be home when your dad gets back."

"Mom." He sounds exasperated.

"What?"

"I know he's away for three months. I know he's taking a break."

Silence. Then, "Dad told you?"

"Jason knows too. He told both of us."

"And you don't care?"

"Mom, we weren't surprised. Dad's been leaving for a while now. He's stopped being corny, stopped joking. He said he just needed a break."

There's that word again. "You don't care that your parents might be getting a divorce?"

"Of course I care. That's why I'm calling. To see how you're doing."

I'm still processing the fact that Bill told both of our sons about our separation.

"Mom? You still there?"

"Yes. Yes, I'm here. Don't worry about me, Bobby."

"Well, I don't want you to freak out or anything. Please don't stay cooped up alone. Enjoy the Beltline, play tennis, do your flower stuff. You know, walk in God's garden."

"What?"

"That's what Rasa says. She says every day is a chance to walk in God's garden. Everyone's patch of the world is just a part of His great big garden."

"And who is Rasa again?" I recall the name from an earlier text.

"She's this awesome girl I met at the Oasis. I've invited her to walk the Camino with me."

"You what?"

"You know. The Way. The pilgrimage in France and Spain."

"I know what the Camino is, Bobby. That isn't what I was asking."

"Well, I invited Rasa to come along. We're going to begin the pilgrimage in this town in France called Le Puy-en-Velay. It's one of the main starting points."

I feel my pulse accelerate. "You're planning to walk the Camino with a girl you just met in Austria? Just the two of you?" Bobby's voice may have dropped, but mine has suddenly risen to a squeaky pitch.

"Mom, it's no big deal. We'll stay in hostels along the way. Dorm rooms with a bunch of other pilgrims. All together. An adventure."

I'm still trying to place Rasa. "So you met this girl at the refugee center where you've been helping out?"

"Yes. You know, the one Stephen talks about. Where he and Tracie met . . ."

Yes, I know this. "So is this Rasa girl"—the name sounds strange, foreign, but not Austrian—"is she a . . ." I clear my throat. "Is she a *refugee*?"

He laughs. "No. She was just volunteering there. She lives in Linz, and she just finished high school too."

I let out a sigh of relief.

"She *was* a refugee, though!" This he says as if it's a great bonus. "From Iran. When she was a little girl—"

I've heard enough. Bobby is going to walk the Camino with an Iranian refugee?

"And when exactly are you planning to take this hike?"

"Oh, in a week or two. We haven't nailed down any dates yet."

"I don't approve, Bobby."

"Mo-om." He gives his best two-syllabled grunt. "Please just chill."

When I say good-bye thirty seconds later, I'm chilled all right. Right down to the bone.

I try to piece together this conversation with my son. He sounds so happy. But he knew about Bill leaving? Bill told the boys, and they aren't totally broken up about it? Certainly, Jason has not let on that he has one iota of worry about anything other than if he'll make the first-string football team.

Dad's been leaving for a while, Mom.

When did my on-the-brink-of-becoming-a-young-adult son suddenly get so good at reading between the lines? He's not worried, I tell myself, because he knows Bill is just taking a break. *Breathe, Abbie.*

Then I think no, maybe Bobby isn't worried because he doesn't want to be worried. He's living his dream, traipsing around Europe, seeing museums and artists and refugees.

Especially refugees.

Bobby, with his bleeding heart for desperate people and his lack of discernment.

Another name floats into my memory. Anna.

I feel like throwing up. Instead I grab my laptop, and there on the floor of the condominium, with Poncie snuggled beside me, I start Googling the Camino and looking for flights to get to a place called Le Puy-en-Velay.

I'll fly to France and walk the Camino with Bobby. I never imagined I'd have the time to go to France before Bill's fiftieth birthday. Now I guess I have all the time in the world, if I step back from tennis for the month. And ask Sarah to replace me at the Garden Club. And a thousand other details that suddenly don't seem to matter. Not with my husband gone and my son running off with an Iranian refugee.

BOBBY

In truth, Dad's leaving worries me a lot. I don't blame him. Living up to my mother's expectations is impossible. But I do feel bad that all three of us escaped at once. He messages me on WhatsApp every day to check on me. But yesterday, when I asked if he'd talked to Mom yet, he made it very clear that that was between the two of them.

Whatever.

About an hour after I tell Mom about my Camino plans, she texts me all the flight information. She'll be here in two weeks.

Me and my big mouth. I shouldn't have mentioned anything about Rasa.

I don't want my mom sitting home alone, but that doesn't mean I want her coming over as my personal chaperone!

I spend about fifteen minutes screaming internally, *Stop trying to control me!* She just has this way of wriggling into every aspect of my life. But I know better than to call her and say that out loud. I don't want to complain to Dad, either. That would make everything worse.

Once I accept that there's no getting rid of her now, I decide on another angle. In all probability, Rasa's parents wouldn't let her go off with some American kid she just met anyway. Maybe Mom coming along can work to my advantage.

Meanwhile I dutifully text Caroline, as I promised Stephen I would. *Hey! I'm heading out on the Camino in two weeks. Stephen said you'll be doing it later in the fall. We need to discuss a few ideas for photos and blog posts. Your brother's suggestion, of course.*

Caroline texts me back short and sweet. *Sounds good.*

ABBIE

I am once again sitting on the open porch at the condominium in Ponte Vedra. The ocean air feels heavy, but the sun is perfect for my task: designing the French royal coat of arms for Bill's cross-stitch. I created the elaborate pattern for the complete cross-stitch on my computer, using my new cross-stitch app, but for this one emblem I decide to create the design by hand. A pamphlet I picked up at the welcome center featured a small coat of arms, and I trace it onto the graph and begin the mind-numbing task of filling in each square with a tiny cross. Or half a cross, if I won't be stitching in the whole square.

Crosses, crosses, crosses. Half a cross. I wish my mind would stay quiet, but instead, a Bible verse pounds in my ears. *Take up your cross and follow me. Take up your cross, take up your cross . . .*

I set down my pencil in exasperation and say out loud, "There are too many! I can't take them all up. And anyway, what am I supposed to do with the half crosses? Am I supposed to take up the half crosses too?"

Long ago, Bible verses would float into my mind to comfort me, reminding me of a God who loved and cherished me. Now when I hear them, it seems there's a harsh, accusatory tone behind the words.

I work for several hours, until the sun is lower. I set aside the project and whistle to Poncie, who trots over eagerly. "Want to take a walk, girl?" I ask, knowing the dizzying effect those words will have on her. She gives a high-pitched yap and does a four-footed dance around my legs.

I wish God's words would have the same effect on me.

When I get back to Atlanta, I go to Rachel's penthouse on Peachtree to return the condominium keys. She opens the door and motions me in.

Rachel likes order and is no-nonsense. She's been divorced a long time and lived for years in New York, and she has a tough, practical take on life.

"You're looking fit, Abbie!" she says. "And your highlights look great. You're a bit thin, though."

I can tell she's searching for a nice way to say emaciated.

I shrug and settle into a fauteuil in her spacious living room. "This place is gorgeous."

"Thanks. I'm pleased with it. It has a New Yorkish feel to it, don't you think?"

"I imagine so."

She offers me a LaCroix, raspberry flavored. "So how were Ponte Vedra and Fort Caroline? You promised to explain your hasty departure."

I try to say something nonchalant, but I can't deceive Rachel, so I just spit it out. "Bill left me . . . moved out just when we moved into the loft. He's in Chicago."

She rolls her eyes. "Men. They're all the same." She doesn't seem a bit surprised. But my eyes well with tears, so she adds, "I'm sorry. That explains your need to get away from everything for a few days."

I nod and try to speak past the huge knot in my throat. Finally I blurt out, "So I'm going to walk the Camino with Bobby."

This time Rachel does look surprised, but she quickly recovers and says, "Oh, that's perfect, Abbie. Yes. Do it!"

"It's not really my thing. Blisters and heat and common bedrooms and bathrooms and odd food."

"It'll do you good. Swannee walked the French Camino when she was almost sixty."

"I know, but Mama *wanted* to walk it. I would not willingly choose to go through that discomfort." I am not here to tell Rachel my woes. I just want to give her the keys and escape.

Rachel chuckles. "Well, it's true you can't get manicures along the way or have your hair done. But it's supposed to be very . . . enlightening. It sounds like you could use a bit of enlightenment right now."

I stand up, intending to leave, but instead I hear myself asking, "What did you do when Harold asked for a divorce?"

She doesn't miss a beat. "Ha, I rejoiced! On the night after I signed the papers, I went out and got sloppy drunk and celebrated."

"That sounds a bit extreme."

"Well, I didn't love him anymore, Abbie. Good riddance." Then she catches herself. "But you still love Bill, huh?"

"Yes. Yes, of course I love him."

"That's too bad."

I frown at her and say, "I can't believe he's left. I've got to figure out how to get him back." I launch into the details of the past two weeks.

Rachel takes out her electronic cigarette and says, "Now, don't freak out on me, but could Bill have a lady friend in Chicago?"

I think I might vomit.

"Oh please, Abbie. Surely it's crossed your mind. Harold had a whole string of women he'd visit on his 'business trips.'" She makes air quotes with her fingers, the e-cigarette dangling precariously as she motions. "One in every city."

"I-I don't think he's having an affair."

Rachel flashes her blue-gray eyes at me, a look of pity at my obvious naïveté. She takes a puff on the cigarette and says, "Then go to the Camino."

"What?"

"Frankly, I don't think you'll have any luck getting him to change his mind, or to change at all. Men are so horribly stubborn. But maybe the walk will change you. If you want to stay the same, then just divorce him. That's the easy way out."

We both know that isn't true. Rachel's husband dragged her through the mud and got custody of the kids. It has taken her years to reconcile with them.

"But if you really love him, well, that's a problem. The Camino might help you figure things out in your head and show you if you need and want to change."

Since when has Rachel gotten so philosophical?

She continues, "From what your mom says, it gives time for reflection, helps you find a way forward. What can it hurt? And especially if you'll be there with your eighteen-year-old son. What mother wouldn't jump at that? Ben surely wasn't asking anything like that of me at eighteen."

I know good and well that Bobby isn't "asking" for that either. In fact, he's furious with me right now. But I don't need to say that to Rachel. I do admit, "Um, we won't be alone. He's bringing a girl."

Rachel's face is pure delight. "How perfect." She lifts an eyebrow. "I'm sure you're just thrilled."

Her sarcasm makes me laugh. "Get this. Not just a young American he met backpacking. An Iranian refugee!"

"I love it!" She takes another puff on the cigarette. "I don't know what the fates are up to, Abbie, but it looks like they've pulled every single Oriental rug in your perfect home out from under you."

50

"I don't see much that is funny, Rachel."

"Of course not. It sucks. But you've got to admit something is going on." She crosses her slim legs, her blue silk suit shimmering in the sunlight. "Have you seen a therapist? Or maybe gotten a spiritual director? It's all the rage these days. Mine's fantastic. A Catholic woman."

What? Rachel is Jewish.

"That's a shock. Since when are you interested in Catholicism?"

"Oh, no. It's not church. It's, you know, seeing someone who is wise and discerning and who will listen to you for a long time and then ask pertinent questions. Cheaper than a shrink. I got tired of mine."

"Oh."

"I'm not thinking of converting, Abbie." She puffs on the cigarette, then closes her eyes and exhales slowly. "Your dear mother, she has this amazingly resilient faith. I could almost be convinced by her life." Then she shrugs, and her eyes twinkle with a kind of mischief. "I'm like that ruler in the New Testament somewhere. You know, the one who told the apostle Paul that he was *almost* convinced by Paul's argument?"

Since when has Rachel been reading the New Testament?

"Tell your mom about Bill. Swannee's the one who got me hooked up with this woman. Sounds like you need some direction."

She crosses her legs, uncrosses them, turns off the cigarette. "Enough of these musings, right?"

"Right. I need to get home. Thanks for the condo, Rachel." I stand up. "And the advice."

So I do as Rachel suggests. I tell my mother the next day, while she sits on the floor with me in the family room.

Family room, ha. What family? Boxes are stacked all around us; I still haven't unpacked any except the one with the cross-stitch.

I start out by talking about my time in Ponte Vedra. Then I tell her about Bobby's desire to walk the Camino, leaving out the part about my deciding to tag along. Her eyes light up as she relives her experience, and I'm happy to let her reminisce.

But finally I tell her about Bill. Mama pulls me into a long hug. She is loving and compassionate and disappointed. But not surprised. Why is it that no one seems surprised?

"I've been trying and trying to figure out how to get him back, Mama. I've wondered if we could just go back to Grant Park. He loved that house. I thought we were both excited about moving here, but . . ."

We didn't decide. You begged and begged and begged.

"What if I called Bill and said, 'We aren't moving. Come home.' Would that work?" Of course it won't work—the house has already sold—but Mama knows I'm an external processor, so she lets me talk. "They're all gone. I can't get them back. I can't control any of it."

"I'm sorry, Abbie."

She gets up off the floor and goes to the marble counter in the kitchen area and presses the button on the electric kettle—Nan had insisted on unpacking a few essential items when she was here—to fix me a cup of tea. We sit down at the antique French farm table, on the provincial pillows I sewed from material bought at a French market. Mama sets out my favorite china teacups, which she has carefully unpacked from the box that was, of course, labeled *Limoges, 4 dinner plates, 4 salad plates, 4 cups and saucers.* She steeps the loose tea in the wrought iron kettle from Tunisia, a blend called London Lady. She places two poppy cocktail napkins between us and unwraps a blueberry scone that she purchased at our favorite bakery. This is our ritual: the china, the tea, the scone—huge and soft and crumbly—that we always split between us.

"I am so sorry all this is happening at once, darling." She pours the tea into our cups. I watch the dark liquid slowly cover the little peach and apricot flowers on the interior of the delicate china. She lifts the matching creamer and pours the half-and-half, then takes the sterling-silver sugar tongs, retrieves a cube from the sugar bowl, and lets it fall into my cup with a soft *plop*. She stirs slowly, slowly.

Then she repeats the same ritual for her cup of tea.

"They're all gone," I say again. "Jason at least seems safe at football camp." I recognize the irony of the words. Football is not a safe sport. I've seen *Concussion*. "But Bobby is on his own. I hope he's safe. And Bill . . ."

"So many things we can't control." Mama places her hand over my clenched fist and pries it open.

I fill in the silence. "Rachel said she's got a spiritual director, a Catholic. That's, like, totally bizarre."

Mama smiles. "It is a little bizarre for Rachel, but I think she's in a reflective season, now that she's back in Atlanta."

I take a bite of the scone and try to taste the blueberries. For the past week or two, everything has tasted like cardboard. "Mama, I would have gone to counseling, I would have stopped my volunteer work, I would have done anything. If only he had told me. If only I had known."

Mama is silent for a long moment. She turns her jade-green eyes on me, and suddenly I comprehend.

"Oh, no. Oh, Mama. He did tell me, didn't he? A thousand times he tried to tell me. And I just didn't hear him." I take a long sip of the tea before I ask, "Could he be having an affair, do you think?"

"Tell me what you know to be true about Bill," she whispers.

"He's steadfast and smart," I say, fighting back tears. "He makes me laugh, belly laugh sometimes." Although that hasn't happened in months. "He works hard. Most of the time he loves his job. He's a man of few words and lots of muscle. He can beat me at any board game except Scrabble. He can be stubborn, but he really likes to make me happy."

Bill hates conflict, and most of the time he doesn't have as strong opinions as I do.

"He puts up with a lot of crap. A whole lot. From me. And he's faithful, Mama. He loves me. I think he still loves me."

"Now tell me what you know about Abbie."

"About me?"

She nods.

"Abbie is heartbroken, and Abbie is stuck."

Mama reaches into her purse and pulls out a little business card. "I think Rachel is right. I think talking to Diana, the spiritual director, is a good idea."

CHAPTER

5

CAROLINE

I feel a horrible pinching in my chest, like nostalgia, like regret, as I leave my parents' home north of Lyon and head south toward the little village in Provence. I could have taken the high-speed rail and been in Aix in two hours, but I rented a car, since this trip through the past might be one long last good-bye. I head into the Beaujolais, where vineyard after vineyard greets me from the surrounding hills. On road trips during our French *vacances*, my siblings, Stephen and Ashley, and I used to play "vineyard poker" instead of "cow poker," counting *les vignes* instead of *les vaches* that lined each side of the country roads. Around each curve I see a delightful green grid of vines, dozens upon dozens tucked into the rolling hills.

Two hours later, as I near Avignon, the pinching intensifies as the lavender fields blind me like thousands of sun-drenched amethysts, and sunflowers nod their big, lazy heads my way in never-ending patches of yellow.

My cell buzzes, and when the name flashes on the car's display, another pinching, harder, more painful, ensues. "Hey, Brett," I say, trying to make my voice light. "You're up early."

"Just wanted to check on you, Caroline." When he calls me Caroline instead of darling, the unnamed tension is obvious. "We didn't leave on the best terms."

Hardly. I had narrowed my eyes and said through tears, "I can't tell you what I don't know."

But he'd seen through it.

My parents are turning our vacation home in a little village in Provence into an Airbnb, and Claudette, the lovely woman who has readied it for us for all these years, now will ready it for strangers too. My task is simply to clean out anything of mine that I don't want left in the open. Of course, Stephen and Ashley have already cleaned out their belongings.

But the real impetus that got me on a plane and out of Atlanta was Bastien's email of two weeks ago, inviting me back to France, promising me an end to the mystery.

I can't tell you what I don't know.

"Will you call me when you get there, then? If you don't want to talk now?"

Did I say I didn't want to talk?

Yes, I tell him. We'll talk when I get there.

I make it to our vacation home by eleven, in time to take a quick shower with *Savon de Marseille*—I use the butter-colored bar with the sweet almond scent—and stick my nose in the lavender that grows fat and plentiful in our garden, its sweet smell intoxicating and soothing at the same time.

The bees swarm around me, annoyed but not threatening. "Just need to take in the fragrance, boys," I coo.

I walk to the herb garden and bend down by the basil, its leaves bright green, the peppery and minty smell making me long for a ripened tomato on which to perch a few sprigs.

I arrive at La Maison-Café precisely at noon, as planned.

"You are waiting for someone, *non?*" the waiter asks, rushing past me with a tray of tall glasses held high above his head.

"*Non,*" I say. "I mean, yes."

He returns a minute later, leading me to a table. I breathe in the fragrance of the wisteria dangling from the canopy above me.

If I am going to ruin my life again, there's no better place than sitting in an outdoor café in lazy, lovely Lourmarin, sipping on a *citron pressé*, the French equivalent of lemonade, and tossing black olives into my mouth. I inhale deeply, taking in the perfect summer afternoon, the light casting blinding shadows across the street where a woman is shuttering her *prêt-à-porter* shop. Ah, Provence. Still closing her doors between noon and two so that everyone can take in a leisurely lunch or a nap.

When he arrives, fifteen minutes late of course, I smell him before I see him. He's wearing Aramis as usual, a rich, leathery, and spicy musk, a combination of oak moss and patchouli. He looks the same, black hair falling in his face, searching gray eyes, deep and mysterious. He grabs both of my hands and kisses me three times on the cheeks, right, left, right.

Now not only do I feel another tightening in my chest, but I imagine that my face has turned the color of a vine-ripened tomato.

"You look well, Caro," he says in French. He glances down at my hand, the left one. "No ring."

"No."

"Good." That smile, the one that first enticed me all those years ago.

"Sorry I'm late, but the office, you know. Good, you've gotten a drink." He motions lazily to the waiter. "*Un pastis.*" He takes a seat and stares across the table at me. "You're beautiful. I like the new haircut. Short and sassy."

I swallow and take a deep breath, as my therapist recommended. "*Bastien, arrête!* No flattery. This is not a date. It's business."

He lifts his shoulders and says, "Business and romance, it is all the same when you are near."

My stomach flutters as if those bees around the lavender have taken up residence inside me. The waiter places two menus on the table, and I bury my head in one.

"Caro!" He rolls the *r* in my name in a delicious way, as if he's tasting it. "It only makes you more appealing when your cheeks turn that lovely shade of peach."

"I'll have the *salade niçoise*," I tell the waiter, who has placed a basket of bread—a warm baguette—on the table along with a bottle of chilled water.

Bastien orders the same without even glancing at the menu.

When the waiter hurries off, Bastien cups his chin in his hand so that I can see the hint of a smile peeking out around his fingers. "It's been a long time, Caro. I'm glad to see you."

I take another deep breath. "Bastien, I came back because you invited me. You said you would finally tell me the whole story. I've never known what really happened, and I need it all if I'm . . ."

"If you're what?"

"Going to move forward."

He leans back in his chair and makes a tower with his fingers. "Ah, forward to marriage."

I glare at him.

"I told you what you could hear. The rest is worse. You don't need it."

"I do!"

"Why? To be hurt more than you were all those years ago?

58

If I remember correctly, what you already know put you on a psychiatrist's couch for months!"

"I have to know the truth."

"Ah, the truth. Yes. That word."

"Yes, *that word*."

"But it won't be nice or pretty." His gray eyes are dancing.

"Bastien! You invited me back! You made it sound like you had finally discovered the other half of the story. And I ache for the rest. I didn't know it until I started lying."

Indeed, since I hadn't known the real ending, I had made up one. But my almost-fiancé had not bought it.

Bastien is watching me across the table, eyes laughing, lips turned up in the perfect French pout. "Poor dear. Lying. It's not like my Caro to make up stories. You write them down for others to read in that paper—what is it called again?"

"The *Peachtree Press*," I murmur.

"Ah, yes. The *Peachtree Press*. Because everything in Atlanta has to do with peach trees."

In one short sentence, with that irritatingly delectable French accent, he has belittled me and my job and my city. How could I have fallen for him all those years ago?

I take out a leather-bound journal from my oversized bag and flip to the page I've marked with a pink Post-it. I lay it on the table between us, and before I can remove my hand, his is covering it.

"Such lovely handwriting, my dear Caro, which is no surprise because it comes from such a lovely hand . . ."

I pull my hand away. If I don't change the subject quickly, he'll be giving the restaurant a commentary on my whole body.

"Bastien, listen to me."

That smirk, dark eyes flashing. "Of course, my dear, this is serious. So serious."

How can he infuriate me with only two or three sentences?

I jab at the opened journal. "You said in the email that you had found something else about . . . about the murder."

"I said this, yes." He's taken the journal and is reading the email I've printed off and stuck in between two pages. I snatch it back before he gets to anything I've written about him. "How else could I coax you back? It's been too long—what, three years ago, yes?"

"Yes. Three years ago. Quit being so horrible."

"Ah, now I'm horrible. In the email you sent back you praised my . . . how did you put it . . . my astute observation."

"In the email I was desperate to get some answers, and you said you had more information. But now you're acting like this is a game. You're confusing me, Bastien. You know you are, and it's really not very nice. I thought I could trust you after everything . . ."

I stand up, and he stands too. "Let's not make a scene, dear Caro." And he lowers me to my seat with both hands on my shoulders. "Seriously. Seriously, I will tell you the rest of the story." His eyes soften; his whole face softens.

I let out a breath, relieved.

"But not here. Not now at noon in a crowded café. Tomorrow." He lifts his eyebrows, and I feel my resolve sinking. "Tomorrow night *chez moi* with a good red wine. I will make you your favorite meal and then tell you the story." He reaches for my hand again, pressing his lips to my fingers. "This will be a more appropriate setting, *n'est-ce pas, ma Chérie*? Then, when the atmosphere is right, I will tell you."

I frown. For so long, I was the one who wanted the atmosphere to be right, but it wasn't for him to tell me the story of my best friend's misfortune.

"No." I say it emphatically, but inside I am already wilting a little, and every single excuse I have so carefully planned flies out of my mind, like the bees flitting away when I bent over the lavender.

He lifts his shoulders in nonchalance, puffs his lips in the perfect *ppfff*, and says, "You cannot leave without knowing this. You think it will help your story make sense, and then you will go off and marry that boy—what's his name—Brad?"

"Brett."

"Yes, Brett. And then what will I have but the memory of you? No, tomorrow night. That will give you a little time to get over the jet lag. I will meet you in front of your house." He reaches over and brushes the hair off my brow. "My beautiful Caro. I'm so glad you've come back."

ABBIE

I have never been an out-of-the-box kind of person. I play by the rules. All the rules. I am seeing this woman simply because both Mama and Rachel have recommended her, and those two women, best friends from forever though they may be, are about as opposite as they come. Except for a shared love of literature.

I drive into the parking lot of the Cathedral of Christ the King. When I walk into the foyer, a woman dressed in a sapphire blue suit is talking to the receptionist. She turns, and I am taken aback by her eyes. The very same color as her suit and piercing, in an inviting rather than intimidating way.

"You must be Abigail," she says. "I'm Diana Breeson." She holds out her hand, and I take it. Hers is warm and strong. She looks to be in her sixties, with gray highlights in her short, wavy dark hair. Poised but natural.

"Nice to meet you, Sister Breeson. You can call me Abbie."

Her eyes are laughing good-naturedly. "It's just Diana. I'm not a sister. Just a member of the Cathedral."

"Oh."

I follow her down the hall and into a comfortable room arranged with four dark brown club chairs, the kind you can sink into. She motions to one, and down I go.

In spite of the comfortable chair I feel stiff and want to bolt. "Thank you for agreeing to see me." I stumble through the speech I've prepared. "I'm not Catholic. And I really have no idea what this is, this spiritual direction. But two women I greatly admire suggested it . . . and you."

She nods.

"So here I am."

"That's lovely. Tell me, Abbie, what *do* you know about spiritual direction?"

"Not much. That I come and talk and you listen, for about an hour, and somehow that's supposed to help me resolve my problems. And of course God's invited to come too."

She suppresses a chuckle.

"Oh, and it's cheaper than therapy."

Now she gives a robust laugh. "Spiritual direction is a lot about listening, me listening to you, you listening to the Holy Spirit, us inviting Jesus to be present in our time. It's about being attentive in the present, taking time to hear what God is saying, what is going on inside. I often say, 'Stay with what stirs you.' Once you hear from the Lord, what are you going to do about it?"

I still have not wrapped my mind around Rachel seeing a Catholic. "Uh-huh," I say.

"So today, Abbie, I'm lighting this candle as a symbol of Christ's presence with us. Then I'll offer a short prayer, and you're free to begin. Whatever is on your heart today."

She leans forward and strikes a match, and the flame flickers and catches the wick on the round burgundy candle. She begins to pray, but I'm not really listening. I'm thinking, *Christ candle and Rachel?*

So when Diana pronounces, "In Christ's name. Amen," I blurt out, "I just cannot fathom what in the world Rachel Abrams does here! She's Jewish! She doesn't even believe in Jesus." I am flustered. "Except that He was a good man."

Diana doesn't react. She meets my eyes, a softness in hers. "Well, Jesus was Jewish too. And you'd be surprised at what Rachel Abrams believes. But we're not here to talk about Rachel. We're here for you, Abbie. This is about your spiritual journey, and everyone's journey is different."

I balk. "Now you're going to tell me that all paths lead to God, is that it?"

She nods toward the candle. "Jesus Christ leads us to God, and we have invited Him into our presence."

I have nothing to say to that, but Diana is endlessly patient. I suppose one of the requirements of being a spiritual director is unflappability. I gather my thoughts and plunge in.

"Well, what I really want is to get my husband back. I'm not very convinced that spiritual direction will help. . . ." I gnaw at my lip. "But since my life is falling apart, I figured I'd better do something. You see, we've been married for twenty years. Twenty good years, or so I thought, and we've just moved into a loft on the Beltline, downsizing because our sons are off at school, sort of, and it seemed wise, and in three months my husband, Bill—Bill is his name—in three months he turns fifty. And I've already sent out the save-the-date invites for his surprise party, and I've been working on his gift for two years. And now he's left because he says he needs a break. I don't recognize him anymore. He's been the most laid-back, good-natured type of person you can imagine, and right before we're moving and our sons are leaving, he tells me he needs a break."

I talk for twenty-five minutes straight, and when I finally pause and look up at Diana, she is sitting in a state of total equanimity.

At first I think I must have rendered her speechless, but then she clears her throat and asks, "So Abbie, it frustrates you that he left you while you are making all these plans for his surprise party and gift. Is that right?"

"Yes, exactly."

"Why don't we sit with this for a moment, and you tell me if you hear anything else from what you've shared."

So I close my eyes obediently and sit and try to listen to the silence, but I'm thinking that this is odd and the flickering candle is a little spooky and then I'm wondering about my tennis lesson and then I settle on what Diana has said. And suddenly I shake my head rather vigorously, hearing the implication: Do I want Bill back because I love him or because I've worked so hard to do the right thing?

I've been staring at my hands, but I force myself to make eye contact with Diana. "I mean, of course I want him back because I love him. That's the most important." But it sounds like what it is: a feeble excuse to explain away the ugly truth. I close my eyes. I cannot bear to see Diana's penetrating gaze.

"So my son who's in Europe, I'm going to walk the Camino with him. Have you heard of the Camino?"

She nods. "The Pilgrim's Way. Yes, I'm familiar with it."

Of course she would be.

"Good, because I'm not, and honestly, it doesn't sound very spiritually enlightening to me at all. It sounds like blisters and backaches and being with a bunch of odd people who are probably as mixed up as I am."

She is chuckling again. I had no idea I was so entertaining.

"Oh, Abbie. You do speak your mind, don't you? And your description of the Camino is very apt, but incomplete. Yes to blisters and backaches and other searching pilgrims. But yes also to being alone, to silence, to beauty, to being away from all other distractions."

"So that's the point? Getting away and just walking and thinking?"

"I suppose you could say that. Walking and breathing, listening, soaking in what you hear and sometimes interacting with others. So much has a chance to get through to us when everything else is taken away."

Everything else is taken away. Yes, exactly.

"Have you heard of spiritual disciplines, Abbie?"

I shrug. "You mean like reading my Bible and praying and going to church?"

"Yes, those are wonderful ones."

"Well, I get up at five-thirty every morning to make Bill breakfast so that it's ready when he gets back from his run. And then I read three chapters in the Bible and pray. You know. We used to call it quiet time. Now the kids in our sons' youth group at church call it 'devos.' As in devotions."

"I like it. And are you able to be quiet?"

"What?"

"In this morning quiet time, is your spirit quiet?"

What a strange question. Of course I'm quiet.

But then that tug again. No. No, I'm not quiet at all. I read the pages by rote, a blur, often checking my phone to see if any other human being is up at this ungodly hour. Checking the news, checking my Google calendar, checking, checking, always checking something.

"Spiritual disciplines are all about making room for God. In our fast-paced life, it is often easier to push God into a tight schedule with the rest of our day rather than take time to truly hear Him."

I furrow my brow and look at Diana intently, hoping that I seem concentrated and engaged. But inwardly I'm saying, *Who has time for this stuff? Who really hears from God? How presumptuous!*

"It sounds a bit presumptuous to think we can hear God, but He is everywhere, and He is always speaking—through His Word, through His creation, through people and the community, through prayer."

She just used the exact same word I was thinking. *Presumptuous.* Spooky.

Diana is still talking. ". . . slow ourselves down and find rhythms in our life that help us hear. A quiet time is a lovely rhythm. Attending worship and prayer are also. And there are many other spiritual disciplines we could explore. If you are in agreement, perhaps I can suggest one or two each month and give you some reading material about them, and then you can choose."

"Okay."

"Do you journal, Abbie?"

"You mean like keep a diary?"

"Yes, a record of your thoughts and feelings, allowing God into these."

"No, I don't journal. I stitch."

She cocks her head. "Tell me more."

"I do needlework. That's when I relax. And think." Sort of.

"How interesting."

"Would you like to see the cross-stitch I'm making for Bill?"

She seems surprised, but says, "Yes, yes, I would."

I take it out of my Vera Bradley bag. The cross-stitch is

neatly folded and stored in a Ziploc, and when I unroll it, Diana reaches over and says, "That is remarkable. Beautiful."

Now it's my turn to chuckle. "That's the back." I flip it over and spread out the whole canvas for her to see.

She reaches for a corner, questions me with her eyes. I say, "Sure, you can hold it."

"It's simply breathtaking. The colors, the detail." She focuses on me. "But I don't think my metaphor will work."

"Metaphor?"

"Yes, it's an often-used one, about how a tapestry looks so tangled and pointless on the underside, but the finished work is beautiful, that God is using what looks like all of the tangles in our life to make a lovely work of art." She carefully turns the canvas to the underside again. "But my goodness, even this side is beautiful. I didn't know this was possible."

I whisper, "Maybe the metaphor for me is that I try so hard to make sure no one ever sees any loose threads in my life." I'm shocked that I've admitted such a thing, and then my eyes are watering. "I want everything to be perfect. I try so hard to do the right thing. But to use another needlework metaphor, it's all unraveling."

I want to leave. Surely my hour is up by now. Part of me is thinking, *I don't have time for this*, and another part of me is thinking, *I have all the time in the world*. And then a thought lands softly, gently in my lap. Could this be what listening to God is like? Could He be nudging me into this new step precisely because of where I am in my life?

Diana reaches over and takes my hand, hers resting lightly on my clenched fist. "Abbie, I'd like you to consider that maybe your being here at this time is exactly the right thing for right now."

As our session draws near the end, Diana asks, "Could I take a photo of your beautiful cross-stitch canvas?"

I shrug. "Sure."

"It's quite interesting, Abbie, what I see in this. Have you ever heard of a Rule of Life?"

"No, but I like rules! Tell me about it."

"It's actually an ancient way to schedule our lives, our days." Schedule. Another word I like.

"It started in the fifth century with Benedict. A Benedictine 'rule,' but it isn't something rigid at all. The word *rule* comes from a Latin word that means trellis. It's something that helps us move in a life-giving way, in a good direction.

"What strikes me when I look at this cross-stitch is that it is, in a sense, a Rule of Life. You have made a family tree, as you said, not only of Bill's ancestors and immediate family, but also of all the things that give Bill life."

I try to follow her. "The things he likes. Is that what you mean?"

"Yes, but it's more than that. It is what is good for his soul. Without having the faintest idea of the Rule of Life, you have depicted the things Bill likes in a life-giving way, incorporated in the leaves that are hanging from these limbs. It strikes me, Abbie, that you know your husband very well to have lovingly stitched his life into the canvas." She sets it down. "Now I am going to give you some homework."

Diana opens a file drawer and retrieves a photocopied page. "I want you to make a Rule of Life for yourself. You can read more about it here, and you'll see there are online links with examples of what others have done. Give careful thought to what brings you life, daily, weekly, monthly, seasonally." Then she hands me a small gray journal with the words *Be Still* written in cursive across the bottom of the cover. "Spend some time contemplating what brings life to you, and then jot down your ideas in this journal. A small gift for you to take with you on the Camino."

I realize she hasn't given me any idea at all of how to get Bill back. When I blurt this out, she says, "Let's get Abbie back first."

Back in the loft, I dial Bill's assistant. Judith, a fiftysomething single mom, has worked for him for fifteen years. She's good at her job and deeply loyal. Has he told her about leaving?

"Hey, Judith, it's Abbie."

"Oh hi, Abbie! How are you? How's the loft? Bill says it has an amazing view."

Bill is talking to Judith?

"It's great. We love it. Um, I was just wondering, have you said anything to Bill about the trip to France?"

I can hear her smiling through the phone. "Of course not! Our secret! Not a peep about the trip or the party."

"Well, I was a bit concerned. With him taking that three-month assignment in Chicago."

"I know. I figure you'll think of something to get him back home early on that Friday. He'll be almost done by the time you were planning on leaving."

"I thought maybe you could hint at something. . . ."

"Oh, no. You know he's not even coming to the office at all. And when he calls, it's all business—he is so excited about this project. You know how he gets." She laughs. "But now that you mention it, I think you should tell him. Just sit him down this weekend, give him a beer, let him watch the Braves, and tell him all about it. I'm sure he'll arrange things once he hears all the awesome stuff you've planned."

But Bill and I aren't talking. I have no idea that he loves his project. And it's all supposed to be a surprise. A big surprise.

"Anyway, you know how much Bill hates surprises."

Bill hates surprises? He does?

A memory assaults me from a few years back, when Bill got a hefty promotion and award as a top consultant in his company.

"Hey, Abbs, please don't organize some big thing for me," he said. "The promotion is all I need. Don't announce it to the world."

But I paid no attention and threw a surprise party with about thirty friends.

I wince inwardly.

"If I were you, I'd tell him," Judith is saying. "That way he can plan around it, and he'll probably enjoy the party and the trip more anyway."

I cannot find my voice, so she continues. "But of course, it's your call. Whichever way it turns out, he'll love it. He's always bragging on you, Abbie. If only I were so lucky to find a guy like Bill."

CHAPTER

6

BOBBY

I'm sitting in the main room of the Oasis, where all the refugees have congregated for the evening coffee bar, a time to play
games and drink coffee and mint tea. I'm sketching the scene
before me, as I've done each day. That was Stephen's first assignment for me: make sketches. I email them to him. He's running
an update on the refugee center, as he does every few years.

It was at the Oasis that he "met his wife and changed his
life"—that's how he puts it, rhyme intended. That was in 2005.
Nowadays the refugees are mostly Syrian, but I've met plenty
of other nationalities as well during these two weeks. I'm concentrating on a toothless turbaned man, probably in his late
sixties, who keeps slapping the table with his hand and roaring
with laughter. He's playing a game of Uno with three boys. I
actually don't think any of the three speak the same language.

I love this place—its aura of energy and hope. Kindness too.
Kindness and *refugee* aren't two words I'd ever think to put
together. Words like *persecuted, rejected, impoverished, homeless* come to mind. But here I see kindness in the international

staff who run the center, and a reciprocal kindness in the eyes of the refugees . . . like they're swallowing the atmosphere whole and then bursting out in laughter at the simple pleasure of it all.

I'm trying to capture this in my sketch when Emad, a Tunisian kid, wanders over and points to the drawing. "It is good," he says in heavily accented English.

"Thanks." I shrug. "Just a sketch."

"*Brouillon?*" He knows I understand French, although I've not been very successful at speaking it.

"*Oui, brouillon.*"

He sits beside me, nodding as he points out each figure I've drawn and its resemblance to my unknowing models across the room. Then he points to a young woman I've sketched. "*Où est-elle?*"

I feel my face go red. "Inspiration. She's not here."

He laughs and winks. Emad knows very well who this is. He comes to the coffee bar every night it's open, and he's seen Rasa here.

"Very beautiful, this girl." He pats my back and walks over to the group playing Uno.

I flip back through my sketchbook. My great-grandmother was an artist too. She was known for cleverly inserting her loved ones' faces into her sketches, even onto the gargoyles on Notre Dame Cathedral. I had followed her example, inserting Rasa's face on that of a tourist watching the Lipizzaner stallions perform, on an art student admiring the works of Rembrandt, on a refugee mother cradling her baby in this very room.

Wow. I haven't done anything like this since Anna. I push the thought away.

In this most recent sketch Rasa is staring straight at me, her thick black hair falling almost to her waist, her eyelashes and brows thick and dark. And her eyes! Her lovely eyes holding secrets I am determined to uncover.

At least this is what I am trying to depict. I reach out and touch her face on the pad and sigh. I'm glad none of my friends can see me now.

Love-sick, they'd say. I've never felt this way before. Of course, there was Anna. . . . But I'd never really understood being love-sick until now.

I have this weird feeling in my gut all the time. I keep track of how many days it's been since I've seen her. Five. And I still need to convince her to come with me on the Camino.

I text her about my mom coming with us, and she replies right away.

Oh! That is nice. That is a different-colored horse then.

I'm glad she's not with me to see how I chuckle at her comment. And then feel all warm inside with hope.

My phone beeps with a text from Jason. Finally. He's sent me all of three short messages the whole time I've been gone.

Hey!

Hey back! How's football?

He texts back a string of emojis and then *Hot. And coach is super strict. But I'll get by.*

I have no doubt about that. My little brother is a master finagler.

How's Europe?

I know that he's not asking for details, but this might be the only time he shows any interest at all, so I text, *I met a girl.*

What?! I don't believe it. Followed by a dozen question marks and emojis.

It's true. She's amazing. Her name is Rasa.

And?

And what?

And what's her crisis? She must have something really bad going on.

No crisis. She's beautiful and fun and mysterious.

Of course. You like mysterious.

She's Iranian.

That sounds exotic. I knew there had to be something different about her. But hey, I'm glad for you. You haven't talked about a girl since Anna.

He types her name so casually, as if a thousand memories aren't attached to it. As if I'd gotten past that nightmare years ago.

But Jason is that way. He refuses to look at pain, his or anyone else's.

I'm thankful when he changes the subject. *Why did you tell Mom about that pilgrimage thing? Did you WANT her to come along???*

No, I don't want her here! I screwed up. I insert several choice emojis.

It's making her freak out about everything—including football injuries!

Sorry it's falling on you too. At least she didn't decide to join the football team.

Ha ha.

I am worried about her, though, with Dad gone.

You worry about everyone.

At least somebody cares about his parents, I want to text back, but I refrain.

Have you talked to Dad lately? he texts.

A few days ago. You?

Last night. He's coming to my first game in two weeks. Flying in from Chicago. He said he could spend the weekend in town if I want.

Cool.

He probably won't like my friends.

What, are they druggies or something?

No.

I wait for more of an explanation, but instead Jason texts, *Do you think they're gonna get divorced?*

I don't know.

It sucks. Why can't Mom just chill a little? She's ruining everything. Gotta go! Have fun with your refugee.

I'm walking back to the guesthouse when Stephen calls.

"The sketches are great, Bobby. And I just published your 'Mint Tea and Migration' piece. Good stuff."

"Thanks. And guess what? I've met Rasa. It took a little while to connect the dots between her and Tracie's Aunt Bobbie, but I figured it out."

"Rasa! Wow. When I first met her, she was about six or seven—the most precocious kid, in a spiritual way—like she had a direct line to Jesus. Last time I saw her she was a gangly teen."

"She's not gangly anymore."

He chuckles. "Sounds like someone has a crush."

It spills out. "I think I'm in love, man. I'm going to visit her in Linz, at the House of Hope."

"Hamid's ministry? Wow, Bobby. You're stirring up lots of memories here. . . . Okay then, take some photos when you're there, if you can get permission, and do some sketches. And could you write up three hundred words on the House of Hope? We've never done an article on it."

I like the enthusiasm in his voice. "Sure, boss."

"Great." He pauses, then adds, "And behave yourself. I don't want your mother railing on me about you falling in love on your gap year!"

"Ha! She already knows all about it. She's invited herself to hike the Camino with me."

Stephen waits a few seconds before saying, "Wow. That's kind of a bummer, isn't it? I mean, you were looking for a bit of independence."

"Totally. But I made the mistake of telling her I'm walking the Camino with Rasa."

Stephen laughs again. "The plot thickens."

"You can say that again. Not only is Mom coming, but Rasa *isn't* coming—yet." Then I explain my plan of using Mom's presence to convince Rasa and her parents that we'll have a chaperone on our hike, so all will be well.

Stephen gives a low whistle. "You sound like Jason, knowing how to play all the angles." But then he adds, "Well, if you're going to get Rasa to walk the Camino with you, it's probably a good idea to let your mother come along."

Stephen's good that way, all youth-pastorish. He hangs pretty well with us, but he'll throw in a subtle commendation for our parents too. "Which part of the pilgrimage are you planning to walk?"

"From Le Puy in France to somewhere down near Spain. I texted Caroline the approximate dates. She was cool with that."

"Thanks, Bobby." He's quiet for a moment. "I've suggested that she start her Camino in Le Puy too. Maybe y'all could start together."

"I thought you wanted us to do different routes, me in August and her later in the fall."

He gives a sigh, which always means Stephen is trying to decide how much information he can share with me. "I did. But Tracie and I really think it'd do Caro good to get away from Lourmarin as soon as possible. It's not a great time for her to be alone there. And I don't think she'll mind pushing her plans forward a little. You know how she is."

I do. Caro perfectly encapsulates the word *unpredictable*. She's a lot of fun, but not the most dependable person. Although Stephen never said so, rumors at the *Press* suggest that Caro has quite a past.

"I'm thinking out loud here, Bobby, so bear with me. But what if I let her know you'll be starting the pilgrimage soon and encourage her to join you?"

Jason does anger, I do avoidance, so I don't say what I'm screaming in my head: *Holy crap, no! I'm going to be stuck on the Camino with my mom AND your sister? And possibly without Rasa? No way!*

But Stephen gets it. "Listen, maybe having Caro along will give you time alone with Rasa. Your mom and Caro might bond."

"Sure. Totally." But I don't try to hide my displeasure.

"Sorry to throw this at you, Bobby. You work on Rasa. I'll work on Caroline."

I grunt my accord.

"What day will you be in Le Puy?"

"I don't know. Ask Mom. She's already got the whole thing planned."

Anna. How I wish Jason hadn't said her name. Not that she wasn't already on my mind, but his glib text bore a hole in me.

Anna Harris was in my ninth-grade chemistry class. She was a loner, the kind of girl others avoided. There were rumors of an alcoholic father, no mention of a mother. But I liked Anna. Maybe I felt sorry for her, but I also thought she was pretty and smart and interesting. I began to worry for her. She never went into detail, but she'd say things like, "My dad can be really cruel, you know?"

I didn't know, couldn't begin to imagine a cruel father, but the way she looked at me, her eyes hinting at something almost evil, dug into my soul.

One day she mentioned that she was afraid to go home, so I invited her to our house for dinner. After that, she started coming over every week or two. Jason thought she was weird, but Mom and Dad liked her. Mom took Anna under her wing, did little things that made her feel special. Mom was great that way.

But more than once she warned me that I couldn't solve all of Anna's problems. "She's a dear girl, Bobby, and she is always welcome at our house, but please don't you try to reform her father. Promise me that."

I don't remember what I promised, but Anna's face started finding its way into some of my sketches.

Twice a year, from the time I was really little, Mom organized something called the Picnic in the Park for the poor and homeless in Atlanta. I think my grandfather actually started the event back in the sixties, and Mom took over when his sight started going.

People from different churches around the city worked together, getting donations of clothes, food, toys for the kids, and household items. The year that Anna and I became friends, I invited her to join me as a volunteer. Stephen and Tracie were there too, sponsors to our church youth group. Anna played games with the children, laughed alongside the other teens while serving lunch, and helped Mom with all the logistics of distributing clothes and food.

"You know you can come to youth group sometime if you'd like," I told her at the end of the day.

She smiled at me—I didn't see that smile very often—and said, "Sure. Maybe."

Late in the afternoon Mom was still busy cleaning up, so

Stephen offered to drive Anna home, and I went along. "You can drop me off here," she told Stephen, motioning to the parking lot of a convenience store in a rough section of town.

But Stephen insisted on taking her to her house. When we arrived, there were several cars parked out front, and I saw her wilt.

She opened the car door and said, "Thanks for the ride, Stephen. And for including me. It was really awesome."

"Let me walk you to the door," I said.

"No. Please go. I'll be okay."

Stephen hadn't heard much about her background, but he picked up on the fear in her eyes. "Anna, are you feeling in danger?"

She shrugged.

"I'll be glad to talk with your parents if you think they'll be mad about you going with us today," he offered.

I'll never forget the look of panic on her face. "No. Please. Just leave. It'll be okay if you just leave."

She hurried out of the car and to the house.

We heard the commotion immediately: screaming and cursing and the sound of breaking glass. Oblivious to Stephen calling after me, I jumped out of the car, ran across the yard, and began banging on the front door. When no one answered, I threw it open and took in the scene: beer cans littering the front room, two men passed out on a worn sofa, Anna cowering beside the TV cradling her arm, a gash above her eye, while a bearded man with tattooed arms screamed curses and swung a baseball bat at her.

I plunged into him, and he turned the bat on me. It came down on my left shoulder with the force of a cyclone. I think he would have killed me, but Stephen rushed in. He'd already called the police on his cell phone.

Stephen took us to the hospital. Anna had a broken arm and a concussion, and my shoulder was dislocated. When my parents arrived, Mom put her hand on my face and said, "Oh, Bobby. Bobby. Sometimes you just care too much."

Her father went to jail, and Anna went to a foster home.

Yes, I cared, I cared a lot. How does a person know when "a lot" becomes "too much"? I only knew that I broke out in a cold sweat and my heart beat really hard whenever I thought about Anna and her crazy father.

CARO

I arrive back at the old *mas*, the farmhouse that my parents lovingly restored years ago. Late summer is my favorite time here. I walk over to a rosebush, Augusta Luise, planted by my mother and now lacing up a trellis on the side of the house, and breathe in the sweet smell.

"Hello, Luise," I say. "You've outdone yourself this year."

The rosebush is boasting hordes of apricot-colored blooms—several are buds, others are opening petal by petal to the heavy sun, and one rose has already become salmon-pink, the petals splayed out in perfect delicate layers. I stick my nose into it and inhale the strong, fruity, sweet fragrance. "Thank you, Luise. I needed that."

I punch Brett's number into the phone. "Hey," I whisper.

"You okay, Caroline?"

"It always takes so much out of me to be back here."

"I know." And he does. But he doesn't know I've already met up with Bastien, and I'm not going to tell him. Yet.

"Look, darling."

Ah, that word!

"Take your time. I'm sorry you feel like I'm pressuring you."

I'm still breathing in Luise, slowly filling my soul, and I whisper, "Thanks. I'm sorry too. I just, I just have to figure these things out. You don't want to be hitched to a question mark all your life."

"Caroline, you're not . . . But you're right. You must be sure. I'll wait."

How ironic that most of my girlfriends are totally annoyed with their guys who can't make up their minds about marriage or anything else. And here Brett says that he knows I'm the one.

I tell myself that my reservations aren't because of Bastien. It really is the story of Lola. Right? But I'm a mess, a completely undone mess as I sort through my wardrobe and pick out a little black dress for the meal with Bastien tomorrow night.

My next call is to Tracie. "Well?" she says across the static.

"Well, I saw him, and it completely undid me. But he didn't tell me the rest of the story."

"What? I thought that was why he summoned you." Her annoyance with Bastien, whom she's never met, is loud and clear.

"He said he would tell me later, at his place. Tomorrow night, over dinner and candlelight."

"And you said . . ."

I let out a sigh. "I said okay. I tried to tell him no, I swear, Trace. I did. But he's such a horrible, horrible charmer."

"You can't go."

My sister-in-law is my accountability partner. She's allowed to say things like that. "Are you still sober?" she adds.

"Yes. Promise. I haven't touched a drop."

"You can't go tomorrow night," she repeats.

"I have to know, Tracie. Wouldn't you want to? Wouldn't it be important to your story?"

"Not if I had the kind of history you have with this Frenchman!"

"I'm just doing what my therapist suggested—letting myself grieve, really grieve, by learning what really happened."

"Yeah, I know. Grieving is good. But I'm afraid you won't do much grieving when you're face-to-face with Bastien over a romantic dinner."

"You're right. You're right. Thanks, Tracie."

I hang up, glancing at the little black dress lying innocently across the bed.

Seven years earlier

I had finished my last year of university in Lyon studying communications and come back to Lourmarin to rest, to have one month alone at our vacation home, without my parents or siblings. I was still smarting from a recent breakup with a Greek guy I'd dated since we'd met on the island of Kefalonia the previous summer. The latest in a long list of bad boy choices. All I wanted was some peace and quiet and a whole lot of wine to wash away my heartache.

I had planned on spending long lazy afternoons with my best friend, Lola. I missed her during the year and worried when she'd stopped sending her signature long emails. Her family was well-known in the village, her father French, her mother Iranian. Lola was two years younger than me, and we had bonded over our French fathers and foreign mothers who still spoke French with a strong accent. Hers I thought particularly lovely, with its Middle Eastern trills. My mother's was all American deep South.

Bastien knocked on my door the first afternoon I arrived. "*Bonjour.*" He was holding an envelope in one hand. "I'm your new neighbor, Bastien."

"*Bonjour* back," I answered. "I'm Caroline."

"Caroline." He looked surprised, then flashed a smile. "I'm new with Peugeot. Had to get away from Paris, and Lourmarin has a great reputation."

"Have you ever been here before?"

"No. Not to Lourmarin or Aix." We stared at each other for a moment. Then, "I heard that the owner of this house also works for Peugeot."

"My father, yes, Pierre Lefort."

"I've got a few tickets to a private party in Aix this evening. Dinner and jazz. You know, part of Fête de la Musique. I was going to invite your parents."

La Fête de la Musique was a big free music festival held all over France on the twenty-first of June, the first day of summer. Any amateur or wannabe musician could find a corner of a street in a village and perform. Of course there were really good bands and chorales and symphonies performing too. And there were private parties like the one Bastien was proposing. It was one of my favorite outings. Wandering around Provence, village to village, sipping wine and listening to music. Especially jazz.

"Sorry, but my parents aren't here." I couldn't take my eyes off him, dark hair spilling into his dark eyes. Energy practically radiated from him. And the scent of Aramis. He seemed the tiniest bit disappointed by my comment and lifted his shoulders.

"*Dommage.*"

Oh, yes, it is too bad, I thought. "This is their vacation home," I hurried to explain. "They're in Lyon. Just me here alone. *Les vacances*, you know. No parents, no siblings," I laughed a bit awkwardly.

"*Très bien*. Well, do you like jazz? I mean the tickets are here," and he handed me the envelope. "It's supposed to be a nice party—if you like jazz."

"*Merci*. As a matter of fact, I do." I opened the envelope

and retrieved an invitation—gold lettering on thick ecru paper. *Une soirée jazz. Chateau de Beauregard. Black tie.* Two little ecru rectangles were tied with a pale ribbon to the invitation. I cocked my head. "Um, should I just go there and show my invitation?"

He smiled and lifted an eyebrow. "Well, I am going there too, of course. If you would like, I can take you."

"You don't have a date?"

He studied me. "*Non.* Not for tonight. I just moved down here. I don't know anyone yet."

"Okay, then. Sure, I'll go with you."

"Good. *Pourquoi pas?*"

I felt my face redden and beamed at him in a ridiculous way. "Yes, why not?"

I loved parties and jazz and good French food. I dressed in a sequined sapphire blue gown that had a silk collar in the front and plunged down low in the back, and I wore matching suede heels. I piled my dark brown hair—it was shoulder length at the time—high on my head in a French twist and added a delicate diamond and pearl necklace and matching earrings to the ensemble—my mother's jewels I'd found in the family safe. I finished off with a hint of my favorite perfume, Cachette, surveying myself in the antique oval mirror in my parents' bedroom. I felt young, sexy, and carefree.

Bastien arrived in a black tux and a white bowtie. "You look lovely," he whispered in my ear.

Then we both laughed, really almost giggled like two starstruck high schoolers ready for their first prom.

"I feel like I'm sixteen."

He raised his eyebrows. "You don't look sixteen. You look like a beautiful young woman. Perfect." Then he added, almost as an afterthought, "How old are you?"

"Twenty-one. And you?"

"Thirty."

He led me to his forest-green Alfa Romeo, and when he held out his hand to help me in I felt like Grace Kelly in *To Catch a Thief* stepping into Cary Grant's fancy car for a drive along the Grande Corniche in Monaco.

We drove toward Aix, but before getting to the city, he turned off the main road and onto a long drive bordered on each side by rows of olive trees. A chateau, lit up with candles everywhere, glowed in the distance. "Oh, Bastien. It's a dream!"

He glanced over at me. "I hope you will enjoy it."

I did. Champagne and canapés and candles and jazz. And amid a crowd of ex-pats and French bourgeoisie, we were essentially alone. Neither of us knew a soul.

"How did you get the invitation?"

He'd raised his eyebrows. "Connections."

Much later, we left the soirée and wandered the cobbled streets of old Aix, where Fête de la Musique was still in full swing. Sometimes silently soaking up the sounds of music around us, sometimes taking a seat at one of the many outdoor cafés, where we ordered drinks and then coffee. He listened, seemingly entertained, as I told him stories of growing up in a Peugeot family and all the different countries we'd lived in because of my father being transferred regularly.

Bastien occasionally piped in with a cynical comment, or even a criticism, the way the French do, and he looked at me, really looked in my eyes in a way that made me feel sexy and beautiful and appreciated. But I also felt free and heard and cared for by a complete stranger.

Aix was magical at night, with twinkling lights embedded in the plane trees that form a canopy of leaves over the Cours Mirabeau. The whole town was out at the party, young and old, children dashing around and old couples strolling hand in hand. We turned a corner and there, in a hidden alcove with a string quartet playing, couples of all ages were waltzing to the music.

Bastien looked at me and shrugged. "Would you like to dance?"

"I would, *bien sûr*."

When we arrived back in Lourmarin at three in the morning, he parked his Alfa Romeo and walked me across the street to my parents' house. I expected him to invite himself in, but he didn't.

"Are you busy tomorrow? Do you like to hike? Mont Sainte Victoire?"

I was delighted at the prospect of another day together. "I'd love to hike Mont Sainte Victoire with you."

And we did, in shorts and T-shirts and backpacks. "Cezanne's territory," he said when we stood near the top, with the sun casting shadows across the valley below. We'd perched on a rock that overlooked the valley and had grapes and Comté and goat cheese with a baguette and a bottle of rosé. He talked of art and history in that comfortable way young French men have. Polite and cultured and yes, charming.

"Do you have a girlfriend?" I asked after our picnic, because I had never been very good at guarding my heart.

He looked at me, reached over, and brushed my cheek. "I don't know. Do I?"

I was startled, thrilled, and completely besotted when he leaned over and kissed me ever so lightly. Then stood and held my hand.

But he never suggested anything more, not during our first three days together. At the end of the third day, which we'd spent in Les Baux de Provence, an ancient village perched high on a craggy hill, I invited him back to my house. And he actually hesitated. "Are you sure?"

Did I really want to run into another affair?

I did.

I fell for him so hard that I never even considered walking down the street to Lola's house. Not until he and I were eating breakfast in our garden the next morning. When I did traipse down to find her, I walked with my hand interlaced with Bastien's. I could not wait to introduce him to Lola.

I knew the button to push on the other side of the wall to open the wrought iron gates. We walked, tangled together, up the dirt road, lined with plane trees that canopied above us. Lavender fields spread to the east and an olive grove to the west. The stuccoed house was the color of terra-cotta, and that same pottery lined the front porch, with verbena and lantana tumbling out of the huge clay pots.

I threw open the Mediterranean-blue door. "Lola! Lola! I'm back."

No response. Finally Salima, the caretaker of their house and garden, came from the back. She looked harried, her hair unpinned and falling loosely under her scarf.

I dropped Bastien's hand and ran to her, kissed her three times, right, left, right, on the cheeks.

"It's so good to see you, Salima!"

She grabbed my hands and pulled me into the *salon*, casting a suspicious look at Bastien. She put her finger to her lips. "Shhh. Not a word! Not a word!"

"What is it?"

She motioned with her eyes to Bastien.

"He's a good friend. He's fine."

Salima shook her head.

"Would you mind leaving us alone for a sec?" I begged him.

He frowned, then shrugged. "Of course. I'll wait in the front yard."

When he left, she grabbed my hands and burst into tears. "Something terrible has happened! I came to the house this morning to clean. I knew Malika and Lola had left for the weekend, but I expected them to be back today. The house was empty. But . . ."

My heart started thumping in my chest. Salima pulled me to the curving marble stairway, and I followed her up to the bedrooms on the second floor. Everything in the bedrooms was overturned, drawers emptied on the floor, pillows slashed. And there was blood everywhere.

I caught myself on the bannister, my head spinning, my heart hammering with fear. "Salima! Where are they? Have you called the police?"

"Yes, I called them. Just before you arrived. Someone is coming. Soon. I'm so afraid."

I held on to Salima even as she clutched me, both of us in shock. We stumbled back downstairs to the salon.

I spent the rest of the day with Salima at Lola's house, terrified that the gendarmes would find a body as they scoured the grounds. At some point, Bastien must have left. It was only hours later, when I trudged home, that I thought of him.

If I hadn't been so caught up in the impromptu affair, I would have seen Lola, been with her, noticed if anything was wrong. That day, guilt crawled up inside me, winding itself around me like Augusta Luise on the trellis by the house.

7

ABBIE

"Let's get Abbie back first." What a strange thing to say. I'm here, in living color; it's Bill who's gone away.

Diana had asked me to sit with what stirs me. I don't like that expression, so I change it to *Think about something that is bugging you to death.*

It is bugging me to death that Bill has just up and left. It is bugging me to death that he won't answer my calls. It is bugging me to death that he gets to work on a project he loves, according to Judith, while I am stuck here in a house full of boxes and a broken heart.

I feel so angry I'd like to yank out every stitch in my "remarkable" canvas. *"It strikes me, Abbie, that you know your husband very well to have lovingly stitched his life into the canvas."*

Exactly. So how in the world could he leave?

Well, I have always been one to do my homework. No Cliffs-Notes for this girl. I take out the cloth-bound journal Diana gave me and start making a list. I know exactly what I like. I like a clean house and none of Bill's clothes on the floor. I like it when the members of the Garden Club show up on time, no excuses, and have actually done what they promised. I like it when the boys do well on their sports teams and finish their assignments and attend youth group.

I look at the list and feel sick to my stomach. Is this who I am? Are these the things I find "life-giving"? When did I become so neurotic? When did I begin to worship my lists and grab so tightly to what I want for my family? It's true, I have suffocated them.

But what do *I* like?

When I was a girl, I loved camp, the spend-the-night-away-from-home-for-a-month kind of camp, with bugs and shared cabins and lots of sports and competition. I also liked camping out in a tent. When Bill and I were first married we went camping several times a year, until Bobby came along and I just couldn't manage all the paraphernalia that comes with a baby.

I love flowers, every kind. When we moved into the Grant Park neighborhood in 2000, our house was a true fixer-upper. We had a small plot of land that housed an unbelievable amount of junk left by the previous owners. I'd take the boys out back with me, and while they were playing, I'd garden. I turned that overgrown, junk-filled space into a little slice of paradise. It was my absolute favorite thing about the house. So why had I decided to move to a loft on the sixth floor of an old mill, trading in my backyard for a balcony?

I keep going with my list. I love beauty—fine china and lovely linens. But I used to cherish it, not possess it.

I love planning surprises. But Judith says that Bill hates surprises. And she's right.

Oh, this is all way too painful to think about.

"God's truth hurts. It pierces."

Oh yeah. I know who that piece of wisdom came from. How I miss her.

The boxes are stacked neatly, but I pull one off the other until I find the box I've labeled simply *Miss Abigail*.

I set it on the floor and plop down beside it, hands shaking. Poncie pads over and collapses beside me, head in my lap.

"Hey, girl. It's okay. It's okay." But dogs have a sixth sense, and she knows I am definitely not okay.

Miss Abigail. The inner-city missionary Mama met in 1962, the one who introduced her to true faith. The saint I was named for.

I open the lid and stare down at three beautifully framed poems by Amy Carmichael. Miss Abigail loved Amy Carmichael, the missionary to India, so I cross-stitched the poems and had them mounted and framed for her. When she died, her family insisted I take back the poems as well as the scrapbook I had made for her surprise eightieth birthday party. I pull the scrapbook into my lap, and Poncie begrudgingly gives me space.

I bury my face in my hands and whisper, "I miss you, Miss Abigail. I miss you!"

A hundred memories parade before me. Me as a tot, perched on a stool, stirring pots of spaghetti sauce as Mama prepares a meal to take to Mount Carmel Church. Me standing between Mama and Miss Abigail, ladling that same sauce onto mounds of spaghetti noodles while a skinny teen or a sagging older woman with no teeth waits patiently for a plate.

Nan and Ellie eventually came along too, all three of us helping out, but I loved it the most. Before I knew what it meant to worship God, I worshiped my namesake. I followed her all around that old church as a four-, five-, six-year-old. And she loved me. She loved me for exactly who I was.

Miss Abigail was nothing if not eccentric, with her long

gray ponytail and her beat-up station wagon crammed with giveaway clothes and cans of beans. The front porch of her house, located right down the street from the church, held used furniture and appliances that people would bring by as donations for her to pass on to the poor. Inside, her little house was crammed with boxes of used clothes, diapers (unused, thank goodness!), secondhand kitchen utensils, and just about anything else in the world that a household might need.

I wanted to be like her because she was perfect. Perfectly strange, perfectly saintly, perfectly imperfect with a perfect heart of gold. At thirteen or fourteen I remember lamenting, "I'll never be like you, Miss Abigail."

"Well of course you won't, Abbie girl. And why would you want to be?"

"Because you're perfect."

She grabbed my hands and bent down to look me in the eyes. "Abbie, we have the same name, and that is precious to me. But God made each one of us unique, and He doesn't want you to be anyone but who He made you to be. You just keep those eyes fixed on Him, and He'll make you more and more the Abbie He wants."

I understood what she meant. She loved me as I was, and so did this big and mysterious God she served so faithfully. But she was my mentor, and I spent many a Saturday following her around the Grant Park neighborhood offering its residents the love of Jesus and "goods" from her overflowing house.

I leaf through the scrapbook, the photos and careful calligraphy and cutouts . . . a love letter to this woman who had helped shape me.

I turn a page and see a photo from the summer after my sophomore year of college. There are five of us crowded around Miss Abigail in front of her '74 Buick station wagon, which we were sure ran on a blend of gas and prayer and angels' wings. We're leaning over and planting kisses on Miss Abigail's cheeks.

I can feel my chest constricting. Serving as an intern with these four other college women—two African American, one Asian American, one Latina—was one of the best summers of my life. They nicknamed me Triple A for Absolutely Accurate Abbie. My perfectionism was useful that summer; it countered the self-proclaimed starry-eyed idealism of the others. We worked well together, amid laughter and prayer, sweating in the muggy heat as we unloaded clothes or played softball with the neighborhood kids or painted the church doors or a hundred other projects. I was Triple A, needed and loved and appreciated.

Twenty-five years ago, I had tasted something so pure and good. What had happened?

Near the back of the scrapbook I find one of the few photos with Bill and Miss Abigail together. My stomach cramps as I stare at the photo and remember. Three months after Bill and I got married, he held me in his arms when I learned of her death. He stood so close at the funeral.

It hums in my mind again: *I miss you, Miss Abigail.*

I'm not sure I want to keep turning pages, but I always finish what I start. Always.

On the scrapbook's last page I've pasted a collage of photos of Mama and Daddy, Nan, Ellie, and me with Miss Abigail. I touch the photo of all of us when I'm nine. Ellie is four. It's before the accident.

Let's get Abbie back first.

Oh yeah.

The first time I remember trying to control life was when Ellie was scarred. Nan and I were at school the day of the kitchen fire. In the matter of a single day, Ellie went from being my curly-haired, five-year-old, blond firecracker of a little sister to a scarred and scared little girl.

I was scared too. This was a little child in the safest place she could be, her own home. If something so bad could happen to Ellie, anything could happen to anyone. I would have to figure out how to protect everyone I loved.

What a heavy burden it became!

Daddy's scars from Vietnam had bothered me. I could picture the shrapnel and hear the bomb exploding and imagine him waking up without an eye. But Daddy never acted wounded. In a way, his scars made him a perfect hero, just as Miss Abigail's eccentricity made her a perfect saint. But Ellie? Her scars drove her crazy for a long time.

When Mama almost died of breast cancer back in 2001, Bobby was a toddler and I was pregnant with Jason. Fear for Mama and for my little family overshadowed my ordered life. Then in 2012 Nan's first husband, Stockton, died in a car crash, leaving her widowed with three little girls. I clutched Bill and Bobby and Jason tightly, literally and figuratively. If Daddy and Ellie could be scarred, if Mama could have breast cancer and Nan's young husband die in such an awful way, what might happen to my men?

Maybe that was the last straw. Maybe that was when I went from an ordinary perfectionist to a control freak, hypervigilant and fearful. And then came Anna.

My fears grew. I had nightmares of Bill dying of a heart attack or being in a terrible accident.

How perfectly ironic that what drove him away was me trying so hard to make sure he never ever left.

I close the scrapbook, feeling as hollow and devastated as I did the day I stood near Miss Abigail's casket, as a gentle rain fell on the mourners gathered 'round.

CARO

We are sitting outside at a round wrought iron table. Votive candles in small jars are everywhere, flickering on the stone wall. Tiny white Christmas lights are twisted throughout the olive trees, and they twinkle romance down on us. Bastien is in the kitchen, putting the finishing touches on the meal.

Seven years ago I was sitting at this same table in the garden, my face splotched with tears, remembering the blood, remembering the glaring lights as four police cars descended, screaming tragedy, upon the dusty road that led to Lola's home.

I had tried to comfort Salima, tried to help her answer the onslaught of questions from the police. I'd called my parents and my siblings and begged them to come to Lourmarin. When I finally walked back to the farmhouse, in a complete stupor, Bastien was waiting for me by our front door. He wrapped me in his arms and spoke softly, led me to his house and to this very table.

"Sit down, Caro, let me get you a drink. You're in shock."

I was shaking violently, and my head was splitting. Why was I here with this man whom I barely knew? I wanted to be with my mother. She would hold me, and we would sob together for Malika and Lola, our friends.

Deep shame and guilt weighed me down, as if my arms held the draping wisteria that hung heavy and pungent on the latticework above Bastien's terrace.

When Bastien spoke, his voice sounded small, the smart, sexy, sophisticated tone completely gone. "Dear Caro, I'm so sorry." He actually looked devastated, yes, and deeply concerned. "*C'est terrible*. Terrible."

He brought me a glass of water, which I gulped down, then rushed to the bushes and threw up, along with what little was in my stomach. Heaving, I cried, "These people were my friends! Our friends. I played with Lola every summer for ten years. And then, out of nowhere, they disappear? Why would they simply disappear? And all the blood! You didn't see it! It looked like a slaughter!"

He wiped my mouth with a damp washcloth and brought me another glass of water, kind gestures that suddenly seemed too intimate. I felt naked and exposed before him in a completely different way than I had the night before. I gathered my arms around me. He read my body language and did not try to touch me. He doubtless saw a mixture of terror and anger in my eyes. I wanted to scream at the top of my lungs for the horror of what I had seen, but I also wanted to scream at Bastien. To tell him that he was the reason I had not visited Lola over the weekend, scream that he was the reason I had lost her.

But even though he was the reason, I was the one to blame.

My parents arrived a few hours later from their permanent home in Lyon. My sister, Ashley, too. Stephen flew in from America the day after the news broke. We sat in shock and watched the police go back and forth to Lola's house, questioning Salima and the other neighbors and us. And Bastien. But no one had any information at all. No one had seen Lola; her mother, Malika; or her father, Jean-Claude, in the forty-eight hours preceding the break-in. No one had heard anything.

Stephen found me that first night. "Had Lola spoken to you about anything that worried her?"

"No. No. I would remember. I only thought it strange that about two months ago she stopped sending me emails. We usually wrote once a week. I figured she was busy with school and exams. I didn't worry."

"They converted. Malika and Lola."

"What?"

"Last summer when I was back here, we talked often about the different faiths. Jean-Claude too. We sat out around the table and talked. Do you remember?"

"Of course I remember! All very respectful—Islam, Catholicism, evangelicals, Jews, agnostics."

"Later, Lola wrote to me." Stephen looked pained, as if he knew this might hurt me. "She wanted to know more about the Jesus of the Bible."

"So?"

"So she did a lot of reading, talking to a priest, to a pastor, and to a woman at a little evangelical church in Aix. And of course, Mom shared her whole story with them. Lola wrote me about two months ago to say she and her mother had become Christians. She was very happy."

"You're kidding!" I tried to assimilate this news, what felt like an enormous betrayal. Lola had confided in my brother, but not in me.

In 2005, my brother had reverted to religion after spending time at a refugee center in Austria, all very strange. I had no interest in any kind of religion. I was a third-culture kid, raised in five different countries, uprooted so many times that I finally stopped trying to make friends. When my father left my mother, I moved out too.

But Mom and Stephen had some type of spiritual experience in 2005. I was in my second year of high school at a boarding school in the north of France. I partied and drank with my friends, and I grasped at things to fill up the emptiness. Guys, parties, alcohol, drugs. So when Stephen and Mom talked about their experiences, it just made me furious. Mom had plunged into a depression for years. I didn't buy any part of a religious change.

And yet, they did change. Stephen broke up with his control-freak girlfriend, and Mom got out of her depression. And I guess they were really convincing, because my father came back to my mother, she stopped drinking, and, if what Stephen was saying was right, six years later Lola and Malika bought into whatever Mom and Stephen had gulped down.

Now I stared at my big brother and dared him with my eyes. "You think that their conversion had something to do with all of . . . all of this!"

"I don't know."

But as soon as I said it, I did know. Over the past few years, Lola had grown increasingly worried about her cousin, Khalid. Her mother's family in Iran were devout Muslims. Lola and her mother were faithful and conservative in dress, although not particularly devout.

Lola and I often went to the hammam and had our hands dyed with henna. I remembered one conversation from about a year earlier. "We're worried about Khalid. He has joined a radical group in Iran."

Lola and I had many discussions about the dangers of religion, any religion. But she especially worried for Khalid.

"Surely no one would want to hurt them because of their conversion!" I said to Stephen.

"I hope not."

"You're all the same, you evangelicals!" I had blurted. "Seeing Muslims as terrorists. Seeing anyone who believes differently from you as a threat and a sinner. Condemned."

Stephen's face reddened, and I prepared for a rebuttal. Instead he said, "Sis, I'd be fine to have this conversation with you at another time. But right now"—his eyes met mine—"right now this family whom we love seems to have met with something terrible. Let's work together to try to figure out what that could be."

I never saw Bastien in the following days when I was with my parents and siblings. But one afternoon he found me alone.

"Caro. Caro, I'm so sorry about all of this." He was searching my eyes. "I don't know what to say, and that's rare."

I wanted to fall into his arms, and at the same time I was repulsed by the thought. So I stood stiffly away from him.

"Would you like to go somewhere to talk?" he'd asked. "We could get a drink. . . ." All I heard was a type of sympathy or maybe pity in his voice.

"*Non! Non*, Bastien, please. Please."

"I'm so sorry, Caro," he'd said again and then gently touched my cheek with his hand. "It was a mistake."

I'd stared into his gray eyes for a few long seconds, then turned my head down and nodded.

Those four words would haunt me for years. What did he mean? Was our wonderfully romantic weekend a mistake? Was sleeping with me a mistake? Or was it just that he agreed with me, that the timing of it all was a mistake?

It was my fault to have fallen for him. I was to blame. I couldn't even accuse him of a friendly seduction. I was the one, on Sunday night, who invited him to my house and up to my bedroom. For all his French charm, cynicism, and allure, he had not seduced me.

Un concours des circonstances, the French say. It just happened by coincidence, Americans agree. It was pure coincidence that I was in Lourmarin alone when Bastien came over to offer tickets to my parents. A coincidence that he'd just moved in and didn't have a date, that we both liked jazz and spoke three languages and had lived in the same countries. Just a coincidence that we had even attended the same French university, years apart.

But coincidences aren't mistakes. Why was it a mistake? I

wanted to ask him that many times, but I never dared. Because maybe he'd meant that I was the mistake.

Instead, that day I hid my heart and said, "Yes, it's all been a mistake. I shouldn't see you again. Please. Please just leave me alone."

And I'd fled.

Now here we are, in the present, with the candles and the smell of summer and fresh bread, and Bastien says, "I promised I would tell you all I know. Are you ready to hear it, Caro?"

My throat has gone dry and my stomach is cramping with these memories. Through blurry eyes, I nod. "Yes, Bastien. I came all this way because you promised to tell me the whole story."

"You heard about Khalid," he says. "That he joined Isis. You know he's a very dangerous man."

"Of course, his face was all over the news after the Bataclan attack, and then he was thought to be somewhere in Belgium."

Bastien nods. "You know that for years I've tried to find answers from the authorities. But they won't tell civilians anything that we can't find on the news. He's dangerous, but still, as far as I can tell, they have never linked him to any crime with Malika and Lola."

"But there was a crime!" I whisper. "I was there when they found Malika's body."

He nods again, and his hand comes across the table and grasps mine. "Yes. *C'était terrible*, Caro. I'm so sorry."

I'm shaking with the memory. "They asked me to identify the body first because it took two days for Jean-Claude to get back from Japan with his business. And Salima was too distraught to view it. . . ."

I am waiting for Bastien to volunteer more information, but he is silent.

"What do you know? What else have you discovered?"

He gives a shrug and looks momentarily uncomfortable. Then he recovers and meets my eyes. "I have no more news about Lola, Caro. But I know that you must let go of the guilt. It has crushed you. You are carrying it around like a heavy cross." He shifts his long legs under the table, leans way back in the chair. "You do not have to solve the question of Lola. This is not your problem."

I start to protest, but he continues, oblivious. "I'm afraid I am still your problem." He gives the beguiling smile. "I am sorry I have caused you such problems. You are wondering if you love this Brett, if there is the passion we had. It is good to come back to figure this out." He sits forward, and with his finger traces a soft line down my face, and I flinch.

"After the terrible events with Lola's family, you descended into guilt."

This is not new news. We've discussed it plenty of times before.

"My poor Caro. You are not a guilty woman. You have a lust for all that is beautiful. You want to try it all on. You don't want to be tied down to marriage to this boy."

The heat on my face feels unbearable. Yes, guilt. Yes, he's right. The questions. The longing for a passion I had felt with him. I think I love Brett, but I miss the passion that I knew with Bastien.

"You wrote me! You said you had more news, and so I agreed to come over, but you had no intention of doing anything but seducing me," I say, my voice sharp with accusation.

"Have I ever seduced you, dear Caro?"

His look stabs me with the truth. Because he hasn't. Ever. Only once had we slept together, that one time. My initiative. I've seen him many times since, but never as his lover. Each visit was preceded by something I wanted more desperately than

Bastien: finding Lola. I'd spent days and weeks and months searching for her, writing letters to the government and to every NGO that looked for lost persons. There had been trips to different detention centers. From the summer of 2011 until I finally left for the States in the fall of 2014, I had helped Jean-Claude search for Lola.

I had even gone to Interpol, whose headquarters are in Lyon, and asked for information.

Inevitably, I'd let Bastien know when I had returned to Lyon or Lourmarin, and he'd come find me. Yes, I'd thought I didn't ever want to see him again, but he was the one who lived that tragic weekend with me. The horror and the guilt and the fear of what happened to our friends got all tangled up with Bastien. It made me want to run away from him and it begged me to draw him back. Somehow, reliving the tragedy with him felt like a step toward healing, even as it kept the wound gaping open and gushing blood.

In truth, I longed for Bastien to be more than a confidante. I wanted him as a lover.

Bastien understood the problem with my subconscious reasoning long before I was willing to admit it. "Of course we can talk, Caro. But this is not helping you get past those traumatic events. Anyway, Caro, I am not a safe bet." He'd told me the same thing the first time we met after the tragedy.

Well, obviously. Anyone could see that. He had the fine aquiline French nose, the penetrating eyes, the slim, muscular body that looked casual and at the same time sensual. And he had a thousand smiles in his repertoire—a pout, a smirk, a cynical turn of the lips, a sensual curve accompanied with half-opened eyes, a tender softening of his whole face into a genuine smile. He knew art and history and philosophy, but he also knew how to make me feel important, special, attractive.

We hiked Mont Sainte-Victoire again and again. We visited the lavender fields in July at the height of their splendor, and Bastien bought me every lavender lotion and spray and perfume and essential oil at the farm because he knew how it filled up my senses and my soul.

"You live life through your nose, dear Caro," he'd joke, and then tweak my nose to make his point. "You should be making perfume or tasting wine for a living."

He saw my soul, he pushed me to think in that irritatingly critical French way that I knew all too well from my years in French schools. Criticism can be good or bad or neutral. At first his criticism seemed negative, but gradually I found his questions and remarks stimulating and helpful.

So often, in those days together, I wanted to say, *Would you have me? I would settle down with you, if only you'd have me.*

But Bastien was always honest. "I will never marry. I am a loner, Caro." Once he had even shared a bit about his up-bringing. "I was raised in the bourgeoisie. Everything based on appearances. My parents had a very unhealthy marriage. I will not do that to anyone." His face had gone white for a split second. "Sometimes I wish for a family of my own, but I do not trust myself. My dear Caro, I am afraid I'm good for you only in small doses."

When my eyes had filled with tears, infuriating me, showing my weakness and disappointment, he'd taken my hands. "Caro, you are beautiful and smart, and you have a good soul. We have a strong connection, but I am not reliable. I wish I were."

Then change! I'd wanted to scream at him.

Sometimes when he'd say this sort of thing, his eyes were tender, loving, soft. Sometimes he would let down his cynical veneer—yes, it was a veneer—and let me peek into his soul too. I wanted him to declare his love for me, but he would not.

I suppose I respected him for this, in a way. He didn't lead me on. With him, I knew.

And then, inevitably, he'd pronounce these words, "Caro, why are you still frantically searching for Lola? Let it go. It's not your fault. Please."

He was begging me with his eyes to let it go. In those moments, I felt there was something else, something almost desperate, that he wanted me to see. *But what?*

"Caro, for all your spur-of-the-moment ways, deep down you want stability. You want to marry. It is in your DNA. You must marry the right man, to be sure. But Caro, it is not me." How had he read me so completely?

Once when I'd come to Lourmarin after Lola's disappearance, we ate at our café, we walked the streets of Aix, his arm slung around my shoulders. "Caro, please don't waste your life on these things." For I told him about the other men and what was becoming a real problem with alcohol. "You are beautiful and talented. You see beauty with those eyes, you are gifted with the photography, you smell life in all its intricacies. Your eyes and nose, they work perfectly. But this"—and he had tapped his finger against my head—"this is not working well. You must get your mind straightened out, dear Caro."

I would write Bastien and beg to see him and he would come. He'd cock his head and smile and tease, but he wouldn't touch me in a romantic way. *Was I so bad, so disgusting that you don't want me again?* That was my fear. And yet, I knew he cared. Maybe I was like his little sister now. Maybe the horror had scarred our relationship so much that he didn't want anything more.

Once he had even whispered, "You don't want me as a lover, Caro. I will only make you sad. And Caro, I don't want you to be sad."

One night shortly after the Bataclan debacle, when I was watching the news with my parents, a photo of Khalid appeared on the news. He had somehow been involved in the bombing at Bataclan. He was linked to two other terrorist groups in Belgium. I screamed and Mom began to cry and Papa cursed in French. And then we sat there in a stupor and all the horror of that weekend came rushing back in. It made me all the more determined to find out what happened to Lola. But it also drove me crazy.

Stephen begged me to move to the States, and my parents pleaded the same. I was slowly losing my mind. Bastien, whom I saw a week later, was the one who really convinced me. "Caro, let it go! Let it go! You cannot solve this, and you see that this man, this Khalid, is a terrorist. He is bad. Please, for the love of God, let it go."

When I told him that I was moving to the States, that Stephen had begged me to go into a treatment program, Bastien said, "Yes! Yes, do this, dear Caro! Please. Get sober and then find your life, your real life."

"So I'm telling you good-bye," I'd said. *Please, if you would only say you love me.*

"Yes, you are right, my Caro. Please. Sometimes you have to say good-bye to so many things, good things, but sometimes they get in the way of your real life."

I wanted you to be part of my real life. Am I a mistake? Am I?

So I let go, and I left. I let Lola go and Bastien too. No more emails, no more calls. No more rendezvous in Lourmarin where I longed for him to take me in his arms and kiss all the confusion away. I was slowly letting the dream and the nightmare die.

Until he wrote me, three weeks ago.

I cannot think of these things, so I shout, "You lied to me! You told me you had something more to share about Lola!"

I am trying not to cry. Why have I come? What in the world did I think I would discover with Bastien? I know he's right. I have come back here to see him one more time.

Dinner is over. The night is muggy and calm, the cicadas chirping madly. He walks me across the road to my house, his arm slung carelessly around my shoulder. "I am leaving tomorrow, Caro, for Paris. How long are you staying here?"

"I don't know. Stephen wants me to do a story on the Camino, so I'll be backpacking for a week or two at least."

I don't mention how adamant Stephen and Tracie are that I leave Lourmarin and get my butt on the trail—with Bobby Jowett and his mother.

"Good for you, Caro. This will be a perfect thing. Very enlightening." He comes close and cups my face in his hands. "Two weeks. You will walk and think. Then you will know what to do." He takes my hand and holds it fiercely. "Then, if you decide you would like to see me again, you must only call, and I will come down at once."

We are standing in front of my door, and I expect him to peck me on the cheeks as has become his habit. But instead he leans in close, and I think his eyes are asking me something. I can feel my heart ramming my ribs. I don't budge. I simply meet his eyes. But then I tilt my head upward and lean forward until my lips meet his. He takes me into his arms and kisses me, hard, passionately, until I, breathless, manage to break away. "Please, Bastien," I choke out. "Please leave me now."

I watch him amble across the road, his fragrance lingering in my mind, his passion still tingling on my lips.

CHAPTER

8

BOBBY

"And exactly why do you want to go to Linz?" asks Marie, one of the Oasis workers.

Over the course of the two weeks I've been helping at the Oasis, I've come to appreciate Marie. She's one of the administrators, obviously devoted to the refugees.

"To help out at the House of Hope, like I've done here at the Oasis."

She looks up from the computer and over her glasses and says, "You know, you're not the first short-termer to be swept off his feet by Rasa."

I'm so shocked I can't find anything to say. Heat creeps up my face.

Marie notices my discomfort and changes the subject. "You can't just show up and do whatever you please, you know. They have protocols just as we do. You did fill out a form to come here."

I've never been big on details. Head in the clouds, Mom often says. "I can fill out forms again. Whatever you need."

"How long do you plan to be in Linz?"

I clear my throat. "Just for a week. I really do want to help at the House of Hope. Stephen wants me to write an article about the House like I did for the Oasis. But then I'm going to walk part of the Camino . . . with my mother. She's going through a bit of a hard time."

Marie brightens. "The Camino with your mother! How wonderful." She looks back at the computer. "Well, you'll need lodging in Linz, and meals."

I swallow and stare at my running shoes. I notice one of the laces is untied and bend over to fix them. "If you tell me what I need to do I'll be happy to comply, Marie. Of course I'll pay for my food and housing."

She looks up again, and a faint smile is hovering on her lips. "Relax, Bobby. I'm just giving you a hard time. You remind me so much of Stephen all those years ago. He was older than you in years, but much younger in the faith." She sits back in her chair, and I read nostalgia on her face. "We are ministry partners with the House of Hope, Bobby. I believe I can talk with Rasa's father and a few of the other full-time workers. A week, you say?"

I breathe a sigh of relief. "Yes, just a week. Mom gets here on August 9."

"Well, I'd better get to it then. I'll text you what I hear."

"Hey, buddy. How's everything going?"

"Good, Dad. Really good. I mean great, really."

"Sounds like you've enjoyed helping out at the Oasis."

"Yeah. It's been awesome."

"And you've visited all around Vienna." Dad has uploaded a tracking app on his phone so he can follow my adventures.

"It's been really fun, Dad."

"You doing okay with money?"

"Yep. So far I've hardly spent anything." I hesitate. "Um, Dad. I'm taking the train to a city a few hours away tomorrow. I know you're stalking me on your phone, so I don't want you to freak out when you see me heading west."

He laughs. "Noted. I won't freak out. Which city?"

"Linz. A friend who was volunteering at the Oasis lives there. Her dad is a pastor and runs a refugee center too, like the Oasis. I'm going to do a short article on it for Stephen."

"Got you." I can hear him smiling through the phone. "Going there just for Stephen? Not for this friend?"

"Da-ad."

"Just asking."

I want to change the subject. "Have you talked to Mom yet?"

"No."

"You don't think you should call her?"

Silence.

"I know it's supposedly none of my business, but she sounds really depressed, Dad."

He doesn't say anything for a few seconds. I can almost see him wiping his hands over his face, the way he does when something is troubling him.

Things don't usually bother Dad, at least they didn't seem to. But this past year, Mom has bothered him. I don't know any other way to say it. He seems to be wiping his hands over his face every day, usually while he's talking to her.

Now he's the one to change the subject. "What's this about doing the Camino with an Iranian refugee?"

"I thought you said you hadn't talked to Mom!"

"I haven't, but she sends me plenty of texts and emails."

"Then you know she's coming too."

"So she says."

"She'll be here in a week. My friend—Rasa's her name—and I are going to meet her at the beginning of the French Camino in Le Puy-en-Velay."

At least I hope Rasa will be with me. And Caroline might be there too. I don't even want to think about that.

"I know that will be very special for your mother, Bobby. I'm sure you'll all have lots to talk about and learn from the experience." He pauses, a sure sign of a reprimand coming. "But Bobby, it's not up to you to rescue her. Neither she nor I expect that from you. I've told you that this is not your problem."

"I didn't invite her to come, Dad. She absolutely did freak out about me doing the Camino with Rasa. I shouldn't have said anything." But then I add, "Actually, it's okay. I doubt anyone would approve of me taking Rasa on the Camino alone. And Mom sounds very lost. I guess I'm just worried."

Another long silence. Finally he says, "Maybe going over there will do her some good. But Bobby, I don't want you ruining your gap year trying to take care of your parents."

I don't say that wondering if my parents are getting a divorce is already going a long way toward ruining my gap year.

"Dad, how are *you*? I mean, are you planning to stay in Chicago, like, for a long time?"

He gives one of his signature sighs. "I can't really say, Bobby. I'm pretty much taking it a day at a time. I'll be here through mid-October, though, for sure."

We chat for a few minutes about Jason and football. Dad doesn't usually have a lot to say, but when we end the call, I have the distinct impression that he's leaving a whole lot of things unsaid. Somehow, I don't feel reassured.

The train ride to Linz takes two hours because we stop in every village along the way. I am impatient, so I take out the

110

sketch pad and start recording the countryside, the onion-domed churches, the geraniums cascading out of window boxes in homes that look like Swiss chalets.

I get off at the train station, totally nervous. *Chill, Bobby!* I tell myself. I pull up the map of downtown Linz on my phone and begin navigating the streets. Marie has assured me it's a very short walk from the train station.

The House of Hope is a two-story building painted a happy shade of green and sitting behind a Baptist church. A woman about Mom's age greets me at the door.

"Bobby Jowett?" She sounds totally American.

"Yes."

"I'm Lisa. Marie phoned the other day, and fortunately the apartment upstairs is vacant." She's reading a sheet of paper. "You've been helping out at the Oasis and want to volunteer for a week here, I understand?"

"Yes, ma'am."

She grins. "Don't 'ma'am' me, please! Makes me feel old. And Southern. I'm not Southern."

"Oh, okay. Sorry."

"Let me show you around." We go inside the foyer, and the first thing I notice is a large rectangular sign on the wall that has *Welcome* painted in different colors and at least ten different languages.

"We have many ministries here," Lisa is explaining. "Some are similar to the Oasis—like the coffee bar and the Bible studies—but we also have sewing classes and art classes, German classes, sports activities. Marie mentioned you're an artist."

I feel my cheeks redden. "Well, I'm studying art, yes."

"She said you've done some lovely sketches of the Oasis and you've been commissioned by an American newspaper to write a blog about the House of Hope."

"An online paper. Yes, my boss has visited the Oasis several times throughout the years. Stephen asked me to take photos and write blog posts on both the Oasis and the House of Hope. Of course, I won't put any of the refugees' faces on the Internet. I'm familiar with the rules."

"Articles about the House of Hope in an American online newspaper." She lifts her eyebrows and smiles. "Not bad. Where are you from again? The South, obviously," she adds.

"Atlanta."

"Atlanta, yes, the busiest airport in the States. Can't say that's endeared the city to me, but I've never actually left the airport, so perhaps I don't have a clear picture." She grins. "Well, along with your writing, would you be interested in giving a few art lessons? The classes are on Wednesday and Friday afternoons. In fact"— she glances down at her phone—"one starts in two hours."

"Sure, I'd love to help! Anything you need."

"Great. Well, come upstairs to your room and we'll let you get settled. Then I'll introduce you to some of the staff." She gives a wink. "I hear you've already met Rasa."

I accept then that my time in Linz will go from one awkward moment to the next.

I'm staying in the upstairs apartment, which has a bedroom, a sitting room, and a kitchenette with microwave and sink. I set my backpack against the bed and reprimand myself. My hands are shaking. *Calm down, you idiot.* I do a few sets of crunches, trying to shake my nervous energy. Then I make myself a cup of instant coffee and try, failing miserably, to turn my mind to what I can offer in the art class.

When I come back downstairs Lisa gives me a tour. We peek inside a sewing room, where several women are diligently working the machines. Outside on the asphalt parking lot a group of boys are shooting baskets.

"And here's the art room," she says, opening a door.

"Wow," I say as I step into the room. The walls are covered in multicolored, bright splashes of paint. I walk over to the far wall to inspect what's written inside each splash—the name of a country and then a signature.

Lisa notices my interest and says, "We ask all our visitors to sign their name and country."

"I like it! It gives a feeling of belonging and hope."

She nods. "Many people say that." We walk across the hall. "The German class is meeting in this next room," she whispers as she opens the door. I let out an involuntary gasp as I see Rasa standing in the front beside a whiteboard. A dozen young teens are sitting at a table. She glances at me and smiles, and I feel all gooey inside. And very foolish.

"You can talk to her after your classes are done," Lisa says. "Ready for your students?"

"Sure." But I feel disoriented and light-headed.

When I walk back into the art room, Lisa introduces me to a teen from Afghanistan, a young father from Nigeria, and an older man from Syria. They look expectant. I close my eyes and think of my art classes at home and begin. We communicate with our hands and our pencils. We laugh, we create, and I feel something warm and affirming.

Near the end of the hour, Tabor, the Nigerian, nods to my sketch pad, which I've been using, and I hand it over without thinking.

Suddenly he is smiling and pointing to a sketch I'd done at the Oasis. "Girl! Here! Rasa!"

I want to hide under the table, but the other two have crowded around Tabor as he leafs backward through my sketches of these past weeks. They are laughing and patting me on the back and saying, "Bobby loves Rasa."

I'm sure they can read my complete embarrassment and mortification. Are they going to run across the hall and tell her that I'm obsessed?

But Tabor comes beside me, puts his arm around my shoulders the way Dad might do, motions to the three of them, and says, "Our secret. Yes?"

The other men nod, laughter in their eyes. "Yes. Our secret."

When my students leave the room, Rasa comes in. Fortunately, I've closed the sketch pad. "Hi," she says, obviously trying to sound American.

I laugh. "Hi back."

We stand in silence. She seems to feel every bit as awkward as I do, which makes me feel oddly relieved.

"The House of Hope is amazing." I swallow. "Lots of original ideas, like the walls in this room."

Rasa points to a framed newspaper clipping. "This was in an American newspaper years ago. A journalist interviewed one of the full-time workers at the Oasis. We believe the same things."

I read the article, digesting the quote from a man named Tom. *A value that is deeply engrained in me from my time in the Oasis is Presence. We welcome refugees into the Oasis, our homes and our lives. We offer them a safe place where they can come and know they are welcome. We move toward refugees even when language is a barrier. We share meals, stories and celebrations. We visit them. We pray together. We want to know their names.*

I finish reading and Rasa says, "So we had the idea of having a place where the refugees not only tell us their names and where they are from, but they leave it with us, as a blessing, as proof they were here, and they were seen. They are not invisible."

As usual, I don't know what to say.

"You can paint a splash too."

"But I'm not a refugee."

She shrugs. "But you are. We are all refugees—pilgrims on the earth. We are awaiting our eternal home. Peter, the disciple of Jesus, says we are aliens and strangers."

I have already learned that Rasa doesn't enjoy small talk. I am drawn to the intensity in her voice and her words.

"By the way," she says as we leave the art room, "you're having dinner with my family tonight."

"Oh, okay, great. Thank you."

Mortified. That's how I feel a few minutes later as I search through my backpack and dig out a fancy hand towel covered with images of Atlanta. Mom made sure I had a dozen of them to give as gifts. Just in case. I certainly won't give one to Lisa, with her commentary on Atlanta, but hopefully Rasa's mother will appreciate it.

"My parents don't speak a lot of English," Rasa informs me as we ride the bus to her home. "Baba gets by, but Mamaan won't say much. But my little brother, Omid, he'll jabber on and on. He's thirteen and thinks he's thirty."

We climb a narrow stairwell to the fourth floor and go inside the apartment. It's small and very clean, with tiled floors. Immediately I feel as if I've stepped into a Middle Eastern home. I guess I have. I follow Rasa's actions and remove my shoes. A boy with black hair slicked down with gel slides into the hallway in sock feet. "Hi there!" he says, with an accent that sounds totally American.

"My little brother, Omid." Rasa winks at me.

"Good to meet you, Omid."

"I heard you're an artist. Do you want to see some of my drawings?"

"Omid! Don't be rude. He just arrived."

"I'd be happy to look at your drawings, Omid. Later."

Rasa leads me into the den, furnished with cushions all along the four walls. "We have kept some of our Iranian customs."

"Of course." I'm trying to appear calm, but the thought of meeting her parents has me sweating. Just then, a stocky middle-aged man with graying hair comes into the room.

"Hello, Bobby." He offers his hand. "I'm Hamid, Rasa's father."

I swallow the ball in my throat. "Good to meet you, Mister . . ." I realize with total embarrassment that I don't know Rasa's last name.

"Just call me Hamid. Americans sometimes have a hard time with Middle Eastern surnames." But he's laughing good-naturedly. "So, you want to take my daughter away from me. On a hike?"

Once again, I cannot find my voice.

Rasa giggles and points at me. "Your eyes, Bobby! They're huge! You look terrified!" She takes her father's hand in a loving gesture. "Baba, don't scare poor Bobby."

"You are scared? But I am not a scary man."

Indeed, he has a gentleness about him. I only manage a nod.

"Why do you want to do this pilgrimage?"

"Well, uh, um, I think it will be spiritual, and there will be many chances to share our faith with pilgrims who are searching spiritually. You know." Beet red.

"Rasa has many opportunities to talk of Isa to the refugees right here."

"Yes, of course. It will be a different experience."

"How long?"

"Just two weeks."

"Two weeks is a long time to take my daughter away."

"My mother is coming too."

"Ah."

"Baba," Rasa interrupts. "He's worried for his mother and wants to care for her." She then begins jabbering in Farsi. I just wait, heart jittering.

The mother, Alaleh, answers back in Farsi, and they all laugh.

Omid says, "We know why you want to take Rasa. You're in love with her!"

I want to crawl under the table.

But I don't.

I make it through dinner without too many more embarrassing moments. Rasa walks with me to the bus stop, and as we wait she says, "I cannot go with you on this hike, Bobby. I'm sorry. You see, my father needs me at the church. And I cannot risk falling in love with a boy who will tempt me to go away from where God has called me."

Risk falling in love!

"Where is that?" I manage.

"Here," she says. "I am to stay here. I lead the worship on Sundays and I teach the German classes three nights a week. And I start university in town in September."

I try to hide my disappointment. The mountains are crested with a snow that never melts, far in the distance. But the air is warm, and the river runs soft beside us. "Would you pray about it?" I ask.

She turns her eyes toward me. "Pray about the hike?"

"Yes." I search for the words. "You're like the wind . . . The Spirit blows and you follow. You live by faith. But I have faith too, and I don't believe it's an accident we met."

She cocks her head and looks perplexed. "What kind of boy goes to Europe for his grandmother, walks the Camino with his very sad mother, and draws my face in sketches when I am not there?" She glances at me, smiling, and I know someone has told her about that. "Perhaps he is a very special boy. Perhaps he is someone I must get to know better."

ABBIE

I'm exhausted long before I ever start walking the Camino. I've spent the better part of the last week preparing for this trip, and now I think I am just about crazy. I cannot believe I'm doing this.

I changed my ticket, and that cost a pretty penny. Instead of flying with Bill to La Rochelle in October to research his ancestors and celebrate his fiftieth, I'm flying to Paris in five days and taking a train to that town called Le Puy-en-Velay.

Who knew there were thousands of sites online about the Camino. It's almost as if this pilgrimage thing is as in style as the whole spiritual direction thing.

I've informed Bobby about the day we'll start this adventure. I can tell he's not overly excited about my coming. To put it lightly. Actually, I think he's pissed at me, to use one of his more colorful expressions.

What are you doing, Abbie? a voice is whispering. *You're suffocating him again. The gap year is about his getting away from you!*

But I argue with the voice. He cannot go traipsing around Europe with a girl he just met! I'm making it possible for him to do something he really wants to do.

I shut down those annoying voices by going through a book of French verbs that I found on a bookshelf. I took high school French and spent a semester in France in college. My French is rusty, but by golly, I will get it back. Bobby took French too, but I've never heard him pronounce a word.

I'm in the process of reviewing the subjunctive when, to my surprise, he calls.

"Guess what, Mom. Caro's going to join us on the Camino too." He does not sound very enthusiastic.

"I thought her name was Rafa."

"Rasa."

"Yes, Rasa."

I'm relieved to hear him laugh. "No, I mean, yes, Rasa's coming with me. But Caro is going to find us in Le Puy."

I'm totally confused. "Who is Caro?"

I can practically hear Bobby rolling his eyes. "Mom. You know Caro. She's Stephen's sister. She works at the *Peachtree Press*."

"Oh, oh yes. Caroline Lefort. Yes, I remember." I've met her once—a very hip young woman with a flair for the dramatic. She did write good stories. "What a coincidence" is all I can manage to say.

"I know. She's over here doing research for Stephen and planning to walk the Camino in a few days. Stephen thought we might meet up."

"Hmm. Very nice," I say and immediately forget about her . . . until the next morning, when I find an email from Stephen in my inbox.

Dear Abbie,

Delighted to hear that you're going over to be with Bobby for a walk on the Camino. It was life changing for me.

I wanted to ask you for a favor about my sister, Caroline. I think you've met her once or twice. She's in France right now, at our parents' home in Provence. She's planning to walk the Camino too. Doing a story for me.

She's had a bit of a rough patch lately—say, the last ten years—and she doesn't seem to be making the best decisions.

I was wondering if you could look out for her if your paths cross. No pressure. She's gifted as all get out, but she has a real knack for getting into trouble. Not making the wisest choices.

Okay, yeah, I'm worried. When I found out that you'd be over there, I must admit I was relieved. I know there will be thousands of pilgrims walking the trails, but I thought maybe you could suggest that Caro start with you and Bobby. She sometimes needs a little shove to get her moving in the right direction.

I hope this isn't a burden. I don't want to spoil your fun. It's just that if you could help her stay on track, well, I'd be grateful.

Warmly,

Stephen

He adds her cell number at the bottom of the email.

Well, of all things. My first thought is that she sounds a lot like Jason. But then I remember she's in her late twenties, not sixteen. My second thought is that if I'm already going to be looking after Bobby and Rasa, one more needy soul won't be a problem. And my third thought is that of course I will do this for Stephen. We owe him big time.

I have asked to see Diana again before I go. It annoys me to break the rules—you're only supposed to meet with a spiritual director once a month—but I feel so undone by my life that I quash my pride and call her.

I get to her office—this time she's wearing a very stylish summer suit, apricot—and wish I didn't need this. But I do. I just do.

After Diana lights the Christ candle and offers a brief prayer, I launch into my story.

"I'm leaving in two days for the Camino. Perhaps I should feel excited, but I don't. I just feel ill. All the time. Like I'm going to lose my son too because I'm running after him, if that makes sense. But I have to." I tell Diana about Rasa.

"Anyway, I have a huge ball of regret eating me up on the inside. There's still no word from Bill. I text him every day, and I've emailed him about my travel plans. In case he cares." I'm pretty sure he doesn't. "But I've done the Rule of Life."

I obediently pull out the journal Diana gave me and open it to where I've used many different colors of felt-tip pens to create my Rule. Diana looks at it. For a long time. It's something I like and dislike about her. She's obviously not in a hurry.

The good part is that she is really studying what I've written and drawn, but the bad part is that she is taking so much time that this precious hour is ticking away, and I have so many other things to talk about!

"This is lovely, Abbie. The colors, the shapes, the words you've chosen to describe your Rule. A work of art."

"I enjoyed putting it together."

"That's good to hear."

"Thinking back about things I enjoyed, 'life-giving things' as you say, was hard. It took me back to the woman whom I considered to be my spiritual mentor."

"Tell me about her."

"Miss Abigail," I say. "I'm named after her. She was an inner-city missionary here in Atlanta and the most unorthodox person you can imagine. And I loved her. I loved her for all her crazy, unorthodox ways. Maybe that seems surprising, given how straitlaced I am. But she had a heart bigger than all of Atlanta and just exuded joy. As I got older, I helped her out a lot. She didn't have an organizational bone in her body." I laugh. "She recognized my gifts and talents and applauded them. When I was with her, I didn't feel like a control freak or a perfectionist. I was Triple A."

"Triple A?"

"Absolutely Accurate Abbie."

Diana chuckles. "Love it."

"It was a compliment, and I enjoyed being accurate. I helped to organize fundraisers and neighborhood food drives and picnics for the homeless. I felt most useful in a group when I could help others come up with a plan."

"Do you still feel that way?

"Rarely. Now I just drive everyone crazy with my planning and my control."

"And how do their reactions affect you?"

"I resent it. Why can't they just appreciate my gifts the way Miss Abigail did? When she died I was already married and getting on with my life, but . . . I guess I felt like I'd lost my mentor."

I look over at Diana. She is sitting on the edge of her chair, anticipation in her eyes, as if I'm going to do a big reveal.

"I hadn't thought of it this way before, but she died a few months after I got married. I was devastated, of course, but I was also a newlywed, madly in love. And then life got busy and I never found another mentor."

"And never really grieved the one you had?"

"Perhaps."

"What does that feel like now?"

I wish she would stop asking me how I feel, but then I surprise myself by admitting, "It feels like I'm losing my father, too, in the same way that I lost Miss Abigail." I bite my lip. "He's losing his memory, and he's almost blind. He's a Vietnam vet. I feel fear," I blurt out. "We've had a lot of losses in the family, and it's left me scared and vulnerable and determined to keep everyone okay. To make things perfect for my family. Of course, it doesn't work."

I can tell she is absorbing every word. "Tell me about this fear."

"I'm afraid that if I don't do things right, something bad will happen. I feel protective. And now I've driven my family away. That was my greatest fear—losing Bill. And boy, have I lost him." Tears spring into my eyes. "He doesn't even care what's going on with me. I've had no word from him since the day he walked out of the house. Don't you find that strange?"

Diana says nothing. Then, "Do you?"

"Heck yeah! He's my husband. How dare he just leave and not give any sign of life, of caring about me? I text him and email and get complete silence."

"What did he ask of you, Abbie, when he left? What exactly did he say?"

"He said he needed a break. To just give him a break."

"And do you think sending him texts and emails feels like a break to him?"

How dare she? I feel my defenses surge, and I want to scream or punch something. Then, almost immediately, I calm. She's absolutely right. "Okay, no more texts or emails. I'll leave him alone."

"I believe that will be a good next step." We sit in silence for way too long. Then she looks back at the Rule of Life I've created. "Perhaps we can talk about a few other disciplines to practice while you are walking on the Camino."

"Okay."

"Will you be carrying a Bible?"

"Only the one on my phone. And I'm going to take the felt-tips pens and this journal. And my cross-stitch."

"Good to the journal. But the cross-stitch? You aren't afraid of misplacing it?"

"I think it needs to be part of this whole process."

"Fair enough." Diana gives me two handouts and briefly explains each one: The Prayer of Examen and Lectio Divina. Both seem really . . . Catholic.

"Have a blessed trip," she says. "I'll be praying that our Lord Jesus makes His presence very known to you as you travel along the Pilgrim's Way."

CHAPTER

9

CARO

My cell phone awakens me. "Yeah."

"Hey." It's Tracie. I squint to read the time. Seven in the morning in France.

"Trace, what are you doing up at one in the morning?"

"Worrying about you."

Great.

"Where are you?" she demands.

"At the house."

"Still? You were supposed to be starting the Camino."

"I got delayed." Three days later, I'm still smiling about Bastien's kiss.

"That does not sound good."

"Oh, Trace. This isn't going to work. Bastien is right. I didn't really come back for Lola. I came back for him. And he kissed me, Trace!" *Well, actually I initiated it, but he seemed to enjoy it thoroughly.* "I'd given up on that, you know. Maybe he's changing his mind about us. I think there is something more he wants me to see."

"Don't be stupid. Get out of there!"

"Chill, Tracie. He's gone back to Paris. I'm here alone."

"Have you talked to Brett?"

"Yes, I have talked to Brett. Several nice, predictable conversations."

"So you really aren't looking for more information about your friend? I thought Bastien told you he had something to share."

"He did. He said he wanted me to get over my guilt."

"You aren't seriously thinking of hooking back up with that Frenchman, are you?"

"Trace, quit yelling. I can hear you." I have gotten out of bed, have put the phone on speaker, and am making a pot of coffee. "Let's just say that I feel more confused than ever. Not less. But he's right, you know. My therapist said the same thing. That I have to forgive myself."

"Look, Caro. Yes, to forgiving yourself for not being there for Lola. But a huge *no* to continuing to see Bastien."

"I'll think about it, Trace." I find the cream in the fridge and take it out. "Thanks for caring. And please, don't say anything to Stephen. Promise?"

"You're impossible! Your brother is worried. But I won't say anything to him if you will promise me to get your tail onto the Camino."

"I will. I will. Bobby and I have been in touch. I know his mother's coming along too. He gave me her cell."

"Good. So when are you meeting up with them?"

"Soon. Not sure exactly, but you know. Soon."

"Caroline. Call Abbie Jowett now and figure it out! And let me know your plans. I'll give you till tomorrow. If I haven't heard from you by then, I will not be held responsible for what I tell your brother."

But before I get around to calling her, Abbie Jowett calls me. I can tell that Stephen has asked her to watch out for me.

Admittedly I have a knack for creating drama, but it irritates me that he still treats me like a teenager.

"I fly out of Atlanta on the eighth and will take a train to Le Puy the morning of the ninth. I'll be meeting Bobby and his friend at the train station that afternoon and—"

Finally I break in. "Okay, I'll plan to catch up with you at some point."

Vague doesn't sit well with Abbie Jowett. "Which day and which town?" she asks.

Stephen had mentioned Le Puy as a spot for great photo shoots, so I tell Abbie I'll meet her there.

I have five days to clean out the house, which should be plenty if I don't waste them, as I've done these first few. Bastien is a very bad distraction, even when he's not physically present. As I told Tracie, his kiss has me more confused than ever.

I go through my clothes and personal items. Then I move to the salon, where Mom has left me several things to look through.

Caroline, here's a folder I found from years ago. There are a few photos of Lola. I didn't want to toss it out before you had a chance to go through it.

I sink into the worn leather couch and take a deep breath. Do I want to remember more? There are mainly newspaper clippings about my father's work with Peugeot. And there's one from the little local paper, a feature story about the growing population of "summer people" who have found Lourmarin such a lovely spot to vacation. A photographer shot pictures of Lola and me picking grapes and hunting for champignons and riding ponies, and we thought we were the next best thing to famous. We look young, carefree, innocent.

Had Lola really converted to Christianity? Could that be true?

I remember a conversation with her when we were teenagers. We were stretched across my bed, looking at fashion magazines.

"Your brother has gotten very religious, hasn't he?"

"Yeah. He's driving me crazy with all his God talk."

"I know. Me too." But Lola blushed.

I sighed. "Please don't tell me you're in love with Stephen!"

"Okay." She smiled. "I won't tell you."

We both giggled like silly girls, but then I said, "Look, Lola. He's a great guy, even with his little religious tangent. But he's dating another girl. Very seriously. A girl who got religious at the same time and place as he did, in Austria."

She faked a pout. "I know that too. He's told me all about Tracie. Don't worry, Caroline. I'm not really in love with him." She brought her knees under her chin, hugging them to her chest. "I'm just in love with the idea of him. And"—her expression grew more serious—"I like the way he talks about refugees. Not many people understand. I think he does."

Lola had told me the story of how her mother escaped Iran in the fall of 1988, soon after what is known as Iran's reign of terror. Malika was a student at Tehran University when the Ayatollah Khomeini began cracking down on political dissidents. Many students broke the law by reading a newspaper that spoke out about Iran's leadership, and little by little they simply began to disappear.

In May of 1988, a three-month reign of terror began, and thousands of students were taken away in groups of six or seven and hung—lynched! Their crime was simply supporting the opposing political party.

The hangings were whispered about in Evin Prison, where Malika's brother was held captive. During a prison uprising he escaped and reported the horror that was happening. Since Malika had also supported this party, he urged her to leave the country with him. They escaped in the night and made their way through Turkey to Europe, starving but alive.

Malika settled in France, where she met and married Jean-Claude Fourcade. Lola was born in France, was a French citizen, had a French surname. Still, she experienced racism because she looked Arab. Jean-Claude worked for Peugeot, like my father, but our families really got to know each other when we both bought vacation homes in Lourmarin.

I pick up another newspaper clipping from the Aix-en-Provence paper, with a photo of Mom in a floor-length ball gown and Dad in a tux at a fancy Peugeot affair. They're smiling, their arms around each other, and standing next to Lola's parents. Malika looks youthful and radiant.

Then I suck in my breath. In the background are other men and women in party attire. And there, staring back at me, with a cigarette hanging from his mouth and his arm slung around the shoulder of a gorgeous woman, is Bastien.

I shiver and look for the date. May 2007.

Bastien was in Aix-en-Provence, a stone's throw from Lourmarin, in May of 2007. At a black-tie Peugeot affair. That can't be right. It was *four years later* when I met him for the first time, when he told me he'd never been to Lourmarin or Aix before. *I'm new with Peugeot. Had to get away from Paris, and Lourmarin has a great reputation.*

My head is spinning.

"Hey," Brett's voice on the phone is soft, wounded.

"Hey back."

"Rough few days?"

"I shouldn't have come. It was all a mistake."

"You saw him, didn't you?"

I consider lying. Then, "Yep. Your faithful fiancée screwing it all up."

"Fiancée?"

"Almost. I thought it was about Lola, Brett. I swear I did. But . . ."

"But it's about him."

"Yeah. I shouldn't have come."

"No, Caro. We agreed. I'm not stupid, you know."

"I'm going to walk this Camino thingy for Stephen," I say. "I promised him. Then I'm coming home."

"And?"

"And then we'll see."

"No, Caro. You already see."

"Bastien's not for me, Brett. I know that now."

"That was never my fear. But he showed you that I'm not good enough. That's the part that irks me."

"No. No, it's not that."

"It *is* that, Caro. Look, I love you, but I will not play second fiddle. It's a really lousy part. Take your time. Walk the Camino."

"Will you wait?"

"Maybe."

BOBBY

I've been staying at the House of Hope for four days. As at the Oasis, I'm pulled in by these people, the ones who work there. Teaching art, playing basketball on the cement carport, fumbling through chess with them, sharing kitchen duties . . . it all fills me up. I wish I could stay right here for a while, but in three days Mom will be in Le Puy, and I need to be there.

Rasa is still undecided about the Camino. I suspect that her parents are putting pressure on her to stay, but she shakes her head.

"I can make my own decisions," she says. "But I have a responsibility here."

So I try to keep my mouth shut and just pray, pleading with God to let Rasa come along. I can't imagine God being particularly impressed with these petitions.

My art class is done, and I wander across the hall, following three of my art students who will now study German with Rasa. I smile to myself as eleven students find seats at an oblong table while Rasa writes phrases on the whiteboard.

I take out the sketch pad, pull a chair into the back of the room, and begin to draw. So far Stephen has approved of my sketches, which I send via WhatsApp. I'm careful never to sketch the refugees' faces, for security reasons, only the missionaries' and volunteers'. And Rasa's. But most of those I keep for myself.

Another young woman has joined Rasa up front. She's in worn jeans and a long bright green tunic, and she wears the hijab. But her face is visible. I can see she is older than Rasa, probably in her late twenties, with beautiful olive-colored skin and an oval-shaped face. On her right cheek is a jagged-looking scar, and her eyes seem perpetually sad. I sketch the two of them and entitle it "The Traces of Suffering," but I don't quite know why.

When Rasa glances over at me, she gets a worried expression on her face. She says something to the students and comes to my side. "Don't sketch her, Bobby," she whispers.

"Oh, sorry," I say. "I thought that sketching teachers was fair game."

"Fair game?"

"Was totally fine."

"Yes, usually it is. But Selah is different."

When Rasa doesn't offer any more information, I grin and say, "What, is she in hiding?"

Rasa is not amused. In fact, she looks angry. "This is serious," she rebukes me.

I'm so shocked I don't know what to say. "Wow, okay," I

mumble. "I'm sorry. I promise I won't show this sketch to any-one else. You can trust me on it, okay?"

Rasa calms and whispers, "Yes. I will trust you. I'm also sorry, Bobby. I have maybe jumped at the gun, but we must be careful."

We've finished a dinner prepared by all the Syrian refugees in Rasa's German class when Rasa comes beside me. "My father would like to meet with you tonight, if you can."

I feel my heart plummet. I know he's going to tell me she can't come. But I do my best to look nonchalant and say, "Sure. No problem."

"Good. You can walk home with me, then, and he will talk to you there."

Nothing could make me happier than walking Rasa home. Twenty-five minutes alone with her!

As we walk, she shares a little more of her story. "You know my father was a professor in Tehran before he fled. It is very important to my parents that I go to university. But I will also continue this work." Her eyes twinkle. "My secret work."

She is baiting me. "Go ahead," I say. "Tell me about this secret work of yours."

"I can't," she says, eyes dancing with mischief.

I roll mine. I know she wants to tell me more.

"I will tell you what I can. Besides our work at the House of Hope, my family is involved with the radio ministry that brought us to Isa. Baba teaches on one of the programs, and I am part of something else—a secret Internet community for young people in Iran. Baba teaches them. You cannot imagine their joy to find other Christians. They are very brave."

"You're brave, Rasa."

"When you think you are going to die because you believe in Isa, and then you are spared, you are no longer afraid." She looks away as tears rim her eyes. "Isa let us live for a reason, so we can be what others were for us. A lifeline. A hope."

She pauses. Then, "Do you know about persecuted Christians, Bobby?"

"A little. People from Open Doors have come to our church to share about the persecuted church." I shrug. "But I'm sheltered. We're all sheltered in America. That's why I came to the Oasis—because I wanted to see more." My conscience pricks a little. "I also came to get away from my family."

Rasa's eyes grow big. "You are not allowed to worship Isa in your family?"

"Oh, no, nothing like that. My parents are Christians. I grew up in a church. No, I just mean I needed to get away from my parents for a while."

She looks confused. "But now you are going to hike the Camino with your mother. I don't understand."

"The atmosphere at my home is very tense. Mom has always been pretty controlling, but in the past few years it's gotten much worse. She picked out the university I should attend when I was thirteen! And my father isn't very good about standing up to her. Anyway, I don't want to go to any of the schools she picked out—I want to be an artist like my grandmother. So when Stephen suggested a gap year, I saw it as a way to escape all her crazy expectations."

Rasa's brow is furrowed; she's clearly not following.

"And there's more," I say. "My father left my mother, right after they had moved to a new apartment, and my younger brother has gone to boarding school, so all of a sudden my mom is completely alone. When I told her about walking the Camino, she decided she should join me. Unfortunately." I make a face. "I mean, I'm worried about her, but I was trying to get a breather."

"A breather?"

"The gap year is about being on my own. Not walking the Camino with my mom. I guess it'll be okay, but it would be much better if you would come too."

"That is kind. I'm sorry I cannot go with you, though."

"Why not?" I know I sound exasperated.

"I am needed here, I tell you. There are some of the refugees who have just arrived, and we are helping them find housing. I cannot go."

She sees my disappointment and continues. "Some of these refugees have left everything. Some have lived through violence. Do you know violence, Bobby?"

"No. I told you, I've lived a very sheltered life."

Anna is screaming. The baseball bat crashes onto my shoulder. . . .

"But you are kind. I see it in your eyes. And you have depth. You can read souls too, can't you?"

"I don't know about that. . . ." I can feel my face turning red.

"It is the first thing I see. The soul. Not the face or the color of the skin. Not the sound of the voice. First, it is the soul. I see it through the eyes sometimes. And I always, always want to see Isa in the face."

As she talks, I see pure faith shining in her eyes that are like deep wells. I feel something so very disturbing in my spirit. A tugging, an aching for Rasa, for her heart, for all of her.

"Do you know these verses? They are my prayer for those I meet. For friends." She takes out her cell phone. "I will find it on my Bible here and use Google Translate for you." She beams.

A moment later she begins to read, "Dear friend, I pray that you may enjoy good health and that all may go well with you, even as your soul is getting along well. It gave me great joy when some believers came and testified about your faithfulness to the truth, telling how you continue to walk in it. I have no greater joy than to hear that my children are walking in the truth."

She looks at me so eagerly, as if she has literally swallowed these verses. No, taken them into her mouth and slowly, slowly chewed on them and then absorbed them into her soul.

"Um, no. I can't say I recall those verses. Where are they from?"

"From Saint John's third epistle. I cried when I first read them!"

What kind of teenager reads John's little letters at the end of the Bible? At least I think they're near the end of the Bible.

"How I love praying for my friends this way! I have always wanted to know that my friends are 'getting along well' in their souls and walking in the truth. That they are growing in Christ—this gives me the greatest joy."

She is looking at me with those unbelievably dark eyes of hers, and I can tell she wants me to nod and say, "Yep, me too." But what I really want to say is *I haven't thought about it that way. At all. But give me time, Rasa. Please give me time to catch up to you.*

We've reached her apartment, and the night is raining down romance on us. "Marie said I'm not the first boy to fall for you."

She laughs. "Marie is right, but I am not what they call a flirt. I am sorry if you think so."

"Have you prayed about coming with me on the Camino?" I ask.

We're standing at the entrance to the apartment complex. She shakes her head slowly. "You must talk to Baba," she says. "He will tell you why I cannot go."

We walk inside, and Rasa and her mother go into the kitchen so that I can talk with her father in what I think of as their den. I am terrified of what he will say, expecting a reprimand.

But after we exchange greetings, Hamid looks at me, dark eyes serious, and says calmly, "I will let Rasa go with you."

My eyes are wide with wonder. "You will? I mean, thank you, Hamid."

I put my hand out to shake his and rise from my chair, thinking the talk is over. But Hamid has a far-off look in his eyes.

"Sometimes my daughter has a hard time separating her life from those of other refugees. Sometimes I am afraid she is too devout, too careful. I am afraid she is not really seeking the next step in her life. She is determined to wrap herself around our lives and work. She cares too much."

Everything Rasa has just told me confirms what her father is saying.

"Our journey to Austria back in 2005, our pilgrimage"—he looks as if he has chosen this word carefully, just for me—"was terribly hard. Rasa had more faith than the rest of us. She trusted Isa. She trusted with the faith of the young child she was. But she lived through great trauma. She almost died. She saw horrible injustice. And there are scars. Even so many years later, she still wakes with nightmares of her time with her mother and brother and grandmother on the Refugee Highway." He glances toward the kitchen's closed door and lowers his voice.

"I think she needs the trauma of the other refugees now, the ones she works with. It brings back her trauma, but it also protects her from healing from the trauma." Hamid shakes his head in frustration. "I do not express myself so well in English."

"No, your English is perfect. I understand what you're saying, sir."

His face softens. "Please, don't call me sir. Just Hamid. We are informal here among fellow Christians."

I nod, but I'm hearing the words *trauma* and *horrible injustice*.

"Yesterday I talked on WhatsApp to my friend Stephen. Your boss." He smiles. "He likes you. He trusts you, so I trust you. I want Rasa to do this pilgrimage. I want her to go away from the refugees, if only for two weeks. Stephen says you are an 'old soul,' and my daughter will be safe with you." Then he winks at me and adds, "And your mother."

My palms are sweaty, no longer from fear of a reprimand, but from his trust in me.

"Now you understand that it may not be an easy pilgrimage for her. . . ." He leans forward as if willing me to read between some hidden lines.

I blurt out, "It is physically demanding, but I assure you it isn't dangerous."

"It is a different type of pilgrimage, to be sure, Bobby. But it is still a pilgrimage. It is a time to search your soul. I am telling you these things because I anticipate Rasa's soul searching to be difficult."

Again I think of what she has just shared with me. Rasa is definitely in tune with her soul. I wouldn't be surprised if she searches it every day, even multiple times a day. *Complex* is the word that comes to mind.

"Be very careful with her. She goes by the spirit, but she's fragile." Hamid frowns, as if he hasn't said the right thing. He tries again. "Her spirit is both strong and fragile. Perhaps that is what makes her so empathetic, so aware of everything around her. She goes to cemeteries and cries for unknown people, soldiers, babies who perished. She feels everything in her heart. I hope this pilgrimage will be freedom to her spirit. May she see beyond the duties of the House of Hope; may she see a different kind of hope. Take care of her, Bobby."

I am sweating profusely. Finally I manage, "What if she doesn't want to go?"

"I believe she wants to go very badly. But ask her."

I start to protest that I have asked her, many times, but Hamid gives me a warm smile and his eyes hold kindness.

"Ask her one more time, and if she says yes, then you have my blessing and her mother's too."

I wait to make sure he has finished talking before saying, "Thank you, Hamid. I don't know what else to say except thank you."

I start to shake his hand, but he adds, "One more thing . . . if you take my daughter, I want you to take my son too."

My face falls, the exuberance replaced by thinly disguised dread. And then he is laughing. Hard. "I am kidding, Bobby. I would not entrust Omid to you. That would be quite unfair!"

I suppose it should rattle me, hearing Hamid's somewhat dire prediction for his daughter. But actually it inspires me. I *will* take care of her. I will make sure she finds joy and freedom on the Camino. I'm a boy with dreams, and the words he's pronounced make me dream all the more.

I will protect her. I will rescue her if need be.

Rasa and I stand in the hallway after I've told the rest of her family good night. I tell her about my conversation with her father.

"So it's up to you, Rasa. Do you want to come with me on the Camino? Your father has said yes. He gave me his blessing."

Her head is down. She doesn't look at me for the longest time. Finally I see the slightest nod of her head.

"Yes," she whispers. Then she meets my eyes with hers, dark and tear filled. "I want very badly to go, Bobby. I want to take this pilgrimage with you."

138

CHAPTER

10

ABBIE

My stomach does a little flip-flop as I drive into Ansley Park, the neighborhood where my parents live. I turn onto Beverly Road, and their house comes into view. Way too many memories assault me.

Mama and Dad live in a steep-roofed Tudor cottage that sits on a narrow embankment overlooking a golf course, the house a combination of gray stone and red brick. Today, as I park my car on the street, a thought pierces me. This is not a house for a blind man. The stone steps leading to the front porch are slippery in the rain and ice. Inside, the house is a maze of little two-step stairways where it was added onto. And the second-story staircase is steep. But they've lived here for almost forty years. It's the home we grew up in and the one where the whole Middleton-Bartholomew gang still gathers. I can't imagine them moving.

I knock on the front door and wish that I didn't have to work so hard to keep the worry out of my face. But it's Dad who opens the door, and he can't even tell it's me, so I say, too loudly, as if he's deaf instead of blind, "Hey, Daddy."

"Oh, Abbie. How great of you to come by." He enfolds me in his arms, and I am ten again. His little girl.

I take his arm and we walk to the sofa in the den, which is right off the front entrance. At home Daddy uses a cane to get around, but the wheelchair comes in very handy on other occasions.

I get a glass of iced tea and bring one for my father.

"You 'bout ready for that hike? What's it called again?"

"The Camino, Dad."

"The Camino. Well, are you ready?"

"Getting there, although it may drive me crazy."

"Oh, Abbie, you love all that planning and organizing."

Mama has not told Daddy about Bill leaving, I guess. Fine with me. I don't want him worrying.

We chat for a few minutes about family and then he says, "I hear you're going on a hike. What's it called again?"

I scoot closer to him on the sofa and hold his hand, almost desperately, and my voice sounds far-off and scratchy when I say, "It's called the Camino, Daddy."

After leaving my father in the den, I go through the house to the sun porch, which is also Mama's atelier. She's at her easel, painting. I stand there for a few moments, observing.

When I make a little noise, she looks up quickly. "Oh hi, darling." She sets down the paintbrush—was her hand shaking slightly?—and stands to hug me. "How are you?"

"Hanging in there. Trying to get everything ready for the trip."

"You're brave. I know Bobby will enjoy having you with him."

I raise an eyebrow. "You're getting his texts and emails, right? You know about Rasa and Caro?"

She smiles. "I do."

"Well, I don't think he's overly excited about having either me or Caroline along. But hopefully he recognizes that my presence is what's allowing him to have this little adventure with the girl."

I wait for my mother to volunteer information. She shrugs.

"I've taken control again, haven't I? Forced myself in."

"I'm afraid so, Abbie. I understand why, but . . ."

"But it's still being a control freak, right?"

She reaches over and gives me a motherly squeeze.

"I went to see Diana a few days ago."

"Oh good. I'm glad you got to see her again before you leave. How was it?"

"Well, you know she gives homework. And this week while I was reflecting on something called a Rule of Life, I couldn't stop thinking about Miss Abigail. I still miss her."

"Yes, it comes upon me suddenly sometimes too. She certainly loved you, Abbie."

"She made me believe God was pleased with me. She helped me see the good in my personality."

Mama has closed her eyes. "There's so much beauty in you, Abbie." She sighs and opens them and takes my other hand. "You're going to get through this, darling. I think this trip will give you time to listen, and to grieve, and to move forward."

I feel a chill. "Does that mean you don't think Bill will be coming back, Mama?"

"No, sweetie. I have no idea what is next. But I do know that you have things to grieve."

She gives my hand another squeeze. She has encouraged me, seen my heart, but I can tell she's preoccupied.

"How's Dad, really?" I ask. "Is he managing around the house?"

Her face falls, and we're silent for a moment. Then she

motions with her head, and I follow her out of the sun porch and into their spacious backyard. We walk to the fishpond and take a seat on the cement bench beside it.

"A blind man can't stay in this house, Abbie—there are too many steps to navigate. Your father has fallen twice. Thank the Lord, he wasn't badly hurt. But he scraped himself up pretty good the last time." She stands and walks around the pond, looking down at the lily pads. I follow her out past the pool house where the mimosa is blooming. "It's not just the blindness, you know."

"I know, Mama. It's his memory."

She gives a little sniff, and I can tell she is trying very hard not to cry. "It seems like it's happening so suddenly, the sight and the memory."

I put my arms around my mother, and we stand in a silent embrace. And then an idea comes to me, totally out of the blue. "Would you like to move to the loft while I'm away?" Before she can answer I continue. "The loft is perfect for the two of you. No stairs to navigate, an elevator, state-of-the-art everything. It would give you time to decide what's next without worrying about Dad's every step."

She's still staring at the abundant flowers, the fishpond, the pool.

"I need a reason to unpack things, Mama. This will be the incentive I've needed. And you'll be doing me a favor—I won't have to board poor Poncie. She's gotten used to the loft. This will mean one less upset for her."

Mama holds on to me a little tighter. Now our heads are touching. I inhale the familiar scent of turpentine and oils.

"Thank you, Abbie. Let me think about it. See how to present the idea to your father." She lets go and swipes a finger under her eyes. "Definitely something to think about."

When I leave my parents after dinner, I hurry back to the loft, motivation pumping in my ears. I have two days to make the loft a safe place for my parents. Adrenaline keeps me going as I begin unpacking boxes.

It isn't until the next morning that I see I've got a voicemail. I listen to Jason's football coach informing me that Jason's been caught smoking—twice—and will be kicked off the team if there is another infraction. In which case, I will need to come pick him up from football camp.

But I don't call Jason or text him. He is not going to keep me from escaping! Instead I shoot a quick email to Bill, ending with *This one's your problem. I'm off to France!*

Then I put on my favorite playlist from Spotify, a hodge-podge of songs from the seventies, eighties, and nineties, and I unwrap paintings, place books on the built-in shelves, hang clothes in the armoires, and put sheets on the beds. Donna Summer and Barbra Streisand are disco harmonizing, and suddenly I begin to sing and dance along with them, flinging my arms up and down disco style, spinning around with an empty bottle of Perrier as my mic while poor Poncie cowers in the corner.

By one a.m. I'm sweating and happy. I may be a total mess, but the house looks like a five-star hotel suite.

CARO

I am supposed to be readying the house for renters. Instead I am tearing it apart, looking for more clues about Bastien. I go through all of my parents' papers. I look for Bastien on social media, but he's not there. And he's never really told me what

143

his job is now, has he? Is anything he has told me the truth? I'm furious at him, which is a godsend, because I'm no longer obsessing over seeing him again. But I am obsessing over him.

I call Mom's cell.

"*Allô*," she answers from Lyon in her Georgia French accent.

"Hi, Mom."

"Caro!"

I can picture her face lighting up. I don't call that often.

"Oh, darling! So good to hear your voice. I wasn't even looking at the phone to see it was you."

We chat for a moment, and then I tread cautiously into the reason for my call. "I was looking through those old photos and newspaper clippings that you left out for me. . . ."

"Oh dear," Mom says. "I'm sure that was hard."

"Yeah. Kinda hard. But Mom, I saw in one photo the man who used to be our neighbor—Bastien, right? He was at a party with you and Dad and Malika and Jean-Claude. Did you know Bastien before he became our neighbor?"

"Oh, yes, Bastien and his lovely wife. I can't recall her name. . . ."

His lovely wife! I bristle inside.

"We met them at several Peugeot events, but she never came down once Bastien bought the house. At least I never saw her there. But yes, we knew them a little bit."

"Did Jean-Claude and Malika know him too?"

"Well, yes," Mom replies. "We all knew each other. Not exactly as friends, but the men were colleagues." She lowers her voice, or maybe she isn't talking into the phone, because suddenly I can barely make out what she's saying. "And then he moved down here and became our neighbor, and well, you may not remember how awkward it was when we all were together after all the horror about Malika and Lola. He'd just moved to

ELIZABETH MUSSER

the village in time to be part of a murder investigation. I don't think you ever met him then. Anyway, it was so strange. . . ." She lets the phrase trail off.

"Did he stay around after what happened to Malika?"

Mom hesitates. "Well, it was such an awful time. You know as well as we do—you were there first. I don't remember exactly, but he didn't stay in the village for more than a few years before I think he started renting out the house. As I said, I never saw his wife again. Perhaps they divorced. Now, what made you think about Bastien?"

What can I say? Why *did* I ask?

I decide to tell a half-truth. "I saw him in the village the other day, and we talked briefly. That's all. And then the same day I saw him in that photo. A strange coincidence. He said he was doing some repairs on his house."

I can almost hear Mom nodding. "Getting it ready for new renters, just like us, bless his heart."

I change the subject. "Mom, do you have Jean-Claude's phone number, or know where he lives now?"

"Oh, that poor man. Your father and I were just talking about him. He still lives in Provence, in a little village not too far from Lourmarin. I can't recall the name right now. We were saying we'd like to see him again when we come down in a few weeks." She looks up his address. "Cavaillon!" she proclaims. "He lives in Cavaillon."

"I thought I might call him, Mom. It's been so long. . . ."

"I'm sure he'd enjoy hearing from you." She pauses. "Are you okay, Caro? You sound distracted."

"I'm fine, Mom, but you're right. Seeing all those photos, and then running into Bastien . . . It brought back good and bad memories." I change the subject again. "But I'm heading out on the Camino soon."

"How nice. Stephen said you might do that. Taking photos for the *Press* about the pilgrimage, right?"

"Yep. And I won't be alone. Do you remember the young intern, Bobby, who has been working for Stephen?"

"Yes, vaguely."

"He and his mother are walking with me."

I can hear relief in Mom's voice. "Well, that's just lovely. And when you're done, Caro, please come and spend a few days with us. I'm sure your boss would grant you a few more days in France." She chuckles.

Yes, I'm sure Stephen would be delighted to hear that I am going to visit our parents. It doesn't happen very often.

After I get off the phone with Mom, I sit in a trance. Bastien knew my parents from way back. Bastien knew Lola's parents. Bastien had been in Provence many times. My mother had met his wife. . . . His wife! He lied to me again and again and again. What more will I find out if I keep digging?

I try to recall exactly what happened that day in 2011. We'd gone to the Fourcades' house, and he'd given no indication that he knew the family. Salima certainly had not recognized Bastien . . . or had she? I think of the fear in her eyes, and how she refused to share anything with me until Bastien stepped outside. Because he was a stranger. Right?

I go into the breakfast room and plop down at the French country table, the one I used to color at as a kid, the one I've eaten a thousand breakfasts at, smearing sliced baguettes with butter and homemade strawberry confiture and then dipping the baguette into a bowl of hot chocolate. Now the table is littered with photos and my notes. I put my head in my hands and cry.

My parents have lived all over the world, five different countries during my growing-up years. Their last stop was Lyon, so I did high school and university in France. But after that weekend with Bastien, after Malika's murder and Lola's disappearance, I fled. I left Lourmarin, and then I left France.

I never breathed a word to my parents about Bastien and me, and I knew Bastien had kept silent too. Not that they'd be surprised by another fling, but this was different. Bastien would forever be tied to tragedy. And guilt.

I fled and traveled for a year, then I spent two years with two different guys in two different cities in Europe, all the while playing around with photography and drugs and alcohol. Of course, my parents knew that I was a mess, flitting from one relationship to another. They weren't dumb. But they didn't know about my relationship with Bastien and the guilt I lived with that woke me in the night when I thought about Lola's disappearance and Malika's murder.

When Stephen begged me to come to the States in 2014, he paid for me to enter a very expensive rehab program, after which I lived with him and Tracie and their girls for six months. I went back to school, got another degree, this one in graphic design, met Brett, and started working at the *Peachtree Press*, but my life continued to be haunted by Bastien.

Although my parents never knew anything, Stephen and Tracie knew, as well as the therapist at the rehab center and my AA support group. They all called my relationship with Bastien an obsession. My therapist said, "You must get sober first. And your obsession with Bastien will lessen too."

I wanted to scream that I wasn't obsessed, that he was someone special, someone different from the other guys I dated. But she'd ask, "Do you think the obsession has come because he turned down your advances? Are you determined to bring back the passion of that first weekend?"

I didn't know. It truly was all tangled together.

And now with this most recent kiss and his lies, I am more confused than ever.

Before he became our neighbor, Bastien knew my parents. Bastien knew Jean-Claude and Malika. Maybe Bastien even knew Lola. I'm turning all this over in my mind for the hundredth time when my phone beeps with a text. It's Abbie Jowett.

Hey, Caroline. I'm looking forward to meeting up with you tomorrow.

I've been so caught up in my search that I haven't even bought supplies for the Camino. I have my camera and a backpack—at least I'm pretty sure there's a decent backpack somewhere at the house. But I'm not ready to meet Abbie. I text her that I'll be a day or two late, to go on without me, I'll hope to catch up with her soon.

Please send your arrival time so I can make the necessary sleeping arrangements.

I text back, *No worries. I'll figure out my own lodging.*

Somehow I don't think this sits well with Abbie.

A few hours later, Tracie calls me. "What have you decided?"

"I'm going on the Camino. You can assure my dear brother that I've talked to Bobby's mother and we have a plan—I'll be meeting up with her soon."

"Soon?" That one word is loaded with Tracie's unspoken thoughts. *What exactly do you mean by soon? As in today or tomorrow? Or in a week or a month or a year?*

She's been my sister-in-law for over ten years, and I know all of her subtle and not-so-subtle insinuations.

"Soon means in two days." I hear one of her kids crying in the background. "Look, I found out more things. Very upsetting stuff. Evidently Bastien knew my parents and had been in Aix for a lot longer than he let on when we first met. And . . ." I almost don't say it. "And he has a wife! Or at least he had one."

I spend a few minutes going over everything with Tracie that I've discovered in the newspaper articles and on the Internet and through my conversation with my mother. The child's screaming grows louder. "It sounds like you need to check on some impending disaster, Trace," I say.

"You're the only impending disaster I'm worried about," she replies.

BOBBY

Jason texts: *Two warnings from the coach. If I get another one, he'll kick me off the football team.*

I text back: *What is your deal, anyway?*

I got caught smoking. Smoking! Just a dumb cigarette. Not pot or anything.

You're the one who's dumb. Come on, Jason.

Dad is furious—of course they sent him the news. Mom is just going to France anyway. He adds a few choice words. *They don't give a **** about me!*

I want to respond that he cares so much about himself no one else needs to bother. Instead I type, *Of course they care, but have you noticed they have some hard things going on in their lives too?*

His reply is a bunch of angry emojis.

Rasa and I have stayed up late the past two nights, me listening entranced as she told stories about the persecuted church and revival among the youth in North Africa and the Middle East. I've made the reservations for the train from Vienna and at the youth hostel in Le Puy. I've even gotten most things ready in my backpack. Together we have pored over several of the top Camino sites, and I can see her excitement growing.

So I'm in no way prepared when she finds me the morning of August 9, only a few hours before we're supposed to leave. She is shaking, and her beautiful eyes have lost their shine. "I can't go," she whispers.

"What?"

"I can't go with you. I'm not ready. I don't have the right things. . . ." She rattles off several almost incomprehensible phrases and then stops, staring at her feet, and says, "I used to have an attack of panics."

I screw up my face. "What?" Then it registers. "Oh. You mean panic attacks?"

She nods, her eyes down. "They were very scary. And for the last two nights I've had the nightmares about them." She dares to look up at me. "The nightmares began right after I agreed to do the Camino. And I am afraid that the attacks will come back too."

I frown, trying to grasp what she's saying. When she stares back at the ground, I ask the first thing that comes to mind. "Do your parents know? About the panic attacks?"

She nods. "Yes. Of course. I used to have medication that helped, but I haven't needed it in so long. I thought I was healed of these attacks, but the nightmares make me afraid. Afraid to leave."

"Okay. Wow." Hamid's warnings are throbbing in my head. *She's fragile, strong and fragile.*

"I have an appointment with my doctor this afternoon. To get more medication. So you see, I can't leave. I'm *afraid* to leave, Bobby. I'm sorry. I'm so sorry."

I don't know what to say, but I feel disappointment lodged way down in my gut. Then a really heavy cloak of responsibility descends on me, so heavy it feels suffocating. I'm supposed to watch out for Mom, take care of Rasa, and keep an eye on Caro. How do I choose? I have no idea what to do.

Hamid looks defeated when I meet up with him later at the House of Hope. "You see what I mean," he says. "She's fragile."

I think he's going to admit she shouldn't go, but instead he says, "If you could wait just one day, see what the doctor recommends. He knows her history. She hasn't had a panic attack in years. She does have nightmares off and on, though. I think the doctor will calm her down. I really do."

The desperate way he says these things unnerves me.

But what about my mom? She's already on the Atlantic flight and should be landing in Paris in the next hour or two.

I still don't know what to do, but then I do. I call Swannee.

"Oh, Bobby! How nice to hear you." But she sounds distracted.

"Hi, Swannee. How are you and Granddad doing?"

"Well, we got your mother off, and you won't believe it, but your granddad and I are moving into the loft."

"What?"

"It was your mother's idea that we stay there while she's away, and it gave her the gumption to unpack."

"But why would you want to?"

"Well, you know how your granddad's eyesight is going. He's had a few mishaps lately."

Only my grandmother uses words like *gumption* and *mishap*.

"Has he gotten hurt?"

"Oh, nothing to worry about, but as your mother pointed out, the loft has no steps and an elevator."

Her voice sounds a bit too cheerful. Off in some way.

"What else is it, Swannee? Tell me, please."

"Honey, nothing for you to worry about."

"Are you going to have to move for good?" I can't imagine my grandparents leaving their home on Beverly.

"No, no. Don't you worry. We're going to take care of Poncie and have a lovely time." Now she really sounds off, superficial. Not like my Swannee. "Tell me about how you're doing. Ready to meet up with your mom today?"

But now I'm thinking about my grandfather's loss of sight and his memory problems, and Swannee's hand shaking as she holds the paintbrush, and I don't want to burden my grandmother with my problems. So I say, "Yes, we're about ready to begin our adventure."

"Well, keep texting me and also posting the photos on Instagram, Bobby. It's like I'm right there with you."

When I click off the phone, I feel the cloak covering me, smothering me with worry. I feel old. Not just like an "old soul," Mom and Dad's description of me, but old like all the fun and adventure and cool stuff I hoped to experience has been ripped right out of my sketch pad, wadded up, and discarded.

CHAPTER

11

ABBIE

I don't sleep a wink on the plane, and by the time we land in
Paris I feel high on caffeine and exhaustion. And this backpack. It weighs a ton. If Bill had been with me, well, he would
have said, "Abbs, you don't need to pack the kitchen sink, for
heaven's sake," and he'd start pulling things out.

But Bill is not here, and I have planned this whole trip alone.
Fiercely alone.

I take the train to Le Puy-en-Velay, one of the four main
starting points for the pilgrimage in France. It is almost ninety
degrees outside. Thank heavens there is air conditioning on
the train.

I step off the train, hoist my pack on my back, and pull my
small suitcase behind me, searching for a taxi. I stop to take
in my surroundings, looking up at the huge rock—more like
a very narrow mountain—and gasp. I've seen photos spread
across the Internet, but there she is, in real life. Or I should say,
there *they* are. Mary and Jesus, way larger than life, perched
high on a rock that dominates the city.

She's called Notre Dame de France, and Wikipedia tells me that she was erected in 1860, standing in her glory way up there on a volcanic spur 130 meters high. The red statue was created and cast from the bronze metal recovered from 213 cannons captured from the Russians during the Crimean War. Leave it to the French to make the Virgin Mary from cannons! She's huge—22 meters high—and weighs a ton. No, make that 835 tons. And she's holding baby Jesus in her right arm.

I find it interesting that everything I've read about this statue calls it "Our Lady," as if baby Jesus isn't even there. But He's there all right. The babe is pointing with His hand out across the valley, or maybe the world. Mary's head is hallowed with a crown of gold stars, which seems so odd to me, the idea of Mary's majesty, when only a few decades later that baby in her arms will be wearing a crown of thorns. But I've read that these stars are symbolic, from somewhere in the book of Revelation. And if I squint, I can see that Mary is stepping on a serpent. In the Bible I think it's Jesus who does that in the prophecy, but in this setting Mary is quite convincing.

The sight is breathtaking, and beautiful, in a way I cannot even try to explain. I stare at them and think, *Okay, well, maybe this is a good place to start a pilgrimage.*

I'm staying in a tiny studio on a cobbled road in the old part of town. The room is way up on the third floor. No elevators, of course. I drag my backpack and suitcase up the narrow, winding, very old cement staircase, which has a vague aroma of cat urine.

The studio seemed like the perfect location, but there is one hiccup. The French have this Camino thing working like a well-oiled machine. A minivan from a company called La Malle Postale will pick up my suitcase tomorrow morning and take it to the next place I'm staying, fifteen kilometers farther down the trail. Of course, many pilgrims only carry a backpack for their long journey, but I have not signed up for torture, and evidently lots of other people feel the same way. But it was only *after* I'd paid for my lodging on Airbnb that I discovered one minor inconvenience: La Malle Postale does not pick up bags from Airbnbs, but only from hotels and hostels specifically registered as part of the Camino.

I groan, thinking of the early morning run I'll have to make across town tomorrow morning to deposit the suitcase at the acceptable spot, and let the backpack slip from my shoulders onto the wooden floor. I need a cup of tea. A strong cup of tea. It is two in the afternoon in France, and I've been up for twenty-four hours straight.

I go out onto rue Pannessac, cobbled and quaint. Something twitters in my soul as I amble along this ancient street. I pass a *boulangerie*, catching the scent of fresh baguettes, and a *bou-chérie*, where hunks of different types of meat, all red and raw, hang in cords from the ceiling. And I feel it, joy welling up from way, way down inside.

Across the street I notice a yellow stone building with two thick arches framing the large storefront windows where the words *salon du thé* invite me into Les Beaux Thés du Monde—*beautiful teas of the world.*

A young woman in a T-shirt, jeans, and a white apron greets me with a "*Bonjour, Madame,*" and I greet her back. She hands me the menu and I see immediately what I want.

"*J'aimerais avoir le thé gourmand, s'il vous plaît,*" I say, although the words feel like cotton in my mouth.

She smiles and says in perfect English, "The gourmet tea, an excellent choice."

"*Qu'est-ce que c'est?*" I insist. I will not speak English!

She smiles again and complies, in French, explaining that I'll have my choice of tea and then three mini desserts.

When she brings out the tea and treats, I give another little gasp. It is so very French. The tea comes steaming in a lovely china teapot, Limoges, I'm almost positive, with a matching china cup, and the miniature desserts are laid out on a matching china platter: an almond pear tart, a curved glass jar filled with panna cotta and some kind of crumbly topping, and a chocolate cake—which I suspect will be gooey deliciousness in the middle—with a dollop of whipped cream beside it. A tiny dark chocolate spoon sits beside the desserts. The young woman points to a contraption that holds three minuscule hourglasses, the sand inside bright yellow, bright pink, and bright orange. She points to the orange sand, which is sifting down into the bottom of the hourglass, and says, "Let it steep for six minutes."

So I do. I'm enchanted.

While I wait, I take out my phone and check my texts. Bobby and Rasa should be arriving at the train station in an hour. I've planned to meet them there and walk with them to the hostel where they are staying.

Hey, Mom! Um, I'm afraid we aren't going to get there today. Rasa's having some health problems, and the doctor says she needs to stay put for a day or two. So sorry! But you go ahead. We'll meet you in Monistrol and take it together from there.

The delight of thirty seconds earlier disappears into a ball of fear and then anger. How dare they!

I reread the text and fume. *So sorry???* I've broken my neck getting all this organized, down to the last detail of where we'll eat tonight, where to pick up the pilgrim passports, everything! Of all the nerve . . .

The next thought that floats in is *I don't want to do this alone.*

And then Diana's soft voice and annoyingly bright eyes are flashing in my memory as she says, *Let's get Abbie back first.*

I am still fuming as I leave the tearoom, but I have managed to devour the desserts and drink every last sip of Earl Grey. I had no intention of doing any part of this Camino alone. In fact, the idea terrifies me. I imagine myself hiking up these steep, steep hills on a rocky trail with biting wind and rain and not another pilgrim in sight. With my luck these days, I'll fall and sprain an ankle. Wouldn't that serve them right?

Serve *them* right? Where did that come from? It's not like Rasa deliberately got sick to annoy me. I shake my head and try to concentrate on how Bobby must feel. I shoot him a text. *Wow, that's disappointing. But I'm sure I'll be fine.*

It's only three p.m. Instead of going back to the train station, I'm free to walk around the old part of town, take photos, and admire the statue of Mary and Jesus from every angle. Then I decide to walk to the cathedral, an immense structure built over the period of some ten centuries, the fifth to the fifteenth, so I've read. That's old.

The short hike from my studio to the cathedral goes up and up and up a sharp incline. I walk along the cobblestones, noting a few cozy restaurants and tourist shops lining the narrow road. The cathedral's façade, striped looking with alternating white and black stones, is imposing, almost intimidating, towering over me with its three massive levels of stonework. The bottom layer—my destination—is the cathedral's porch with its arched arcades. I stand, already out of breath, at the bottom of the sixty steps.

Good grief, we pilgrims will be worn out before we ever start our journey if we have to climb up here with our backpacks!

But for today I'm unencumbered, so I walk up and up and up all those steps. It's worth the view from the top, though, as I turn around and look past the alcove and the vaulted openings to the whole valley below.

I enter the church, dark, majestic, and very gothic, demanding reverence. I stand there for a few minutes, letting my eyes adjust. Then I look up and ahead of me at the painted cupola with its black virgin. I feel chills. An elderly couple enter, genuflect, and cross themselves, Catholic style. After a few minutes of silent contemplation, during which I am still hearing too much noise in my mind, I pass through the cathedral bookstore, where I have read all pilgrims must go to get their "passport." It's called a *créanciale* and is a folded booklet that pilgrims get stamped at each place they stay. A proof of their pilgrimage, I guess. The suggested donation is five euros. I get one for Bobby, Rasa, and Caroline too, and leave the enthusiastic cashier thirty euros.

"*Merci, Monsieur.*"

He rewards me by answering in French. "*Je vous en prie, Madame.*" Then he adds, in English, "Do you know about the welcome meeting later today?"

In fact, I do. I've saved a thread from a Camino forum on my phone that talks about this as well as the early morning mass: *There is a friendly group of Friends of the Camino in Le Puy who welcome new pilgrims. They meet every evening between April and October starting at 5:30 p.m. at 2 rue de Manécantare.*

Every day at 7 a.m. there is mass in the Cathedral with the Pilgrim's Blessing at the end. It is rather nice to start your Camino experience leaving from the Cathedral with the other pilgrims, through the old streets.

For now, I leave the cathedral alone and wander around town, up and down, up and down. I could walk up to the top of the Corneille Rock, where the view is surely amazing, but I decide to save my strength for the start of the hike tomorrow.

Late in the afternoon, as the sun is descending, gleaming off of Mary as if she's on fire, I make my way behind the massive cathedral to the little street, rue de Manécantare, where I find a door marked *Camino* and *Acceuil*. Welcome. I step inside the room and find a group of pilgrims seated around a table on which sit little glasses and a pitcher filled with what an American would assume is weak Kool-Aid. Not at all. It's a *kir*—white wine with crème de cassis added. The French! Welcoming pilgrims from around the world with a glass of wine!

I pass on the kir and settle into a chair while the group leader, a fiftysomething man named Laurent, launches into an animated discussion of all the wonders of the Camino, alternating between French and English as he talks. He doesn't mention anything religious exactly, although he admits this pilgrimage can be "very spiritual." He's walked all 1,200 kilometers from right here in Le Puy to the end of the Camino on the farthest western piece of land in Spain. According to Laurent, the place, Finisterre, literally means the end of the world.

Twenty of us are present: ten Germans, two young men from Italy, a father-son team who are French, a young Polish man, and four American women who look to be about my age.

We go around the room, sharing where we're from and how far we hope to walk.

The young man has already been walking for two months, from his home in Poland, and he's going to walk two more months at least until he gets to Finisterre. Alone.

The women are from Washington State. They are planning to walk the Via Podiensis, the part of the pilgrimage starting in Le Puy and ending at a picturesque village called Conques, two hundred kilometers farther south in France. It's the same path that Bobby and Rasa and I are planning to take. And Caroline, I remind myself. Maybe. I've calculated the length as one hundred twenty-five miles.

When it's my turn to share, I say, "Hi, I'm Abbie. I'm from Atlanta, Georgia, in the southeast of the United States. I'm walking with my son and his friend, but I just heard today that his friend is sick, so they aren't joining me until I get to Monistrol." I give a nervous laugh. "So I guess I'll be alone for these first few days."

Laurent leans over from where he's sitting, eyes dancing. "Abbie," he says, and his accent is strong and clear. "This is what is so beautiful about the Camino. You are never alone."

I think he may launch into something about God being with us, but instead he says, "You will find many, many friends on the Camino. I guarantee it."

As we leave the welcome center, one of the women comes over to me. "Hi, I'm Jamie. That's a bummer about your son's friend."

"Well, it's a disappointment, for sure. And especially for them. But"—and I turn up my palms—"Laurent says I won't be alone. That's good to know."

She chuckles. "Indeed." Then, "Abbie, would you like to join us for dinner?"

"Oh, no. I don't want to bother you all."

"No bother! We're all pilgrims, right?"

"Well then, sure! Thanks!"

These women, Jamie, Brenda, Barbara, and Lynn, each give me a big smile and a welcome. Then Lynn adds, "Let's go ring the bell for good luck on our pilgrimage!"

We head out into a garden that adjoins the building, where I immediately spy the large bell that I've read about on the forum. Each of us rings it, recording the photo on our smartphones. I take a deep breath and say a silent prayer, "Thank You, Lord, for these women. I really didn't look forward to being alone tonight."

We eat dinner at a restaurant tucked into a nook near my studio. "Oh," I whisper, as we step inside a large room with vaulted ceilings and stone walls, similar to the stone in the cathedral. "It's so charming."

A waitress hands me a menu, a real French *menu*, meaning four courses. Really five courses if you count the first one, what the French call an *amuse bouche*—literally something to amuse your mouth. After that there's a choice of salads, then a choice between trout or leg of lamb for the main course, then the cheese course, and finally another choice between an iced mousse with lemon verbena (the specialty of this region) or shortbread with caramel ice cream. My senses are ready for this feast.

The evening is progressing well. Bobby has texted to make sure I'm okay. By the time we leave the restaurant, it is after nine and I am wiped out.

"Will we see you at mass tomorrow morning, Abbie?" Jamie calls after me.

"Yes, of course. I'll be there bright and early."

"Why don't you come back afterward and have breakfast with us at our hotel—it's delicious. Homemade jellies, cheeses from the region, yogurts, and of course, French bread. And fresh fruits. I've already checked with the host, and he says it's fine. We need to start out with a big breakfast if we're going to make it."

"Thanks, girls. You've been so kind. I'd love to join you tomorrow morning."

As I head to my little studio, I can almost hear Laurent whispering, "You're never alone on the Camino, Abbie." I guess he's right.

BOBBY

I don't sleep well, but at least I have heard from Mom. She sounds upbeat and ready to tackle her first day on the Camino.

I spend the day at the House of Hope, anxiously waiting to hear what Rasa's doctor will say.

Late in the afternoon, I'm sitting with Lisa outside the art room. Two new refugees have just added their names to the splashes of color they've painted on the walls. "Hamid told me about Rasa's decision," Lisa volunteers. Before I can respond, she looks at me hard. "Bobby, have you ever heard the term 'vicarious trauma'?"

I'm so surprised to hear those two words that I don't have time to disguise it. *Anna.* "Yes, as a matter of fact I have."

"Then perhaps you can understand a little of what Rasa experiences. She went through real trauma as a child, and now hearing similar stories of refugees here seems to cause vicarious trauma."

I do understand. But instead of sympathizing, I surprise myself by asking, "If she relives her terrible journey on the Refugee Highway each time she's with these refugees, why does she continue?"

But I know why. I see myself desperate to help Anna, again and again and again.

"It's an odd type of safety she feels, being here."

Yes, exactly.

"And she has such a heart for this ministry. For years when she was a young teen, she had nothing to do with the House of Hope or refugees. She's made incredible progress, but there is, of course, lingering damage."

Lingering damage.

Each word Lisa pronounces is a stab, a vivid memory.

It's time for the art class to begin. Seven men have joined me in the room, and Lisa nods my way and leaves. I welcome them, pronouncing each word slowly in English. "Today we're going to paint with our fingers." Of course, no words are necessary as I demonstrate this childhood delight that, Lisa has told me, has been very therapeutic for adult refugees. The men nod and smile and nudge each other.

While they diligently work on their finger paintings, I take out my sketch pad and flip through the pages, remembering all the vicarious trauma I lived through with Anna.

I'm cleaning up after the afternoon art class when Rasa finds me. "My doctor says it would be a good thing to go on the Camino," she tells me, her dark eyes dancing with their usual excitement again. "He says I care too much sometimes. I have too much"—she searches for the word—"too much empathy. I must step back." She is blushing, which only adds to her charm.

Too much empathy. Yep.

Mom is always telling me I care too much, I feel too responsible for myself and everyone else. "You were born with two consciences, and Jason was born with none." She smiles when she says it, but I know she isn't joking.

I push the thought away and concentrate on the good news: Rasa can go on the Camino!

We walk into the little kitchen area to get glasses of cold water, which we take into the lounge. Rasa does not do small talk. She sets her glass on the floor beside her chair and peers at me, her gaze so penetrating that I feel a bit intimidated. I may be an old soul, but Rasa is older still.

"I have told you my story, Bobby, about our flight along the Refugee Highway. I was young, and I had just found Isa." She closes her eyes briefly. "A kind American woman told me about Isa when I was at my Armenian neighbor's home. And then everything went wrong. Baba had to flee. I went into hiding with Mamaan and my grandmother. But Isa was with us, there in hiding, and all the way on our journey. He saved us.

My mother should have died in childbirth, my little brother should have died of a fever. But I prayed and Isa healed them. I prayed, and even though the journey was horrible, I *believed* and I felt Him with us. I *felt* Him, Bobby."

I can hear in her voice a plea for me to trust her. "I believe you," I whisper.

"I almost died too. But we lived." Her eyes cloud. "Except for my grandmother, but she was ready to live in a different way. In heaven. And we got to Austria. It was good here. Until I started having the attacks of panic and bad dreams . . . nightmares. You know?"

I nod, not daring to correct her.

"For a long time." She takes a deep breath. "But then I saw a doctor, and I learned to do things to help me. And Isa healed me. Again." She gets a look of fierce determination, as if daring me to disagree. "He healed me of the dreams. And the attacks. I wanted to be at the House of Hope. Before, I avoided it. But I always knew in my heart that Isa would heal me so I could help here."

"And you're really great with all these people. You understand them. You bless them," I say.

She twists her hands—those lovely, delicate hands—in her lap. "But my father believes I am carrying the burden of the refugees too much." She furrows her brow, a deep V between her thick, expressive eyebrows. "I try to give this burden to Isa." Her lips are tight, as if she's trying hard not to cry. "He healed me. But now I have these bad dreams. Will the attacks of panic come back too?"

I let the silence answer her question, but I wonder, could it be the idea of a pilgrimage, a journey, that is causing the fear?

"Sometimes I wonder, where is God now? Sometimes it seems like He has gone away." Now her eyes fill with tears. "Like everything I do does not help these people. It seems dark when I think this way."

I feel like Rasa has pulled back a curtain to her soul and invited me to step behind. I choose my words carefully.

"I had a friend in high school who had a bad life. She was abused. By someone close to her. I tried to help. But then I cared too much and I *carried* too much. I let myself feel everything she went through, so much so that I couldn't help her or myself. So I had to step away. For a while."

I had to step away forever, I think. *I lost her.* But I don't say this out loud. I concentrate very hard on Rasa, on her beautiful eyes, so that I don't see Anna's terror-stricken face screaming out at me again and again and again.

We stay in the lounge of the House of Hope until the sky becomes a multicolored pastel painting out the window. Occasionally Lisa or Hamid pokes a head in, but they never comment. I think they are collectively holding their breaths, probably praying that I can convince Rasa to go on the Camino with me.

"I know what you are saying and what my father is saying. I need to go away for a while. I need to break." She frowns, then gives her embarrassed smile that melts my heart. "I need *a* break so I won't break." She grins, pleased with her play on words.

"Exactly."

"So I will go with you, Bobby. But not tomorrow. Tomorrow I will rest and get ready. Do you think your mother can wait for us one more day?"

Later I text Swannee a video of the refugees' hands as they mash them into gobs of brightly colored tempera paint and then create their "finger masterpieces," as we've dubbed them.

She texts right back. *Love it! Finger painting like Jean-Paul.*

Swannee told me how her artist friend had been diagnosed with a degenerative disease—a strange form of arthritis. He could no longer travel, and more importantly, he could no longer hold a paintbrush—the worst fate imaginable for an artist. But he retrained himself to finger paint. She showed me some photos of his newer work on his website, and they were every bit as detailed and breathtaking as the old.

She texts again: *Speaking of . . . have you confirmed your date with him?*

Oops! I'll do it now, I respond. *And one of our first items of business will be visiting that museum so we can see your painting.*

I find Jean-Paul's number on my phone and write my text message, thumbs moving rapidly over the screen. Then I pause a moment, cradling the phone in my left palm and gazing at my hands. Young hands that work—no tremor, no arthritis, no fear. And I bow my head and think, *Thanks, God, for my hands.*

CHAPTER

12

ABBIE

I sleep like a rock—the blessing of the first night before jet lag really sets in—waking to the alarm on my phone at six a.m. I dress quickly and gulp down a cup of coffee before dragging my suitcase to the designated place for La Malle Postale to pick it up. *Ouf!* The first thing checked off my list.

Back at the studio, I reclaim my backpack and take the short walk to the cathedral. In spite of only containing the necessities of the day, the backpack feels heavy as I climb those steep stairs. The cathedral looks foreboding in the early morning light, like a giant inmate in his striped prison clothes. But once I'm inside, a combination of peace and excitement settles on me. By the time the mass begins at seven, the cathedral is literally overflowing with pilgrims, all our backpacks leaning against the cathedral's walls.

I search frantically among the crowd for the women from Washington I'd met—and finally see Jamie and Brenda motioning to me from a pew across the way.

When the young priest begins the sermon in French, I secretly congratulate myself on understanding almost everything he says. His reflections from the gospel of Luke and Paul's epistle to the Galatians draw me in as he talks about welcoming Jesus into the pilgrimage. I'm pleased. Somehow I thought the mass would be all about the Virgin Mary. *Chalk it up to evangelical bias*, I think. Already I can tell that this Camino is going to be about me letting go of many preconceived notions I have of others and myself.

At the end of the mass, the priest pronounces the Pilgrim's Blessing. We all stand together near the front of the cathedral, and as he speaks in French, the words are projected on a screen in several different languages.

"Almighty God, You never stop showing Your goodness to those who love You, and You let Yourself be found by those who seek You; show Your favor to your pilgrims as they pursue their pilgrimage and guide their path according to Your will. Be to them a shade in the heat of the day, a light in the darkness of the night, a relief in the midst of their fatigue, so that they can happily finish their journey under Your protection. Through Jesus Christ, our Lord. Amen."

I recognize echoes of Psalm 121, one of my favorites. "The Lord is your shade on your right hand; the sun will not smite you by day nor the moon by night. . . ." I am pretty sure that many of the pilgrims would not consider themselves Christians, but I am impressed by the sense of reverence and joy that surrounds the mass. I feel buoyed up and excited.

Diana has suggested that I read what she calls the Psalms of Ascent, Psalms 120 through 134, as I go along the Camino. These are the songs that the Jews recited as they made their own pilgrimage each year to Jerusalem.

The priest begins stamping the first square in each pilgrim's créanciale—our passport. I hold mine out and he says, "Go in the peace of Christ! We give thanks to God."

I murmur, "*Merci.*"

Several gray-clad nuns are giving out little plastic rosaries to those who want them. They also direct us to a wooden box containing copies of the Pilgrim's Blessing in various languages. I pluck the small card in English, admiring the lovely calligraphy.

I am trying to assimilate all I've already experienced this morning. I'm tempted to have the priest stamp the créanciale for Bobby and Rasa and Caroline, but no, they aren't here. I think about how Bobby wants to rescue everyone, including me. I wonder how I can help him see that I don't need to be rescued. But as soon as the thought comes, another follows: *Oh, but you do. You need to be rescued from yourself.*

Was that the voice of the Spirit? I haven't paid attention to His whisper in a long time.

The breakfast with my new friends is exactly as Jamie promised: coffee and fresh fruit and cheeses and breads, along with yogurt and several homemade jams served in big bowls. We talk easily as we leave Le Puy, following the white and red *traits*, the French markings on walls or wooden posts that assure pilgrims we are on the correct trail.

The first part of the walk begins on a road that winds up a steep hill, out of town, giving a panoramic view of the city, with Mary gleaming far in the distance. Up and up and up we walk. Many of the pilgrims left the cathedral immediately after the mass to begin their hike, but it's nine thirty before the Washington Women and I reach the top of the first hill. As I look back down I see a few stragglers, and somehow this pleases me. I don't want to be last.

After the first steep climb, the next part of the walk meanders along flat country roads. Then we cut through a field on a narrow path that climbs again, so that we are eventually hiking on the edge of rolling hills in a spot called La Roche, giving breathtaking views of the valley below.

Brenda, it turns out, is a walking encyclopedia. Or perhaps a walking Wikipedia, I should say. As we stare into the beauty, she says, "All of this area has buildings built of basalt—it's the black stone you see. This is a volcanic region. The red stone is from the volcano and the black is what was in the ground."

We've been walking for a few hours, and the sun is getting ferocious. Thank goodness I'm wearing a sleeveless T-shirt and exercise capris and sunscreen. I've loaded my backpack with water bottles, and my boots seem to be holding up well. We arrive in a town called St. Christophe-sur-Dolaizon, where we come across a dozen or more pilgrims lounging beside an ancient chapel, enjoying bread and cheese and *saucisse*. We learn that the group from Germany has provided the food for any and all, and they urge us to join in. We happily comply.

You're never alone on the Camino. I feel warm and filled up.

The Germans are from an evangelical church near Frankfurt. They've been doing parts of the Camino together for ten years. Each day one of their group takes a turn driving a van that follows them with food and drink at different stops along the way. After they pack up what remains of their bounty, they go into the ancient chapel, and we follow. They sing hymns in German while I stare at the basalt stones and the luminous stained glass.

Something comes over me when I recognize the tune of "How Great Thou Art." I hum along as they sing in German. Lynn looks over at me and says, "I remember that hymn from when I went to church as a kid." We stumble through two verses in English with the Germans encouraging us on. By now, other pilgrims have made their way into the chapel, enticed, I suppose, by the singing. Little by little, they make their way forward and join us in the pews. Before long, the hymn is being sung in many languages, some I don't recognize.

I close my eyes. This is the Camino. Norwegian, French, and Polish students, retired Germans, and a group of American housewives singing in different languages in an ancient chapel in France. I'm only halfway through the first day, and already the Camino has surprised and blessed me and filled me up with wonder and gratitude.

The magical quality of my first day continues as I listen to the easy banter of the Washington Women, obviously close friends for years. I appreciate their letting me tag along as we walk past pastures with cows chewing their cud and horses sticking their soft gray muzzles over fences in search of a carrot from a kind pilgrim.

When we stop for a water break later in the afternoon, Barb looks at her phone. "Oh, brother. Jack is tracking me on this app on his phone, but when will he figure out that it isn't necessarily accurate?" She laughs. "This morning he was sure I was going in the wrong direction. Now he's freaking out because he thinks I've been sitting at a café for three hours straight. He's sure that I've either been kidnapped or fallen and broken my neck and can't move." She texts him, *I'm fine. Your phone is bugging again.* "What's the point of tracking if it just makes him worry all the more?"

I listen to her story and try to smile.

Then Brenda says, "Don't feel bad, Barb. Phil is following my every step with the GPS on his phone. He's sure I'm going to get lost too."

Jamie laughs and pulls out her phone. "I think Thomas is delighted to have me gone for ten days. He'll be eating beets from a can and watching sports 24/7." Then she gives a little giggle. "But he's tracking me too."

I want to disappear. Does Bill even have any idea where I am? Well, yes, I've written him my detailed plans. With no response. Does he even care?

Maybe it's true that I won't be by myself on this pilgrimage, but at that moment, as the women laugh and compare tracking devices on their smartphones, I feel lonelier than I have since the day I first met Bill twenty-two years ago.

"Y'all have been great," I say when we arrive in a village called Montbonnet. "I can't thank you enough for making this first day so fun. Here's where I've reserved my first night."

We exchange good-byes and text each other our phone numbers, and the others continue on their way, five more kilometers down the road.

I'm thankful to leave them. I need time on my own, time to think. Isn't the Camino about thinking?

But then, I don't want to think about my father, who's going blind and losing his memory, or my mother, whose hands are trembling; I don't want to think about Jason getting kicked off the football team or Bobby stuck somewhere in Austria with a refugee. I especially don't want to think about Bill and the way he ignores me. I don't want to think about how I'm not supposed to get in touch with him.

I can hear my exchange with Diana. Has it only been five days? "I'll be praying for you, Abbie."

No more texts or messages. That's what I said.

But I haven't stopped. Old habits die hard. I want him to feel sorry for me. I want him to miss me. I want him to care.

I want somebody to be tracking me.

I see a wooden sign directing me to La Barbelotte, the *chambre d'hôte* where I'm staying tonight. It's the French equivalent of a bed-and-breakfast, and though it's only two in the afternoon, I'm thankful that I've made these fifteen kilometers in good time. My hostess, Geraldine, shows me to my room, and I literally let out a sigh of relief. The room is spacious, clean, and neat, and I have a private bath.

I shower and sit in the garden, sipping a cup of mint tea with the sun on my back and petunias and zinnias blooming all around. A lavender plant splays its purple tendrils in every direction, and I inhale the sweet perfume while plump ripe raspberries peek over a stone wall. This. This! This is France.

Diana has suggested I do something called a Lectio Divina—reading a short passage of Scripture out loud several times and paying attention to any words that resonate. It sounds a little weird to me but, desperate to get my mind off of Bill, I'm willing to try anything.

So I read the first text that Diana has suggested, from the gospel of John, three times out loud, pausing after each reading to contemplate.

> The next day John was there again with two of his disciples. When he saw Jesus passing by, he said, "Look, the Lamb of God!" When the two disciples heard him say this, they followed Jesus. Turning around, Jesus saw them following and asked, "What do you want?" They said, "Rabbi (which means "Teacher"), where are you staying?" "Come," he replied, "and you will see." So they went and saw where he was staying, and spent that day with him. It was about four in the afternoon.

The first thing that jumps out at me is the word *follow*. John points out Jesus, and His disciples immediately start following

Him, leaving poor John in the dust. I'd be a bit miffed if I were John. Anyway, it says the disciples want to be where Jesus is, so much so that they "remain with him for the rest of the day."

Here I am with the rest of the day in front of me. Hmm. Could I remain with Jesus? Invite Him into all my mess? That scares me. I don't want to think too much about that.

So I move on to something else I noticed. *It was about four o'clock in the afternoon.* I've read the gospel of John many times, and I've always wondered why in the world he included that trivial information—the time of day. But today, reading those words brings tears to my eyes—because as I read it, I glance at the time on my phone, and it is literally four o'clock in the afternoon—4:05 to be exact.

I get that annoying pinching in my chest. As if the God of the universe knew I'd be reading this passage at exactly this time on this day. Ridiculous.

But Miss Abigail wouldn't have called it ridiculous. She called "coincidences" like these winks from a God who loves to remind us of His presence. A God who knows what we're doing every moment of every day. I get out the journal Diana gave me and record my thoughts. I feel a mixture of emotions: excitement, doubt, anticipation, annoyance. I write: *God, I don't really want to "remain with You" for the rest of the day. But I'll try to spend a little more time with You. I'm thankful for the Washington Women and their kindness. It's as if You put them here to encourage me after the shock of not having Bobby and Rasa.*

I think this Camino is going to be about trusting You again, God. I can almost hear You say, "Abbie, you've made the plans, you've done your best to get everything just right. But you can't control everything. So just trust Me and go forward."

When I reread what I've written, I am frankly quite shocked.

I sit in the garden for several hours, listening to my thoughts while I continue stitching the Huguenot emblem from Fort Caroline. Then, amazingly, I start praying . . . for my parents, for Jason, for Bobby and Rasa, and finally, yes, for Bill.

"Bless him, Lord. Give him the break he needs. Let him connect with You. And please, God, help me let him go and trust You as I try to find myself."

Why in the world did I pray *that*? I want him to miss me and care! I want him to be miserable without me. But the prayer came from somewhere down deep.

Dinner is delicious—everything organic: cabbage and green beans and saucisse and potatoes with cheese from the region. Amazingly, I am completely alone in this refuge, since Bobby and Rasa and Caroline aren't here. I turn the lights out at nine p.m. and sleep and sleep and sleep.

CARO

"*Allô?*"

Just hearing Jean-Claude's voice on the phone brings back so many memories of my summers with Lola. Following bike rides and pony rides and swimming in the pool, we'd inevitably end up at the Fourcade domain in the late afternoon, laughing and hungry. Jean-Claude would greet us at the door, a smile on his lips and his eyes tender with charm and kindness for "his girls." And I felt the same; Jean-Claude was like a second father to me when my father was away on business trips during our summer vacations.

"*Apéro?*" he'd ask. We'd nod enthusiastically, hurry into the sprawling salon, and collapse on the brown leather fauteuils, giggling. He'd bring out fruit juices or Coke for us along with chips and pretzels and pistachios. While we recounted our adventures, Jean-Claude sipped his pastis, swirling the ice in the glass so that it clinked against the sides.

I swallow back the memories and say, "*Bonjour, c'est Caroline.*"

"Caroline!" I hear pleasure in his voice. "*Comment ça va, ma Chérie?*"

"I'm okay." But there is a desperation in my voice that I'm sure he notices. I blurt it out, "Could I come see you today?"

He hesitates, then quickly recovers and says, "*Bien sûr*, my dear Caroline. Come."

He looks much older than his sixty-five years. It's been three or four years since I've seen him. I remember how his hair turned white practically overnight after Malika's death. Now his always-tanned face is lined with wrinkles. But his eyes are the same soft blue, and when he smiles, they radiate warmth. He gives me the mandatory three kisses, right cheek, left, right.

"*Apéro?*" he asks with a smile.

I grin and nod.

"Shall I show you around the property first?" The house is a renovated mas, an old farmhouse that now boasts handmade tiles from Italy and a salon to dance in, but the furniture is the same—the leather sofa and fauteuils, the ancient farm table that seats twenty.

Out back there are groves of olive and apple trees, and lavender grows in thick, perfumed rows of purple. Basil and oregano and thyme and chives are fighting for attention in an herb garden. I inhale the mixture of fragrances of my beloved Midi and smile. At last, we visit his *cave*, stocked with three hundred bottles, French wines from every region. Back in the salon I have fruit juice, without explaining my sobriety, and Jean-Claude is too much the gentleman to question. I laugh when he brings out the pistachios. He cradles his tall glass of pastis. "To you, Caroline," he says, and we touch our glasses together in a toast.

But I cannot do small talk today. In the space of fifteen minutes, I pour out my story. I tell him everything, the things I have never shared with my mother or father, the things that only Stephen and Tracie and my therapist know.

All the while he's watching me, his blue eyes changing from teasing to surprise to concern. When at last I end my monologue, or perhaps it is a diatribe, with "Can you tell me anything about Bastien?" he takes my hand.

"*Je suis desolé, ma Chérie.* These things are of course deeply disturbing." He clears his throat, once, twice, three times. "Yes, we knew Bastien vaguely, as your mother said. We met his wife, again as your mother said, at one soirée." He searches his memory.

We sit in silence, and I grab a handful of pistachios to calm my nerves.

"It's a bit complicated, *ma Chérie*, but I will tell you what I can."

I almost stop him because I read the pain in his eyes. But he sees the questions, the sense of betrayal in mine, and he begins.

"You know that for years Interpol was coordinating the efforts between the police in Iran and France, searching for Lola's cousin, Khalid. He lived in Iran and visited us in France for several weeks each summer. He felt very close to Malika—she was much more than his favorite aunt. She helped raise him." He shakes his head slightly, the pain etched so deeply in his eyes. "It was believed he was setting up a terrorist hub somewhere in Provence, perhaps even in our little village of Lourmarin." He takes my hand.

"That weekend"—I know exactly which weekend he's referring to—"Interpol organized a sting. The French police planned to apprehend Khalid at our home. He had told Malika he would arrive on Sunday, so Interpol arranged for Malika and Lola to go to a safe house on Saturday. They were just leaving when Khalid showed up a day early."

He gazes out the window where a breeze is rippling through the olive grove, but I know his mind has wandered much further away. A lone tear slips down the crevice in his tanned cheek. He clears his throat again.

"Khalid had a personal vendetta. He loved Malika like a mother . . . and then he hated her because of her conversion to Christianity."

I suck in my breath and feel the bottom drop out of my stomach. "You mean he killed her because she converted?"

"It appears to be so. Yes."

"And Lola was kidnapped?"

He ignores my question and simply says, "We've had news."

Now I feel a surge of hope. "News from Lola?"

He looks away. "Not directly. For all these years, I had no idea if she was alive. Then last year I got word that she was safe."

"You mean she escaped Iran?"

"Yes. That is all I was told. And I was asked to keep it quiet."

"She's alive!" I throw my arms around him, unabashedly, American-style. He holds me close, my head buried in his chest, which rises and falls with his emotion.

I back away, still holding his arms. "So you haven't seen her?"

He wipes a finger under his eyes. "No, not yet."

"But you know where she is?"

"She's in hiding. But I have heard that Khalid is back in Europe and being followed. When he is apprehended, then Lola will be free to come home."

"This is such good news, such wonderful news."

"Yes." But his smile is tight, worried. "But you must keep the news for yourself, Caroline. Say nothing. Not to your parents or brother or sister. We cannot be too careful."

"Of course!" I have to ask him the next question before I lose my nerve. "Do you think Bastien was involved in any of the horror?"

Jean-Claude struggles with the question. Clearly I have made him uncomfortable. Finally he nods. "*Oui.*"

CHAPTER

13

ABBIE

The phone alarm wakes me at eight. I've slept well. I dress and then head out to the breakfast room, which has been transformed from an ancient stable complete with a huge trough—fit for baby Jesus—and barn tools hanging on basalt-stone walls. I enjoy a breakfast of yogurt, bread, and homemade apricot and strawberry jellies, and a fresh pot of coffee. Geraldine comes in and says, "Enjoy your day. Be careful—there are some violent windstorms going on."

My fear must show on my face, because she smiles and reassures me. "You'll be fine. Just pace yourself."

Back in my room, I decide to read Psalm 121, the one I thought of at the mass yesterday, to calm my nerves. I am nothing if not an obedient pilgrim!

I will lift up my eyes to the mountains; from where shall my help come?

Here I am, lifting my eyes to the mountains in front of me. I suppose they are literally extinct volcanoes.

My help comes from the Lord, who made heaven and

earth. He will not allow your foot to slip; He who keeps you will not slumber. Behold, He who keeps Israel will neither slumber nor sleep. The Lord is your keeper; The Lord is your shade on your right hand. The sun will not smite you by day . . .

Well, the sun may not smite me, but what about the wind? I take a deep breath and read on.

. . . Nor the moon by night. The Lord will protect you from all evil; He will keep your soul. The Lord will guard your going out and your coming in from this time forth and forever.

I take another deep breath and feel the quiet settle upon me.

Yesterday was all small talk, simple camaraderie with new friends, and that had lowered my stress. I'd been surrounded with people, and I'd felt safe. But today—today I'm alone.

I think about what Diana said to me, that loneliness and solitude are not the same thing. "You can be lonely in a crowd of people. It's an aching, a type of grief. But solitude is different. It's gathering up what the Spirit is saying, a chance to meditate on the beauty of all you've been given. Solitude is a gift."

I take one more deep breath and welcome the gift.

As I head out, I receive a text from Caro. *Will meet you tomorrow in Monistrol. Thanks!*

She doesn't specify a time. Of course not. Am I supposed to wait around all day in the village for her to arrive? I text back. *I'm arriving in Monistrol-sur-Allier this afternoon. Please give me the hour your train will arrive.*

No idea. I'll be riding the Camino bus. Will text you once I'm on the way.

A text from Bobby arrives soon after. *Hey, Mom. Rasa is better, and I hope she'll be well enough to travel tomorrow, but it will probably be more like Monday. I'm really sorry.*

Deep breath. Solitude. And a short prayer. *Lord, may I spend this day with You.*

I leave the bed-and-breakfast and follow the red-and-white markings on the trees and fence posts as I head out of the village. Just as Geraldine has warned me, the wind is blowing fiercely, tangling my hair in my face.

I feel a trill of fear. How strong is this wind? I can't even see the path in front of me, my hair is blowing so crazily. I take the bandana hanging from my jean shorts, twist it around my neck, and pull it over my head. I probably look like a Muslim woman, but it works. I can see the path. I'm thankful for the walking poles and plant them solidly in front of me. The wind rushes from the north, pummeling me so hard I fear my pack will tip me over backward.

I'm suddenly wishing I would catch a glimpse of the Washington Women or my German friends up ahead, but the trail is empty of pilgrims. Just me and the wind and the wide-open fields. I pass a crossroads, and as I turn to follow the trail, I spot a lone boot hanging by its tied laces over a fence post, flapping eerily in the fierce wind. I walk closer and notice that the sole is ripped open. Someone has literally walked himself out of his boots. I hope that poor pilgrim had an extra pair of shoes in his backpack!

Eventually the narrow path winds up and up into a forest of tall evergreens. The tall pines shelter me from the whipping wind, and sheaths of sunlight peek through the trees. I take off my makeshift hijab. I'm totally alone with the ancient volcanoes. I inhale the scent of evergreens.

The perfection of creation, the calm in the forest, the sound of trilling birds, a flicker of a blue wing teasing me. A praise song echoes in my mind, and I feel myself filling up with something benevolent and peaceful.

Wow, where did all this positive emotion come from? Ten minutes ago I thought I might be carried away like Dorothy up into the sky, and now I am soaking in an ethereal peace, happily traipsing along the Yellow Brick Road.

As suddenly as I entered the forest, I am now leaving it. The wind has calmed, and I am on a paved road with harvested fields on either side. Bales of hay stand rolled and waiting for a tractor. In the distance windmills turn, and further out are rolling hills and mountains. Somewhere in between the fields and the hills, stone villages with red-roofed houses are tucked on hillsides.

I'm in the Mont of Devès, perched above the Allier and Loire Rivers. The *burle*—the bitter winds of winter—keep inhabitants inside, according to my guidebook. I can only imagine how vicious they must be as I think of the forceful summer winds I've just encountered.

I walk through a tiny village on flat land and then start down the path toward the village of Saint Privat-d'Allier. The trail is fairly steep and filled with loose small rocks and pebbles interspersed with bigger rocks. I'm thankful for my boots and walking poles, ordered at the last minute from Amazon Prime.

He will not let your foot slip. . . .

I hope the psalmist's words are literal, and meant for me, right now.

Most of the homes and shops in the village are made from volcanic stone. I soak in the contrast of the ancient black stones and the red-tiled roofs against a background of rippling, green-carpeted mountains. I feel like I'm standing in paradise. I take a photo on my phone, though I know full well I cannot capture the unique beauty of this place.

I find a café and take a chair, ready for a cool drink and

lunch, perched above the Allier River with a view of undulating mountains in every direction.

Thirty minutes later I leave the village, back on the trail, anxious to make my destination eight kilometers away before the predicted rain. I follow the trail farther up into the hills until I reach a paved road. The red-and-white markings indicate that I should now turn down a steep narrow path, what the French call a *chemin de chèvre balisé*—literally a goat path.

I peer down. It looks like loose rocks will accompany me the whole way. A safe path for goats, maybe, but not so much for humans. A sign in French says that, in case of strong rain, there's an alternate path. But the sky looks clear, and for once I'm glad to be alone. If dozens of pilgrims were trying to descend this narrow rocky path, one after another, it would create a real traffic jam!

I'm only five minutes into my descent when shadows move across the mountains. The storm comes out of nowhere, the rain pelting me. That vicious wind accompanies the slicing rain, and it suddenly feels chilly for August. Very chilly. I plant my poles and brace myself against the wind. The rocks have become slippery like ice.

He will not allow your foot to slip. . . . The Lord will guard your going out and your coming in. . . . I repeat the words over and over in my head like a plea as I concentrate on descending the path, carefully choosing where to plant each pole so that it holds me as I place my boot on a slippery boulder.

Three times my poles save me from landing on my rear end. I make it to the bottom and the path widens. A few trees provide a little shelter, so I stop, throw off the backpack, unzip it, dig through my provisions to find the plastic liner, and use it like a poncho to cover myself and my pack—even though we're both already soaked.

I stand among the trees, shivering, and feel my resentment building. No one cares that I'm out here alone in a thunderstorm. No one cares that I am all alone.

BOBBY

My father calls about every other day to check on me. I wish he would do the same for Mom. I've just come in from playing basketball with a group of missionaries and refugees in the House of Hope's parking lot when my cell sounds the ringtone I assigned to Dad.

"Hi, Dad!"

"Hey, buddy. How was your first day on the Camino?"

"Um, I haven't started yet." I briefly explain about Rasa.

"So your mother is doing it all alone?"

"I think so. Stephen's sister is supposed to join her—I mean us—soon."

He says something under his breath. Then, "She walked about twenty kilometers yesterday."

"How do you know that?"

"I'm following her on my phone. Nan set it up for me before your mother left. She doesn't know I'm tracking her, unless she notices the app, which I doubt she will."

I force myself to say nothing, but I am very relieved that he's involved, even if secretly.

"Bobby, there are violent storms in the area where she's walking today. Have you talked to her?"

I've been so distracted with Rasa—and basketball—that I haven't. "No, I didn't see that."

"Well, please check on her."

"Okay, I will."

Then he says, more forcefully, "Check on her now!"

He cares! My dad cares! He's tracking Mom. I'm still not sure why he can't simply check on her himself, but I decide to leave that subject alone. "Okay, I'll call her as soon as I get off the phone with you."

"Thank you, son." He sounds relieved but distracted.

"Is something else wrong, Dad?"

He hesitates. "I hope not, but she's been stopped for quite a while—two hours or more—in a very remote spot. Now that I know you're not with her, well, I'm concerned she could be hurt."

"Okay. I'll call now and let you know as soon as I hear anything."

I'm a bit rattled when I get off the phone. I feel guilty for staying back with Rasa. But Dad tracking Mom on his phone gives me a great feeling of relief as well. I click on Mom's number and listen to the buzz as it rings once, twice, three times, another time, and then the voicemail kicks in.

"Hi, this is Abbie. I'm off on an adventure, but I'll get back to you soon!"

I leave a message. "Mom, call me as soon as you get this."

Then I text her. *Mom, how are you? They're announcing bad storms around where you are.* I wait thirty minutes, an hour, more. No answer. I text my dad and feel a knot slide down and land with a plop in my stomach.

CARO

All day Saturday I fume and worry and cogitate. I don't call Brett or Tracie or Stephen or anyone at all. I rehearse all the ways that Bastien has betrayed me.

Nothing was coincidental! He planned to meet me, and he did it to keep me away from Lola so that Khalid could kidnap her and kill her mother!

I slow down. This is not *exactly* what Jean-Claude said. He simply said *oui* when I asked if Bastien was involved. But I could tell he knew a lot more than he was telling me.

I am so undone about Bastien that I haven't given Brett a moment of thought. Shouldn't I be at least somewhat preoccupied about my almost-fiancé, who may or may not have broken up with me the other day on the phone?

I am tempted to go to the cave and pull out three good bottles of wine and chug them down one after another until the hot sparks of hate are extinguished by the deep burgundy liquid that will kill my soul.

I've been sober for two and a half years. Two and a half excruciatingly hard years.

I know what I'm supposed to do—call Tracie. But I can't. I sit huddled in a ball on my bed, yanking my bare feet back from the tile floor every time I'm ready to trek down to the cave.

Lola is alive! Lola is somewhere safe!

I repeat this over and over, hoping to calm the furor in my head. But I can imagine it, the heady mix of scents when I swish the wine in my goblet, watching it slide down the crystal glass like a slow romantic ballad.

My throat feels parched. I set my right foot onto the cool floor and shiver with anticipation.

Punch in the number. Call, call, call!

Call Tracie!

I place my left foot on the tiles and stand, already feeling lightheaded, anticipating the delight of that first sip.

ABBIE

I should have been better prepared. I thought I had planned well, but the storm came out of nowhere. Now I'm sopping wet, and I've already slipped and fallen twice. I sit down on a rather uncomfortable rock, exhausted, a mixture of sweat and rain dripping from my brow and a thin trickle of blood sliding down from a scrape on my knee.

Evidently every other pilgrim had enough sense to stay off the trails today. Sitting on the rock, annoyed with myself for my poor choice, a memory surfaces that I'd prefer to forget.

"We have to move the party inside. It'll be okay. You can't control the weather, Abbs!"

Bill held me tight, but I fought to get out of his arms, furious that my seated dinner under tents in our backyard for his office buddies and their spouses had to be moved inside.

Bill's idea had been to reserve a room at the Club. "Nice and simple, Abbs."

But I wanted it at the house and then, when the crazy storm practically flooded the backyard an hour before the guests were to arrive, I rushed around in rain boots and a windbreaker, desperately trying to redirect the water and screaming at Bill and Bobby and Jason to help me, for heaven's sake!

Why was I always making them pay for my craziness?

A thunderclap shakes me from my self-incrimination. Then a bolt of lightning splinters the sky, frightening but eerily beautiful. A song from church, a simple melody with profound words, whispers in the storm: *Be still and know that I AM; even the wind and waves obey my will. Why do you fear? Where is your faith? Lo, I am with you forever and always. Be still.*

I get back up, rattled with all this noise in my head. I do not want to hear any more voices, encouraging or recriminating.

I make it down another steep slope, my legs wobbly with the effort. The trail veers to the left, and I find myself in a copse with the ruins of a stone house where a group of laughing youth are huddled together. They've created a makeshift tent with their ponchos and walking sticks. I notice the kerchiefs around their necks. Scouts! I've run into a troop of French Boy Scouts. Twelve of them.

I'm dripping wet, but they are dry.

"*Madame!* Are you alone?" a boy asks in French.

"*Oui.*"

A young man, evidently the leader, says, "Come under the shelter. You can stay with us until the storm ends."

I am so grateful that I have to force myself to keep from hugging this man.

"Would you like some bread and chocolate?" another scout asks.

I almost laugh out loud. Bread and chocolate. The proper *goûter* for every French kid. Yes, yes, I want this simple snack!

Before long I'm perched on the ruins, under the makeshift tent, eating a wedge of dark chocolate that's been stuffed inside a thick slice of baguette. When they bring out thermoses filled with hot chocolate, I can't help but smile. The French are always prepared with food and drink.

The boys ask me questions, and when I explain my situation, I think I see admiration in their young eyes. *Wow, lady. You've tackled one of the harder portions of the Camino alone!* If French Scouts earn merit badges, I'm sure I've helped them check *Rescue a wandering pilgrim* off their list.

I'm not alone. That shivering realization, that feeling of protection wells up in me again, and I acknowledge what *might* be God's presence.

After a fairly impressive lightning show, jagged white bolts illuminating the sky, the storm calms.

"You'll stay with us, then, Abbie," the young leader says, more statement than question. For now we know each other's names and are fast friends. It's that inexplicable bond that happens on the Camino.

I nod, deeply grateful, and say, "*Bien sûr.*"

The remaining kilometers to Monistrol alternate between passages on paved roads, each with beautiful vistas of the surrounding mountains and valleys, to more of the wooded and rocky downhill paths with different types of vegetation. Down, down, and down we hike, the Scouts patient as I plant my poles with painstaking care and slowly make my way behind them. Several times my right knee threatens to buckle under me thanks to an old skiing injury. The boys look back up at me with eager, hopeful eyes, as if I'm their inept den mother for whom they hold sole responsibility.

The downpour has turned into a steady drizzle as we head straight downhill. I stop to glance over the side of the road and see *Monistrol* written in flowers far, far below. The Allier River looks busy and very small.

When we reach the town an hour later, the Scouts leave me. They still have ten kilometers to get to the next town where they'll spend the night, tucked in their tents.

"Good-bye, Abbie," they chorus in heavily accented English. My heart soars. These are *my* boys, like my sons' friends whom I adopted long ago when Bobby and Jason were Scouts. And this is the Camino. So I take each boy in a big old American hug. The French don't hug—they do cheek kisses. But after the first two startled boys receive my hugs, one by one the others turn their bright pink cheeks up to me and engulf me with their skinny arms.

As I watch them walk across an enormous bridge, occasionally turning back to wave, I swallow down a bunch of bottled-up emotions. Then I get out my phone and see that I have three texts from Bobby.

Mom, are you okay? They're announcing bad storms around where you are.

Mom, can you please answer?

Mom! I'm worried. Call me.

And seeing those words, I cry.

14

CARO

Recovering addicts in the twenty-first century have a tool that didn't exist in centuries past. *Have your cell phone with you at all times!* That was the mantra drilled into my head. Call, call, call!

As I make my way down to the cave, I try to ignore its buzz. The first time I am successful. Now I'm standing in front of the cave door. I open it, the wine bottles happy friends greeting me from where they are stacked on iron racks around the whole outer wall.

My phone buzzes. I click it off. I browse through the bottles. If I'm going to fall off the wagon, I'll make it worth it. I pull a dusty bottle off the rack, a Bordeaux from 1964. A ping sounds from my phone, alerting me to a text. I ignore it.

Another ping and another and another. I pull my phone out of my pocket, exasperated. I'm just about to shut the cell down when it rings, catching me completely caught off guard. I answer it angrily. "What?" I seethe. "Who is it?"

I don't recognize the voice on the other end. "Caro? Caroline? It's Bobby."

"Bobby?" Then, "Oh, Bobby." My mind flits from the desperate anticipation of that taste on my tongue to an equally desperate voice on the phone.

"Sorry to bother you," he says, "but Mom is on the Camino, and there are violent storms where she's walking, and she hasn't answered my calls and texts or moved from one spot for several hours, and we're worried."

The spell is broken as I listen to Bobby's panicked voice. I place the bottle back beside the one from 1959, another Bordeaux, and concentrate on what he is saying.

"I was hoping that maybe you could go really soon, even today, to join up with her. I'm in Austria, and I can't get there till tomorrow night or maybe Monday morning. Could you please try to reach her? Could you go now?"

So instead of chugging down three bottles of vintage wine, I close the door to the cave, go back upstairs, search through the rooms until I find my old backpack, and begin gathering random items for the Camino.

I text Abbie to say that I'll meet her tomorrow morning at the train station in Monistrol. I don't hear from her until two hours later.

Great. Thanks! I'll be waiting.

She sounds just fine. But I know, *I know*. It's time to go. Tracie is probably on her knees, in between the tantrums of her children, begging God to intervene.

Well, I guess He did.

BOBBY

Mom finally calls late in the afternoon. She had no idea we were all so worried. She blabs about French Boy Scouts rescuing her, and I feel annoyed and relieved at the same time.

My backpack has been ready for days, but Rasa has still not verified that she even *has* a backpack suitable for this venture. I try to be patient.

"She needs to prepare in her own way." This Hamid shares with me as we are repairing a broken pipe in one of the refugee apartments a ten-minute drive from the House of Hope.

I'm not a handyman by any means, but I've watched my father—he can repair anything—and so I volunteered to go along. What else can I do with myself? Thinking about my mom and Rasa and Caroline has my insides all tied up.

So I'm in this tiny apartment, more like a studio with a mi-nuscule kitchen and a bathroom, which Hamid informs me is home to a family of seven.

"Do you think Rasa's nightmares could be more about doing the pilgrimage than being too involved with the refugees?" I ask him. In truth, I'm scared of her having a panic attack while she's with me.

"Possibly," he concedes. "I believe there is much mixed in together."

I hand him the pliers he's requested, which, I can tell, won't do the trick. He fiddles around with them for a few minutes, then sets down the tool without fixing anything, and looks at me. "I am sorry if I have put too much burden on you, Bobby. Rasa will have her anti-anxiety medication with her. But please know that Alaleh and I do not expect you to work miracles. We want Rasa to get away, have the scenery changed. But if she decides after a few days that it is too much, I will come get her. I will not ruin your trip."

Doesn't he understand that all I want is simply to be with Rasa? Anywhere. I scrounge around in the toolbox, retrieve a couple of wrenches, and say, "Can I give it a try?"

Five minutes later I've tightened the pipe and there is no

longer a leak. Hamid grins, pats me on the back, and says, "You will get along fine on the Camino."

In the afternoon I sketch Lisa, along with two African women, one from Nigeria, the other from the Ivory Coast, as they sit in the shade of a huge plane tree, stitching. These sketches are only for me, I've reassured the missionaries. I won't send them to Stephen; I won't even share them with others. But sketching these refugees is my way of tiptoeing the tiniest bit into their suffering, noticing their quiet dignity and fierce courage as they converse and stitch, using bright threads to create scarves and mittens and slippers.

Watching them now with their needles and thread, I think of Mom and the cross-stitch she's making for Dad's fiftieth birthday. I wonder if she'll even end up giving it to him. I know Dad would say that's not my problem . . . but I think of the relief and joy I heard in Mom's voice when I spilled the beans—another one of her favorite expressions—about Dad tracking her.

You'd have thought I told her I'd seen Jesus in the clouds. She giggled like a little girl. "Oh!" she said. "Imagine that! How do you know?"

"Because he called me, and he was out of his mind with worry. He saw you were stuck in some remote spot during the storm. He was freaking out, Mom. You know Dad never freaks out."

Maybe I exaggerated a little, but it worked. I had no idea what it meant and neither did she, except that Dad had broken his silence. And she was giggling with relief.

I glance back at the women and their needlework and continue to sketch. For the first time since I laid eyes on Rasa, I feel an excitement in my gut that isn't about her. I actually miss my mother, and I'm looking forward to seeing her soon.

Later that evening, I'm still thinking about my mother stitching. From my earliest memories, I picture her with a needle and thread. She's not crazed like Madame Defarge, but she isn't exactly happy either. She's busy. It's her hobby, yes, but I can't say that it relaxes her.

At any rate, the memory that floats into my mind starts out happy and ends up tragic. After Anna was sent to a foster home, she continued attending my school, for which we were all extremely grateful. Her father went to jail, and his sentence brought great relief. For months afterward, she came to our house, to church, to youth group. She laughed, she never had to wear long shirts to cover up bruises, she truly seemed free.

I had just gotten my license, and several evenings a week I would pick up Anna at her foster family's house and bring her to our house for dinner. When we arrived, we'd inevitably find Mom stitching an intricate canvas as she waited for us.

Anna learned to cross-stitch from Mom, and after we had eaten dinner and finished our homework, she would sit with Mom, both of them halfheartedly watching a sitcom, both intent on stitching. Whereas Mom stitched somewhat frantically, Anna took it as a lazy and lovely parenthesis in her life. She wasn't particularly trying to create or prove anything; she was just happy to be with us.

In my junior year, Anna's father got out of jail, which seemed like a huge crime to me. But there was no way he would get Anna back, so we thought she was safe. Anna knew differently. Her stitches became erratic and a lost look came into her eyes. She started wearing long sleeves even though she had not set eyes on her father.

Trauma. That was what she had been through. She'd seen

a therapist for almost a year after she was removed from her father's house. I'd been in counseling too, for what they were calling *vicarious trauma*. But in the end it didn't work.

I'm home. Mom is stitching, Anna is stitching, and then she's not.

I force myself to think of something different. I force myself to stand up. I shake my head, and I look at my sketch pad. These ruminations have made me crazy with grief, and the ladies bent over their needlework in my sketch pad are unknown, except for one who looks straight at me with Anna's face.

ABBIE

The sun has broken through the clouds as I make my way to my chambre d'hôte in Monistrol, located in the *bourg*, the old part of town, perched on the opposite side of the Allier River. To get to that side, I cross the Eiffel Bridge, constructed by the same Mr. Eiffel who designed the famous tower in Paris.

The bridge is a massive green structure that actually looks a bit like part of the Eiffel Tower turned on its side. Standing in the middle, I gaze at the water rushing far below me, swollen after the storm, then to the basalt stone houses on either side, tucked into the mountains. Joy wells up in me—but not only because of this breathtaking beauty. Bill has been tracking me! I twirl around, backpack, poles, and all.

I pass a yellow arrow with the familiar red-and-white lines indicating the next leg of the Camino, and instead follow the small hand-painted sign directing me to my destination. Geraniums and petunias tumble out of flower boxes in windows along the way. Bells toll from an ancient church. People emerge from where they've been waiting out the storm. With the sun now peeking through the clouds, they buy ice cream from store-fronts that display multicolored flavors.

I'm still smiling as I climb the last narrow cobbled street to where I'll be spending the night. All the fatigue and worry and fear fall off my shoulders along with my backpack when I enter the lovely little room I've reserved. My suitcase, which La Malle Postale delivered during the day, is awaiting me inside.

I head to the shower in my private bathroom and soon I'm belting out Elton John's love ballad, "Your Song," as I try to wrap my mind around this day. I've lived through a year full of emotions in about eight hours.

I sing and laugh in the shower until I remember the sign on the door asking guests to please be very frugal with the water. I towel dry and dress in capri jeans and a soft pink sleeveless shell, feeling light and carefree.

Bill has shown signs of life. Bill is worried about me.

I blush to think of my annoyance when the Washington Women talked about their husbands tracking them. I suppose if I'd taken the time to study my phone, I might have figured out that I had a similar app. But I hadn't bothered to do anything but writhe in self-pity.

I almost email Bill a long note about my harrowing day. Then I stop myself. Instead I get out the canvas and let my thoughts carry me away while I cross-stitch.

Give him a break. Give him a break. Give him a break. I repeat it in my mind like a mantra.

I exhale a mouthful of bitterness at his silence and inhale a calming breath of gratitude at his concern.

He cares. He was freaking out.

I stare at the cross-stitch, running my fingers over the intricate patterns, holding on to that feeling of thankfulness as I contemplate the way the design defines not only Bill's life, but my own.

The dozen pilgrims staying at this chambre d'hôte meet for dinner, crowding around an old pine table in the salon of the main house, which is tucked into a row of stone residences. Our host, Pascal, serves up specialties of the region, a simple soup, then *boeuf bourguignon* ladled over steaming pasta, fresh bread, and later, cheese and fruits.

Back in my room, I click on the Bible app on my phone and scroll through to Psalm 122, the next Psalm of Ascent. *I was glad when they said to me, "Let us go to the house of the Lord. . . ."*

These words actually cause me to smile. This was probably the first Bible verse I ever memorized, way back in vacation Bible school when I'd barely learned to read. Tomorrow is Sunday. I won't be going to church, but I am going *up*, just as the Israelites were doing on the pilgrimage to Jerusalem.

I spent much of today slipping and sliding my way down into this valley. Tomorrow's hike begins with a steep climb out. But tomorrow I won't be alone. In the morning, I'll be meeting Caroline at the Monistrol train station.

I fall asleep feeling an excitement that has nothing to do with the climb or with Caroline. It has to do with one little word. Bill.

CARO

I walk outside and breathe in that mingling of fragrances after a thunderstorm. While I've been seething about Bastien, the same storm that threatened Abbie on the Camino has whooshed through Lourmarin. As the sun sets behind the village, I stand and watch until the bold crimson fades to pink pastels. I get my camera and shoot photo after photo of raindrops perched on Augusta Luise's petals, then lizards emerging from under rocks to catch the last fleeting snatches of sun and honeybees swarming again around the lavender.

I breathe deeply, the way they instructed me in rehab, and force myself to let go of the wrath that has wrapped itself so completely in my mind. Yes, I feel betrayed, worse than betrayed, by Bastien. But he was not the last thing Jean-Claude and I talked about.

"*Merci, chère Caroline,*" Jean-Claude had said, "for everything you've done for Lola these many years. You have loved her well, searching for her at great personal expense. I'm sorry I cannot tell you more right now. But I promise you will know first, when it's safe to share."

I know now that my intuitions, most all of them, had been correct. Khalid was responsible. And he had murdered Malika not from a terrorist's motive but from a fundamentalist's ire, the bane of extreme religion.

I make my way past Bastien's home, where dark green ivy covers the stucco façade and the thick wooden shutters are painted the olive green of Provence. Where I sat with him ten days ago and felt his lips on mine. I stand in front of the darkened structure and let the guilt fall off. I had been young and foolish, headstrong, selfish, and many other things during that weekend of 2011.

But now I know that Bastien had purposely kept me away from Lola.

Maybe I can do what he's been begging me to do. Let the guilt go. How ironic that he's the one who finally convinced me to get help.

"I'm not a safe bet," he'd told me. Well, for all the lies, that surely is the truth! But why the recent kiss when he'd been Mister Hands Off for so long? What does it mean? *You initiated it, Caro. It means you're still obsessed.*

But Lola is alive! In truth, I had given up hope of ever seeing my friend again. Now hope bubbles just below the surface and soon, when I actually *see* her, it will burst forth in a spray of joy. Lola is alive!

I continue down the road to where the Fourcades' house stands, out of sight behind all the olive groves. Someone else tends the property now. I let myself in the unlocked wrought-iron gate and walk up the long dirt drive, inhaling the fresh night air. The sky has turned dark, the moon peeks around an olive branch, and the cicadas begin their mad chirping. I sit down, my back against a tree, letting my senses soak up this moment.

I feel like I've come through an intense and intensely personal battle. I've been whipped and thrown around, but not defeated.

I feel the traces of a smile turning the corners of my lips upward.

Lola is alive. I am still sober. And tomorrow I am starting a new adventure.

CHAPTER

15

ABBIE

I wake with that same feeling of excitement in my gut, humming a hymn and then saying out loud in the room, "'I was glad when they said unto me, "Let us go into the house of the Lord."'" I wash my face and put on my makeup and clothes and am ready to head to breakfast with the other pilgrims.

But first I pick up my phone, and when I open my email, I see a message from Bill. My stomach literally twitters with the same anticipation I used to get when he'd call to invite me on a date.

Dear Abbs,

I think it's time to explain my silence. I'm sorry to have left you like I did. But the thing is, I knew you'd be fine. You're always fine. It has felt to me for a long time that you don't need me anymore. Or maybe I should say, you only need me so you can organize my life.

I've always admired your skill, Abbs. The way you set up the house so beautifully, the way you give yourself 200% to any task and do it so well. And the way you've cared for your men, as you call us. You did it all.

But somewhere along the way, it felt like I lost myself. Like I didn't have a say in any decisions. I know we talked, but sweetie, you can be so doggone convinced and convincing, and you argue me into the ground.

For years it really didn't bother me too much. I don't have strong opinions like you do. You know I'm a pretty easygoing guy.

I don't know exactly when it started eating away at my soul. Or maybe I do. Maybe it was when Jason started pushing hard for boarding school, and then Bobby wanted a gap year. They wanted to get away. They felt controlled and manipulated and suffocated. As I did. I know that's hard for you to hear.

And Abbie, I will admit that I'm partly to blame. I let you control, I let you manipulate, I let you figure it out.

But finally, I knew something had to change. I started seeing a therapist, told him about our lives and what was happening and how much I longed to escape. And the more I talked, the more I realized how much of me had died a slow and subtle death.

So I had to get away. And in some way, I think you needed us to all be out of your life for a little while too.

I don't know what else to tell you. I needed this breather. I have to say that I've so appreciated this month away. And I'm very afraid to come back.

I do love you, Abbs. I just don't know what that means for us in the present. I absolutely refuse to run back to where we were.

I'm sorry.

Bill

I can barely breathe. I read his email three more times, and each time I feel a knife stabbing my heart and then twisting in deeper and deeper. I frantically force myself to see the good things in his words—the fact that he wrote me in the first place, the fact that he still calls me Abbs. He even says he loves me.

But none of that resonates, of course. Instead, what I hear is *I lost myself . . . felt controlled, manipulated, suffocated . . . died a slow and subtle death . . .*

I think I am going to vomit. My stomach cramps, and I sink to the bed, gathering my arms around my midsection to squelch the pain.

I don't know what else to tell you. How about "Hurry home! I can't wait to see you!" Instead it's *I needed this breather. I've so appreciated this month away. I'm very afraid to come back.*

The words are screaming in my head so loudly that I can hear nothing else. Except this: he's right. And that is what hurts the most. I feel the sickening strike of conviction in my soul. *He's right!* I have been admitting it to myself, to Diana, to my mother and Nan and Rachel. But when I read it from Bill, anger simmers and boils over, and I rush to the bathroom and heave all the wonders of the Camino into the toilet.

When I stand and splash water on my face and glance in the mirror, I see that I'm pasty white. I feel a deeper grief than when I learned about Anna, deeper than with Nan's tragedy. I feel fury and hatred for Bill. How dare he say these things? How dare he ruin my time away?

How dare he tell me the truth?

The truth does not move me to repentance and freedom. It crawls up from my gut to my throat and then back down to my heart, where it tangles itself around all that is good.

I'll fight back! I am determined not to let this spoil my day. My life. I breathe slowly in and out. I will regain control. I will make it all okay. He can't hurt me. I won't let him hurt me like this!

Thirty minutes later, I've reapplied the makeup that washed away in my shock, I've pulled my hair back in a ponytail, I've packed my suitcase and set it outside where La Malle Postale will retrieve it and carry it along to my next destination.

I grab my backpack and head to the garden, where breakfast with the pilgrims awaits.

CARO

By morning, all my delight at being sober and knowing Lola is alive has evaporated like last night's puddles of rainwater on the stones around the house. The morning is heavy, oppressive, the thermometer already reading eighty-six degrees at nine thirty. A similar heaviness weighs down my shoulders long before I hoist the backpack onto them.

Bastien has invaded my thoughts, and I cannot get rid of him. If he knew about Khalid, if indeed he was somehow working with him, well then, he's dangerous. He's a criminal.

I have thought of Bastien in many different ways, but never as a criminal.

I retrieve my camera bag, filled with the camera and extra lenses, fully aware of how heavy this will make the pack, but my job is to take photos and send them daily, along with a blog post, to Stephen. I briefly consider leaving the camera and attachments behind and just using my smartphone, then decide to carry the real deal. But my enthusiasm has slipped away. Why walk the Camino when I could be helping Jean-Claude locate Lola?

The bus leaves me at the train station. I hop on with two hours to calm down, two hours to change from a hot mess into a friendly backpacker.

Abbie has long wheat-colored hair that she wears in a ponytail. She has donned the perfect pilgrimage outfit. In fact, waving to me from the quay, she looks like an ad for a luxury walk on the Camino with a fancy bright pink-and-gray backpack, brand new top-of-the-line hiking boots (that don't look broken in to me), a V-neck periwinkle-blue Under Armour shirt that matches her eyes (swollen a little?), the latest in black workout shorts, and Ray-Ban sunglasses perched on her head. I think she even has designer walking poles, for crying out loud. When she looks at me, I try not to notice the tiniest bit of condescension in her eyes.

"Hi, Abbie. Nice to see you."

She gives a tight smile. "Hey, Caroline. Good to see you too. Thanks for joining me." Then in the next breath, "You're wearing those?" She's staring at my Keens.

"Yep, sandals. I'm wearing sandals." I want to yell at her that I didn't have time to think through anything because I was trying to solve a murder case and then came dangerously close to getting completely stoned and losing my hard-earned years of sobriety. But I don't. I just think, *Yes, I'm wearing my Keens, my extraordinarily comfortable Keens.*

She smiles a very white-suburban-house-mom smile. She's tanned and fit, and her backpack is filled with "only the necessities for the day," she explains. Evidently you can pack a suitcase with all the rest of your stuff, and they deliver it from place to place for a small fee.

"A very small fee," Abbie specifies.

After our initial awkward greeting, she says, "If you're ready to begin, the trail is this way."

"Sounds good."

I think to myself that I don't know why Bobby sounded so panicked yesterday. Obviously this woman has everything under control.

ABBIE

I feel completely out of control. Something in my left boot is rubbing the wrong way, and Caroline is rubbing me the wrong way too. She's wearing jean shorts that barely cover her very small rear end, a pale green T-shirt that hangs off one shoulder, showing a plethora of tattoos, and sandals—*sandals* to walk the Camino! Her thick dark brown hair is cut short, and it looks at once relaxed and sexy. She's a slim, casual beauty. Her backpack is, to put it lightly, anything but light, stuffed, it seems to me, in a very haphazard way. And she has a real camera, with a crazy long lens, hanging around her neck.

Yep, this is the girl I remembered. Has she even planned anything for the Camino? Honestly!

When I explain about La Malle Postale, she laughs. "You're doing the luxury version of the Camino, aren't you?"

I look at her, hoping to disguise my annoyance. *There's nothing luxurious about this pilgrimage!* I want to shout, but I refrain. I force myself to stop thinking about Bill's email, but it doesn't really help my mood. Because seeing this girl—a young woman, really—with that effervescent but lost look in her eyes, obviously doing things on the spur of the moment . . . it all feels like nothing close to luxury. Just one more person for me to have to try to control.

My hiking boots are not completely dried out from yesterday's downpour, and I've put on two pairs of socks that I hope will keep my feet dry. But after only two kilometers, hiking straight uphill, I feel the blisters coming.

Although Caroline is not prepared, she seems more than ready to get going. She has an energy that bowls me over, climbing the crazy-steep ascent out of Monistrol as if she's prepping for a triathlon. Fortunately she also has this alarming sense of smell, and so, randomly along the trail, she'll stop in her tracks and bend down over some plant or flower, sniffing. Then she takes her camera from around her neck and changes the lens—she has at least five different ones, I think, stuffed in the backpack—so that she can get the perfect shot of whatever flower or leaf or tiny drop of dew or bumblebee in midflight has caught her fancy.

Her olfactory and photo obsessions are my salvation. Otherwise I would not be able to keep up with her as she effortlessly climbs the almost ninety-degree ascent to what's known, according to my map, as the Chaos de L'Escluzels.

Chaos! Ha! My whole life is one big piece of chaos.

Caroline's holding on to rocks, the camera dangling around her neck—surely it will bang against something and shatter a lens—while I plant my poles carefully between each boulder, far behind her. I'm perspiring and huffing and puffing like the big bad wolf when she suddenly stops again, balancing a bit precariously on two semistable rocks, while rattling on about some wonderful smell emanating from an odd-looking weed that is poking its way up between them.

I catch my breath and offer what I've read about the landscape before us. "What we're seeing over there—those huge eroded boulders that look like the humps on a giant camel—were actually formed from extremely violent volcanic eruptions along the fault lines in this region."

"Amazing! Love it," she says while she clicks numerous photos and then resumes her mad pace, climbing up, up, up, completely oblivious to my discomfort.

The blisters have worsened, and I'm limping. We're on a road now that zigzags back and forth, no less steep. We pass a strange-looking chapel of sorts, built into the basalt rocks. "It's a troglodyte chapel," I say, consulting the Camino app on my phone.

"A what?"

"A place where hermits lived—below the ground. Evidently prehistoric human bones have been found inside."

"Stephen is going to love this! Volcanic boulders and an underground prehistoric burial site! And all these crosses along the Camino—every shape and size and texture." She motions to a small granite cross perched along the path and surrounded by pebbles left by pilgrims.

Click, click, click, change lenses, *click, click, click.*

To be fair, I am taking my share of photos too. And yes, the crosses—thick stone or thin wrought iron, whether one foot or ten feet high, they've enchanted me too. My favorite so far is a pietà that stands outside the chapel in Monistrol.

Off she goes again with me trailing. I note rather proudly that although I am far behind Caroline, I've passed two groups of pilgrims moving slow as turtles and stopping every few minutes to wipe their brows.

"Caroline, can you please slow down?" I call out at last, exasperated. "I'm having a hard time keeping up with you."

She stops and turns to me. "Oh, Abbie, I'm sorry. I guess I am walking rather fast."

I surprise myself by saying, "You're climbing this very steep ascent as if you're mad and trying to get all the anger out through your sandals."

She laughs. "Well, you've got that right. I *am* mad. In fact, I'm furious." She stops, places her hands on her skinny hips, and takes a deep breath.

I surprise myself again by saying, "Well, if it's any comfort, I'm furious too."

She looks at me, startled. "At me?"

"No," I lie. "At some pretty crappy circumstances."

"Really? Wow, that's pretty cool. I mean, not cool, but, um, interesting . . . that we're both in bad moods."

"Yeah, a bad mood is putting it lightly. I don't know what to do," I confide.

Caroline stares at me as if I've told her I'm a seamy predator. "What?" I say. "You look shocked."

She recovers, laughs a bit self-consciously, and says, "It's just I was about to say those exact same words. I don't know what to do either. I really don't know what to do."

Wow, indeed. The Camino is working its magic. And just like that, we become fast friends. For the remainder of the day, all twenty kilometers, we tell each other our tales of woe.

We've given each other a descriptive thumbnail sketch of why we're both *livid*. We've decided that's the word that best describes our mood. She's told me about Brett and Lola and Bastien and what she calls the murder mystery and her stints with alcohol and drugs and therapy and her past week in Lourmarin, which sounds like a place I'd like to visit, and even the panicked phone call from Bobby last evening while she contemplated swallowing what she calls "Papa's best bottles from the cave." She ends her monologue with "Bastien's a ****** crook and an accomplice to murder!"

Then, without taking a breath, she asks, "So what's the news with Bobby and the girl?"

"The *refugee*, the refugee who is *sick*," I specify.

She lifts an eyebrow, hearing the irritation in my voice.

"They're hopefully coming tomorrow. But it may be the next day. You never know with those kids."

"Not too thrilled with this relationship, I take it?"

I shrug. "Just one more thing to worry about. And try to control." I stop to catch my breath, and we let a group of pilgrims—chattering away in Italian? Spanish?—pass us by. "Control is my top vice."

She grins. I start to bristle until she adds, "And my top vice is a total lack of control."

And for some reason, we both begin to laugh.

"So how did you meet Bill?" Caroline asks a little later.

"By accident," I say.

How odd that I call it an accident when up until now I have always seen it as the hand of God.

"I was at a party my junior year . . . or maybe it was my sophomore year."

I've always known the exact day, month, and year. Have the details floated off on their own, or am I intentionally suppressing them?

"It was a fraternity party that his younger brother was hosting at their house. Bill had finished school several years earlier and worked for a while in banking. He was back at school getting his MBA. We were all enjoying the music and dancing, the food and drinks. Bill came home from who knows where"—actually I did know—"and his brother introduced us."

What I didn't say was that his brother, James, had already asked me out. But I wasn't interested in James.

"We chatted for a while," I tell Caro, "and at the end of the evening Bill walked me to my car and asked me to dinner the very next night, and I accepted."

I don't go into the feud that started between James and Bill, but I ponder that whole idea of an accident. Was our marriage an accident? What a crazy idea! Without Bill, I wouldn't have Bobby or Jason.

I refuse this dangerous train of thought and continue my story. "Most of the time dating Bill was just plain fun, but occasionally he'd surprise me with something unusual, a more serious side. He's a history buff, and he'd come out with a reference to the persecution of his Huguenot ancestors or a little-known fact about the civil rights movement. He'd show another side of him, and it excited me that there was more than just fun-loving, business-minded Bill.

"He calmed me down—you know—the old thing, opposites attract. But after a while, of course, opposites can also drive each other crazy. So we had our crazy years, and the more I organized our lives, the more he grew silent. He went along, he nodded, but he laughed a lot less. And then he stopped laughing at all, and he left."

CARO

We're nearing a town called Sauges when we come across strange sculptures along the path. "What in the world?" I say, as a huge iron sculpture of a wolflike creature comes into view. It's big enough for me to stand under, between its front and back legs.

Abbie is laughing. "Ah, of course. The Beast of Gévaudan." She's looking at her phone. "Evidently some terrifying animal ran rampant in this region in the 1760s, devouring more than a hundred women and children."

"*Quelle horreur!*" I inject.

She grins. "Yes. There are several different accounts of who finally slayed the beast."

I snap several photos of Abbie under the beast and then she takes a selfie of both of us under it—which doesn't really work, since all that shows is the underbelly and our smiling faces. But here we are, standing together, arms around each other's shoulders, taking a selfie. How strange this Camino—binding people together in such a short time.

We've been sharing true confessions for about four hours,

213

the last two at least concentrating on our sob stories with men. After Abbie tells me about her first meeting with her husband, she asks, "How did you meet Brett?"

"We were set up by Stephen. We had stuff in common. He's a photo buff and loves the outdoors. But he's careful. Put together."

"Boring?"

"If I compare him to Bastien, yes, but I know it's not fair to compare. I actually have no idea why he loves me. I'm such a mess. I know Stephen and Tracie thought he could bring a bit of stability into my life."

"Do you love him?" she asks.

I stop in the middle of the trail, and a herd of pilgrims passes us on either side. "I've tried," I say. It comes out as a hiccup of truth, and I'm mortified. "He's a good guy. He's responsible, he's funny, he's cute. We have a good time together, but . . ." I swipe at my eyes. "I almost said yes when he proposed the first time, but then when I tried to imagine my life with him, all I could see was Bastien. They're so different. If I did that old pros and cons thing, well, I suppose Brett would come out on top. But who wants to decide about marriage with a sterile pros and cons list? Shouldn't it be fireworks and passion?"

Abbie cocks her head, undoes her ponytail, and lets her thick, perfectly highlighted blond mane fall to her shoulders before securing it again with a pink elastic. "Maybe," she answers.

"Well, did you feel passionate about Bill?" I realize too late how desperate I sound to hear her answer.

"Yes, oh my word, yes. He was my polar opposite, and as I've said, I guess opposites attract. He made me laugh, he knew how to tease me, in a good way. I was absolutely crazy about him." She glances my way. "So yeah, it was fireworks and passion, but also some kind of soul connection." For a moment she closes her eyes, completely gone from me, recalling, I suppose, those first days and months and years with Bill.

"That's how it was with Bastien," I say. "There was passion, of course, but it seemed like he really cared about me. He can be cynical and critical. But sometimes he'd look at me with the tenderest expression. Almost . . . almost like he loves me," I whisper, embarrassed.

I'm a little shocked to be telling Abbie all this, but what else will we talk about for eight hours a day? And I'm beginning to like her no-nonsense, practical, organized self. What she calls her Triple-A-ness.

I can't tell her the rest, how whenever that certain look came across Bastien's face, he would get up from the table or power ahead on our hikes and find something to do with his hands. And then he'd become a stone wall, his face blank, as if he had suddenly let his deepest, darkest secret be seen and he needed to backtrack real fast.

The thing is, I never told anyone about those tender moments, not Tracie or Stephen or my therapist. They all thought Bastien was one big fat jerk, and in truth, I wanted them to think that so they could convince me of the same thing. But I was wrong too. I was the one who kept running back to him again and again and again, hoping for something that he had decided not to give me. Hoping for love.

Abbie has come back from her reverie about Bill, and she's actually been listening to me. "Well," she says, "I don't know about this Frenchman, but I can tell you one thing. Don't marry someone just because he's a nice guy." She blushes a little. "As if I'm an expert on marriage," she says and gives a clipped little laugh.

I try not to show my shock. Her blunt assessment rings absolutely true. I am actually considering marrying Brett because he's a nice guy. I'm not starry-eyed "in love." I'm not even sure I love him.

I say in a small voice, "Maybe the only reason I've considered marrying Brett is to protect myself from Bastien. I'm a mess, but once I get married, I'll be faithful. I know that about myself." To my surprise, tears come. "And now more than ever, I need to protect myself from Bastien."

ABBIE

We're six hours into our walk and now we're talking like bosom buddies. Confidantes. We've slowed our pace considerably, as my blisters are making the whole hike excruciating. I've called to cancel the chambre d'hôte in Le Sauvage—at my slow pace we'll never make eight more kilometers before nightfall. Instead we'll spend the night in a tiny village called Le Villeret-d'Apchier.

I've layered both of my heels with Band-Aids, changed socks twice, and put on my running shoes. My boots dangle off the back of the pack. To her credit, Caroline shows sympathy when we finally sit down at a picnic table beside the road.

I share my picnic—Caroline didn't think to bring any food along, and now that we're bosom buddies, I understand why. We munch on a fresh, buttered baguette filled with saucisse, provided by my last hostess.

"I guess I kept holding on tighter and tighter and tighter to Bill," I explain between bites. "We've had a lot of losses in the family, and I think the last two—the tragic death of my sister's husband and then the equally tragic death of my son's girlfriend—well, they undid me. Of course, all the previous losses had affected me deeply. But with these, I freaked out.

My sister and my son got help, but I just lived out their pain vicariously and then went about my days with an iron grip on Bill and Bobby and Jason. Big mistake."

"It sounds like you need to give things up," Caro says after snapping a photo of what looks like a huge stone menorah planted beside the road. "What I need is to take the risk of finding stability, of trusting people again. I flit from one thing to another." She sits back down and takes a bite of baguette. "The problem is, when I'm with Bastien, I feel so alive. So passionate. Life is filled with endless possibilities. Frenchmen don't like the words commitment or accountability. They don't believe sensuality is a sin or that beauty is reserved for certain occasions."

Just mentioning him brings renewed enthusiasm to her voice. I'm thankful we're sitting, or I imagine she'd be off hiking like a marathoner.

Around four in the afternoon we reach our destination for the day. This time we're at a true *gîte*, as in common showers and toilets. Caroline and I will be sharing a room with two other pilgrims who have yet to show up. The room has four cots. I'm simply thankful that this gîte still had room for us.

Our hostess, Lucette, greets us, and she and Caroline start babbling in French. It always surprises me to hear Caroline's perfect French, but she did grow up here, as she reminds me.

Lucette instructs us to leave our boots and backpacks in the outer hall—nothing in the rooms—a precaution against bedbugs and who knows what else. She gives us each a bucket to put our essentials by the bed, but she does allow me to haul my suitcase, deposited earlier in the day, up the narrow stairs. I'm thankful that La Malle Postale was willing to reroute my bag when I called to inform them of my change in destination.

We shower, me loaning Caroline a towel because, of course, she hasn't brought one with her. We sit outside at a little picnic table with a beautiful view of the forest, sipping on bowls of hot tea. I start cross-stitching while Caroline uploads her photos to her tablet.

A while later, who should show up but the Washington Women. As Laurent had explained my first night in Le Puy, one of the beauties of the Camino is crisscrossing with other pilgrims all along the way, back and forth, back and forth.

I introduce them to Caroline, and they admit that they stayed put during the storm yesterday. Around the dinner table, again with delicious regional fare, ten of us pilgrims share bits and pieces of our stories.

That night, lying on my cot with sweat dripping off me in the ninety-degree heat, I think about Caroline. We walked twenty kilometers together today, Caro in those strappy sandals and me in my brand-new but broken-in boots, and I'm the one with blisters. I'm the one, in spite of my sunscreen, who is burnt on the back of my neck, and I'm the one who wakes up in the middle of the night to Barb's snoring beside me.

Caroline, on the other side, is zonked out cold.

But I'm awfully glad she's here.

CHAPTER

16

BOBBY

We've been on three different trains in three different countries—this last one a night train from Zurich to Lyon—when I wake in the pitch-dark somewhere between Sunday night and Monday morning. Fifteen hours of travel has worn us both out. At first Rasa babbled along, sharing story after story of Isa in her life. But around eight o'clock she drifted off to sleep, her head bobbing back and forth when the train swept around a wide bend.

Lisa drove us to the train station after we attended the Iranian church that Hamid pastors. As we waited in the car for Rasa to say her final good-byes to her father and mother, Lisa said, "Several years ago, Hamid, along with eight other Iranian students from all over Austria, began a three-year training program. They came to the Oasis for a week four times a year to study the Bible under Iranian teachers. Seven of them are now in full-time ministry, and there are dozens of Iranian-led fellowships throughout the country. Hamid not only directs the House of Hope, but as you saw this morning, he's also an ordained pastor."

I had soaked in the simple, buoyant joy of these Iranian believers—over a hundred of them—as they worshipped in Farsi.

"I enjoyed being part of that experience," I told Lisa. "What an amazing story."

"It is, and we have many such stories. It's what keeps us going when ministry gets tough. Rasa has led worship in her father's church for the past few years."

Watching Rasa up front, dressed in a modest, bright, flowing dress, her hair under a scarf, had been distracting, to say the least.

"Besides teaching German at the House of Hope, she also helps with the youth group. Has she told you that she plans to go to law school?"

"No, I don't think so."

"She hopes to become a family court judge in the future and work with refugee families in Austria."

I'm not sure why Lisa added that detail. In my postworship reverie, I'd simply nodded amicably. But considering it now, as dawn dangles far beyond the horizon, it sounds almost like a warning: *Don't become too attached, Bobby. Her place is here.*

But I *am* attached. I study Rasa's tiny wrists, one crossed over the other, her black hair tangled behind her where she's twisted it into a loose knot, tendrils falling beside her face, her thick lashes quiet against her skin, and I feel an overwhelming sense of protectiveness. It flutters in my gut between worry and delight. I stare until fatigue overtakes me, and I close my eyes. . . .

Mom is stitching, Anna is stitching, I'm strumming a few chords on the guitar. We're making light conversation. Then we hear a fist banging on the front door, ringing the doorbell multiple times. Mom glances at me, whispers, "Call 911!" Anna sits frozen, panicked. Then, rising from the chair in slow motion, she sets down her cross-stitch canvas.

Somehow she knows.

I can't remember how he gets in the front door, but I remember his red-glazed eyes, the way I scream, "Leave! Run, Anna!" The way her father grabs my arm, twisting it.

Then I see the gun and hear Mom screaming to someone on the phone. Her father threatens to shoot me, and Anna hesitates, turning around, terror in her eyes.

"Go, go!" I yell as her father's fist rams into my cheek.

Anna shrieks, "Bobby! Bobby!" and I stare at her through blurry eyes, hunched against the sofa, gasping for breath as my mother lunges toward this madman. But he shoves her aside—as if she's a feather pillow, as if she isn't even there—and I desperately try to pull myself up as I watch her father drag Anna through the den and out the front door.

My father is at one of Jason's basketball games an hour away, but I call Stephen and he shows up five minutes after Anna is taken away. I kneel down beside my mother. "I'm fine," she murmurs. The police arrive, and a female officer sinks to the floor beside Mom while the man listens to my description of the car and radios ahead for backup before taking off, siren screaming.

Stephen and I are in his car as he careens after the police, with me begging God to let us catch Anna and her lunatic father. We come upon the car in a ditch. I remember the explosion, my screams as I rush toward the excruciating heat, and Stephen tackling me, forcing me to the ground, and holding me there for all he's worth. "It's over, Bobby. I'm so sorry. It's over. . . ."

The sirens from the police startle me from my nightmare, but it is actually only my cell ringing. I shake myself awake, shocked to see my grandmother's name appear on the screen. "Swannee?"

"Hello, dear Bobby." Our connection is bad, or perhaps she's just talking very softly. "I've got to get hold of your mother. I've been trying for an hour now."

"We're not with her yet, Swannee. Still on the train. We should be meeting her in about three hours."

Then I realize just how unusual it is for my grandmother to call me. It's after eleven in the evening in Atlanta. "Is everything okay?"

"Yes. Nothing to worry about." But Swannee's voice is easy to decipher when something is wrong.

"What's the matter?" I say, a sliver of fear sliding into my gut. "What's happened to Granddad?"

Her voice is small. "We think he's had a stroke."

I can barely talk. "Where is he?"

"He's at Grady Hospital. I'm heading there now." She sounds as if she's in a parallel universe.

"Oh, Swannee! I'll text Mom, and I'm sure she'll call you right back. But what can we do?"

"Pray."

I text my father. It's only ten Chicago time. *On the train to meet Mom in a few hours. Swannee just called. Granddad had a stroke!*

Does your mother know?

No, Swannee can't reach her. It's only 5 AM over here. Mom and Caroline are together, but they're probably still asleep.

Don't worry. I'll find out exactly what's up.

Promise?

Of course.

And you'll let me know.

Of course.

Did Jason get expelled?

Not from school, but he's off the football team.

Oh, great. That sucks.

Don't worry about Jason either. I'll reach Swannee and get back to you. Try not to worry.

He's right, of course, but my stomach is in knots as the train chugs slowly through the mountain passes of Switzerland and into France. I stare at the snowcapped mountains and then at Rasa sleeping beside me. I try to soak in the wonder, but all I succeed in doing is replaying that horrible last day with Anna in my mind.

I have to do something to distract myself, so I get out my sketch pad and switch on the small light above my seat. I think of a conversation I had with my grandmother a couple years ago, when I finally admitted to her that I wanted to try to make a career of painting.

"It won't be easy," Swannee said to me. "It will be hard, a crazy-hard challenge. You'll question yourself multiple times in your career."

"But I have to paint, Swannee. I can't *not* paint. It's stronger than I am, this desire."

She'd smiled at me knowingly. "Then you must paint. You must pursue it until the hand of God stops you."

"I'll disappoint my parents."

She'd nodded. "You'll probably disappoint most everyone for a while. But that is the choice." Her eyes softened. She looked away into the backyard. "You see the pond, don't you?"

"Of course."

"You see the fountain?"

"Yes."

"They weren't always there."

I shrugged. That seemed quite obvious.

"When your grandfather decided to put in a pond with a fountain, he came up against many obstacles, and he was just about ready to give up. But the thing that kept him going—at least it's what he's always told me—was that he knew I needed the sound of water as I painted. It soothed and inspired me when the task seemed too hard. Even now, when I'm discouraged, I sit here in the sunroom, the glass doors wide open, rain or shine, and listen to the trickle of water, constant, reassuring.

"So find *your* fountain, Bobby. Hold it when you find it, keep it near to remind you that your life and what you're doing are important. That it counts."

I have often come back to those words and now, sitting on the train, nearing the Camino, with Rasa asleep beside me, I ask myself, *What is my fountain?*

I don't know. But I do know that Swannee was the first one to notice my passion, and she's one of the main reasons I'm doing this gap year. As the train screeches to a halt in one of the many towns on the way to Le Puy, I'm thankful that I'll be heading to Paris in just two weeks. With my grandfather in the hospital, I feel an urgent responsibility to view Swannee's painting of the Swan House as soon as possible.

Responsibility for Mom, for Rasa, for Jason, for Dad, for Swannee and Granddad.

I drift off to sleep feeling overwhelmed.

ABBIE

I awake while it's still dark outside and take in my surroundings. A large room with four cots. To my right, Caroline lying flat on her stomach and cradling her pillow. To my left Barb lying flat on her back, snoring. And across the room, Jamie sprawled out on her cot wearing . . . nothing! I quickly shift my gaze. My feet are killing me, and my heart is a mixture of crazy emotions. I dress in the dark and tiptoe downstairs. All the other pilgrims are still asleep, so I sit outside at a picnic table where a slice of moon is still visible in the dawn.

I'd texted Diana last night. *Do I have to do the Psalms of Ascent in order?*

Dear Abbie, read them in whatever way you wish. Or don't read them at all. It's a suggestion, not a command.

I can almost hear her friendly chuckle through her typed words. But I am desperate. What if I do it wrong and they don't work? What if nothing works?

I know my reasoning is infantile or superstitious, but my faith is so weak. I need this exercise to work.

Blurry-eyed, I scroll to Psalm 126 and read aloud in a whisper.

"'When the Lord brought back the captive ones of Zion, we were like those who dream. Then our mouth was filled with laughter and our tongue with joyful shouting. . . . The Lord has done great things for us; we are glad.'"

During my junior semester in France I traveled by Eurail around Europe with two friends. In spite of my best efforts at planning our itinerary, reserving hostels, and figuring out train schedules, there had been times of confusion and lost directions. Once we found ourselves sharing a compartment on a night train with some seedy-looking characters. But throughout that month we prayed and watched God provide in the strangest, most personal ways. Often someone would randomly cross our path and direct us to the correct train or hostel without our even asking—we called them angels.

I swallow and think of all the "angels" I've met in just three short days on the Camino—the Washington Women, the Boy Scouts, even Caroline. I have felt it, the joy of fellow pilgrims, my fears being replaced by angels showing up to care for me, the undergirding presence of the Lord.

"He's always with you," Miss Abigail used to say when I worried that I couldn't feel His presence. *"He will use you. If you let Him . . ."*

I am no longer a naïve teenager. I know exactly what those words "if you let Him" mean, and I don't like the meaning. Sacrifice. Giving up my dreams for God's. Miss Abigail was always quick to remind me that if I delighted myself in the Lord, He would give me the desires of my heart. She insisted that God was not waiting to make me miserable with His plans; they were broad and big and good.

But I had seen her life. And although I admired her more than any other human, I desperately did not want her life. I would have affirmed in all sincerity that I also wanted to live for Christ, but deep down inside I felt I needed to help Him along with the running of my life.

Then I met Bill, and we said our vows before God, and so I'd gotten marriage *and* God, and I knew I'd let Him do whatever He wanted with our lives.

And it had worked. For a while.

Until I began clutching and fretting and feeling afraid. Just as I am doing right now.

I'm waiting for the Compostel'Bus that daily picks pilgrims up and drops them off at designated spots along this stretch of the Camino. It's the longest I've ever gone without seeing my son, and when he gets off the bus, I have to blink back tears. His reddish-brown hair looks longer, and he has a five-o'clock shadow I've not seen on him before, but his eyes are still soft brown and filled with kindness.

"Mom!" he says, engulfing me in a hug, his backpack slung across one shoulder. Then he turns and holds out his hand to Rasa as she steps out of the bus.

I see at once why Bobby is so taken with her. She looks like a wood nymph from *A Midsummer Night's Dream*. A tiny olive-skinned sprite, with black hair that falls to her waist in a thick braid, and piercing eyes, dark and deep. She looks fragile, maybe a little fearful. Yet there is also something almost flamboyant about her. As if, without warning, she might suddenly twirl around like a ballerina and then leap into the air, her legs in an elegant split.

Bobby's phone starts ringing as he's helping Rasa with her backpack. Absently he hands it to me. "Can you answer it, Mom?"

"Hello."

There's a pause. "Abbie?" It's Bill's voice.

"Bill?"

"Yes. Hey, Abbs." Long pause. He clears his throat. "Listen, I guess Bobby's told you by now about your dad."

"My dad? What? No, they arrived just this second. I've barely even said hello to them. What happened to Dad?"

"He's had a stroke, Abbs. Swannee called Bobby at five your time. She tried to get through to you, but I'll bet your sound was off."

My heart is racing in my chest for two completely different reasons: Bill and Dad. It's the first time I've heard my husband's voice in over a month. But I push that thought away. "A stroke? Are you sure?"

"Evidently he fell when he got up in the night. He's at Grady. But he's okay, Abbie. He's okay. There's a little paralysis, but he's awake and talking. They're calling it a minor stroke."

In my mind I'm already grabbing my backpack and suitcase and hopping on this bus and somehow getting back to Atlanta.

"Abbie, listen to me. I've been talking with your mom. She doesn't want either you or Bobby to come home. Nan and

Ellie and Ben are with her, and I'm flying in tomorrow from Chicago. It would only upset your mom and dad if you and Bobby cancelled your trip." A long silence passes, then he says, "I know you're already figuring out how to get home, but please, darling . . ."

Darling! Abbs!

". . . please don't."

I don't know what to say. I'm standing on the quay with Bobby and Rasa staring at me.

"We'll keep you informed, Abbs," Bill says. "I know it's very hard to hear." He pauses. "I know you're both terrified, but you've got to trust me."

But I don't trust you! You walked out on me! You said you're happy without me.

"Ellie will call you in a couple hours from the hospital with an update."

"Okay," I say, but I'm thinking, *What about us, Bill? What about us?*

"Everything's okay, Abbs," he says. He's using the same calm voice that has talked me off ledges for years. "Everything's okay. Wait for Ellie to call."

"Okay," I whisper and end the call.

17

CARO

Talk about a downer. Between hearing Bill's voice, meeting Bobby's refugee, and learning about her father's stroke, Abbie is in a frightful humor. She hobbles along the first few kilometers of the trail until Bobby, who can obviously read his mother well, encourages Rasa and me to go ahead. I agree for two reasons: I know Abbie has a lot she wants to talk to her son about, and I cannot bear the snail's pace.

I feel sorry for Abbie. She seems like the kind of woman who, once she's in a bad mood, finds it hard to shake. She's limping along with her blisters, but it's really her spirit that's limping. Bill's email yesterday had already worked some pretty fierce magic. Black magic. But now she's heard his voice. And he hasn't given her any more hope.

I can also tell she really loves him. And strange as it seems coming from me, I think some of our discussions from yesterday have done her good. I know they've helped me. My therapist says that speaking the truth out loud is the best therapy, especially if you're with someone who knows how to really listen. Abbie really listened yesterday, and then she asked good questions.

So I'm poring over our conversation, how I finally admitted that I'm not in love with Brett. That feels like relief. But the rest of it, the part where I realize I *am* in love with Bastien, is terrifying. How can I be in love with someone who, for all intents and purposes, betrayed me, betrayed my friend, and perhaps was not so indirectly involved in murder?

No, no, no—this can't be the truth! Bastien wouldn't use me this way!

Or would he?

The more time I have to process in my head, the more concerned I grow. I look back at all the different instances I have met up with Bastien since the murder and kidnapping in 2011. Every time except this last one, which he initiated, I'd been trying to find out new information about Lola's disappearance, and I'd written him about it. And we'd met up. In a purely platonic way.

Did he do this because he knew I had information about Lola? For all these years, has he been keeping track of my every move? Not out of concern for Lola or love for me, not even because he wanted another romantic tussle—which he didn't. Why? He'd listen to me attentively, compassionately, as if he truly cared. Then what did he do? Did he send every last detail to Khalid?

Surely time will let me get over him, now that I know the truth. But of course, there is that dark part of me that doesn't want to simply get over him. I also want to get even. I want him to be apprehended and questioned and locked up. I want him to suffer.

But who should I tell? Does Jean-Claude know everything? He said that Khalid is back in Europe and being followed. Is Bastien being followed too? Am I?

If I listen to these thoughts all day, they'll drive me crazy. Fortunately, I'm forced back to the present as Rasa comes beside me and we head out.

Whereas Abbie wears designer clothes to walk the Camino, Rasa is dressed as if she's headed to a mosque. Her thick black braid is covered with a bright blue scarf, and she has on a long white tunic and white leggings. Her army-green backpack looks like something she dug out of a closet, definitely from the 1970s. She walks with determination and concentration, almost as if she's not walking this trail at all but reliving something else from long ago.

At first we don't talk, each of us lost in thought. I try to determine if I'm walking too fast for her, but she easily keeps my pace. Gradually I start to make conversation. "So where are you from?" I finally ask.

"Iran," she says, and you could have knocked me over with a toothpick.

"You're Iranian," I repeat stupidly.

"Yes," she answers.

"Oh wow."

I stumble through a few more awkward questions until at last, gracefully, she says, "If you'd like to hear about my time on the Refugee Highway, I'll gladly tell you. It is hard, but it is filled with hope."

What a strange thing to say. "Sure. That'd be really . . . interesting."

She begins to tell me her story, and when she does, her whole face transforms. There's something almost like a spiritual energy to her. And as she talks I realize I have heard this story before. Rasa is the girl my brother helped rescue, along with her mother and infant brother. He had convinced his boss at the *Peachtree Press* to let him run stories in the paper about this refugee family, and as a result raised a bunch of money that allowed a whole team of people to buy a van in Turkey and smuggle Rasa and her mom and brother out of Iran. Her father is Stephen's dear friend Hamid. And Rasa, as a mere child, is the one who helped Stephen "come to faith."

I interrupt her, saying, "You do know that Stephen is my brother, don't you?"

Her eyes get big. "No, no! I did not know this." She seems flustered. "At least I don't think Bobby told me that. He said you were coming but . . ." She blushes and smiles and says, "I like your brother a lot. He is very kind and very brave."

I shrug. "Agreed. But please keep going."

Rasa spares no details in telling her story, although she occasionally cannot find the appropriate English word or mixes her metaphors. When she says, "We escaped by our teeth's skin," I can't help but smile.

"Sorry!" I say. "You almost got it. It's 'by the skin of our teeth.' Which I grant you is a very odd expression. Please go on."

So she does. But as she talks I'm aware of a growing twitter of annoyance or even anger in my stomach. What the heck? Why am I angry with this poor girl who has been through such a harrowing experience?

And I know the answer. Lola.

Ridiculous as it sounds, on some level I'm blaming her for Lola's disappearance. If Rasa hadn't come to faith along that crazy refugee highway thing, her family wouldn't have ended up at the Oasis. And if they hadn't been at the Oasis, Stephen wouldn't have met them, and if Stephen hadn't become a Christian and then been so insistent on sharing his faith with Lola, well . . . Khalid would have had no problem with his aunt and his cousin. Malika would still be alive, and Lola would be in Provence.

I can cast the blame far beyond my misguided weekend with Bastien.

But it's hard to dislike Rasa. She has a magnetic personality, and eventually her sincerity and enthusiasm overcome my admittedly twisted logic.

Perhaps it's the magic of the Camino or the heady smells of the region—the pungent odors from the cow pastures and the fresh scent of the pines—but finally I decide to tell Rasa my story.

"I have a friend who's Iranian," I say. "A dear friend. She's a Christian too."

Rasa is immediately interested. "Where does she live?"

"I don't know. She grew up in France, and we spent summers together in Provence. We were very close." I hesitate. "But seven years ago she became a Christian, and she disappeared."

Rasa looks at me and frowns. "In France?"

"Yes. Her mother was murdered because she had become a Christian too."

Rasa shakes her head. "No, no, no!" Then suddenly she's shaking all over.

I'm caught off guard. Her reaction seems a bit extreme.

She takes several deep breaths. "I'm sorry. I have sometimes emotions when I hear hard things."

"No problem." We stop within the shade of a small cluster of pine trees.

Then, after Rasa has taken several deep breaths, she asks, "Her mother was murdered in Iran?"

"No, she was murdered by her nephew at her home in Provence. He killed her because of her faith. And he kidnapped my friend."

Rasa has tears in her eyes. Quite a sensitive soul. "I am so sorry, Caroline. And you don't know where your friend is now?"

"No." I'm about to share what Jean-Claude has told me, but fortunately I clamp my mouth shut. Then, "I don't even know if she's still alive. I haven't heard from her in seven years."

Rasa is staring at me with a strange look on her face. I think she's going to grab me by the shoulders, but she stands rooted in place, her thick black braid falling over her shoulders as she wipes sweat from her brow. Then she reaches out and takes my hand and says again, "I'm so sorry, Caroline."

Seeing her deep empathy prompts me to tell my story about Bastien. It spills out as we start back on the path, probably not that coherently, but she never interrupts. I tell her about my foolishness and our weekend affair and the guilt I've lived with for years because of what happened to Malika and Lola. Of course, I don't mention the crazy way that learning of Bastien's involvement has alleviated some of the guilt.

As I tell the story, my grief becomes her grief until at last she says, "This Lola, this friend of yours, does she know you're looking for her?"

"No. Like I said, I don't even know if she's still alive."

When I look at Rasa, her brow is knitted, and she looks confused and maybe even afraid, and I have no idea why.

We start out again, walking along open plains with the occasional gray stone house along the way. As we cross a cobbled bridge over a stream, we are greeted on the other side by doe-eyed cows chewing their cud and nodding our way while the sun beats down on us. We trudge on until the road narrows to a dirt trail, and suddenly we are in an evergreen forest.

I am clicking photos and taking in deep breaths of pine, and I think of a John Denver song my mother used to like. I hum the chorus of "Annie's Song."

Rasa hears me and smiles. Then, hands lifted to the sky, she twirls around with her out-of-date backpack and her flowing white tunic and begins singing a song in what I suppose is her native tongue. I recognize the melody. She looks over at me, takes my hand and says, "You know it? This church song."

"A hymn?"

"Yes! A hymn. About how God is great and how nature tells us of His hands' work. We see this, and we must sing how He is great."

"Yes, I've heard that hymn."

I don't currently share Rasa's enthusiasm about the song or God, but I can agree with her on one thing. The panorama of the Camino is stunning.

We stop to rest, sitting at a picnic table that overlooks the Margeride Mountains, munching on the crusty, saucisse-filled baguettes that Abbie asked Lucette to prepare for us. We rest for probably an hour, eating, napping, and filling our senses with the beauty, until Bobby and Abbie appear.

BOBBY

"Mom, are you okay? You're limping."

"Blisters," she says, furious. "I paid $234 for these boots. I broke them in. Five miles a day walking, with my backpack mind you, around Piedmont Park. And still I get blisters." The boots are dangling from her backpack. "But wearing my running shoes today is a big help. I'll be good as new soon."

She calms down as we walk, and I breathe a silent prayer of thanks that Caroline has gone ahead with Rasa so I can go at Mom's slower pace.

"This is as awesome as people say online, isn't it? I want to get one of those scalloped shells with the St. Jacques symbol that I've seen on other pilgrims' packs."

"And I've got your créanciale—the passport you'll want to get stamped at each leg along the way."

"Yeah, thanks."

She seems resigned to our slower pace, and I figure I can keep her mind off Granddad in the hospital and dodge any questions about Dad or Jason by telling her about my time in Vienna and Linz.

We make our way into the Margeride Mountains, a very gradual climb. I tell her about the Oasis and the House of Hope and Rasa's journey to Austria. I tell about all the sights I saw in Vienna, and fulfilling my dream of going to the Kunsthistorisches Museum on four different days. But then I make a blunder.

"There's a modern art museum in Linz, the Lentos, and also something called the ARS Electronica Center. Both are really cool, Mom! There's a great art institute in the city too. I'd like to study there and help out at the House of Hope a few times a week, teaching the art class. I could stay there forever."

Mom comes to a dead stop. "Forever?"

I should have curbed my enthusiasm.

She takes a swig from her water bottle and wipes her bright pink bandana over her brow. "But what about all the dreams you had for college? In the States?"

I frown, hesitate, and, as Mom would say, "tiptoe up" to my next comment. "Mom, those were your dreams, not mine. You know that all I've ever really wanted to do is paint. I promise I'll get an education. I'll get a degree. But please, Mom, just let me live this year. I'll do the Camino and then take the art class in Paris with Jean-Paul and then study in Linz—"

Mom finishes my sentence. "So you can be near Rasa."

I blush and run my hand through my hair. "Yeah. That's part of it, I admit. She's great."

"Well, I haven't gotten to talk with her yet, so I'll withhold judgment. I'll withhold everything for a while. Let's not make any rash decisions, Bobby."

I read her loud and clear.

Thankfully, Aunt Ellie calls right then to report that my grandfather is stable and will likely be released tomorrow. Mom visibly relaxes.

"How is he right now, Els?" she asks.

She has the phone on speaker, and Aunt Ellie's voice comes out scratchy but intelligible.

"Hanging in there, but it's hard to see him like this. But he's not in danger of dying. It was a relatively minor stroke. But it's—"

"It's the first of many, you think?" Mom is always finishing other people's thoughts. One of the many things she does that bugs me.

"I mean, what do I know?" Ellie replies. "And I think Mama's grieving in advance. She sees what's coming. But she's also very relieved that he's talking; he's making sense. The paralysis is gone. And mostly, she begged me to insist that you stay. I know that's hard to hear, but it would tear her up, and Daddy too, if you canceled your trip."

"I can't imagine staying."

When she admits this I'm not surprised, but still I feel my stomach sink. *But we just started the Camino, Mom. Don't quit now.*

Ellie's voice is insistent. "Please, Abbie. Just wait. And whatever you decide, Bobby has to stay."

At this Mom glances over at me.

"Mama is living everything vicariously through him. She's counting on him visiting Jean-Paul and going to see her painting in that museum. I promise you, Abbie—the best thing you can do right now is for you and Bobby to enjoy the Camino. Bobby needs to keep texting Mama and posting his photos on Instagram. Just include us in whatever way you can."

"Can I talk with Daddy?" Mom asks.

"He's asleep right now, but in a few hours Mama will be back and I'll have her call, and you can talk to them both. I forced her to go home and get some sleep."

Mom lowers her voice, and I walk ahead to give her privacy, but I can easily distinguish what she tells my aunt.

"Bill called on Bobby's phone, and I answered. First time I heard his voice in a month . . . Yeah . . . I have no idea what he's thinking. Well, actually I do. I think he wants to leave. For good."

I stop and stare at Mom, but she is just shaking her head and practically whispering to my aunt. I wish I hadn't heard any of their conversation. Surely he's not going to leave for good!

Mom is still behind me, talking, as I come upon a young couple with four really little kids. The littlest one, a boy, is wailing. His knee is dripping blood all over the path and on the dad's shirt as he holds his son. The other children surround their little brother, obviously fascinated and repulsed by all the blood. They're talking in another language, maybe German. I hurry toward them and ask, "Can I help?"

CARO

When he comes into view, Rasa and I automatically look at each other, shrug, and laugh. Bobby is carrying two backpacks. At first I think he's got Abbie's, but no, she comes around the bend with her backpack placed solidly on her shoulders as she limps along.

"What in the world?" I say out loud, but more to myself than to Rasa.

She smiles self-consciously, her face lighting up, and she says, "I like that about Bobby. He always wants to help people. I think he *needs* to help people."

For as much as Abbie's told me that Bobby has a crush on Rasa, I think it's pretty mutual.

When Bobby reaches us he says, "Rasa and Caroline, I'd like you to meet this cool family." He nods to a couple. "Henk and Marieke from the Netherlands."

Henk is a tall, muscular blond in his midthirties with a child of about four perched on his shoulders. He's also carrying two backpacks. He smiles at his wife, who's cradling a smaller child in her arms and laughing as she introduces her brood. She's attractive, with thick strawberry-blond hair and a perfect complexion.

"Bobby here saved our lives. Jilles took a tumble and got a bit scraped up, and then Jelle got the upchucks and well, we were having a hard time managing." The four children are all perfectly blond and rosy-cheeked. "Thank heavens for the Camino! Never alone!"

The family joins us at the picnic table, chatting merrily.

Bobby sits beside Rasa. "How's it going so far?"

She gives a shy smile. "It's okay. A nice walk."

"I'll do the next leg with you," he says, and I think she looks relieved. Then he says to the Dutch family, "I'd be happy to carry the backpack until we reach our stopping point."

Henk laughs and says, "We can manage now. But thanks."

We head out again. Abbie has once again shortened our trek because of her blisters.

239

"I'm sorry we won't get too far today," she says.

I can tell it infuriates her to be a burden. Poor Abbie—limited by her humanity.

But none of us mind. I'm taking photos and lingering over the varying fragrances of the trail, even the cow manure smells, and Rasa and Bobby are deep in conversation.

Farther along the path, I take out my phone to snap a photograph to post on Instagram and see I have a text from Brett.

Caroline, I think our silence speaks for itself. I care deeply for you, and I had envisioned a life together, but I can tell you're not ready. I should probably have called to say this, but I needed to put my thoughts in writing. I want you to do all the soul searching you need on your Camino. I'm glad you're there, and I just want you to be happy and free. So I guess I'm just saying I'll always care for you, but I think it's time to let you go. Love, Brett

I'm taken completely by surprise, I admit. I reread it, stopping in the middle of a fairly narrow passage while pilgrims navigate around me.

Obviously I've hurt him deeply. Well, I tell myself, at least he sees the truth that all my insecurities and my mad crush on Bastien have indeed made me unsuitable for him. He's right to let me go. But rejection is never pleasant, and I could second-guess myself all day long.

I think, *I should talk to Tracie*, but oddly, the person I want to talk it over with is Abbie. Amazing how two short days—or actually two very long days—can knit souls together. Maybe it's because she's the one I finally admitted the truth to. I'm in love with Bastien, and Brett is just a nice guy.

But look at me now. Bastien has betrayed me and Brett has broken up with me. Not of my own doing, I'm free. I'm free to figure out my life, and I know that somehow the mystery of Lola is my next big step.

I wait for Abbie to catch up with me, and we talk.

BOBBY

As we walk along a dirt road with mountains in the distance, I can hardly keep my gaze from Rasa.

I think about Mom's obvious disapproval when I mentioned staying in Linz. I try to be objective. What if one of my friends told me he'd just met a refugee and wanted to move to her city and study? Different cultures, different languages, different traditions, different . . . just about everything. But different doesn't have to be a deal breaker, does it?

I don't know how long we've been walking in silence when Rasa asks, "How well do you know Caroline?"

I shrug. "Not that well—I see her at the *Press* now and then, since Stephen started giving her work."

Rasa is frowning. "I did not realize she was Stephen's sister until she told me a little while ago."

"I never mentioned it? I thought I had. Anyway, what happened? Did she say something rude to you?"

"No, not rude." Rasa looks perplexed. "Confusing." She shakes her head. "No, she tells me a strange story that I don't like."

Oh, great, I think. I can hear Hamid warning me that Rasa is fragile, to watch out for her. "I'm sorry if she dumped a lot of her problems on you, Rasa. She's a bit wild, I guess."

"Do you trust her, Bobby?"

"Trust Caroline?" I'm taken aback. "Um, I guess. I mean, I don't know her very well. She works for Stephen but rarely comes into the office. I like her well enough."

Now I am hearing Stephen's words again, asking Mom and me to watch out for Caroline on this trip.

"You've got a really nasty frown on your face, Rasa. Do you want to tell me what's up?"

"What is up is that I do not think I trust Caroline, but I trust Stephen very much." Her face softens. "Stephen is good. He helped save my family. He helped save me." Now she has tears in her eyes.

I am failing miserably at protecting Rasa and helping her forget all her trauma. I blurt out, "Did Caroline unload a lot of her trauma on you?" Why did I say the *T* word out loud?

"Yes. She told me about her Iranian Christian friend who disappeared."

I have no idea what she's talking about. "Look, Rasa, Americans can be . . . we can be so naïve. I'm sure she didn't mean to offend you."

Rasa has been leaning on an ancient wall. Now she stands up straight, taking several deep breaths. Her eyes hold fear, and I shudder. She looks like Anna whenever she mentioned her father.

Trembling, Rasa whispers, "I know her Iranian friend. I know her well! That is why I don't trust Caroline."

Now I am completely bewildered. I also feel responsible for whatever Caroline has said to Rasa. Surely she hasn't made anything up, has she?

"I don't understand, Rasa. I have no idea what you're talking about."

She takes more deep breaths and closes her eyes. When she opens them and looks at me, her eyes hold a penitent expression. "I'm sorry, Bobby. You are right. I've made you be dark."

I grin in spite of myself.

She furrows her brow again, then sees the teasing in my eyes and actually laughs. "I said it wrong."

"Just the tiniest bit." I can see she wants me to correct her. "It's 'you're keeping me in the dark.'"

She grins back. "Yes. Forgive me."

"Forgiven. But hey, feel free to tell me what you're upset about. I'm good to hear it."

Rasa doesn't continue the conversation, so I'm left to wonder. How in the world can she and Caroline have the same Iranian friend?

18

ABBIE

I'm exhausted—more from mental strain than physical. Mama convinces me not to go home. She even puts Daddy on the line, and his voice sounds strong.

"We love the loft, Abbie! It's perfect. I can't wait to get out of this hospital and get back to those stunning views of the Atlanta skyline."

Mama confides, "Honey, yes, it was a big scare, but he's okay. And we do love being at the loft."

But it's Nan's call that sends me plummeting. "Bill got here a little while ago. He's moved all his stuff out of the loft—you know, to make more room for Dad. I guess he's taking it to his apartment in Chicago."

"What? He has an *apartment* in Chicago? He's not staying in a hotel?"

Nan hesitates. "Oh, Abbie. I thought you knew. He didn't act like it was a secret."

I think I may vomit all over the trail. I stop, motioning for

Bobby and Rasa and Caroline to keep going. "No. I don't know anything, Nannie. I don't know anything anymore." I end the conversation, barely able to whisper good-bye.

I try to regain my composure as I hobble along, catching up with the others.

Put it out of your mind.

At first I don't succeed, but Caroline insists on walking with me while Bobby heads out with Rasa, and I find her sob story a welcome distraction. She rattles on and on about Brett and Bastien and guilt and relief, and I listen to her confused monologue. I'm equally confused by my life, so it takes extreme concentration to focus on hers.

Finally I blurt out, "Bill's moved out permanently. He's gotten an apartment in Chicago. He took all his stuff. . . ." I give a little hiccup and force the tears away.

"Oh, Abbie. That really sucks."

We're on a flat dirt road, and as we round a bend we both stop. In front of us a shepherd is guiding a flock of sheep down the trail with pilgrims mingling ahead and behind them. It is such a simple, profound picture of our lives on this pilgrimage. The town of Le Sauvage lies in the distance, an agglomeration of stone houses with blue slate roofs.

Pilgrims have stopped and are taking photos. And I think this is why we came on this pilgrimage. To run completely away from our modern, connected life (with the exception of our cell phones). The sheep, the shepherd, the stone houses, the pasturelands with the pine-covered mountains all speak of a different life. The simple scene calms me.

You can't control Bill. Let go, let go, let go.

But I have to know what he's doing! I have to.

I've stopped calling, texting, and writing him. I've tried to leave him alone. And now, it's not my fault that I've heard his voice and know he's in Atlanta with *my* family. Or that he's moved all his stuff to an apartment in Chicago.

Let go, Abbie. Let it all go. Let him go.

I give such a loud sigh that Caroline glances over at me. I shrug, turn my back to her, and pray. *Okay, Lord. I'll try, really try to give him the space he needs. I'll try to do it out of love, not revenge and resentment, not hoping he'll feel lonely and miserable. Out of love.*

I'm amazed at my own thoughts, but I continue. *Change me, dear Lord. I can't change Bill. I can't change my heart. But You can. So please, change me.*

I take a deep breath and feel peace.

Caroline is squatting down as she photographs a butterfly perched on a pink wildflower.

"We're in the heart of the Massif Central," she says. "The Margeride Massif here and the Aubrac Massif, which we'll reach tomorrow. They're not exactly mountains—more like a series of high plateaus. You know, extinct volcanoes and stuff like that."

I raise my eyebrows, and she laughs. "You're not the only one who can Google." She is snapping photos as fast as the butterfly's wings flutter, a blur of bright orange and black. "It's a rugged beauty, isn't it, Abbie? Harsh and wild, especially in winter. Definitely a mountain climate." She motions with her camera. "Those are mostly Scotch pines. And some European oaks too."

"You've become a regular Wikipedia page," I tease.

She laughs again. "If we're lucky, we may see some wild boars and deer."

I make a face. "Yes to the deer. No thank you for the boars."

We fall into a companionable silence, soaking in the scenery and forgetting our grief for a few moments.

The blisters aren't healing as quickly as I'd like. When we find Bobby and Rasa waiting in the town of Le Sauvage, I tell them all to go ahead without me. "I'll ride the Compostel'Bus to our next location."

I don't want to keep canceling the reservations I've made at the chambres d'hôtes and the gîtes. We're in high season on the Camino and finding beds can be a real problem, I've read, if you don't plan ahead. When there's no room in the inn, many pilgrims simply walk farther down the road, five or ten kilometers, until there are vacancies. But that won't work for me.

"Are you sure, Mom?"

"Yes. You've got at least eight kilometers to go. If I rest now, tomorrow will be better." I pull up an app on my phone. "The bus will be here in an hour."

"I will wait and ride with you," Rasa offers.

I'm surprised but pleased. Bobby raises his eyebrows as if to ask Rasa if she knows what she's getting into. She gives a shy smile and nods.

So while Bobby and Caroline continue ahead, I find a little café in Le Sauvage, and Rasa and I sit in the shade of a parasol and sip a citron pressé.

I like Rasa. She's a darling girl. But the thing that sends a shiver up my spine is that she reminds me an awful lot of Anna. Would my son subconsciously fall in love with the same girl twice? Rasa doesn't look or talk like Anna, but she has known terrible trauma. Like Anna. And she is just the kind of girl Bobby would want to rescue. Like Anna.

The Compostel'Bus lets us off at La Bergerie de Compostelle, an ancient farm-turned-gîte for pilgrims. Each room has its own private toilet and shower, and everything is sparkling clean and modern. It feels like luxury after last night's communal showers. The contrast between the ancient stones and the slick white porcelain sinks reminds me of something out of *Country Living*. Although it's much more likely that the magazine got its ideas from here.

I offer to stay with Rasa in the room with two beds, which she agrees to with relief in her eyes. Bobby and Caroline haven't arrived yet, but I know Caroline won't mind being in a room with five other people. And Bobby will get to sleep in the *tsabone*.

"It's like the original tiny house," he tells me, pleased with my choice for him when they show up an hour later.

"You know what it was used for, right?" Caroline asks.

He shrugs. "A house, right? A tiny house on wheels."

"It's *la cabane du berger*!"

"What's that?"

"It's where the shepherd spent the night with his sheep!"

Again we enjoy the fellowship of other pilgrims at dinner, but Bobby's and Rasa's eyes are heavy. I make sure Rasa is comfortable in our room, and then Caroline and I sit outside at the picnic table, sipping on tisanes while we resume our conversation about the men in our lives: Bill, Brett, and Bastien.

"The Triple Bs!" Caroline quips, giving me a wink as we head to our rooms.

I am awakened by a shriek. I sit up in bed, jolted out of sleep. Disoriented, I rub my eyes. Rasa is sitting on her cot, hands pulling at her long hair.

I rush to her side. "Rasa! Rasa!" I whisper. "It's okay. Just a bad dream."

But she is shaking violently.

I sit on the bed beside her. "This is Abbie. You're with me and Bobby and Caroline."

She comes out of her fog, her eyes bright, almost translucent in the dark. She turns and looks at me and begins to babble in a language I don't understand.

I try again. "Rasa. Rasa, it's me, Abbie. Bobby's mother. We're on the Camino. We're staying at a hostel. You're safe. You're okay. Everything's okay."

I take her in my arms and rock her back and forth, back and forth, like a baby. She calms, and before long she falls back asleep. But I am wide awake, replaying every event of the past few days in my mind over and over and over again.

I wake before dawn, exhausted, thinking through yesterday's experiences with a mixture of gratitude, confusion, anger, and relief. Rasa is sleeping peacefully, but there's no chance I'll fall back asleep, so I pull on my exercise shorts and a top and leave the room. In the kitchen area I place a filter and coffee grounds into the *cafetière* and pour in the water. As the coffee brews, I force myself to breathe with the rhythmic sound of the liquid dripping into the glass pot. *Drip, drip, drip.* I inhale the freshly brewed fragrance as I make my way outside, where white plastic chairs and a table invite pilgrims to sit and observe the mountains in the distance.

The dark sky gradually comes alive with streaks of auburn and fiery yellow, and the sun peeks over the mountains, casting tangents of apricot and crimson into the violet blue sky.

"Oh!" I say aloud, momentarily astounded by the piercing light. I breathe deeply again. It's been a very long time since I've enjoyed a luminous sunrise. Oh, I was aware that the sun was rising outside as I maniacally read my Bible and started the coffee and breakfast and my workout. But to enjoy it?

The air still feels cool and refreshing. I take out my phone and go to the Bible app. I think of how joy lifted my heart yesterday as I read Psalm 126, and I hope for the same reaction this morning. But as I read Psalm 127, I feel instead a surge of anger.

"Unless the Lord builds the house, they labor in vain who build it. . . ." I grit my teeth and continue. "It is vain for you to rise up early, to retire late. . . ."

This psalm is berating me for being an early riser. I don't need this condemnation.

I read on. "Behold, children are a gift of the Lord; the fruit of the womb is a reward. Like arrows in the hand of a warrior, so are the children of one's youth. How blessed is the man whose quiver is full of them. . . ."

Well, Jason is an arrow all right, piercing the target of my heart. He's been kicked off the football team for smoking. Ellie volunteered that information yesterday, information she had heard, of course, from Bill. And Bobby's declaration yesterday stings, somehow threatening my motherhood. My sons' arrows fill my quiver all right. With pain.

But it's Bill, oh, Bill, whose arrow hits the bull's-eye. To borrow the earlier metaphor in this psalm, he's knocking down our house one stone at a time, our house which I thought impermeable to life's craziness. Built on a firm foundation of Christ, right?

Right, I snarl to myself. He's off building his house in Chicago!

I thought we'd built our house together on faith and love. But everything I thought—maybe it's a lie. Maybe our house or loft or whatever is crumbling because we were working so hard at building it.

But how can working hard be wrong? Of course we had to work hard!

Through some small miracle, I feel a nudge to read the psalm again. And I'm struck by that one little word: *unless*.

Oh.

The psalm doesn't say it's wrong to work hard and get up early. It's only in vain if we leave the Lord out of it.

But I haven't! I haven't, Lord! I argue . . . knowing full well that lately, in these past four or five years, I have.

I decided a while back that I'd make sure my house was solid. That no tragedy would befall us. Like what happened to Nan. Like what happened to poor Anna. I push it away.

But they come back, the memories of my attempts to control. I set down the phone and stare out at God's masterpiece coming to life all around me, and I whisper, "Please, Lord, please. I don't want my life to be in vain. Please show me what I need to do to get Abbie back."

And in the quiet of that moment, I hear God's voice. *Exactly what you're doing right now.*

BOBBY

We turned in early last night, but Rasa doesn't look rested when she greets me at the white picnic tables where all the pilgrims are gathered, each one dipping a buttered-and-jellied baguette into a bowl filled with strong coffee.

"Did you sleep okay?" I ask her.

"A little difficult." She glances over at Mom, who gives her a nod. "But okay."

Whatever is bothering Rasa floats away after breakfast. She leaves the table and holds out her hand to me, eyes twinkling. "Come on! I want to show you something."

I don't need to be asked twice. I take her hand and follow her past the terrace and into the field. She is wearing her long white tunic with a loose-fitting pair of capri pants. Her hair is also loose, falling almost to her waist. I know she will braid it before we begin the day's journey, but seeing her from the back, her black hair flowing against the white tunic . . .

She stops beside the road and turns her face upward. "You can almost feel Isa here with us, can't you, Bobby?"

I look skyward. Isa isn't on my mind at the moment. "Um, I guess so. How do you mean?"

"This place makes me think a little of my home country. We have forests too, you know, in Iran. And many mountains. I get that feeling in Austria too. It is like God's nature everywhere tells us He is big and wonderful and worthy for us to give Him praise. I feel it here in this place, Bobby. Do you?"

In truth, I just feel a bit worried about my parents splitting up, my granddad having a stroke, and Rasa not trusting Caroline. "Sure. I guess. Being out here in this landscape with the scenery and all, it's pretty cool."

"Then you must draw it. You tell beautiful stories with your pictures. I want to see the story of today. I do not want that frown."

I tilt my head. Somehow Rasa has discerned that all my worry is crowding out the creativity. Whereas melancholy can inspire me, igniting my desire to draw, worry always seems to snuff it out.

I grin at her. "Trying to read my mind, are you?"

"You are sometimes easy to read, Bobby Jowett. You betray your heart with your face." She twirls around and says, "Later today, when we take a rest, I want you to draw me something. Draw away the frown on your face." She laughs and runs back to the farmhouse with me trailing behind, dazed.

Mom proclaims her blisters much better. "It's an easy walk today—very flat. We have twenty-three kilometers to reach Aumont-Aubrac, and hopefully I can keep up."

The four of us start out together, but fairly quickly Rasa and I take the lead. I'm still recovering from the way my gut kept jumping around when she took my hand in the field.

"Would you like to tell me anything else about the story you started yesterday—how you and Caroline know the same Iranian girl?"

"I will tell you if you say nothing to Caroline. I don't want to hurt her feelings."

"Of course. And if you don't want to talk about it . . ." I'm afraid she may think I'm asking her to gossip.

"No, I do want to tell you, Bobby, because I do not like it when my heart feels cold to someone. I want to like Caroline. Perhaps you can help me understand."

With that enigmatic reply, she begins.

"Caroline feels guilty because of what happened to her friend Lola many years ago. They were very close friends and spent summers together in the south part of France. One summer, Lola and her mother became followers of Isa. Soon after this, Lola disappeared and Lola's mother was murdered by her nephew, a fundamentalist Muslim who was very mad about them leaving Islam."

I nod. "Go on."

So she tells me a horrible story about the day Caroline goes to visit and there is so much blood, about how Lola's mother, Malika, was found days later, buried on the grounds.

And then she gets to the part that has angered her. "Caroline had an affair with a Frenchman she just met, and that is why she didn't go to see Lola right away. She could have saved Lola and her mother."

"So Lola is dead too?"

"No, she is not dead! I told you she disappeared! And something Caroline does not know is that finally, finally, Lola has escaped. But if Caroline had gone to see her, heard her fears instead of having a time with that man, well, maybe none of the horrible things would have happened to Lola. Maybe her mother would still be alive. Caroline has been searching for information about her friend for many years, and I have answers. But I do not trust Caroline."

I'm still trying to follow, still processing this strange coincidence. "You didn't tell Caroline that you know this girl?"

"I did not. You know her too!"

Before I can reply, Rasa walks off the trail and sets her backpack on the ground. "Can you get out your sketch pad?" she asks.

I don't ask questions. As soon as I've dislodged it from my pack, she takes it and flips to a page where I've sketched her teaching a class of refugees. I've sketched the refugees from the back, but I've drawn Rasa very detailed (lovingly, if I dare admit it), and beside her I've drawn the other young woman who was teaching the class. Also Middle Eastern. The young woman named Selah.

"This is Lola," she says, pointing.

"I thought her name was Selah."

"That is what we call her. Some refugees change their names for safety reasons when they escape. Lola lived through terrible things and escaped by miracle, like I did. Khalid had kidnapped her and taken her back to Iran. She was going to be forced to marry a Muslim, but she escaped. A very harrowing escape. By her skin's teeth." She stops, and her cheeks turn crimson. "No, don't correct me, Bobby. Caroline told me. By the skin of her teeth."

"Wow."

"Our stories in some ways are similar. Both Iranians who learned of Isa through Americans. Both of us traveled almost the same way on the Refugee Highway. It connected us. And when she finally trusted me enough, she revealed that Lola is her real name. She chose Selah because it means pause. She sees this time in Austria as a pause until she can return safely to France."

"And Selah is Caroline's friend Lola?"

"Yes. Can you believe it? And there is something more. Some of the same people who helped rescue me have helped rescue Lola too."

"That is quite amazing, Rasa."

She nods and looks down to her sandals. "One of those people is Stephen." She glances at me, her cheeks flushed.

It takes a moment to register what she's just said. "What? Stephen helped rescue this friend of yours? How?"

"He has many connections to people around Europe who help refugees. He gets the word out. He is very good at it. I told you how he raised money to buy a van and chickens to help my mother and brother and me escape Iran in 2005!" And she actually lets out a giggle. "He did similar things for Lola."

"Huh?" I reach for the sketch pad, trying to digest this information. "Are you sure? The Stephen I know, Caroline's brother?"

Rasa nods again. "Yes. That Stephen."

19

CARO

Around four in the afternoon we enter the village of Aumont-Aubrac, our final destination for the day. The hike has been breathtaking; we meandered in wide-open spaces with the Margeride Mountains all around. The buildings in the village are made of light-colored stone, a type of ancient granite. Even the roofs have scalloped stone tiles. As we pass a fountain, I say, "Oh, it's that wretched Beast of Gévaudan again, Abbie!"

Bobby and Rasa stare at me, as do the Washington Women, who once again are part of our party. So I give a brief and gory explanation and am rewarded with their horrified responses.

The fountain consists of a small stone tower from which four wrought iron spouts pour water into a round, stone-walled pool. A reddish-brown wrought iron representation of the grisly beast is perched on top like a weather vane. The beast is standing on its hind legs, teeth and tongue eerily visible, and his front right paw is clutching a flag while his left paw rests on a coat of arms.

"He looks fierce!" Brenda says, but Bobby, indifferent, cups his hands and fills them with water.

I've walked for three days now on the Camino, and somehow it's working the kinks out of me. I don't feel an ounce of temptation when the wine is placed on the table at dinner. We feast on the traditional *aligot*—a combination of boiled potatoes with melted Tome de Laguiole cheese poured over top.

My legs are sore. I even have a few blisters and a small rash on my left leg where I walked into a patch of nettles while chasing a butterfly. But it all feels good. A good kind of tired. A good kind of conversation along the way. A good kind of satisfaction with the photos I'm taking. A connectedness with other people. Even a relief to share in their problems so that my focus isn't always on myself.

After dinner we find seats in the *salon de détente* of our gîte. On one wall is painted a map of the part of the Camino that we're walking. We fix ourselves tisane and relax with the other pilgrims. Abbie takes out her cross-stitch project. I admire her for continuing to work on it, in spite of what she heard from Bill. As she stitches, the other pilgrims stand around her in an awed silence.

It is an astounding piece of tapestry, intricately woven with a kaleidoscope of colors. Abbie's told me the names of some of the threads—medium celadon green, very dark wild blueberry, light cornflower blue, dark antique rose—the names are exotic, like the cross-stitch itself.

The canvas is at least one foot by two feet. There's a tree in the center, and cross-stitched on its limbs are symbols of Bill's fifty years, things like his college football mascot and an Atlanta Braves banner. She's even stitched tiny black cameos of herself, their sons, and even their dog!

She's created and graphed many of the patterns herself. The

whole canvas is almost completely covered in stitches, and the most amazing thing is that when she turns it over there are no loose threads. It looks almost as perfect as the front. It must have taken hundreds of hours already.

And now he's left her.

But Abbie just keeps right on stitching, every evening. At the moment she's finishing up a Huguenot cross, all the while calmly explaining to some pilgrims how she hides the ends of her threads to keep the back of the canvas looking so neat.

Bobby has seen it all before and is decidedly unimpressed. He takes out a small notepad and shows me a sketch from earlier in the day. "Rasa commissioned me to draw something," he explains.

The sketch is of a wooded trail littered with pebbles and rocks. Written on one rather large oval-shaped rock in beautiful calligraphy are these words: *It's about the journey, not about the destination.*

"I saw that rock on the trail," I tell him. "I love what it says. The journey is what counts."

He gives a little shrug and begins sketching the pilgrims who are gathered around Abbie, with the Camino map on the wall behind them.

Rasa entertains everyone with her stories. She's a natural evangelist. She can be commenting on the boeuf bourguignon we had for dinner or the blister on her left heel, and somehow she just naturally works in a remark about Isa.

I find it fascinating that, because she uses the name Isa instead of Jesus, people seem more willing to listen. I certainly do. Somehow *Isa* doesn't feel quite so personal and uncomfortable—more like a foreigner whose presence in the room is noticed but not acknowledged.

As the sun sets late in the evening, I wander out into the

sizeable vegetable and flower garden, relishing the jumble of scents and dizzying display of colors. After I take a few dozen photos I come back inside, satisfied. I download my photos, jot down notes from the day, and write a short blog post for Stephen, which I email him along with the photos. I leave the main room and go into the bedroom I'm sharing with Abbie and Rasa—they are both sound asleep. I tiptoe into the private bathroom and soak my blistered feet in a tub filled with warm water and drops of lavender essential oil. The private room and lavatory and bath feel like luxury.

I fall into bed, content. I don't mind Abbie's planning in the least.

The next two days of hiking have us huddled in sweaters in the middle of August. We're on one of the many worn volcanic plateaus—the steppe where cross-country skiing and other Nordic sports are enjoyed in the winter. It's not hard to imagine—we almost expect to see snow in the distance as the wind whips along the plateau. Abbie's blisters have improved. Mine haven't, but I've doubled up on this thick foamy type of Band-Aid that the Washington Women shared with me.

We start our days in a tight-knit community made up of the four of them, the four of us, two Australian couples, and Henk, Marieke, and their kids. I think both Abbie and I need a break from rehearsing our woes, and the Washington Women keep us entertained with light banter that demands little effort or involvement.

Bobby and Rasa hike ahead of us, although we can usually see them in the distance. At one point we find them admiring a herd of beautiful palomino-colored cows with horns in the form of a lyre. The coat on the cows' chest and legs and around their eyes is lighter-colored, but their eyes are a rich dark brown like their hooves and muzzles.

"Aren't these Aubrac cows magnificent?" I say. "The French say that they're wearing makeup. Look at their eyelashes—it's like they've applied thick mascara."

"You're right! Love it," Brenda says, snapping photos. "I should ask them what brand they prefer."

"The Aubrac herds come up to this plateau region after the transhumance at the end of May," I continue, while Rasa skips across the tufts of wild grass to pet a few of their wet muzzles.

"Someone's been Googling again," Abbie says, but I protest.

"Not this time. I grew up in France, remember? This is part of my heritage."

A little farther down the road, we come upon an odd-looking structure made of all different sizes of stones with a steep slate roof. "Look, guys," I call out to the group. "It's a real *buron*! There are tons of them in this area. Authentic mountain shelters for the shepherds in summertime."

"Oh," Bobby jokes, "so the tsabone is the shepherd's tiny wooden house, and this is where he stays if he doesn't have a tsabone. A big stone teepee."

I laugh as we enter the buron. "It's used to make cheese—like the yummy kind we had in the aligot last night. Upstairs in the attic is where the shepherds stay."

"Cool! Are we going to stay in one tonight, Mom?"

Abbie rolls her eyes. "Fat chance." But we are all enamored with the friendly and sleepy-eyed cows and the burons.

I have fallen into a happy rhythm of tour guide. I remember my father telling stories of the region, and I search on my phone in the evenings to recollect its history. As we hike into the town of Aubrac the next day, I point out what's known as La Domerie d'Aubrac.

"It dates back to the twelfth century, when it was known as a refuge hospital for the pilgrims who were en route to Saint Jacques de Compostelle in Spain. They were the first people who did the Camino."

"A refuge hospital," Jamie says, admiring the rectangular configuration of stone buildings as we trudge by. "My feet could certainly use a refuge."

"Mine too!" several others chime in.

"Unfortunately, the next eight kilometers are some of the hardest on the whole Camino," Abbie informs us.

We give a collective groan. "Let's get some coffee and rest our weary bones," Brenda pleads.

We find a little café-bar-brasserie near the town center and collapse for a half hour at the outdoor tables, relishing the sun, which has suddenly appeared, warming us comfortably. We shed our sweaters, sip on coffee, tea, and hot chocolate, and munch on cereal bars that Abbie has stocked in her backpack.

Then we keep walking.

Soon after leaving the town of Aubrac on the afternoon of this, my fifth day on the Camino, we come upon a group of French Scouts having a picnic, leaning against a stone wall with the Aubrac cows munching on their own picnic in the background. Abbie lets out a little cry of joy and rushes over, kissing each one of the boys on each cheek.

"These boys saved my life," she proclaims, and if any of us doubt her, the boys nod enthusiastically and say, "*Abbie, quel plaisir!*"

I babble along with them in French, chuckling to hear their version of rescuing Abbie. They join us on our final leg of the day, which, they confirm, will be a bit more challenging than the previous three days.

"You go straight downhill for almost five kilometers," one boy volunteers. "Keep your *batons* ready!"

Rasa squints at the boy. "What are batons?"

He grins, his face turning pink. "You know." He holds up his walking sticks, which look exactly like ski poles. "These!"

Rasa nods, equally embarrassed.

The same Scout looks over at Abbie and says, "You'll be careful, won't you, Abbie?"

She laughs good-naturedly. I'm thankful to see her smiling. She's been talking with her parents each day, and her father seems to be recovering. And I think she's resigned to having no more information from Bill.

BOBBY

The sun is blazing hot, which feels pretty good after the chill of the last two days on the Aubrac plateau. We've hit a rough patch of rocky terrain that heads steeply downhill, but everyone proceeds with caution, using their poles.

I'm pleased to see how Rasa has bonded with my mom. They're talking and laughing together. It bothers me that she still isn't comfortable with Caroline, though of course I understand why. Rasa assures me that she will mention their mutual connection eventually, but each time I question her she says, "So far it has not felt right in my spirit."

How can I argue with that?

I'm helping little Jilles down a steep slope, carrying his pack, when I hear a shriek, a literal blood-curdling shriek. Those of us who have already made it down the steepest part stop dead in our tracks, glancing back behind us where the noise has come from.

There is Rasa, at the top of the incline, doubled over as if in pain, her hands covering her head, shaking violently.

I drop my pack, set down the boy's, and hurry back up the hill, stumbling on the loose stones.

Rasa is on her knees, moaning, rocking back and forth. My mother has taken off her pack and is kneeling down beside her.

"Rasa!" I say when I reach her. "It's okay. I'm here." When I touch her hand, it's sweaty.

"Can't breathe," she whispers. She's clutching her throat, making a gargling sound. Her eyes are wide, distorted, terrified.

Her backpack is hanging off her left shoulder, swaying precariously and pulling her off balance, and she's right next to the steep descent. I'm frozen for a moment.

She leans over farther with her hand on her chest.

"Let me get your pack off," I say, but it takes a moment to remove it because she's clutching her arms around her chest.

"I think it's a panic attack, Mom. She's had them before."

Mom nods. "I think so too. She's having such a hard time breathing." She leans down and asks Rasa, "Does your chest hurt?"

"Attack. Heart. Pain."

Mom stands up and says to a group of pilgrims who are gathering around us, "Please stand back. She needs space." Then Henk and Mom and I gently lift her away from the precipice and into a clearing.

I'm trying to recall what Hamid has told me. Mom has opened her own backpack and is hurriedly searching through it. "I know I've got some cool wipes in here somewhere." Finally she hands them to me, and I place several on Rasa's forehead.

"Can you look in her pack for medication, Mom?"

She finds the bottle, and I whisper, "Rasa, this is your medication. Your father said it can help. Will you take it now?"

But when she turns toward me, her eyes still appear terror stricken. "Can't . . ." She is motioning to her throat.

"You can't swallow?"

She nods.

Caroline appears from out of nowhere and kneels down with us. "Listen, Rasa, breathe with me. Like this." She takes a deep breath. "Slowly, slowly. I'm going to breathe, and all you do is copy me."

She gently cups Rasa's chin and looks at her dilated eyes.

"Close your eyes, Rasa," Caroline instructs. "I'm going to count to four as you breathe in. One . . . two . . . three . . . four . . ."

Rasa closes her eyes and does as Caroline says.

"Now breathe out. One . . . two . . . three . . . four. Yes! You're doing a great job, Rasa," she says. "Really good. Stay with me. Keep that slow breathing."

Rasa whimpers softly, her whole body shaking violently, but after a minute of slow breathing she begins to calm.

Caroline glances at me. "Bobby, open my pack and get out the bright yellow zip bag. There are essential oils in there. Find the lavender oil. It really helps with panic attacks."

When I hesitate, she looks at me in a way that says, *Believe me, I know.*

"She hasn't taken the meds, right?"

"No, not yet."

"Okay, then the lavender is safe."

I fumble through Caroline's pack, open the yellow bag, find the little brown bottle of lavender, and hand it to Caroline. Mom and I move away as Caroline lies down next to Rasa, explaining, "I'm dabbing this on your wrist. It's lavender. As you breathe, inhale the fragrance. That's right. Good job, Rasa."

Caroline continues talking softly to Rasa. They are both

lying with their backs on the ground, both breathing slowly, each with her left wrist up to her nose.

Eventually Caroline helps Rasa to a sitting position. "Now I want you to focus on the scalloped shell on your backpack." Caroline gets up and detaches the shell and hands it to Rasa. "How does it feel? Touch the ridges. That's right. Now touch the smooth underside. That's right. You're doing great."

Caroline never takes her eyes off of Rasa. I'm astounded by the firm confidence in her voice, the strength and kindness there.

"We're going to get through this together. It will end soon. I know it's really scary, but you're not in danger." She reassures Rasa, and I find myself breathing more calmly too.

At last Caroline says, "Do you think you can walk now?"

Rasa nods.

"Great. We'll go super slow. Abbie and I will walk right beside you."

I leave them there and encourage the group of pilgrims huddled at the bottom of the descent, watching and waiting. "She's okay. She's going to be fine. We'll be taking it slowly, but y'all go on ahead. We'll meet you in town."

Fifteen minutes later, Henk and I are carrying Caroline's, Mom's, and Rasa's backpacks along with our own while Mom and Caroline stand on either side of Rasa. They slowly make their way down the descent, each using one pole while the other arm supports Rasa. She's a bit wobbly, but she plants her poles and breathes slowly and gives a timid smile at us all as she walks.

It takes us three more hours to reach our destination of Saint-Chely d'Aubrac. Caroline and Rasa have walked and talked the whole way together. As we enter the town, Rasa falls in step with me and says, "I trust Caroline now. I trust her."

CARO

The four of us and the Washington Women are all staying in this amazing medieval gîte that dates back to the fifteenth century. It has a stone tower complete with a winding staircase, a main room with an antique farm table that seats sixteen, three bedrooms with stone walls and beautiful wooden beams, and two rooms below—a library and a billiard room—with vaulted stone ceilings. The whole place is a photographer's dream.

Rasa has completely recovered, and she and I are enjoying tisane and cookies, sitting around the table with the Washington Women, when I stand and say, "I'm going to check out our room. Abbie is already up there."

They nod, and Barb says, "I hear the rooms are the height of luxury, but I'm still recovering from today's hike. We'll come up in a little while."

As I enter the beautifully remodeled medieval bedroom I'll share with Abbie and Rasa, I stop and stare.

"What on earth are you doing, Abbie?"

She's sitting on the floor, grabbing things out of her bright pink suitcase and tossing them randomly around her. Her backpack lies with all its contents scattered over the whole floor.

"What does it look like I'm doing?" she snaps. "Emptying everything out of these godforsaken pieces of luggage."

"Okay. And why are you doing that?"

She turns her periwinkle-blue eyes on me, anger written in bold red splotches across her face. Then she bursts into tears. "I've lost it. They told me not to bring it. Everyone told me!"

"What have you lost?" I ask, but even as I say it, I have a sinking feeling.

"The cross-stitch. I've lost the cross-stitch."

I curse. "Oh, Abbie. Surely not!"

"It's not here! Do you see it anywhere?"

I join her on the floor. We unpack every plastic bag with makeup and toiletries and unroll every piece of clothing without success.

Eventually Rasa comes into the room, along with Brenda and Jamie. They stare until I explain, then they too begin to hunt. But it's no use. We turn the room inside out as well as all of our backpacks and suitcases. Then we search the whole gîte. There is no cross-stitch.

When Jamie and Brenda motion to me, we leave the room together, and Jamie whispers, "I'm sure there's some kind of lost and found on the Camino. We'll call around and find out what to do."

"It's crazy," I say. "I mean, how could she lose that masterpiece?"

"Maybe somebody stole it," Brenda offers.

We look at her, astonished. "Who would do such a thing?"

Brenda shrugs. "No idea. When did Abbie even have her backpack out of her sight?"

"It must have fallen out on the trail," Jamie says. "She threw her pack down and was rifling through everything when Rasa had the panic attack. Remember, she took out those wipes? It could have fallen out then, right?"

"True. We need to have somebody go back to that part of the trail and look for it."

I shudder. That part of the trail had several precipitous drops, and there were so many pilgrims crowded around after Rasa's attack. I think to myself, *Somebody could have taken it then*. But out loud I say, "You know how she had it rolled up in that pink and green pouch? Anybody who saw it would recognize it. We need to get the word out to everyone who's been hiking in this vicinity today."

"Good idea," Jamie says. "I don't think anyone stole it, but if it fell out, I'm sure someone would have picked it up."

Poor Abbie begs us to leave her alone, so we spend the next hour getting the word out about the cross-stitch. I'm feeling claustrophobic and need to get away from everyone, so with camera around my neck and camera bag over my shoulder, I set out to explore our hostel. I photograph the ancient doors and furniture, the walls and ceilings, and, from a window, the breathtaking countryside all around the village. I am desperately trying to calm my erratic heart, trying to concentrate on specific objects, as I'd instructed Rasa to do on the trail.

Rasa's panic attack has brought back vivid memories of my own.

"You were awesome with Rasa," Bobby told me afterward. Perhaps, but I'm shaking now, wanting a drink, *needing* a drink.

I open the massive wooden door to the library—thank goodness it's empty—and settle into a cushioned chair. Setting down the camera bag beside me, I call Tracie.

I find it hard to believe that it's only been a week since we've talked. It feels like years.

The connection is spotty, but in a flourish of garbled words I explain everything that's happened in the past five days. "Trace, I could really use a drink. They serve wine at every meal. I haven't felt tempted at all. But now, with all that's happened today with Rasa and Abbie, I'm really struggling."

For the next few minutes, Tracie talks me off the ledge . . . again. "Of course Rasa's panic attack has brought back so much. But you know what to do, Caroline, and you're putting the plan into practice. You even called me!"

I wince at her barb. "Sorry, it's been a bit intense. But you'll be happy to hear that some things are beginning to get through my thick head. Like helping Rasa. It felt, I don't know, it felt really good. And natural. Like maybe some of the junk in my life can help me know how to help others. If that makes sense."

"It makes perfect sense. And I'm glad to hear it. You have a lot to offer, girl. Hopefully the Camino is helping you begin to believe it."

"Maybe. Breaking up with Brett and getting away from Bastien are also freeing up some ram on my hard drive."

"Great analogy, but it probably feels pretty destabilizing to have all that free space."

"Exactly."

Tracie pauses. "Dear Rasa. Stephen and I haven't been back to Austria for a visit in several years. I'm so glad you were able to help her."

"Me too. And I was totally shocked to learn she's Iranian. That was a bizarre coincidence."

"Did you tell her about Lola?"

"Yeah. It just spilled out, the whole story, even the juicy parts about me and Bastien. I'm afraid I shocked her. She's a strange girl—a mystic or something. But I like her. She's been through a lot."

We chat for a few more minutes and I say, "You've kept me sober again, Trace. Thanks. You're the best."

When I get back to our room, Abbie is sprawled out on the bed, sound asleep. I shower and dress and then wake her up, and we head downstairs to dinner.

Much later, after a feast served around the massive oak table with the fire in the fireplace blazing, Abbie, who has consumed multiple glasses of wine, moans. "It's my baby! I've lost my baby! I've been birthing it for two years, and now it's gone."

No one knows what to say. We're well aware that no platitudes will suffice.

She fills up the silence with slurred words. "I guess I've lost

270

him completely now." She gives a pitiful laugh. "I knew I had to let him go. Wow. Well, it's done. It's really all over now."

Bobby inches in on the bench beside his mother and pulls her close. His face shows a combination of worry, embarrassment, and shock.

The Washington Women give me a questioning look, but I just shrug. I'm not going to say anything about Bill. Then Brenda offers, "Abbie, we're letting pilgrims and hosts throughout the region know. I'm sure someone will find your cross-stitch."

Abbie nods. "Of course. Sure. Easy as pie. It'll just magically show up!" She gives a pitiful laugh and says, "I better turn in before I make a complete fool of myself. Nighty-night."

"Bless her heart," Lynn whispers as we watch Bobby help his mother slowly climb the spiral stone stairs. "She's not going to feel like doing anything in the morning, with the headache she'll have."

CHAPTER
20

ABBIE

It's gone. Even if others had gotten the word out, it probably washed away in the flash flood that assaulted this region in the night.

I weep.

Both my heart and my head feel like they're breaking. I have no idea how much alcohol I consumed at dinner, but my pounding head this morning gives me a pretty good idea. Until last night, I'd never drunk more than a single glass of wine in an evening in my life.

Henk, who is staying with his family in another gîte in town, got up early, and he and Bobby walked back the way we had come, searching for the cross-stitch along the steep and now slick and soggy path. Caroline and the Washington Women have called all the auberges and gîtes and hostels and chambre d'hôtes within fifty kilometers, asking if anyone has found a bright pink-and-green Vera Bradley bag holding a cross-stitch canvas inside. And I've posted on the Camino lost-and-found forum.

Many of the pilgrims who've been walking with us for the past few days have taken photos of the tapestry and, hearing the news, they text the photos to any other pilgrims with whom they've mingled and exchanged phone numbers. It feels like a massive search party, a completely different type of tapestry being woven across the Camino—everyone, pilgrim and host and café owner and Compostel'Bus driver united, a multinational solidarity with one thought in mind. *Find the poor American woman's amazing cross-stitch.*

The word spreads like wildfire, but bless their loyal hearts, Bobby, Rasa, and Caroline keep their mouths closed about the fact that Bill has left me. The message that is circulated is that I've spent the last two years stitching the most intricate and colorful cross-stitch as a surprise fiftieth birthday present for my husband. Throughout the day, I receive numerous texts asking if I've found it.

Even if I hadn't been so hung over and devastated, I think I still would have cried at the kindness of my fellow pilgrims. They all try to encourage me. Occasionally I receive a text or someone posts on the forum a miracle story of having lost a passport or a wallet or a treasured photo and how it showed up days or weeks later in a hostel dozens of kilometers down the road, retrieved by a pilgrim.

But even miracle stories can't dislodge the feeling of dread in the pit of my stomach when Bobby and Henk return empty-handed.

Rasa has apologized about a thousand times for having a panic attack. I almost wish I could be mad at her, but I'm not. Instead, over and over, I picture myself beside her. Then I'm throwing things out of my backpack, frantically digging around until I find the wipes, rushing to Rasa, leaving the backpack on the path, paying no attention to whether or not anything has fallen out.

I can only blame myself, and boy, am I good at that. I curse myself all morning. *You idiot! You fool. You never should have brought it!*

I'm full into self-incrimination when I make the phone call to Bill's assistant.

"Hey there, pilgrim!" Judith answers, surprising me.

"How do you know where I am?"

"I don't know where you are, but Bill said you're doing a pilgrimage somewhere in France. So that makes you a pilgrim, right?"

"Bill told you that?"

"Yeah. I thought it was weird when he kept staying in Chicago every weekend, until he explained that you'd taken off for a pilgrimage with Bobby."

"Judith, Bill's staying in Chicago because he left me," I say.

"What?" She sounds shocked. "What do you mean?"

"I mean he walked out a month ago, told me he needed a break, and got an apartment in Chicago."

Prudish Judith lets out a string of expletives. Then, "That's unbelievable! I don't know what else to say, Abbie."

"Well, you can say whatever you want, but unfortunately it's true. Anyway, I'm calling to tell you to cancel his surprise party. I know the save-the-date went out, and I know you've got the formal invitation ready to mail. I'm sorry for all the work you've done, but can you please just cancel it?" Hearing my voice pronouncing those words, I can't make it through another sentence.

I click off the phone before Judith can protest.

Around two in the afternoon we head out on the next stretch. I keep screwing up this whole Camino thing for everyone. First my blisters slowed us all down, and now it's the blasted cross-stitch. No one has even been able to fully appreciate this luxury medieval gîte we're in, one I found and reserved online from Atlanta. Nope, everyone is too busy worrying about me.

Well, by golly, I'm not going to mess anything else up. I. Will. Not.

Lost cross-stitch or not, we'll make it to our next destination on time, so help me God.

BOBBY

The next few days are the low point in our Camino. We all have blisters, and we're super bummed about the cross-stitch. We halfheartedly enjoy the beauty of the mountain regions. Even Rasa stops petting the cows. It goes from fifty-three degrees and pouring rain to ninety-five degrees and boiling hot in the course of about twelve hours. Mom never puts on makeup, and she wears the same clothes for three days straight. She looks like death warmed over. There's another of her favorite expressions, but I wish I didn't need to use it.

After three days, there's still no word that anyone has found the cross-stitch. I think she is going to unravel before us. My mother has always been on the thin side, but now her cheeks are gaunt and she looks like those really old women who are skinny and wrinkled. And worse, she is now physically attacking the Camino. No joke. Like all her anger and frustration and self-hate are poured into power walking twentysome kilometers a day. She has a look of grim determination on her face. I've seen it a hundred times. You don't dare cross Mom when she looks like that.

After a while, the rest of us don't even try to keep up. We figure she needs to be alone.

And Rasa looks fragile to me, almost broken. I think she's blaming herself for the lost cross-stitch. She doesn't exactly come out and say it, but I can tell she's carrying a lot of guilt.

"I wish it would be like in the Bible," she says to Caroline and me, when Mom is far ahead of us. "When Joseph meets his brothers and hides a silver cup in one of their backpacks."

Caroline obviously has no idea what she's talking about. But after she tells the story from the book of Genesis, Rasa explains, "I wish you would find the cross-stitch in my backpack. Maybe she could have put it there to blame me because I caused such problems for everyone."

"You're not the one causing problems," I assure her. Heck no. Rasa is by far the brightest light in my life. But I don't think my words are very convincing.

I feel relieved when later she pronounces in her faith-filled way, "I just know we're going to find her cross-stitch. I know it!"

But her words aren't very convincing either.

For these few days we're all walking together, but we're alone in our thoughts, each of us processing way too much stuff in our heads. The silence is deafening, and my only hope is to draw, furiously sketching the beauty around me. But those sketches can't mask the angst inside.

Several days ago I decided to sketch every cross I came upon on the Camino. I ran the idea by Stephen, who thought it was brilliant. But Mom was already ticked off at the way Caroline takes photos of the crosses and the vegetation and comments on every fragrance. Now she is ticked off at me.

"You're wasting time. What is the point in crosses and flowers and everything else? We're supposed to be walking."

She's looking for a fight. Of course nobody blames her for being upset, but I think we're all relieved when she powers ahead of us.

My drawings look frantic, and every step of the way my mind is juggling multiple worries: will we find Mom's cross-stitch, will Rasa have another panic attack, will Granddad fully recover from the stroke, will Swannee be okay, will Jason get kicked out of school? And last but not least, will Dad really leave Mom for good?

It feels like I'm carrying everyone's backpack of crap on my shoulders all at once. It's totally ruining everything. But whom can I admit that to? No one. Everyone has way too much to deal with. I guess what I'm longing for is a little bit of peace. If I could just look around and know that everybody is going to be okay . . .

Finally I call my grandmother, hoping she will offer some advice.

I start with the obvious first question. "How's Granddad doing, Swannee? I need to know the truth."

"He's much better. There doesn't seem to be any lingering paralysis."

"And his memory? And his eyesight?"

"Bobby, some things are probably not going to get better, but I don't believe it's something the Lord wants us to be worried about."

She's sounding like my grandmother again. Sharp, sensitive, spiritual, sensible. I tell her what happened.

"Mom lost the cross-stitch."

"What? Say that again?"

And I launch into the story of Rasa's panic attack and Mom's response and the lost tapestry.

"Oh my word!" That's all she can say. Then, "Dear Abbie! She must be devastated."

"Yep, she's so mad at herself! I don't know what to do, Swannee. She was already having such a rotten time about Dad. She thinks he's left her for good, you know. I don't know why she even kept doing the stupid cross-stitch! It's ruining everything, just like Dad has ruined everything."

I hadn't expected that to come out. "And please don't tell me not to worry, or that this isn't my problem. Because it is, Swannee! It will certainly affect me a ton if they get divorced. I know I can't make things okay, but it all sucks. It's a bunch of crap."

My grandmother doesn't reprimand me. She just listens, and she listens so well that by the end of our conversation I'm not talking about the Camino. I'm not talking about Mom or Dad or a lost cross-stitch, but I'm talking about art, telling her that I'm excited to see Jean-Paul in Paris, and I'm thinking about asking Rasa to be my girlfriend.

Before we hang up she says, "Bobby Jowett, you go forward. Take the Lord with you. I know it's a lot right now. You're not called to rescue your mother or your father, but of course it's heavy on you. Remember, too, that you're not called to rescue Rasa."

"Well, I'm not trying to *rescue* Rasa, Swannee. I'm in love with her!"

Swannee takes a few seconds before she replies. "Yes, I can hear that, Bobby, but there is something in you that cares so deeply. You must remember that Rasa is not Anna."

Why did she have to say that? I stew on that statement for the rest of the day. Why does she think Rasa is so much like Anna? Why does Mom?

I give a long, exasperated sigh. Why do I?

CARO

I'd heard it said that the Camino strips you bare, forces you to look at the junk inside, and then gives you a new start. Well, I guess it's true. At least about the stripping part. We've all been stripped bare. We walk the next days in a kind of stupor. I guess we're processing.

Abbie is grieving everything she's lost, and man, is it a lot. It feels like the cross-stitch tapestry was the last dangling carrot for Bill's return, and once it was gone, everything she's depended on was taken away.

It's a lot more uncomfortable to examine my own life. I'm being stripped bare too. No more Brett, no more Bastien, no more alcohol, no more pity parties. But maybe, maybe at the end there will be Lola.

Rasa and I are walking together while poor Abbie charges on ahead, walking out her fury. *You go, girl!* I shout in my mind. Attacking the Camino is a lot healthier than chugging down bottles of wine or popping pills. We let her speed walk with our unspoken blessing.

"Do you know when you're going to have a panic attack?" Rasa asks me on the steep descent as we're nearing a town called Saint-Côme d'Olt.

"Not usually," I admit. "Occasionally I can look back and see that I was stressed out about something, but sometimes it just comes completely out of the blue."

"Out of the blue?" She looks perplexed.

I smile. "Another great American idiom. It means without any warning. There's no way to tell."

"I really wanted to come on the Camino. I wasn't afraid and then I was, and I couldn't breathe. And now Abbie has lost her cross-stitch and it's my fault. I don't know what to say to her. I've tried to apologize, but—"

"Hold on a minute, Rasa. First, it is not your fault. You had no idea you were going to have a panic attack! And Abbie is not blaming you. She knows it wasn't the wisest decision to bring the cross-stitch with her. She's not blaming anyone but herself."

"But I'm sorry to see her so sad."

"Yeah, me too."

"I haven't had a panic attack in a long time. I thought Isa had healed me."

I give her a funny look and say, "I don't know anything about Isa, but I know I've thought the same thing—that I wouldn't have any more attacks. And then another one comes along. Out of the blue."

She gives me a shy smile. "Your lavender helped a lot."

"I'll give you some to keep with you."

"That would be nice." Then she asks, "Why do you not like Isa? Why don't you want to know about Him?"

Talk about out of the blue! I'm caught off guard, but I shouldn't be. As I've said, Rasa talks about Isa every spare breath. "I'm just not very interested in religion."

"But Isa is not religion." She has the most naïve look on her face. Or maybe it's not naïve. It's angelic—she's a little angel who believes in supernatural silliness.

"Well, whatever you call it, I'm not interested in that. I don't seem to be a good enough person."

"But no one's a good enough person."

I wince. I remember Stephen's sermons, his long explanations about how I can't earn my way to God. I wish I'd kept my big mouth shut.

Of course Rasa says, "You're right, we can't be good enough for God. That's why Isa came."

"I'm sorry, Rasa, I'm just not interested."

She lets it go. At least she stops trying to persuade me, but she still keeps talking about Him. "I am very disappointed. I thought Isa told me to come on the Camino. Maybe I was wrong."

I start to say who in the heck can really hear from God? But I catch myself, and instead I think of what I've told Tracie, that all my junk might be able to help someone else. So I say, "Did you see Bobby's sketch, the one with the saying painted on the rock? 'It's about the journey, not about the destination.'"

She nods. "This is part of our journey. We're like the Israelites in the Bible. We're walking toward the Promised Land. Toward our future."

"Yeah. Something like that. I think that's why you're on the Camino, Rasa. Why I'm here too. To get us a little further down the road. And we get to meet a lot of other good people and share our stuff and help each other and somehow, somehow it all matters. The Camino is good for our souls. But I don't think anything is magically healed. It takes time. A lot of time."

Several expressions parade across Rasa's face as I talk. Now she cocks her head and shrugs. "You are very interesting, Caroline. I like you. And I like what you say. The Camino is good for our souls."

ABBIE

I leave the addresses of every place we'll be staying on the lost-and-found forum and text them to the previous places we've stayed, but each afternoon when we show up after a long day's hike, there's no news about the cross-stitch. I continue to receive texts from different pilgrims asking if I have found it. And each day my expectations and hopes diminish. It's like what you hear on a TV show when a child goes missing. The first twenty-four hours are always the most hopeful, and the longer the delay, the more doubtful a happy ending. I berate myself for comparing a lost cross-stitch to a lost child. But it doesn't make the thought go away.

In the evenings I sit and talk with Barb and Brenda and Jamie and Lynn. They seem eager to share more of their stories with me, maybe to distract me from the cross-stitch. I learn that Lynn is in the middle of a pretty messy divorce and Jamie is on her second marriage and struggling and Barb is a cancer survivor and so is Brenda. All of a sudden, once the truth comes out, things go deeper, and I finally get the courage to tell them about Bill. I mean, they have a pretty good idea after I blubbered who-knows-what when I got drunk.

Bobby is worried about me, I know. I'd hoped for long conversations with him about his dreams and future, but instead I'm scowling and pushing him away.

After I have spent all my anger on myself, after I have walked dozens of kilometers at breakneck pace, after I've tried my best not to let my foul mood infect Rasa and Caroline and Bobby, after all this, it's my mother who calls to pronounce a little bit of truth.

"Bobby told me about the cross-stitch. I'm so sorry."

"Devastating, Mama. I feel like heaven's lobbing endless crap at me." I rant for a good ten minutes, telling her how inanely dumb, furious, and heartbroken I am. Mama just listens.

Finally, when I take a breath, she says, "That's a lot of debilitating self-criticism, Abbie."

She knows that phrase will stop me in my tracks, her being the first one to show me the verses from First John in the Bible paraphrase called *The Message*. I've memorized those verses. She doesn't have to quote them.

My dear children, let's not just talk about love; let's practice real love. This is the only way we'll know we're living truly, living in God's reality. It's also the way to shut down debilitating self-criticism, even when there is something to it. For God is greater than our worried hearts and knows more about us than we do ourselves.

"There's a whole lot of loss in your life right now, sweetie. Try to give yourself a little grace. But it's good to get all the anger out. Yell as much as you have to. You know our God isn't shocked by our anger. Your dad and I will be praying for you, for all of these things."

I silently berate myself that I haven't even asked about him. "How is he?"

Mama weighs her words. "He's a little weak, a little foggier. I thank the Lord we're here in the loft right now. No stairs to negotiate. Bathroom wheelchair accessible. It's a gift to be here. And he's as thankful as I am."

"I should just come home and help you care for him."

"No. Absolutely not. It would be crowded with three."

This is a blatant lie, but I don't correct her. Then I dare to bring up Bill. I know it's not right to put Mama on the spot, but it comes out after all the other junk has escaped. "Have you heard from Bill, Mama?"

"He was great while your dad was in the hospital."

"Nan told me he moved all his things out of the loft."

"You just keep walking, Abbie. Let Bill deal with his stuff while you're dealing with yours. The Lord's right there with you, Abbie, no matter what. You remember that, okay?"

I can tell she's getting ready to hang up, and I don't want her to go. I need to hear her calming voice. So I tell her how Caroline was able to help Rasa and how Bobby is carrying backpacks for strangers and about the humbling joy I've felt with the solidarity of all the other pilgrims.

"Thank you for telling me these things, sweetie. Thank you for finding the good in the situation too. It's okay to be mad, to be heartbroken, but it's not okay to incriminate yourself. You wait, trust, and pray."

And if I hadn't known for sure that I was talking to my mother on the phone, I would have sworn that it was Miss Abigail speaking to me from the grave.

CHAPTER
21

BOBBY

It's been a while since I've heard from Jason, so I shoot him a text. *Hey, how's school? You started on Monday, didn't you?*

Crappy. Everything's crappy. I got kicked off the football team. Dad was freaking furious. I don't care. It's his fault anyway.

How do you figure?

Nothing.

Go on.

If he'd just stand up to Mom once in a while, I wouldn't have been so desperate to leave.

You didn't want to go to boarding school, did you?

Heck no. But I thought it'd be better than hanging around Mom with her noose around my neck.

Have you told Dad?

As if he cares.

Jason was fourteen when Anna died, just getting the feel of a little more independence. But Mom shut him down. She had to know precisely where each of us was going to be throughout every day. She gave us smartphones when many parents wouldn't let their kids have one, but they came with a steep price. She had to be able to reach us at any minute. Sometimes I wonder if Mom didn't need counseling back then more than I did.

Next I call Dad. The phone call starts off awkwardly, till finally I blurt out, "Everything is going wrong for Mom! I thought the Camino would do her good, but now it's making everything worse than ever." I can't stand hinting anymore. "She lost the cross-stitch."

I expect him to ask me what in the world I'm talking about, but he says, "Oh no. The one she's making for my fiftieth?"

"How do you know about it?"

He chuckles. "Come on, Bobby. She's been working on it since forever. We decided way back that I'd ignore her when she stitched. Never peek. So I haven't seen it. But I know it exists."

"Yeah, well, it's gone now. She lost it trying to help Rasa. Not that you care." Jason's wrath is infecting me.

"Whoa, buddy. Slow down. Start from the beginning."

"You'll just tell me it's not my problem. Well, maybe it's not my problem, but you're not around to solve it, so it sure feels like my problem."

Dad is silent for a moment. Then he says, "I'm sorry, Bobby. You're right. Pretty ridiculous of me to think you could spend all this time with your mom and not have to deal with our junk. No, not ridiculous. Selfish. I think I hoped that while I've been working out my stuff, she'd be working out her own and be glad for the space."

"Fat chance. Maybe she was making progress, but now she's in over-the-top anger mode. I wish I could make her go home, but there's no way she'll do that now. She'll finish what she started. Just like always." I take a breath. "I mean, of course she's upset. You should see the thing she was making for you. It's awesome. Other pilgrims would crowd around her at night watching her work, admiring it. She's heartbroken, Dad. Not just about the cross-stitch, of course. It's all about losing you. It's crazy grief. Like when I lost Anna."

I know pronouncing her name will slam into Dad. None of us likes to remember the spiral of depression I fell into after Anna's death.

He sighs. "Okay. I'll call her."

"I'm not sure that would help right now. She'll probably just yell at you."

"And I probably deserve it, son. I'm sorry about all of it." There's another long moment of silence. I can practically feel Dad trying to find a safe subject to talk about. "How's Rasa?"

"I'll tell you tomorrow. I'm asking her to be my girlfriend tonight."

I feel somehow empowered after expressing myself so strongly to my dad. Lighter. Even if he doesn't call Mom, I've dumped the responsibility back on him. The idea of letting go of responsibility that isn't really mine came from the therapist I saw after Anna. But I've never done a very good job of putting it into practice.

But maybe I can now, more out of desperation than anything else.

I find I have a little space for thinking about Rasa. As we walk alone together on the last stretch of the day, carefully negotiating the steep descent into Saint-Côme-d'Olt, I want to ask her my question. Except I chicken out and say instead, "Sorry things are a mess right now. With my mother and all."

"I think Isa does His best work in messes."

I give her a strange look. "How's that?"

"I know He's asking me to come down to earth. I'm too high."

She sees I have no idea what she means. She furrows her brow so that her thick eyebrows almost touch and her beautiful face deepens in concentration. "I am telling Isa I need miraculous healing. No more panic attacks. I tell Him that this is the only way I will know He is powerful. That is foolish. So I have confessed, and now I know it's okay. Even if I have panic attacks all the time, Isa will never leave. He will take care of me. He sent me Caroline that day on the trail to help me."

"She was awesome," I admit.

"He teaches us through every person and every experience. Caroline said that the Camino is good for our souls. That it is important for the journey. She is right. Even the mess with your mother. But she is working things out with Isa too, I can tell. She is having it out with Him as she walks. And that is good."

I'm really trying to listen to Rasa's words, but her hand in mine feels so warm, so electric, so perfect. I lift her chin with my other hand, and I think I am going to kiss her. I bend toward her, heart hammering. Her eyes are bright and teasing, almost daring me. She gives a shy giggle, drops my hand, puts both arms around my neck, and brings her lips against mine. Sweet. Really sweet.

She pulls away seconds later, still smiling. "You see, Bobby. Good things can come from a mess. It is all part of the journey." She laughs again. "Oh, Bobby! Your face. It is shocked. But I promise I am not a forward woman. I do not give kisses away with light." She furrows her brow again. "I mean, lightly. I have never kissed a boy before. But this you needed. And I am glad. Yes, I will hold your hand and yes, I will kiss you. A little. Only a little. And yes, I will be your girlfriend."

CARO

Once again Abbie is walking ahead of us, alone. Bobby and Rasa have been walking hand in hand for several kilometers now, but I pretend not to notice the silly grins on their faces. None of the Washington Women are with us today. They're taking a slow day to visit Saint-Côme d'Olt, recognized as one of the most beautiful villages in France. We've decided to slow down too, and every cross we come to, I photograph from many different angles while Bobby perches on a fence or rock or whatever is available, and sketches. We figure Stephen will enjoy our idea of writing a blog post in which these crosses tell the story of the Camino.

"Oh, wow! This one is amazing!" I say. I kneel down, shooting upward at an intricate wrought-iron cross that's at least six feet tall, its northern point puncturing a sapphire-blue sky. "Look how the sun is illuminating it!"

The setting sun breaks through in a blindingly bright circle, shining through an empty space right in the center of the cross where Jesus is usually hanging, and its rays, like sparks of fire, radiate all around.

The three of us stand in silence.

Later Rasa says to me, "You don't want to know about Isa, but you like the crosses?"

"Love all the different crosses. How can you not? Whether it's beautiful wrought iron like this last one or a thick ancient stone or even a pilgrim's offering made of two sticks held together by a shoestring. They're important. They tell a story."

"You know it's a symbol of our faith? Of Isa's death. And His resurrection."

"Of course I know that," I say. "But I can appreciate the crosses without buying into all that. For me, they're symbolic of the spiritual, but not just Christian spirituality. They tell a story of real people on a real journey."

But I know I sound defensive.

Even as I try to explain, I get that annoying feeling I've had ever since we started this Camino. No, in all truth, ever since Stephen and my mother came back from Austria in 2005, all high on God. It'll lie dormant for a few months, even a year or two. And then whoosh. It comes in, something scratching around in my heart. Each time, I push it away.

But as I stare at this latest cross, with the sun's rays exploding all around it, for some reason I feel my eyes brimming with tears.

ABBIE

I still get up early every morning and read a Psalm of Ascent. Actually I usually read two a day, and I scribble down my thoughts in my journal. The first morning after losing the canvas, I had to squint at the screen because my head was throbbing and the sunlight was piercing my eyes. But still I obeyed. I gulp the psalms down each day, drinking in the words, miserable and desperate, and I make each psalm personal, as Diana suggested.

I lift up my eyes to you. . . . Have mercy on us, Lord, have mercy on us, for we have endured no end of contempt.

—I've endured a whole lot of crap.

If the Lord had not been on our side . . . the raging waters would have swept us away. . . .

—Oh, brother. I'd rather have been swept away than lose my cross-stitch.

Those who trust in the Lord are like Mount Zion, which cannot be shaken but endures forever.

—But I am shaken, Lord. Shaken to my very innermost

290

being. You've taken everything away! I don't trust You to be good right now.

They have greatly oppressed me from my youth. . . .

—Who are "they"? It's perfectionism, it's control, it's fear, it's so many things, Lord . . .

But they have not gained the victory over me. . . .

—But they have, Lord. They have! I give up!

Today I turn to Psalms 130 and 131.

Out of the depths I cry to you, O Lord.

—Yes, help! Help!

If you kept a record of sins, Lord, who could stand?

And here they are, all my sins parading before me. And I'm slinging hatred over my back, like the ancient monks who flagellate themselves.

And then the voice: *Stop it! Stop it, Abbie. Read the psalm.*

—What, Lord?

Read the rest of the psalm.

So I continue reading.

But with you there is forgiveness. . . . I wait for the Lord, my whole being waits, and in his word I put my hope. I wait for the Lord, more than watchmen wait for the morning.

—I wish I could believe that right now. But I have seen the beauty of the sunrise on this Camino, Lord. So I'll keep waiting for You to show up again too.

Oh, Lord, my heart is not proud nor my eyes haughty; nor do I involve myself in great matters or in things too difficult for me. . . .

I throw down the phone. This is the worst one yet! I've always, always involved myself in things that seemed great, or at least important.

I hear myself pushing Bobby to retake the SAT—just a few more points and he'll be in the top bracket.

I'm standing outside Jason's room, assuring him that he will most definitely *not* be going out with his friends until the essay is done.

I'm telling Bill all the reasons we should move to the loft and paying no attention to his attempts to disagree.

I'm rushing around before leaving Atlanta, contacting the Garden Club and my tennis team and the church committees I'm on. Making sure all my *i*'s are dotted and *t*'s crossed.

I'm madly unpacking the boxes at the loft, dancing and singing and still getting everything in order in record time for Mama and Dad to move in.

I'm emailing and texting Bill, again and again, trying to coerce him to come back.

I'm setting up the gîtes where we'll stay and contacting Caroline and Bobby.

I'm managing the whole Camino, with blisters. . . .

It was all difficult, but if I admit the truth, it hasn't been *too* difficult for me. I'm Triple A, and I can handle anything.

Until it's all taken away. That thought slams into my spirit. Yuck.

The cross-stitch. Daddy's health. My sons' presence. Bill. My ability to control anything.

All taken away.

This Camino journey is beginning to feel like the wilderness the Israelites wander around in on their way to the Promised Land. They don't just lose a cross-stitch. They lose forty years for their grumbling. And they just keep on grumbling. These psalms are being sung as they are finally coming out of exile.

I don't particularly like anything about this part of my journey. But it is just *a part* of the journey. I agree with what that painted rock said the other day: It's the journey, not the destination that matters.

Or at least the journey matters *as well as* the destination.

I want to believe that. I want to let this journey, no matter how painful, be enough. I had figured out my destination. I'd been planning how to get there for years. Do the right thing, control everyone and everything, obey God, and it'll work out.

Miss Abigail used to say, *"Every part of the journey is important, Abbie. Even the dying-to-self part. You'll see. It's worth it."*

I used to lap up the paradoxes of the Bible. Dying to self so I can truly live, the last being first, strength coming from weakness. And joy coming in the midst of sorrow.

And now, it's Diana's words echoing another paradox in the Bible: *"So much has a chance to get through to us when everything else is taken away."*

It's still early morning when I finally read the last verse in this short psalm.

Surely I have composed and quieted my soul; like a weaned child rests against his mother, my soul is like a weaned child within me. . . .

—Oh brother. Two little verses, and all this conviction! Not only am I to let go of responsibility, but I'm supposed to be still and rest?

"That's hard to do on the Camino!" I say out loud—in case the Lord isn't paying attention to my thoughts. Diana's voice sneaks in again. *"Let's get Abbie back."* It isn't physical stillness but mental and emotional and spiritual stillness. Solitude. Listening.

I click off the phone and sit for a long time in the quiet before sunrise.

A weaned child.

All those years ago I loved nursing my baby boys. I was quiet; they were quiet. I was not madly accomplishing and organizing things; I was just a mommy, just Abbie, with a baby in my arms, humming a melody, content, in awe of my child and the joy that danced in my soul just because we were together, there, quiet, alone.

It felt like such a loss when the doctor said I wouldn't have another pregnancy. Jason was sixteen months old . . . a weaned child. I remember holding him in my arms, sorrowing that my season of nursing babies was over.

But I don't want to think about this anymore.

I close my eyes.

My cell rings, shocking me out of my silence and also shocking me with its ring tone. It's Bill's jingle. Bill, calling me at almost midnight in Chicago because he knows I'll be up this early over here. I let it ring once, twice, three times. My heart is pounding in my chest.

Four times.

"Hello?"

"Hey, Abbs."

I concentrate on his voice. It sounds older than the last time, or softer or . . . or . . . it sounds like regret.

"Abbs."

"Yes?"

"Bobby called. He said things aren't going very well."

I let the silence hang between us. Finally I murmur, "Yeah. That's right."

"It sounds like he's feeling a lot of responsibility, pretty weighed down. I'm sorry. You know how he is—"

I don't let him finish the sentence. Bill is worrying about Bobby, not about me. This phone call isn't about me. I take a deep breath.

It isn't about me, and that's okay.

"Listen, Bill. It's been a rough few days, but I'm better. I know I've been a jerk to Bobby and the rest of you. I'm sorry.

I really am sorry. I'll talk to Bobby, let him know I'm okay. I'm not falling apart." I take another breath and hurry on. "I know you've moved out. I know Mom and Dad are okay in the loft. I know Jason got kicked off the football team. We've only got three more days on the Camino. Then Bobby will go his way and I'll go mine."

"Where will you go?"

"That I *don't* know, but it doesn't matter. I won't bother you anymore. Or Bobby. Or Jason. I'll give all of you the space you've needed for a long time. I promise. I'll let Mama and Nan and Ellie know what I'm doing when I figure it out. And I hope you're okay. I'm going to be okay. Don't worry about me. I'll let Bobby go just like I'm letting you go. Good-bye, Bill."

I am completely undone when I click off the phone. I bury my head in my hands and sit for a long time, trying to catch my breath. Then very slowly I fall to my knees, and I make myself stay there.

"God, please forgive me. This is one messed-up pilgrim talking to You, but I know You'll never leave me. You've proven it so many times in my life. And right now, all I've got is You, so You better be right when You say You're enough. You better be right, God. I'm holding You to it.

"I'm letting go of everything that is most precious to me, Lord. I'll loosen the grip I have on my boys. I'll trust You with them.

"And I give You Bill. I've been learning to let go of him all along this pilgrimage. Now I'll let go completely." This confession comes out in a sob. "I won't try to fix my marriage. I'll just try to let You fix me. And I'll keep waiting, trusting, and praying."

I stay on my knees for a long time, until I hear the sound of other pilgrims in the *salle à manger*. Then I stand and feel the cool of the early morning surrounding me. I make a short lap around the gîte, taking deep breaths and paying attention to the fragrances around me, the way Caroline does. I get a whiff of pine and freshly cut hay.

And I feel lighter. Unencumbered. It's not like it's a new idea, what confession does for the soul, but I haven't practiced it in a long time. Not true spit-out-the-worst-of-me confession. And I haven't really given anything over to the Lord in a long time either.

As the sun rises, I feel forgiven down to the marrow of my bones. None of the circumstances of my life at the moment feel resolved, yet I bathe in what must be "the peace that surpasses understanding." If I could understand it, this peace that is seeping into my soul, I guess it wouldn't be supernatural.

CHAPTER
22

BOBBY

On our next-to-last day on the Camino, we're in the middle of some pretty awesome scenery. It seeps in through my eyes and down into my fingers, till I'm rubbing my hands together, impatient to sketch the scenes before me and eventually do some paintings from those sketches. We get to the top of the hill, and before us stretches a dirt road surrounded in every direction by deep yellow harvested fields scattered with huge round bales of hay. The dusty brown road, splotched here and there by the pilgrims' colorful backpacks, meanders for miles until it falls off the edge of the horizon. The sky is high and a deep blue.

Mom has slowed her pace and is humming a praise song. That seems like a positive sign. I fall into step beside her.

After walking in silence for a while, I get up my nerve and broach the unwelcome subject that's been nagging me. "Do you want me to come back to Atlanta with you, Mom? I don't want you to be alone. I know this whole thing with Dad is really rough."

She stops, leaning on one of her poles, staring at the sky.

"What a gorgeous day!" She takes a really deep breath. "No, Bobby. I want you to fly. Stay here, take your gap year. Enjoy."

Relief and responsibility compete in my mind. Responsibility wins, and I say, "But will you be okay?"

Mom meets my eyes. "I will be okay, Bobby. But even if I'm not, I want you to fly." Her eyes look clear, that familiar violet-blue, calm, no red-rimmed lids, no furrowed brow. "I hope you know that although I am sick to my stomach about losing the cross-stitch, it's not my baby. It's not you or Jason. It's nothing compared to my sons. I love you so much, Bobby, but I'm going to try to open my clenched fists more and more. I don't want to lose you, too, before the message gets through to me."

I feel a scratching in my throat and can't get any words out, so I nod at her. We walk on in silence.

Later I say, "Rasa and I will take the train back to Austria in two days, and then I'm going to Paris. I'll spend the fall taking art lessons from Jean-Paul. After that I'm not sure what I'll do. Part of me wants to take the art classes in Linz to be close to Rasa. But I just don't know."

Typically Mom would break in with advice or a reminder of her plans for my life, though she never called them that. But she doesn't. She keeps stride with me and says, "It's your decision, Bobby."

"Really?" I try to cover my relief by asking, "Did you know what you wanted to do at my age?"

"Yes, I did. What I wanted more than anything else in the world was to get married and have kids." She looks over at me. "And I got what I wanted. The best gifts I've ever received."

She's getting choked up, and I'm about to say something to lighten things up, but Mom goes right on talking.

"I'm sorry I haven't encouraged you enough with your art.

You've known what your passion is for a long time. Don't worry about college right now. Take your year and see what happens."

Is this my mother talking?

"But what about Rasa?" Before she can answer, I add, "Why does she remind everyone of Anna? Rasa doesn't need rescuing! She's amazing. Are you afraid she'll break my heart?"

"Maybe."

"You're afraid that I'll get so caught up in her that if it doesn't work out, I'll fall into a depression again."

"Something like that. No one wants to watch someone they love suffer the way you did after Anna."

I want to point out that potentially having a girlfriend break up with me isn't in the same category as watching a girl you love burn to death in a car. But I don't want to let that gruesome scene invade our conversation or crowd my memory. "Have you talked to Dad about Rasa?"

"No. Have you?"

"Yeah, but he doesn't say much."

"I wouldn't expect him to."

We're walking again in silence. I wonder if I am too attached to Rasa. Is our relationship unhealthy? Am I trying to rescue her or protect her or possess her, instead of simply enjoying her? And why do I have to figure all that stuff out?

Further down the road I get up the courage to ask Mom the elephant-in-the-room question. "Are you and Dad getting a divorce, Mom? Is Dad leaving you?"

She looks off toward the hills and doesn't answer for quite a while, but eventually she gives a sad shake of her head. "I have no idea, Bobby. I have no idea."

But she says it calmly, not frantically, and she looks stronger, a good kind of strong.

"Mom," I say, "thank you for the way you've taken care

of the family for so long. Thank you for letting me decide about this gap year. I know none of this is easy. I'm sorry about the cross-stitch and of course about Dad. I'm really, really sorry."

She stops on the trail and takes me in her arms and holds me, crushingly tight, wonderfully tight, for a long, long time.

CARO

It's been three days since the cross-stitch went missing, and Abbie seems to have walked out all her fury. She tells me about Bill's phone call and her reaction. Her weird "confessing to the Lord" speech makes me really uncomfortable, but I try not to show it. I'm glad she feels better—*lighter* is the way she puts it. I like that. I want to feel lighter too.

She spent a good part of the day walking with Bobby. Rasa, sensitive soul that she is, gave them plenty of space, falling in stride with me and the Washington Women. Now she's out counting stars with Bobby. It's the perfect night for romance. We're in the tiny village of Espeyrac, its quaint gray stone buildings nestled in a valley, and the stars dot the indigo sky with white glints of hope.

I'm stretched out on a worn leather sofa at our gîte, my laptop on the little table beside me and Bobby's sketch pad spread across my lap. I'm comparing my photos of the Camino crosses with Bobby's sketches.

I flip backward in the spiral pad, admiring his sketches of Margeride cows and cobbled bridges and burons and tsabones and narrow goat paths surrounded by evergreens. I continue flipping backward until I find his drawings from his time in Austria. Suddenly I feel the blood drain from my face.

I bring the sketch close and peer at the faces drawn there. "It can't be," I whisper.

Abbie hears me. "What's up, Caroline?"

"This is her!" I choke out.

"What is who?"

"Lola. This is Lola right here!"

Abbie joins me on the sofa and takes Bobby's sketch pad in her lap. It's open to a drawing of a classroom. Two young woman, one of whom is definitely Rasa, are standing up front, and in the foreground are a dozen students seen from the back.

"This is Lola!" I repeat, pointing to the girl standing by Rasa.

"What? Are you sure?"

"Yes! Yes!"

Abbie sets down the sketch pad and stares at me, obviously at a loss for words.

"I thought Rasa reacted strangely whenever I talked about Lola. Now I know why!" I'm trembling with anger and excitement.

I hurry out into the night and turn into the small herb garden to the left of the gîte. I know I need to calm myself before confronting Rasa. I stoop down beside a basil plant, inhaling the smell as if my life depended upon it. I crush some thyme between my fingers, then some mint, letting the strong peppery fragrance engulf me.

Abbie is right beside me, and I turn to her. "Why didn't she tell me?"

"Maybe she's afraid for Lola," Abbie suggests.

"Yes, but she could have told me. How could I put her at risk, out here on the Camino?"

"I don't know, Caro. You'll have to ask her. But what a strange, strange coincidence, that you both know her." She cocks her head. "Or maybe it's a coincidence that isn't just a coincidence."

My chest tightens. "Don't you dare tell me this is something from God!" My words come out so harshly that Abbie backs away. "I don't want anything to do with God! I don't want to hear how He can make my last seven years of misery into something good. Don't you dare say that, Abbie."

She touches me on the shoulder, gives a soft squeeze, and goes back inside.

The moon is high when Rasa and Bobby approach the gîte, walking hand in hand. I'm still sitting on the ground in the herb garden, turning everything over in my mind.

"Hey, Caroline. Everything okay?" Bobby asks.

I stand up, and my determination to stay calm evaporates. I spit out my accusation at Rasa. "You know Lola!"

Bobby pulls Rasa closer as if to protect her from me, but she breaks free. "It's okay," she says. "Caroline and I need to talk."

Bobby looks unsure, but when Rasa nods again, he leaves us and heads back to the gîte.

"It's true, Caroline. Lola and I are friends." I can see tears in her eyes. "I wanted to tell you this, but at first I was afraid. I didn't know if I could trust you." She reaches for my hand, but I back away. "Now I know I can. Now I know you love her."

I bristle. How could she have ever doubted my love for Lola?

She answers me before I can say a word. "You told me about the man who kept you away from Lola. You said it was a bad decision. So I didn't trust you. But now I know you've suffered, and so you must understand suffering. I'm sorry. I should have said something sooner."

My throat has gone dry. Rasa thinks that my affair with Bastien was one of the reasons Lola was taken. She thinks I betrayed my friend. I try to swallow. I close my eyes. If I weren't concentrating so hard on not having a panic attack, I'd choke her.

Or hug her. I say to myself: *This is good news, Caroline! Lola is in Austria. Lola and Rasa are friends!* Breathe. Breathe. And even as I struggle for control, a part of my mind is admitting that this is a whole different level of coincidence.

When I open my eyes, Rasa is staring at me like Harry Potter before Voldemort. Perhaps she's read my thoughts again—the part about choking her. I clear my throat, take one more deep breath, and whisper, "Can you tell me about her? How is she?"

Rasa gives a tentative smile. "I will tell you what I know."

Quite naturally we begin walking away from the gîte, letting the stars guide our path.

"Three years ago Lola managed to escape from her cousin's control in Iran and made her way across the mountains just as my family did. Many people helped her; it is quite a story. She got to Linz about a year and a half ago. She does not feel safe to come back to France until her cousin is arrested."

"But she is well?"

Rasa nods. "She is well." Her tear-filled eyes meet mine.

My chest tightens, and I can't tell if it's a pain of deep hurt or deep joy or both.

She fiddles with her braid. "There is something else I must tell you now."

Her discomfort sends a zip of fear through me.

"Stephen also knows that Lola is in Linz."

This doesn't register at first. "What?" Then, "Are you talking about my brother, Stephen?"

She nods. "I think he has been involved in her rescue—not physically, of course, but I know that he talks often with my father. He has helped many refugees."

"Stephen knows? He's known for a long time?"

"Do not be mad with your brother. What he does is very good. Very brave."

I cannot process this glut of information. Stephen has known about Lola's whereabouts! Does Tracie also know? Have they kept me wondering for *seven years* if my dear friend is alive or dead? This feels like a much deeper betrayal than Rasa's withholding information.

"I'm sorry if this is hard to hear," Rasa says. "I will leave you now."

I walk out into the starry night, punching in Stephen's cell number.

As soon as I hear his voice, I lose it. "You knew! You knew about Lola! How long have you known?" I launch into a curse-filled diatribe, only slowing down when I run out of breath.

When I finally allow my brother to speak, he begins calmly. "I've known for about a year and a half that Lola is in hiding at the House of Hope."

"Why didn't you tell me? Why? I hate you!"

He speaks softly, but I hear both anger and incredulity in his voice. "You think I would tell my fly-by-the-seat-of-her-pants sister something that could get her friend hurt, maybe even killed? You know I've got all kinds of connections with others who help refugees. I think Interpol was in on the whole mission, but I've been listening out for information about Lola since the day she disappeared. Eighteen months ago there was talk on the Refugee Highway network that a French-Iranian gal who had been kidnapped had managed to escape from her captors and was traveling from Iran into Turkey on the same path that Rasa's family took in 2005. I wondered if it could be Lola."

He pauses, but I'm too overcome to say anything.

"Hamid is the one who let me know that she'd arrived in Linz. But Caro, the authorities were adamant that any leak would put her in even greater danger than she already faced. And I found out by coincidence, Caro. Because of my connections with refugees. I kept quiet. And you were in no shape to know anything, even after she escaped and was safe in Linz."

I still don't respond.

"If you'd known, would you have sat back and kept your mouth closed and waited till you were told it was safe? Forgive me, but I couldn't trust you not to rush headlong into disaster. A lot of people could have gotten hurt."

I'm furious at his words . . . but I know he is absolutely right.

"And now, Caroline, you have *got* to keep quiet." I have rarely heard such intensity in Stephen's voice. "Let Interpol do the work. I don't know what they're planning, but at least I know, and now you do too, that Lola is safe."

"She's in hiding. But I have heard that Khalid is back in Europe and being followed. When he is apprehended, then Lola will be free to come home. . . . But you must keep the news for yourself, Caroline. Say nothing. Not to your parents or brother or sister. We cannot be too careful."

I force myself not to blurt out the news I've heard from Jean-Claude.

"I'm serious, Caroline, when I say that that information is none of your business. It's really none of mine either. We must keep quiet."

I'm sniffing and swiping at tears, so many different emotions boiling up as Stephen says, "I should have told you when I realized you'd be meeting up with Rasa on the Camino. But . . ."

"But you didn't trust me to keep my big mouth shut. You didn't trust me to stay put and not go running off into danger."

"Something like that."

I long for a drink, for something to relieve my colliding emotions. I take several deep breaths. In and out. In and out. At last

I whisper, "Thank you, Stephen. Thank you for not trusting me. You were right."

But when Tracie calls me a few minutes later, I bark out, "Did you know too?"

"No. I promise I didn't know anything recent about Lola. I don't ask Stephen questions about his involvement with refugees, Caro. A careless word could be dangerous to a lot of people—including him." She isn't finished. "Your brother loves you, Caroline. He has worried about you and cried over you for so long. He tries his best to protect you."

Deep breath. I know everything they have said is true. My anger starts to melt into remorse. "I just keep screwing everything up."

"You're wrong, Caro. You're doing great now. You've been making good decisions. You're sober."

In a tiny voice I ask, "Do you remember when you told me about God pursuing me?"

"Oh, yeah, I remember. It didn't go over too well."

"True. But it's happening again, Trace." I explain the series of coincidences that aren't simple coincidences, ending with everything I have learned about Lola and Bastien's connection with Khalid. "It scares me, and it makes me afraid and angry. I'm trying to put up a good fight, but it's hard."

"You don't have to fight against Him anymore if you don't want to, Caroline. I never want you to give in to alcohol, but giving in to God would feel like a huge relief. I promise."

"I'm not ready yet. But at least right now I don't want to strangle Stephen. I'm still mad, but I'm grateful for what he's been doing."

"Sometime you might want to let him know that."

She's right, of course. But not yet. After I tell Tracie good-bye, I head back inside and go to bed.

The next morning, our last on the Camino, I'm hefting my backpack onto my very sunburned shoulders when my cell rings.

"*Allô*, dear Caroline, it's Jean-Claude. I hope I am not disturbing you."

"Jean-Claude!" I'm surprised to hear from him. "No, you're not disturbing me." I set down the backpack and sit on the cot in our room.

"We've had news. Khalid was apprehended yesterday."

Yes!

"Unfortunately, he resisted arrest and was killed while trying to escape."

My mind is reeling. *Khalid is dead. Lola is alive.*

"Unfortunate! I'm glad he's dead!"

"Yes. I too am thankful." Silence. "So now my daughter, my precious Lola . . ." His voice breaks. "*Pardon* . . ."

Tears pool in my eyes. "Lola is alive and Khalid is dead, so that means . . ."

"*Oui*, that means she is safe, and she will be able to come home soon."

"Oh, Jean-Claude." Now I'm crying, crying tears of joy. "When?"

"I'll call you again when I know the date. Maybe next week."

"Jean-Claude! That is such wonderful news! Thank you! *Merci!*"

I'm about to head down to breakfast. I haven't even had time to share this news with Rasa and Bobby and Abbie when I receive a text from Bastien.

Bonjour, my dear Caro. How is your Camino going? It has been over two weeks since we parted, and I haven't stopped thinking of you. I will be back in Lourmarin briefly next week. Perhaps we can meet again. Let me know. Bises, Bastien

I can practically feel that cynical smile vibrating through the phone. *Yeah, right, you want to know.* My heart starts ramming in my chest, and I can't tell if it's lust or fear. Of course he'll be back next week. That makes perfect sense. Horribly perfect sense.

I call Jean-Claude back, blubbering about the text from Bastien. "I'm thankful that Khalid's dead, but I think Bastien has been involved with Khalid all along! You think so too. I'm still so afraid for Lola."

I remind Jean-Claude of all the times when I had seen Bastien in the last seven years. "Do you think he's been using me, Jean-Claude?"

Silence. For several eternally long seconds. I hear him sigh over the phone. "Yes, I am so sorry, Caroline." A long pause. "When you came to see me, when you told me about these rendezvous with Bastien, I was greatly disturbed. I told the police—you know, Interpol. They are the ones who have been tracking Khalid for these many years. They do not say things in black and white, you know? They are undercover. They are like spies. But they were not surprised to hear about Bastien. They have been watching out for him too."

He waits a moment before adding, "But the French police have an agent bringing Lola back to Lourmarin. If Bastien is there, he'll be apprehended."

I want him to be apprehended. Caught. Killed? *No, no! Please don't let it be true, Bastien!*

"What should I do, Jean-Claude? Bastien wants to meet me."

I hear the worry in Jean-Claude's voice. "You don't answer him. I will tell the police about this text from Bastien. Not you. You tell no one about this. About Bastien. You let Interpol, the police, you let them figure it. Okay, my dear Caro?"

When I am silent, he speaks again, his voice raspy with emotion. "Caroline, you must leave him alone. No more helping Lola. She's coming. All is well. You do nothing."

I'm still silent.

"You are like my second daughter. I won't have anything happen to you. I am getting my first daughter back. And I will have you both eating pistachios on my front porch. You understand? You stay away from that Bastien. Far away!"

Finally I say, "Okay, Jean-Claude. *Bien sûr.* I promise I won't say anything. I'll wait. And then, you'll tell me when Lola is in Lourmarin. Safe."

"*Oui, ma Chérie.* It will be a beautiful reunion."

I tell him good-bye and then click back on Bastien's text.

Vengeance. Love. Hate. I want to watch when the police handcuff Bastien while I yell the truth, the whole truth in his face.

Then it slams into me. Bastien has tried to tell me the truth. I swallow hard.

I'm not a safe bet. It was a mistake. . . .

He tried to tell me again and again and again. *I don't want to see you sad, Caro. You're not a guilty woman. Let it go!*

I bury my face in my hands and begin to weep. *This is why you wouldn't continue our romance, isn't it, Bastien? This is the mistake you were referring to. Oh, Bastien!*

It takes me a while to dry my eyes. I go to the shared bathroom and splash cold water on my face. I retrieve my backpack and head to breakfast, but I know I won't be able to keep anything down. My stomach roils. Khalid may be dead, but Bastien is alive and well and coming back to Lourmarin. I shudder. I've lost Bastien, and I'm suddenly terrified I'm going to lose Lola again too.

CHAPTER

23

ABBIE

Before the trip I read that pilgrims often bring a small rock or stone from their home. It represents a burden they've been carrying or a loved one they are grieving or a sin for which they're doing penance. At some point on the Camino, they lay down that stone. The most popular place is at the Cruz de Ferro in Spain, the highest point on the Camino Frances. But we aren't going to Spain, so this last day on our Camino will be the place we leave our stones.

I chose my stone the day after I invited myself to walk the Camino, and made sure the others knew about the tradition too. Mine is a small, smooth stone I picked up from the banks of the Chattahoochee River. It's been tucked in the bottom of my backpack.

We're only a few kilometers outside Conques, where we'll spend our last night together, when we come upon another cross. We're standing together at the top of a pine-covered incline, looking down on the village that lies in the mist below, with the ancient church towering over the rest of the city. This village has changed very little since the Middle Ages, with centuries-old cobbled streets in the old part of town. It's the perfect place to end our journey.

As soon as we see this cross, we know it's where we'll lay down our stones.

The cross is thick, made of basalt stone, with patches of moss clinging to the underside. It's about two feet high, planted beside the well-trod path, surrounded by piles of rocks and stones and many other things too. Pilgrims have left boots and poles and notes and T-shirts and scalloped shells.

It feels like a holy moment as we silently stare at the stack of remembrances.

Then we fish through our packs. Caroline nudges me to go first.

I stand before the cross with its silent confessions. Everything the stone in my hand represented to me a month ago has taken on a new, stronger importance: the burden of my marriage, of my control, of my emotions; the burden of Abbie doing life Abbie's way; the burden of grief I carried for so long for Miss Abigail; the burden of fear. All these things, not just one.

I think it's ironic that I easily locate this very plain, small stone in the bottom of my pack, undisturbed by everything I've lived on the Camino, while the cross-stitch I've spent hundreds of hours constructing is lost. I hesitate, feeling the weight and shape of the stone in my hand. When I set it down on one of the piles surrounding the simple stone cross, it feels again like I'm lightening my load. Or, more precisely, setting down this stone symbolizes what I've been doing little by little on the Camino. It's like a prayer and a promise. I whisper, "Here You go, Lord."

CARO

Early this morning Abbie reminded me about the stone. Mine is a little black pebble I plucked from Bastien's driveway before I took the train to Le Puy just ten days ago. It had always been my plan to let him go, ever since I flew back to France. Get whatever new information about Lola he had to share and tell him good-bye. For good.

But so much has happened in the last few weeks. So many hard and good and scary and confusing things—coincidences— have occurred. I feel deep grief and anger and fear as I hold this helpless pebble in my hand. I'm not sure if I *can* let it go, because the real weight is on myself. The guilt that has hung around my neck for all these years, the anger too. Yes, I'm letting go of Bastien, but in the same way, I'm letting go of punishing myself again and again.

I'm letting it go with no assurance of a happy outcome.

And I am getting rid of my anger at a God I said I didn't believe in.

I walk up to that piece of carved stone, get on my knees, and lay down my rock at the foot of the cross. I find the moment deeply ironic. For years I've reacted with repulsion to that ex- pression, "Lay down your burden at the foot of the cross." Ste- phen said it, Tracie said it, my mom said it too. And every time I'd think, *If only these well-intentioned people could hear how silly and trite that phrase sounds, they'd find another idiom.*

But as I place my little black pebble on the pile, nothing feels trite or silly. It feels real. There on my knees with the other stones imprinting themselves in my flesh, I say in my mind, *I give up, God. I give up! I give in to Your constant pursuit of me for all these years. Ever since Stephen and Mom, You know, ever since they "found You" and tried to convince me*

*that You're real. Okay, so I'm telling You, "Have Your way!"
But You better be real, because I'm so afraid I'll screw things
up again. Yes, I'm afraid of Bastien, and I'm afraid for Lola.
But most of all, God, I'm afraid of myself.*

That is all I can manage, but when I get up off my knees,
Abbie and Rasa and Bobby come around me in a group hug.
Not a word, just this deeply spiritual touching of shoulder to
shoulder and soul to soul.

And I know somewhere in my spirit that everything that has
happened on this Camino has been preparing me for whatever
will happen next. That is the mystery that Rasa has danced
before us; that is the mystery that Abbie has run and walked
and crawled toward these past ten days. That is the mystery
for me.

BOBBY

I didn't bring a stone to carry on the Camino, and I see I'm not
the only pilgrim with other ideas. There are photos of loved
ones, flags, a worn-through boot. Several rocks have messages
written on them. There are pieces of paper intermingled, held
there against the rain and the wind by other pilgrims' stones.

It reminds me of what the Bible says about carrying each
other's burdens. Staring at the scraps of paper under the stones,
I realize I need other people not only to help me carry my burdens, but also to help me let them go.

I have always known what I would lay down at this cross,
ever since I read about the Camino, long before Mom, wanting us to do everything just right, texted me to bring a stone.
I open my sketch pad and carefully rip out the drawing of the
women bent over their needlework at the House of Hope. One

lone refugee looks up at me with an expression of love on her face—Anna's face.

"Ripping carefully" is a paradox. When Anna died, my heart was ripped in two even as I gently held the memory of her in my heart.

I take the sheet of paper and lay stone upon stone on top of it in concentric circles, until all that is visible is Anna's beautiful face. Then I find one more stone and set it in the center, so even that disappears.

Rasa goes last. The rock in her hand has jagged edges and barely fits in her small palm. She stares at it and then at the three of us.

"This rock came from the Refugee Highway. Lola gave it to me when we became friends. It is ugly and heavy. It cuts you if you hold it too tightly."

She balances the rock on her palm. "I have been holding tightly to my expectations of God. I have always known what God wants of me, but somewhere I stopped listening to the mystery. I started trusting in myself. Now I will embrace mystery again. I will let go of the fear of what I don't understand. I will also lay down the need to take care of other refugees. I will try more to do it for God." She closes her fist over the stone.

"And sometimes I will choose not to take on their burdens, and that will be for God too. I will not hold to my trauma and theirs. Today, I will lay down these things with my stone. I know it is only a symbol, and if the fear comes back, I will remember what I have done here, and it will be a balm for my soul."

We leave the cross and walk silently for a kilometer or two, each of us processing and admiring the view from way up on high. We slowly make our way down into Conques. The half-timbered structures, remarkably intact, transport us back to

Medieval times. A magnificent basilica dominates the center of town, dwarfing the few pilgrims walking to the site.

Mom stops us in front of it and says, "This is the Abbaye de Sainte-Foye, everyone. We'll be staying here tonight."

"In the church?"

"In the adjoining *hôtellerie*. And we won't be alone. Over sixty other pilgrims will be here."

A feeling of pride and accomplishment wells up inside me. Mom has walked two hundred kilometers, the rest of us a bit less. It feels like the village is welcoming us. Its ancient stones are saying, *Well done, pilgrims. Well done.*

ABBIE

We've finished the evening meal in the spacious refectory, and dozens of pilgrims are lingering over coffee and a simple dessert of fruit and yogurt. It's time to say our good-byes, as many of us have come to the end of our Camino. The Washington Women head back to the States tomorrow. Bobby and Rasa are taking the morning train back to Linz, back to Lola. And if all goes according to plan, in less than a week Lola will be going home to her father, and Caroline will be there to greet her too.

A man hobbles into the dining hall, one leg in a cast, his pack slung over his shoulder as he leans on his crutch. He glances around the room and in a booming voice announces, "I'm looking for a woman."

Brenda winks at me and says under her breath, "Isn't that always the case?"

The man, probably midforties, ruggedly handsome with a dark blond beard that matches his thick hair, continues talking loudly. "I've been in a hospital bed for the last few days. I got caught in the downpour several days ago and slipped down a very long and rocky trail."

"Oh yeah, we heard about you on the Camino forum," Jamie calls out. "You're the 'cute pilgrim with the broken leg.'"

"Calvin!" A middle-aged lady on the far side of the refectory hops up and rushes over. "You poor thing!"

Calvin blushes furiously as the woman gives him a hug.

"We've been asking around about you," another woman calls out. "We haven't seen anything else about you on the forum."

"I lost my phone when I fell," he replies. "Another pilgrim found it and returned it to me at the hospital. But the reason I'm here is to find a woman who lost"—he squints at his phone—"a pink-and-green Vera Bradley pouch that holds an amazing cross-stitch."

I let out a gasp.

"It says she'll be staying at the Abbey of Sainte-Foye in Conques tonight. Is she here?" He fishes a black plastic garbage bag out of his pack.

I stand up and walk across the room on wobbly legs, like I'm receiving an unexpected award. "It's me," I manage to say. "I'm that woman."

"I got that text from a fellow pilgrim the evening after you lost it," he says. "I was right near the area, so I backtracked a little, and I found the pouch. It had fallen way down in a crevice." He hands me the trash bag. "Here you go."

I take it in slow motion and thrust my hand down inside, pulling out the pink-and-green pouch. It's filthy and waterlogged. Trembling, I unroll it. It's empty. I look at him like he's played a sick joke on me, but he quickly laughs.

"I took it out of the pouch—which, as you can see, was mud caked and soaking wet. But the rain hadn't seeped through. The cross-stitch was well protected." He gives me a wink, and my face catches fire. "It's in there."

I reach back inside the trash bag and pull out my canvas, neatly folded inside the Ziploc freezer bag. I pull open the seal, still feeling as though I'm in a dream. When I hold up the cross-stitch all the pilgrims in the room, over sixty of them, start cheering wildly. They burst into applause while I burst into tears.

It takes me a long time to find my voice. "Thank you, Calvin," I manage. I run my hand over the stitches, staring at Bill's name and the boys' cameos and the Huguenot cross. "I can't believe it. I'd given up hope. I don't know what to say. Thank you!"

I find that I'm holding on to this rugged stranger, crying and hugging him, while pilgrims snap photos with their phones and the clapping continues.

Calvin grins. "What's the Camino for but to bring people together?"

I can almost hear Laurent saying the same thing way back in Le Puy, what seems like years ago.

I do manage to ask one question. "Did you break your leg trying to get the cross-stitch?"

He laughs again. "No, no. I knew I was around the area where it had been lost, so I did a bit of scrounging in the crevices, and sure enough, it was there. I was pretty proud of myself." He winks again. "But as you well know, that trail keeps going downhill steeply for several more kilometers. The storm turned brutal, and I took a tumble. I'll spare you the gory details."

"How horrible," I squeak out.

He shrugs. "Anyway, the way the text was written, it sounded like something worth finding. And dang! I'd say so. I didn't dare take it out of the bag. Who's it for?"

I clear my throat. "My husband. For his fiftieth birthday."

"Lucky guy," he says, with one arm braced on the crutch and the other around me. I gather he's enjoying every minute of the attention.

Lucky guy.

Calvin continues his story. "Anyway, I didn't get all the other texts right away because, as I said, my phone got lost. But once I got my phone back and the hospital released me, I saw the posting of the places you'd be staying and the dates. I'm glad I found you."

I finally let go of him and back away, tears streaming down my face. "Me too. I can't begin to tell you how much this means."

The pilgrims start cheering again, and Barb says, "Bring out the champagne. This calls for a celebration!"

I spend the next hour telling my story and showing off the cross-stitch. Thank goodness Bill isn't on social media or he would see how his fiftieth birthday surprise is lighting up Instagram and Pinterest and Facebook and Twitter.

In the midst of the excitement, I keep thinking, *I've let him go, Lord. But You're letting me keep a part of him.*

We're still celebrating, drinking champagne from little glass goblets the monks have happily provided, when one of them announces it's time for vespers. Twenty or thirty of us go into a little chapel. It has ancient stones, worn wooden pews, and a simple stained-glass window. A candle is burning on a table at the front.

"Welcome, again," a monk says in French. Caroline stands beside him, translating into English. "What a lovely way to end this Camino with something that was lost being found." He glances over at me and the cross-stitch, which I have not let go of since I first plucked it out of the Ziploc bag.

"It's the perfect metaphor for what the Camino does for many of us. It helps us find ourselves again. What we're trying to offer here at the abbey is a safe place for you pilgrims to mentally and emotionally unpack your experiences, and what you've found. Whether ending your Camino here or continuing on, may you lay your burden down and come sit with Jesus for a while.

"I'd like to read the Pilgrim's Blessing that many of you heard as you began your walk. 'Almighty God, You never stop showing Your goodness to those who love You, and You let Yourself be found by those who seek You; show Your favor to your pilgrims as they pursue their pilgrimage and guide their path according to Your will. Be to them a shade in the heat of the day, a light in the darkness of the night, a relief in the midst of their fatigue, so that they can happily finish their journey under Your protection. Through Jesus Christ, our Lord. Amen.' I hope this has been your experience."

Heads nod all around the room.

The monk waits a moment and then adds, "Here is another blessing for the end of your Camino. 'May the Lord Christ go with you wherever He may send you, guide you through the wilderness, protect you through the storm. May He bring you home rejoicing at the wonders He has shown you. May He bring you home rejoicing once again into our doors.'"

He opens up the gathering to a time of sharing for the pilgrims, but I am too overcome to trust my voice. I sit with the cross-stitch across my lap, fingering its nubby surface, and listen as, one after another, pilgrims share their stories. And then it's Bobby who is talking.

"I came on the Camino for a couple of reasons. To be honest, it was mostly to spend time with this beautiful girl I'd met just weeks before. I had a huge crush on her, but I knew she wouldn't come with me alone." He's holding Rasa's hand, and the pilgrims seated around them chuckle.

"Fortunately my mom insisted on coming along to be a chaperone." More chuckles. "These eight days have shown me a lot about myself, but they've also shown me how courageous my mother is. She's strong, and she has a great heart. She's been through a lot and she just keeps going. And now she's even gotten her crazy cross-stitch back after we'd lost all hope of ever seeing it again. It's like that sometimes, isn't it? You have to let go of something before you can really have it?"

Of course most of the people in the room don't know the half of it, but he and I know exactly what he means. "I'm proud of you, Mom," he finishes.

The look of love in his eyes melts my heart.

I'm too emotional to make sense, but I take a turn, babbling about loss and giving up and breathing and waiting and trusting, and I think I say it right.

The celebratory mood continues after we leave the chapel, spilling out into the starry night, delighting in God's good gifts of life on the Camino: loss and love, faith and fellowship, pain and perseverance, and a handful of miracles along the way.

CHAPTER
24

CARO

We're all on a type of spiritual high after Abbie's cross-stitch is returned. I feel that high mixed with a sense of dread that has buried itself deep in my gut. Lola will be coming back home to Lourmarin soon, but so will Bastien. Jean-Claude has forbidden me from telling anyone else about their connection, so I can't say to Bobby or Rasa or Abbie what I know. Or what I fear.

Instead I hold on to Rasa a little longer, a little more tightly, as I hug her good-bye, my throat thick with emotion. "You take care of Lola, Rasa, until she leaves. And tell her I'll be waiting when she arrives home."

Rasa's arms are equally tight around my shoulders as she whispers in my ear, "God has been with Lola for all these years, Caro. He will not fail her now. She has seen His faithfulness and so have I." She backs away slightly, arms extended, looking up at me with her penetrating eyes. "Remember your stone and the cross. And I will trust Isa for you until you can trust Him yourself."

As I watch the train pull out of the station, I raise my arm and wave, tears stinging my eyes.

ABBIE

I hug Bobby and Rasa good-bye and watch them board the train. The feeling of lightness leaves, but I refuse to grab him back. I will respect what I have said. I will do the letting go.

Caroline has invited me to spend a few days with her in Lourmarin, and I agree. I can tell that she doesn't want me to leave. She seems a little worried, but when I ask her what's the matter she just says, "It's hard. You know, everything I've let go."

But I'm grateful for her invitation, because I'm not ready to be alone yet either. And I still don't know what I'm doing next. I told Bill not to worry, but the prospect of actually being all alone suddenly scares me.

As I admire the lavender fields and lazy sunflowers nodding at me on our way to Lourmarin, I'm overwhelmed with a sense of gratitude for the returned cross-stitch. Once again it sits in my lap, and I finger it like a rosary, thanking God again and again for the completely unexpected gift of its return.

An unexpected gift. That has been the Camino. So many unexpected gifts. When I voice that thought, Caro nods.

"I want to concentrate on the things given to me during my Camino instead of all the things that have been taken away. I want to keep processing it all."

"Yes. I so agree with you. In many ways we're both starting over, aren't we?"

She nods, and we make the rest of the trip in a comfortable silence.

The next morning we are sitting on the back terrace of her French country farmhouse, and I'm smothering a fresh baguette with butter and homemade jelly when my phone pings. I'd texted Bobby in the middle of the night, saying, *Just let me know when y'all arrive safely in Linz.*

Now I look down at the screen, and staring back at me is a photo of Rasa and another young woman fiercely hugging each other. I recognize her from Bobby's sketch. Lola. Another photo appears, a selfie of Bobby beside the girls, all of them smiling.

I slide the phone across the table to Caroline. She stares at the screen for a long time, her face a kaleidoscope of emotions.

After a few minutes she reaches across the table and grasps my hand. In her eyes I see traces of hope.

"Are there any churches around here?" I ask a little while later. "With so much to be thankful for, I'd like to do some of my thanking in a church."

She gives me a funny look. "Well, there's a Catholic church in every village. But I think there's one of your kind too." She shrugs. "I know Stephen and Tracie and Mom attend what they call a 'fellowship' in Aix when they're here."

I look up "evangelical churches in Aix" on my phone and find several. When I show them to Caroline, she says, "It's that one. *Le Phare.* The Lighthouse."

"Okay, I'll stay in Lourmarin until Sunday. I'd like to go to this church."

"Sounds good."

"But I do have one request. Would you mind going with me?"

Caroline looks almost relieved. "Sure. I'll go."

On Sunday morning we're running late, but we find the little church tucked inside a storefront building on a cobbled street in the old part of the city. Before my feet even cross the threshold,

I feel the chills, the quickening in my heart—or is it my soul? The tears begin to flow.

A young man about Bobby's age is strumming on a guitar and a girl, no more than fifteen or sixteen, is trilling along on the flute. And the congregation—what a heavy word for the thirty or so adults and almost that many children—is singing a song that I recognize from my junior year abroad.

I'd come to France expecting to fit in like a native. I'd studied the language since high school, I'd studied the history, the culture. But to my great consternation, my accent never sounded French, but pure Georgia, and I cringed with anger every time someone laughed good-naturedly at my mistakes. Anger at them, but really anger at me! And everything about France was slower, and I had never learned how to do slow. I was in a hurry.

Then we came into the little church and sang this song that comes from Psalm 116: "*J'aime l'Eternel, car Il entend ma voix* . . . I love the Lord for He has heard my voice . . ."

The young pastor began to preach simply and eloquently how that psalm had become his favorite.

He told us of the unexpected death of his mother, his wife's second miscarriage, the French Minister of Culture insinuating that all evangelical churches are cults, the consequent fear on many students' faces as they told him they wouldn't be coming back to the church . . .

And then he encountered the Lord in this psalm. *"It's all about my weakness and the Lord's strength,"* he'd said. *"Again and again the psalmist praises the Lord, yes, but why or how? It is always linked to the psalmist's confession of his own weakness. He is weak; he can't do it on his own; but the Lord . . ."*

His words had pierced me to the core. I was always trying so hard to be perfect, to be strong. And as the whole congregation read the psalm aloud, I had let go. "I love You, Lord," I said, over and over again in French. I relaxed, moved forward, in France and in my life back in the States. That experience had been real. . . .

When I came home from France and told Miss Abigail about that encounter with God, she rested her frail hand on my young one and said, "Onion layers, Abbie girl. It's like onion layers. Our gracious Lord peels away the layers to draw us ever closer to His heart."

Now those memories wash over me, and my tears begin to flow. Twenty-five years, and I have to learn the same painful lesson all over again?

Onion layers. Ah, yes.

Caro touches my arm and mouths, "Are you okay?"

And I nod yes and shake my head no, because both are true. Yes, I'm okay, more than okay as layers of blood, sweat, and tears begin to slip off my exhausted shoulders—not only from the Camino, but from years and years of trying so hard. But no, I'm not okay. Losing that weight feels like a death— letting it fall away is killing me. Diana and I had talked about this. Dying to something old, a pattern that is comfortable in its dysfunction, so that one can move to a different system, a new freedom.

"It will feel like death at first. But stay with it. It is life. A new beginning."

When the service ends, I escape out the back of the room. "I'll meet you at the house," I tell a mystified Caro. "Please stay if you want." Because as much as I need to be alone, I see that Caro needs to be there with these people.

I walk for an hour or two in the *veille ville* of Aix-en-Provence, soaking in the beginning of fall in the open market. A vendor is roasting chestnuts on an open fire and handing them out in newspaper cones to delighted tourists. I buy a cone for myself and meander through the cobbled streets, then return to the *marché* to purchase two long-stemmed sunflowers.

I get a taxi back to Lourmarin, and as I step out in front of Caroline's home, I glance across the street to Bastien's house. I pick up a black pebble from the driveway and turn it over again and again in my hand.

Poor Caroline. One chance meeting, one weekend fling had unraveled her life for seven years. But maybe she's on the way to wholeness. I picture her on her knees before that moss-covered cross on the Camino and whisper a prayer for her.

Back in her house, I find a vase for the sunflowers and then I sink into a dark green leather armchair. Almost unconsciously, I've retrieved the cross-stitch and it's lying across my lap once again. I stare at it with an awed reverence. One little rectangle is unstitched. The space I saved to stitch the lighthouse in La Rochelle. I feel a quickening in my gut.

The Lighthouse. *Le Phare.* God has winked at me again.

I've found good pictures of the lighthouse online, but I won't stitch it while I'm here. As I stare at the canvas, I know suddenly what I need to do next, what will move me forward. I'll go to La Rochelle and Ile de Ré. Alone. I don't know how long I'll stay. I will entrust Bobby and Jason and Bill and Mama and Daddy and Caro and Rasa and everyone else, entrust them all to God's care, and then I'll step out on my own and see what comes.

Yes, that is it. That little word. *Trust.*

I will let trust replace the fear that has gripped my soul for so long. I will open my hands again and again and again and trust God with the lives of those I love the most.

And my own life too.

Do I expect God to appear on the path with explicit directions for the rest of my life? No. I honestly have no idea what I will do except go to that ancient Huguenot stronghold. But

I know, way down deep, that this knowledge is all I need for now.

CARO

Abbie cries, as though something is bubbling up out of her soul, throughout most of the church service. Well, *service* is a little too formal. But it's genuine, heartfelt. A bunch of students and young couples with kids and some scattered gray heads all crammed into an ancient storefront that in the Middle Ages probably once held huge barrels of aging wine and marauders dancing under the vaulted ceilings.

Afterward she heads back to our house, but I stay for an Agape meal. It's not that I was moved by the singing or the message, but because I bumped into a woman from Lourmarin, Martine, and she invites me to stay.

We stand in line with porcelain plates and real silverware, waiting to serve ourselves lunch from a table laden with home-made salads and fresh meat and sausages and bread and cheeses. The French know how to do a potluck.

"I had no idea you attended this church," I say to Martine.

"Yes, I've been attending Le Phare for quite some time. Your mother is the one who introduced me to this fellowship years ago."

That makes sense. "Years? How many years?"

She frowns for a moment, thinks. "Oh, that's easy. Since the year I became a believer. Two thousand eleven." She cocks her head. "You know it was your brother's fault, don't you?"

I must look as shocked as I feel.

She laughs. "Just kidding, dear. But Stephen came to Lour-marin for a month with his wife—that cute little Tracie. First time I met her. She couldn't speak a word of French. I saw them last summer—and their darling girls . . ."

But I don't want to talk about Stephen and his family. "You came to this church in 2011." I lower my voice. "Did Malika and Lola ever come here?" I whisper.

Martine's countenance changes from excitement to compassion, and she reaches for my hand. "Oh, that's right, Caroline. You were so close." She takes a breath and looks off, as if she can see through the weathered stones into the cobbled streets beyond. "No, they never attended the church. Their conversion was so recent, and then with what happened . . ."

I grab her hands. "But you knew they had converted?"

"Yes, yes, of course. We'd been meeting together with Stephen, and after he left we continued studying the Bible." She smiles. "If you could call it that. I was so new to the faith myself—it was the blind leading the blind. And then your mother introduced us to the pastor here, and he answered questions . . ." She shrugs. "It was a sweet, intense time for them. And me." She looks down quickly. "Before the disappearance." Her voice is heavy with sorrow.

"Did they ever hint at anything? Anything at all that would cause suspicion?"

Martine takes my hand. "It was a long time ago, my dear."

I feel a thud in my heart. But then she continues. "And I remember every detail in living color. But let's not discuss it here, Caroline. Come see me sometime, and we'll talk."

I want to talk *now*. Right now. Martine must see the urgency in my eyes, because she nods. "I'll be home later this afternoon if you'd like to stop by."

We're sitting on Martine's front porch at a little bistro table. I'm sipping chilled grape juice and cracking open pistachios and popping them into my mouth almost obsessively. I feel the nervous energy surging through me the longer she talks.

"Your mother and I had probably been getting together for three or four months when Malika and Lola came over, both beaming, to announce their conversion. I rejoiced, we all rejoiced, quietly."

Rejoice. *What an old word*, I think.

"At the same time they looked worried. When I probed, Malika explained about her nephew—she feared repercussions for her family in Iran if he heard about it. So they kept things very hush-hush. I didn't get alarmed until the new neighbor started hanging around. He seemed too friendly, too nosy with Jean-Claude."

"New neighbor?" I say in a small voice.

"Yes. His house was just across from yours. I can't remember his name."

I swallow.

"I think Jean-Claude knew him a little from work. But that summer, when he moved into the village, he started spending time at their house, and Malika told me she felt like he was intentionally invading their privacy."

"Did she know why?" I manage to squeak out.

"Not at first. But then she remembered having seen him with her nephew one time a year or so earlier in Aix, and she thought it was strange that they knew each other. And then Malika was murdered and Lola disappeared."

"Did you tell the police?"

She fiddles with her necklace. "I told them about the nephew knowing the neighbor and Malika's fear. I mentioned his frequent visits, but I have no idea if he was questioned."

I want to throw up. I excuse myself, and I do throw up— barely making it to the bathroom. Everything, every last thing I have feared is true. Bastien was part of the plan for the kidnapping and murder and for keeping me away!

When I finally come back out, Martine sees my obvious disarray. "I'm sorry to upset you, Caroline, to bring up the whole sordid thing again. I don't suppose you know anything more?"

"For years all I knew was that they found Malika's body and never heard a word from Lola, so she was presumed dead too."

Don't say anything else. Keep your mouth shut!

"Yes, and Jean-Claude sold that beautiful property and moved away. We kept up for the first few years, but then . . ."

"Yes, my parents too. But it was too painful for Jean-Claude, and I think eventually they stopped calling or writing."

"I wonder where he lives now."

I feel my face turn hot, but I don't say a thing. I just shrug. Surely Martine can see through my façade. But she says nothing. We talk for a few more minutes. All I want is to get back to the house.

When I step inside, Abbie announces, "I know what I'm doing next. I'm going to La Rochelle."

"What?"

"Where I was planning to take Bill for his birthday. But I'm going alone. I'm leaving tomorrow morning. I've reserved an Airbnb. It's all set up."

"Please don't leave yet," I blurt out. I need her here. I don't want to be left alone.

Abbie looks at me—first annoyed, then quizzical. "What do you mean?" And before I can answer, she murmurs, "You look awful. Did something happen at church?"

So I launch into my story about my afternoon with Martine. I don't even realize I'm clutching her until she takes my hand off her shoulder and leads me inside, where I collapse onto the leather sofa.

I fight off the urge for a drink for the rest of the day, making small talk with Abbie, walking back to the Fourcades' old house, standing in front of Bastien's place and letting the tears run down my cheeks. The desire to see him one last time is stronger than any temptation to drink I've had since I've been sober. I have to see him. I *have* to!

So I get out my phone and instead of calling Tracie or finding Abbie, I send a text.

Ciao, Bastien! The Camino has been amazing. I'm back in Lourmarin. I'd love to see you and tell you all about it. Let me know what works for you.

His text comes back almost immediately.

Great! Let's meet at our café at noon on Tuesday. Looking forward to being with you, dear Caro!

I stare at those words, my palms sweaty, my temples throbbing, my throat dry. What in the world have I just done?

Then I call Jean-Claude, in tears. "I have to see him again, Jean-Claude. I have to!"

"Non! Impossible!"

"But I've already set it up. On Tuesday."

Jean-Claude, the gentlest Frenchman I've ever known, lets out a long string of curse words. I can practically feel him shaking me by the shoulders, his voice is so distraught. I hang up the phone.

When Jean-Claude calls me back fifteen minutes later, he's angry. "You are unwise, Caroline. I have told the police. They will have a plainclothes agent there, watching. If you go. But don't go. Please don't go."

CHAPTER

25

BOBBY

I've been here in Paris with Jean-Paul for a week now. He lives in this awesome apartment not far from the Champs-Elysée. It has eighteenth-century architecture that Granddad would love, high ceilings, and lots of curlicues. I should know the real terminology; we studied it in art history. Jean-Paul insisted that I live here this semester. It's just him and his wife, Michèle, and their collie, Raphael, in this huge apartment, twelve rooms with floor-to-ceiling windows. I can see the top of the Arc de Triomphe from my bedroom.

That first day, when I told him about my dream of studying in Linz, he said, "Not yet. Stay here with me until Christmas. We'll work up a portfolio that you can submit to several top-notch schools. Including Linz," he added when he saw my scowl.

I really do want to get back to Linz.

I miss Rasa, of course. I told her good-bye seven days ago. Seven! But we talk on the phone every day. Swannee says, "Well, it's not exactly like the long-distance relationships we had way back when, with months-long anguished waiting between letters." But I can tell she thinks it's a good thing for Rasa and me to "have a little space, even if it's only geographic."

I think a lot about what I learned on the Camino, about being responsible. Or maybe about managing responsibility. I mean, I like helping people. It's the only thing that works besides my art. I'd rather be carrying two backpacks than just my own. I'd rather be listening to someone else's problems. But on the Camino, I realized that carrying too many packs can get awfully heavy.

When I covered Anna's face with those last stones, it wasn't to erase her memory. It wasn't to deny the excruciating pain of her death and the loss of her friendship. And it wasn't to forget or deny my depression and darkness either. No, it was to say I've grieved. It will always hurt, but Anna is Anna. I'm not going to drag her into every new relationship.

It's kind of hard to explain, but when I told Swannee about it, she said, "That's progress, Bobby. That's wisdom. That's freeing you even more to fly."

I text with Jason, and he tells me he won't be on the football team but he's trying out for basketball. I'm sure he'll make it. And I think he's learned a lesson or two. Dad is going to visit him soon, and he finally talked to Mom. He says everything is cool.

She's on some French island in the Atlantic with no one to control! She says she's gonna stay there for a while. Isn't that weird?

She's told me the same thing. She's been touring around La Rochelle and staying in a little Airbnb on the Ile de Ré nearby. And she sounds happy. Maybe she really is loosening her grip, as she'd pledged to do.

I'll see Rasa soon. She's coming to visit me in Paris. Rasa with me in Paris . . . I try to take that in. When we talked last night, she said she's still going to teach German, but she's stepping back from some other responsibilities at the House of Hope. I could hear relief in her voice.

The room is large and airy, about the size of my high school gym. The walls are white. Four black benches sit smack in the middle of the room, and four huge paintings adorn the four walls. To see my grandmother's *The Swan House* hanging opposite one of Monet's *Water Lilies* is a bit surreal.

Jean-Paul stands beside me. "You respect your grandmother a lot, don't you?"

"Very much. She's my inspiration and mentor. She's the one who encouraged me to pursue my dream of art during this gap year—and paid for lessons from you."

"She was my inspiration all those years ago too. We traipsed through Paris under siege and she heard my heart, my longing to paint and my fear of disappointing my very well-known parents."

Fear of disappointing well-known parents. I can relate to that. "I think she's got Parkinson's." I blurt this out, having kept it to myself for this first week with Jean-Paul. But standing in front of her painting, it seems like an appropriate time to mention it. "Is she too old to learn to paint as you've done? To learn to paint in a different way?"

Jean-Paul places his hand on my shoulder. "No. If she wants to learn a different method, she'll do it. When you find the art form you love, you cannot stop practicing it. You may have to get creative, but what are artists if not creative? No, she won't abandon her painting."

"Could you maybe give her a few lessons, tell her how you've traded brushes for fingers?"

He smiles. "It would be my great pleasure, Bobby."

We take selfies with Swannee's painting, and then Jean-Paul moves away, giving me space so that I can fully appreciate her work. This rendition of the Swan House is much more impressionistic than most of the others that Swannee has done. It's the kind of painting that you study, because Swannee hides things in her work.

The glory of the Italian manor house in the background is overshadowed by a series of cascading fountains in the foreground. They sit in between a horseshoe-shaped stairway at the front of the house. There are five tiers of round stone basins holding water, starting with the smallest at the top and descending in ever-larger circles as the water cascades from one basin to the next.

I stare, and then I get chills. I can almost hear the sound of the water falling from one basin to another and another. I can almost feel its spray on my face.

Now I know why my grandmother wanted me to see this painting. Not just for her. For me.

"I put it all in there for you, Bobby, the hidden treasures. I know you'll understand when you study it," she'd told me when I promised to visit this museum.

This is what Swannee wanted me to see—where her love affair began when she was a little girl. She lived next door to the Swan House. She would walk through the woods that separated her own mansion from this one. She would sit and listen for the trickle of the water spilling from one huge marble basin to the next and the next and she would dream and paint, dream and paint.

"Find your fountain," she'd said to me that day when we stood together in her backyard. She had found hers all those years ago, as a child, in the water that spilled in front of the Swan House, and it inspired everything she did.

Find your fountain.

I glance down to where I've set my sketch pad on the black leather bench. And I know. I found my inspiration as a child too. It's this sketch pad and a bunch of other ones that have followed me throughout my life, from the first one that Swannee gave me on my sixth birthday. They hold the inspiration that my eyes take in and my fingers translate into drawings. I don't need water. All I need is a pad and a pencil and my old soul.

I sit down on the bench and sketch myself sketching myself, if that makes sense, in this museum with Swannee's painting behind me. I smile at the layer upon layer of symbolism that my grandmother will understand. Then I hold up the sketch in one hand. With my phone in the other, I take a photo and send it to Swannee with a captain underneath. *Here's my fountain.*

We're Skyping now, standing in Jean-Paul's atelier, and Swannee is watching on the other side in the loft. Granddad is beside her in case she needs him to tap something on the keyboard (not that he can really see it) because Swannee's hands are messy, to put it mildly. She's finger-painting, as is Jean-Paul. He's giving her a video lesson, and she's smiling.

"In case I find I don't need a paintbrush anymore." Leave it to my grandmom to put a positive spin on it.

They look at each other, Jean-Paul and Swannee, with a deep understanding. I guess it's that way for artists. I think I'm beginning to understand it too. Life is beautiful, life is surprising, life hurts. And our job as artists, for as long as we're present in this life, is to use our gift to show the beauty and the surprises and the joy and the pain to others.

She was so pleased when I sent her the selfie with Jean-Paul and me and *The Swan House*, and the one of my fountain, as I called it. I know that what I really came to Europe for has happened. I came to find my fountain, my passion . . . to find myself. And I want Swannee to know without a shadow of a doubt that she has helped launch me into the life I want to live.

Jean-Paul leans in and points a vermillion-stained finger at the computer screen. "He's got it, Swannee, you were right. Bobby's got the talent; he's got the way of seeing, of perceiving, of translating life into beauty. We're going to get him a good portfolio, just you wait and see."

The way he talks, I know it's not flattery.

Swannee beams and gives a cerulean thumbs-up.

I'm going to work hard, very hard, during this gap year. And then I'll open my hands, like Mom keeps saying, like Mom is actually doing. I'll open them wide and fly.

CHAPTER
26

CARO

I can smell him coming before I actually see him, that waft of
Aramis drifting in the air. I freeze, not yet ready to meet him.
I am still the same foolish girl, running headlong into disas-
ter. But I've talked to Jean-Claude again and he assures me,
"Interpol has confirmed with me that their man will be there,
watching out."

Bastien appears as always, sexy, charming, a cynical smile on
his lips. He grasps my hands, pulls me close, and kisses each
cheek, right, left, right. "My dear Caro!"

If he notices the way my hands are trembling and moist, he
doesn't let on. Or is he holding on a little too tightly? Excitement, fear, and stark terror seize me.

I've been watching for the plainclothesman, but he's doing
his job well, totally inconspicuous. Why in the world did I set
this up?

We order pasta salads and Perrier, but I am much too distracted to eat. When at last I twirl my pasta around my fork

and bring it to my mouth, my hand shaking violently, Bastien reaches across the table and forces it down to the plate.

"No one's coming, Caro," he says.

I feel my face grow white. "What?"

"The police aren't coming."

I swallow hard and start to stand. But his hand is heavy on my arm.

"Look at me, Caro. Look at me."

I turn terrified eyes to him.

His are tender for a split second. Then all emotion is erased as he says, "The policeman isn't coming, Caro, because he's already here. I'm with the police."

I stare at him, confused, speechless.

I try to remove my hand, but Bastien is still holding on. Finally I yank it away, saying, "I don't believe you!" I try to stand and again he forces me down.

"Of course not. I do my job well. You couldn't know."

I'm desperately searching for a way to escape.

"Caro, I won't hurt you. Please. Just let me explain."

I'm watching the way his lips form the words, trying to find a piece of reality to hold on to. A hundred questions fly to the surface. Fury and fear and heartache collide, and I spit out, "You knew! That weekend! You knew about Malika!"

"Yes," he says.

"You knew about Lola!"

"Yes."

"You lied!" I yell, and those sitting near us at the café turn their heads. I lower my voice. "You've lied about everything; every single thing was a lie."

"Yes."

His one-syllable acknowledgment without shame or remorse or one blink of the eye catches me off guard. "Tell me then," I say, my voice shaky. "Tell me why." I take a gulp of Perrier too quickly and choke, my eyes filling with tears.

Bastien waits patiently for my coughing fit to subside. "Obviously, I'm not who I say I am. I've never been who I said I was."

"So who are you?" I can almost feel smoke billowing from my nostrils, the fury is so real.

He gives a long sigh. "Do you really want to know, Caro?"

I turn it over in my mind. Do I want to know? Do I want to learn that these last years were even worse than what I've lived or imagined?

He sees me hesitate; he almost reaches out to grab my hand, then he hesitates too.

"Who are you?" It comes out almost as a whimper, a pitiful, begging whimper. "Who are you?"

"I'm with the French police. I work for Interpol." This he confesses with a poker face. I've never seen Bastien with a poker face. His face holds charm, cynicism, laughter, seduction, even tenderness, but this face is blank, and in that moment, looking at that blank face, I know he's finally telling me the truth.

Still I refuse to admit it to myself or him. "No! No, that can't be true!"

He sits back in his chair, his arms crossed across his chest, staring at me as if we have only just met.

"That's impossible," I say.

"May I explain, Caroline?"

He's never called me Caroline, except for the first time we met. I've always been Caro. Hearing him pronounce my name in such a formal, disinterested way stabs me in the heart. I glare at him, trying to make my face hard and furious, when inside I'm falling apart.

"Please don't say anything else. I understand."

"It's not like in the movies, you know," he says. "I wasn't

planning on our relationship. I was to get to know you, keep you away from Lola's house for a few days. And then the sting would be over. We would have caught Khalid and you could go visit your friend." He isn't facing me. He's staring across the street, where a woman is walking her dog.

"That's how it was supposed to be. But then it all went wrong. Khalid showed up early. We lost connection with Malika. My instructions were to stay with you. And there you were, forced to be a witness to a gruesome murder and your friend's disappearance. Then the mission was changed, and they put me on it—for the long haul."

Ridiculously, I cover my ears with my hands. "*Arrête!* I get it, Bastien. You had to keep up the charade so I wouldn't suspect anything. You had to make up all those lies." I stand up. "I don't want to talk about it anymore."

"Please sit down, Caroline, and let me tell you the rest of the story."

I feel dizzy. "Not here." I will not fall apart. I will not. I still half expect him to pull out a gun and shoot me. But he doesn't. He helps me up, leaves a twenty-euro bill on the table beside our untouched food, and leads me down the cobbled side street. I vow to myself that I will not get in a car with him.

But we don't go to his car. We walk to a small park with a beautiful rose garden. The woman with the dog is across the way, a mother and two young children are sitting on the grass, sharing a picnic. Young lovers are perched under an arbor laden with apricot-colored roses, taking a selfie.

"Augusta Luise," I whisper to myself, and walk toward the roses, touching a waxy smooth petal, inhaling the crisp sweetness.

I cannot look at Bastien, but we fall into step together.

"Khalid was a suspected terrorist. The Iranian police contacted Interpol and Interpol contacted us—that's how it works. You have to understand, Caroline, that Interpol had been tracking Khalid for years—finally pinpointing where he planned to set up the terrorist branch. That's why I infiltrated Peugeot way back in 2007."

"With your wife," I say.

"I'm not married. I've never been married, Caroline."

I swallow and cannot keep the tears at bay. I'm swiping at them until he hands me a handkerchief. Of course. He can still keep up the charade if necessary.

"In 2011 I moved to Lourmarin. My job was to be the eyes on the ground. I even met Khalid once, earlier, in Aix. The Internet was buzzing with projections for the terrorist hub." He stops suddenly, and I turn to see his face, filled with remorse. "There are many parts of my job that I do not like."

"He kept hanging around." Martine's words echoed in my head. Malika was afraid, she saw him with Khalid. . . .

"Then Interpol got word of the exact date he was coming to visit Malika, and we set up the final arrangements for the sting. We were going to intercept Khalid and the others when they arrived. Malika and Lola were supposed to be leaving to join Jean-Claude somewhere that weekend. Everything was worked out. My job was to distract you, keep you away from the house, keep you safe. We knew all about your friendship with Lola." He meets my eyes, and I think he's begging me to believe him.

"But Khalid had found out about his aunt's and his cousin's conversion and had a personal mission on his mind. The terrorist hub could wait. He came to Lourmarin three days early, in disguise. No one knew—not the police, not Interpol, not his terrorist buddies, not Malika and Lola, who were just preparing to leave. . . ." Bastien looks away briefly. "He killed Malika and kidnapped Lola, taking her back to Iran. The sting flopped and the police were scrambling."

We're on our second lap around the park, and I'm still trying to grasp one thing. Bastien is with the French police.

"So you seduced me to keep me away from the house while Interpol or the police or someone tried to find out what had happened."

"Did I seduce you, Caroline?"

That same question that once again causes my heart to skip a beat. I look away, and Bastien continues.

"By the time you showed up at the Fourcade house, Khalid had come and gone. You and Salima got caught up in the search for Malika and Lola."

"You knew what I would find when I went there! All that blood!"

"No." He takes my hand. "No, I didn't know. Everyone was scrambling, searching. You have to understand, it was under-cover, Caroline."

I let loose of his hand.

"At that time Interpol didn't know about Malika's and Lola's conversions. We were simply trying to catch a terrorist. When the plan went all wrong, I was asked to become involved in trying to locate Lola and eventually help her escape from Iran."

"But why did you keep agreeing to see me each time I came to France? What did I have to do with your hunting for Khalid?"

"You are so determined, Caro. You turned over every stone to find your friend. I had to know exactly what you were doing; otherwise you might turn over one stone too many and discover the truth. It was dangerous. Don't think you weren't being fol-lowed. Khalid knew so many things about you."

Every time we met, it was only a pretense. Only a way to keep track of me. And make sure I didn't find Lola.

"And what makes it safe now?" I demand. "How do you know his cohorts won't come after Lola now?"

"Because Khalid is dead. His vendetta was personal. But Caroline, I had to keep you in my sight. I had to know." He meets my eyes and looks away. There is no seduction in his eyes, there is no sense of relief even, just sadness.

"If I could have done it a different way, I would have." Then he admits, "I'm sorry for our brief affair. That part I could have, I *should* have done differently. It was wrong."

It was a mistake.

He clears his throat and turns toward me again. "I can say nothing else except I am sorry, terribly sorry. I know it will take time, but I hope one day you can forgive me." His bland expression softens, and I see regret in his eyes. "And this: Please don't live with guilt. Nothing was your fault. Start over. You are worth it, Caroline. Whatever else you believe, believe this. You are worth it."

I force myself to give a tight smile. "Thank you for what you were trying to do. It's not your fault that Malika was killed and Lola was kidnapped. And it's not your fault that I . . . that I fell for you. That part really was just a horrible mistake. I was young and naïve. What if I hadn't gone with you to the jazz soirée that first night—what would you have done?"

He shrugs. "No need to ask."

"Oh, so maybe I would have been collateral damage?" I swear. "Well, I'm glad I agreed to the jazz—it's better than ending up dead!" My heart is beating so hard that I have to take a deep breath. "I'll say good-bye now, Bastien."

"*Bien sûr.*"

He's stolen years of my life and all he can say is *bien sûr*? Before he walks away, I ask, "What will you be doing now?"

He shrugs.

"Where do you really live?"

He shrugs again.

"I don't know anything about you, do I?"

His eyes lose their hardness, and the tenderness that I have seen before—the tenderness that's scared me—comes over him. "No, you don't know me," he says finally.

But I think I do. I think there are truths I know about him that he will not admit.

"Good-bye, Caro." He starts to place his hand on my cheek, but instead he turns away and is gone.

———

I am so stunned by Bastien's confession that I sit in the farmhouse for hours, not answering my phone or texts or emails from Jean-Claude. But I cannot do this to him. Finally I text him. *I'm okay. But you probably have already heard that from Bastien.*

Thank God! he texts back. *I was so worried. I have heard nothing from Bastien. What do you mean?*

I'm so sorry, Jean-Claude. I shouldn't have seen him, but I am okay. I'll explain later.

In that moment, I hate them all, Bastien and Jean-Claude and Stephen and Tracie and even Rasa. It is again my twisted reasoning, but each of them has played a part in keeping secrets from me.

For your own good. And for Lola's.

I'm pretty sure that inner voice in whispering truth. If I'll just accept it.

Man, this is hard. It's all hard.

But Lola is coming home.

The only thing that keeps me from trudging down to the wine cellar again is the thought of actually seeing Lola in three days.

I finally call the one person who can understand. Abbie answers immediately.

"Hey! How are you? I've been concerned," she says.

I am so relieved to hear her voice that I tell her the whole story, the story that Bastien has told me and the story I am living now because it is *my* story, one in which I will try to make the pieces fit so I can limp forward.

Abbie is there to speak truth. "You really are getting a new kind of freedom, Caroline. You've gotten the truth. I think that's a gift. You understand. It was twisted and grisly and horrible and heartbreaking, but it was for a higher good. And Bastien, however much you hate him now—perfectly understandable—he was in it for a good cause—to bring down a terrorist hub. And he tried to tell you, in his own way, that the two of you couldn't have a future. Somehow, even with all the lies, that seems, I don't know, noble. Anyway, don't undercover people, spies, don't they have to lie?"

"Don't you dare take his side!"

"Oh, Caro. I'm on your side. I'm just saying there was a reason. Say what you want, but I think it's a gift for you to know why."

Much later she says, "Remember, there's a fine line between love and hate."

And I don't know what she means.

———

I'm standing with Jean-Claude at the station when Lola's train pulls in. We search back and forth, craning our necks to find her as dozens of passengers spill onto the quay. I finally see her far in the distance, holding on to a man. When he turns around, my stomach plummets.

She is holding on to Bastien.

She drops her bags when she sees us and runs down the quay,

bumping into other passengers, and jumps into her father's arms, just like a five-year-old, just like the perfect ending scene in a movie. Then she grabs me so tightly I can hardly breathe. "Can you believe it? I'm home. I'm home!" She twirls around—reminding me of Rasa—but her smile is the same one from a decade ago. Her hair is shorter, and I see lines of fatigue and pain and a deep scar and other things I don't want to find across her face.

She lets go of me and goes back to where Bastien is approaching with her bags and holds on to him again, hugging him tightly. "Thank you. Thank you." He is clearly embarrassed, but Lola continues, "He saved my life, Papa! He saved my life."

She looks like a child beside her favorite teacher or a beloved uncle. And slowly, slowly, it dawns on me, at the same time as Jean-Claude. "You went to get Lola in Austria, right after we met at the restaurant. It really was you looking after her all this time."

Bastien's face is stone again, but I see the color in his cheeks. "Yes, that's correct."

Everything starts to spin and I'm reaching for something and the last thing I remember is Bastien catching me as I fall into his arms.

Bastien has left, and I'm lying in Lola's bedroom—the one she's never seen before, the one her father lovingly decorated in this new house with a prayer on his lips. And that prayer has been answered. Lola is finally home, a new house in a new village, but it is still her beloved Provence. We've talked into the wee hours of the morn—not about the past years, not about the horror. About *before*.

But finally Lola whispers, "It was never your fault, Caro. Never. You believe that now, don't you?"

I chew on my lip and nod.

She gives me a dark look. "They're evil, they're cruel, they're misguided. Khalid. And others." She hesitates. "You know he saved your life."

"What?"

"Bastien saved your life. He kept tabs on you so many times. Every time that you were looking for me, you were in danger."

"How do you know this?"

She sits up from where she's been sprawled out on the bed. "How do you think I know? He told me."

"All these years he's been telling you!"

"Yes, you idiot! Ever since he found me. Don't you think I was grateful to know?"

"And you believe him?"

"Wouldn't you choose to believe the person who saved your life? He saved my life, and he saved yours, and now we're both free to start again. We're going to start over, both of us. It's going to be okay. Please believe it."

I rub my hands over my eyes. "It'll take a while, but I'll try. I promise I'll try."

She hesitates.

"What is it?"

"Nothing." She shrugs.

"No. I can tell you have something more to say. You've got that look on your face when you have something you want to tell me but you don't quite dare."

We smile at each other because indeed this was part of our life all those years ago, reading each other's minds.

"Do you really want to hear?" Lola says.

"Yes, I do."

"Well then, here goes. Bastien really cares about you."

I sit up and grab a pillow, cuddling it to my chest like protection. "Oh, sure! Right! No, the truth is that he just seduces
everyone in sight. Did he seduce you too?"

She looks horrified. "No. He saved my life."

"Yeah, I get that. But evidently he saved my life too by seducing me."

He never seduced me. *"I'm not a safe bet. I don't want you
to be sad, Caro."*

"You're obsessed with Bastien."

"Don't undercover people, spies, don't they have to lie?"

Finally I manage, "Someday I'll be thankful for him, for
what he did for you. But right now I'm just . . ." Heartbroken.
Confused. Obsessed. "I'm just . . ." I cannot continue.

Lola keeps silent. I sniffle and whisper, "I believe that he
cared; I believe that he does his work well. He's a really good
spy." But a really rotten bet as a lover.

I need to calm down, I need to breathe deeply, I need to
concentrate on the joy of being with Lola. But anger against
him is stealing my joy. "It's all been horrible."

She takes my hands and looks me in the eyes. "Horrible
things were done to me too, you know."

I see the jagged scar on her cheek. I grab her then. "I'm sorry!
I'm so sorry! I'm making it about me, when it's about you. I'm
so sorry!" I weep, literally weep for the pain and anguish and
selfishness and joy and awe, all stirred together.

We sit on the bed, sobbing in each other's arms, for a long
time.

We both sleep twelve hours straight. Jean-Claude has been
patiently waiting for us to wake up. He treats us to croissants
and *pains au chocolat* and fresh baguettes and real French coffee, and after he hears Lola's contented sigh, we go for a stroll
around the village of Cavaillon.

Lola says, "You do know why Bastien invited you back this time, right? He told you, didn't he?"

I shrug. "He's told me so many lies, I can't keep them all straight."

"He got word that Khalid had been apprehended. He made the plans to bring me to France. And . . . and he wrote you. Because he was going to explain it all to you. He was going to tell you the truth. It was safe, and he could finally tell the truth. Except, Khalid escaped. And so when you showed up to get more news from him, he couldn't tell you."

But I'm not convinced. "I guess he revealed all that to you?"

"Yes. He was devastated to lead you on, make you think he had news of me."

"Well, it just got all screwed up again, didn't it? How tragic!" I sound as cynical as Bastien.

"Caro . . ."

"Look, if you think he's so great, you can have him! He's no saint, you know. And I've heard you've become rather saintly!"

The words fly out of my mouth and immediately I see how I've wounded Lola.

"I'm sorry. That was a horrible, horrible thing to say." I take Lola's hands. "You're the one I care about. You're here. We got the miracle, after all. You're home. You're safe. Yes, to starting over. But please, please, don't talk to me anymore about Bastien. It's too painful and it brings out the absolute worst in me. I'll get over him in time. But not yet."

"You're right, Caro. I'm sorry too. I won't mention him again."

Later, as we're meandering through the village, one as quaint as any I've walked through on the Camino, Lola says, "Rasa told me about your time on the Camino. You know her story;

you know what she believes. You know that I believe it too. I trust Jesus. I cannot explain it, Caro. I don't know the why of these many years of suffering. But I do know one thing. I was never alone."

You are never alone on the Camino.

You are never alone.

I was never alone.

I decide to stay in Lourmarin for a while, at my parents' place. I told them I'd pay the Airbnb rate, and they laughed and said that could wait. Lola will take turns between Jean-Claude's home in Cavaillon and ours. We have a lot of catching up to do. Stephen says I can work from here. He teases me and says the photos from the Camino have proved my talent.

On Sunday we're going to have a party. A celebration for Lola. My parents and Ashley are coming down to the house tomorrow. Papa will take out some of his best bottles. I've stocked the house with LaCroix and Perrier and am making something festive and nonalcoholic. Jean-Claude will arrive on Thursday. Stephen and Tracie are flying over from Atlanta on Friday. Stephen, my big brother who works for the good of refugees and loves me enough to pay for rehab and protect me from myself. And refuses to tell me the truth when it would lead to harm.

Truth is a hard word.

It's been a week since I met Bastien at the café and learned the truth, the twisted, heartbreaking, and ultimately lifesaving truth. My anger has waned. I understand now what Abbie meant about the fine line between love and hate. I wish I didn't care about him, but I do. I know it will take me a long time to get over Bastien. But I don't hate him anymore.

Abbie has sent me photos from La Rochelle—all kinds of

selfies of her and the cross-stitch and ancient-looking towers and half-timbered houses. And a lighthouse.

A lighthouse! Le Phare! she texts and adds a bunch of emojis.

Bobby has sent me photos from a museum in Paris. He's there with his grandmother's friend, Jean-Paul, a very sophisticated looking sixtysomething Frenchman. There are selfies of the two of them in front of his grandmother's painting, *The Swan House*. That makes me smile.

Rasa has walked me around the House of Hope, giving me what she calls a Whatever tour. She means WhatsApp.

But whatever.

I leave the house, inhaling the scents of lavender and Augusta Luise and herbs as I walk through the garden, and I think of what Lola said.

I was never alone.

I'm never alone.

I know it's true now. I've been pursued and caught. I'll go to Le Phare on Sunday. I'll sit and listen to the young pastor, and I'll thank God for Lola, who'll be sitting beside me. I'll go because I want to go. I'll go because I'm on a journey.

But today I walk to the café, take a seat at the table, and take out the letter that just arrived in the mail. When I open it, I catch that scent of Aramis again. I stare at Bastien's handwritten note.

Salut, dear Caro,

I don't think I will see you again, but I wanted to tell you one more thing before I say good-bye.

I can imagine his eyes tender, begging me for something.

I'm really horribly sorry for everything. I wanted to tell you the truth a hundred times.

I slap the letter on the table and think, *That would have been nice!* Couldn't he have said, "Look, I can't explain things, but I'm watching out for Lola"? Or something? Anything?

He tried! He told me he wasn't a safe bet, that he was only good for me in small doses.

I look out to where the waiter is gathering dirty wine glasses from the table across the way, then glance back down at the letter.

I should not have continued to see you. I should have asked for someone else to be put on the job when I saw that you were becoming . . . when we were becoming friends.

I close my eyes and admit it again. When I was becoming obsessed with Bastien.

It was wrong. But that's not what I need to say. It started wrong and it's ended wrong, but my dear Caro, I didn't want you to go through your life thinking everything was a mistake.

It was a mistake.

You aren't a mistake, dear Caro. You're amazing. You are worth it. I do not think Brett is right for you, but someday, someone will be. Wait for him.

I believe we became friends, dear Caro, but now you have Lola, your best friend, back. And she is a very special girl. You are free now, Caro. No guilt. No shame. No mistake. Please live that way. For Lola. For me. But mostly for you.

Ciao,

Bastien

A few minutes later, Lola joins me at the café. When I hold up the letter, she gives me a sad smile. "How awful was it?"

I give a shrug. "It was only slightly awful." I replicate her smile. "But it was kind of him to write me, to tell me good-bye."

We let the awkward silence surround us, nothing more to say.

Lola hears a ping on her phone. She glances at it and smiles. "This just in from Rasa." She clicks on her Instagram feed and there is Rasa, holding on to Bobby with the Eiffel Tower in the background. Rasa has written, *Flinging one last time before school starts.*

We laugh. "Young love," I say.

We each order a citron pressé and when they arrive, we clink our glasses together as the sun beats down on us. "To a new beginning," Lola says.

"Yes. To the next step on our journey."

CHAPTER

27

ABBIE

I spend my first three days alone in La Rochelle, a jewel of a town on the west coast of France. In the sixteenth century it was a safe place for a burgeoning French Huguenot population. It had its own governance and was prospering until a new king of France, Louis XIII, grew afraid and ordered Cardinal Richelieu to subjugate the town.

Bill had given me this history lesson—it was part of his fascination with his ancestor René de Laudonnière of Fort Caroline fame, who passed away peacefully in La Rochelle at the end of the sixteenth century, several decades before what became known as the Great Siege of 1627–28. At the beginning of the siege, La Rochelle had a population of 27,000, the large majority Huguenots. Fourteen months later, there were only 5,000 survivors.

I stand on those narrow streets and admire the arches that seem to go on forever on either side, architecture dating back to the twelfth century. My guidebook gives me all the statistics. How did the Huguenots hold out for so long when an army of 7,000 soldiers, 600 horses, and 24 cannons assaulted them? When French engineers isolated the city with fortifications that were manned by an army of 30,000 men? When an enormous seawall, a dam almost a mile long, was erected, blocking all seaward access between the city and the harbor? No supplies could get into La Rochelle.

I imagine the Huguenots trapped within the city walls, slowly starving to death with no place to bury their dead. When they finally surrendered, it was because literally four-fifths of the population had either been murdered, starved to death, or died from disease.

There's a famous painting of the siege, *Cardinal Richelieu on the Dam of La Rochelle* by Henri Motte, that's in all the kids' history books in France. It shows an enormous dam, with warships in the background, making it impossible for provisions to get to the starving Huguenots in La Rochelle. And in the foreground, in bold, striking contrast to the darkness of the dam and the sky and the sea, stands Cardinal Richelieu in his billowing, bright red cardinal's cloak, arms folded across his chest, watching the destruction.

"Horrible old Cardinal Richelieu"—that was how Bill always referred to him, when he talked about this history that fascinated him so.

Oh, Bill, I wish you were here. I wish you could see this too.

All the city's fortifications were demolished during the siege except for the town's three towers.

I stare at those towers now from where I'm standing by the port: the Chain Tower, the Saint Nicholas Tower, and the Lantern Tower. This last, the one farthest out toward the ocean, looks like the spire on a gothic cathedral. After the siege of the city some brave, surviving Huguenots escaped with the help of the light from this tower, making their way toward England, the Netherlands, and America.

I make my way up the spiraling staircase of the Lantern Tower. From my perch up so high, I have a breathtaking view of the city.

I think of another song we used to sing at the little French fellowship I attended in 1993.

Like a beacon in the night your light shows us the way
To the harbor of your arms from harm to your embrace

I'm here at the safe harbor in La Rochelle, but more importantly, I'm here in God's safe harbor again. How did that happen? I guess it's when I finally admitted what I had to do: relinquish control after a long battle. Oh, my battle was relatively absurd, not worthy of being compared to religious wars. Still, it was *my* war, and to win my war I had to lay down my heart and stretch out my hands and say, "I'll take a deep breath and wait. I'll give up control. I'll trust You, Lord."

Bill wanted to come here to trace his history, to learn from it. I'm thankful to see it for him, almost as if he's standing beside me. But I'm thankful to experience La Rochelle for a completely different reason. I'm here to be reminded that I am not in control. I am doing my part, and I am relinquishing the rest.

Deep breath. That's what Caroline would say.

Stay in the present. That's Diana.

And from far out somewhere on the wind I hear the voice of Miss Abigail. *You don't have to be perfect because He is, and He loves you.*

Each day after traipsing around La Rochelle, I drive my rental car across the three-kilometer-long bridge onto the island, Ile de Ré, where I'm staying at night. I have a charming little studio with stone alcoves filled with paperback novels in French and English and a light that seeps in to warm me. There's a bistro table in the alleyway, where I sit every afternoon and sip a glass of wine.

The next days are just me and my bike, which I ride on the island's cobbled streets with the whitewashed houses and shops on either side punctuated with varying shades of heavy green shutters, what the French call *volets*. I ride out to the port, which is teeming with people sitting at the outdoor restaurants, eating mussels and French fries, talking happily among themselves.

Vacances! These happy couples and families are on vacation, their last hoopla before *la rentrée*—the beginning of school in just a few short days. But I'm here to figure out the rest of my life.

On my third morning I place the Ziploc with my cross-stitch and graph in my now-clean Vera Bradley pouch, unlock my bike, and turn toward the port, bumping along the cobbled stones and then riding out to the beach, where the ocean is at low tide and the path is filled with pedestrians and bikers. Boot-clad men and women are standing far out in the mud searching for oysters.

I ride along this lovely path until a sign tells me that bikes are not permitted any further. So I lock my bike against a weathered post and keep walking, bag tucked tight under my arm. I'm not going to lose it again!

The sea is out far to my left, the sun is hidden by frothy white clouds, and a fierce wind pushes me along. This island is wild; so different from the pristine look of Hilton Head in South Carolina, where my family has vacationed for forty years. Wildflowers toss themselves frantically in the wind, and instead of a beach filled with sand, the one far below the path on my left is rocky. The water changes colors from muddy brown to deep, deep green to aquamarine and sapphire and sparkly turquoise.

"Okay, Lord," I whisper. I am completely alone. Just me and the Holy Spirit. The path reminds me of parts of the Camino. I think about all that's happened, all I've learned in the past six weeks. I'm ready for a new beginning. I believe I have indeed "gotten Abbie back." I have slowed down. I have learned gratitude again. I have soaked in the kindness of friends, and I have seen that I cannot control much of anything. I have released Bobby, Jason, and Bill in a way that I'd never imagined possible.

And trust. Oh, yes. I am learning to trust the Lord again. It comes on the heels of letting go. I can either grab tight and drive the people I love crazy, or I can let go and trust.

A breath prayer.

Breathe in: *Lord, I relinquish control.*

Breathe out: *And I trust You.*

I've been forming an idea about the future. I will go home. I will move into the loft, and I will care for my parents there, if needed. I will let Bill decide about us. I will not beg him to come back. I sent him an email three days ago.

Dear Bill,

I've walked about two hundred kilometers, with plenty of time to reflect as well as time to pray and interact with other pilgrims. I am writing to thank you. Thank you for leaving so that I had to face the truth. Thank you for encouraging me to let Bobby take a gap year. Thank you for not answering my desperate texts and emails, and thank you for writing me your thoughts and feelings.

I'm so sorry, Bill, for the way I controlled and manipulated you and the boys. I will be working on these things

when I return home. But I will not ask you to come back.
I have seen myself that you need room to grow. I do love
you very much. I have always loved you—I just didn't
know how to get beyond myself to show you. I discovered
that on this pilgrimage, over and over. And so I'm writing
to say I love you enough to let you go, to trust you even as
I say good-bye. I will pray for you every day for the rest
of my life, but I will not clutch you.

Abbs

I retrace my steps and unlock my bike and pedal across the
island to a beach called Sainte Marie de Ré. As I walk along the
shoreline, sidestepping the large stones that have been washed
white by the sea, I hear a sound. There's not another human
in sight, no boom box making music. But I hear it again and
again. A trilling.

And then I realize it's the music the tide makes as it rushes in
and then draws back over the rocks. It sounds like a special kind
of roaring, loud and beautiful, like hundreds of wind chimes,
like a thousand children clapping their hands exuberantly.

I think of what Jesus said when the religious rulers protested
the people's hosannas: "'I tell you,' he replied. 'If they keep
quiet, even the stones will cry out!'"

I step into the chilly water and laugh and then shout over
God's rock symphony, "I won't keep silent, God. You've
guarded my going out and my coming in. I won't keep silent.
Even though I cannot know the next steps, I am here. I am
present with You now. I won't keep silent."

I perch on a rock and take out the cross-stitch and feel that
chill, that prickle of amazement at its miraculous journey. "And
now, what am I supposed to do with this?"

Finish it.

I don't know if the tide and rocks are shouting this or if it is the Spirit blowing the thought into my mind, but I will comply.

Of course I'll finish it.

I just have one last emblem to stitch. Number fifty.

For all these years I have tried to give Bill what he needed—or what I thought he needed. Yes, I have organized his life because it needed organizing. I turn over my two-year-long project and stare at the perfectly crossed stitches on the back. There are no loose threads; it is indeed a work of art. I may never give it to Bill. He may not even want it, because it's filled with the memories of twenty years of us.

I've known for a while what this last pattern will be. I look at my graph, so carefully gridded and plotted. Not only do I know *what* I am going to stitch, but I know *how* I'm going to stitch it—as Abbie the thirteen-year-old did, stitching her very first project. It was a Bible verse for Miss Abigail: "Delight yourself in the Lord and he will give you the desires of your heart."

Far from perfectly done, but every stitch was made with love.

So I stitch as the sun gets high in that almost fierce blue sky. A warm early September breeze billows my blouse while the ocean tickles my toes.

I stitch my love for Bill, for what I have learned from him, for the life we've had together. For the way he gently and good-naturedly mocked my organization when it became frantic and controlled and unhealthy.

I stitch it with love because now I see his love for me. His leaving forced me to a crisis. The crisis has been going on for several years, but his leaving forced me to acknowledge it.

I whisper to the kids, to the sky, to the Lord, to Bill, "I've gotten Abbie back now."

Will my husband come back? I don't know, but as I put down my cross-stitch after three hours at work, I am pleased. La Tour de la Lanterne—La Rochelle's lighthouse—stands at the bottom of the canvas right beside Bill's name. When I turn the canvas over, that one gridded square is a tangled mess.

I take out my phone and snap a picture of the front and of the back, and I send it to Diana. In the subject line I simply type, *I'm back*.

I make my way back to the little studio, pedaling on the bike, the cross-stitch wrapped and covered in the basket, a smile on my lips. I inhale the fragrance of the ocean, the salt air, the slight breeze, my nose ruffling up as I pass the fish market.

I have three more days here on the island. That I feel calm instead of heartbroken, grateful instead of bitter, is a miracle in itself.

When I get back to the cobbled alleyway that leads to my little Airbnb, I see two of my elderly neighbors at my door. They catch sight of me and begin talking over each other, so that I understand nothing. They are gesticulating, pointing out to the road I just came from.

"What?" I say, confused.

They are still chattering, and then I hear someone calling my name. Or part of my name. The name that only my husband uses.

I twist around and there he is, towering over me, dressed in his ratty T-shirt and shorts and leather sandals.

"Hey, Abbs." His face softens, and he whispers, "Surprise."

My eyes widen. "What are you doing here?"

"Coming for my birthday celebration." He gives a little shrug. "Your mom told me where to find you."

My mouth has gone completely dry. I eye him warily, heart ramming my ribs. "But . . . why are you here?"

"I told you. To celebrate my birthday!"

"Your birthday isn't for another month."

"I want to celebrate early. In the place I've always wanted to visit. With my wife."

The neighbors are still standing in the alleyway, as I try to take in the vision of Bill. I prop the bike against the wall, take the cross-stitch out of the basket, and unlock the studio door. He follows me inside.

"I can't believe you're here," I whisper, as I push the door closed. I want to melt into his arms, but instead I say, "What about the apartment in Chicago?"

He cocks his head. "I rented it for the time I was working there. It was cheaper than staying in a hotel."

"But you moved all your stuff there."

He shakes his head. "What? No, Abbs. Where'd you get that idea? I moved all my stuff into the house on Beverly. We're trading houses with your parents for a while."

"We are? *We* are?"

"Yep. It's decided. I decided it for all of us." He holds out his hand to me, and I take it.

Bill made a decision! Bill decided for us.

He leads me to the little sofa. "I understand that one of the reasons you bought the loft was because your father helped design it. It was a way to hold on to a part of him. I get that now. But your parents are really enjoying living there. So I told them about my plan. Your dad liked it a lot. It's all decided."

I see it in his eyes. And then I know it in my very soul. *We have a lot to work out, Abbs, but I'm here, and I love you.*

He sits down beside me. I'm still holding the cross-stitch pouch. "Happy birthday, then. This is for you," I whisper, and I set my masterpiece in his lap.

He takes the canvas and runs his hands across the surface. He nibbles his lip, a habit he has when he's at a loss for words. He looks from the canvas to me to the canvas and back at me. He rubs my cheek with the back of his hand. I begin to cry.

"I've missed you, Abbs."

"I've missed you too."

The cross-stitch slips off my lap onto the floor as he takes me into his arms.

Author's Note

I asked Nate and Faith Walter, the directors of Pilgrim House, to give a brief history of the Camino and of their work with pilgrims. Here's what they said:

The Camino de Santiago pilgrimage has exploded in popularity in recent years, with over three hundred thousand pilgrims making the journey to Santiago de Compostela last year. For more than one thousand years it has been an important pilgrimage in the Catholic tradition. These days, people of many faiths and cultures walk the Camino for different reasons. One common thread is the many pilgrims who mark a life transition by going on pilgrimage. Some are leaving one job and starting another, some have just graduated from school, and others are grieving the loss of a loved one. By creating time to walk and pound out the miles, pilgrims can reflect on their lives and have solitude while also meeting others who are walking for their own reasons. All in all, walking the Camino can be a deeply spiritual, personal, and communal experience.

Being pilgrims ourselves, our team wanted to offer a place in Santiago where fellow pilgrims could continue to gather together, find solitude, and connect with God, even as their pilgrimages were coming to a close. In 2014, we opened the Pilgrim House Welcome Center, deeply influenced by Henri Nouwen's vision for hospitality in his book *Reaching Out*. Pilgrim House provides hospitality, practical support, and spiritual resources to pilgrims finishing the Camino. Over the years, we've seen the importance of taking the time to engage with whatever has been stirring in our hearts, and we hope that through Pilgrim House pilgrims find a welcoming place to do just that.

In our experience, pilgrimage is best understood as a state of the heart that is enriched by a physical pilgrimage. May pilgrims of the heart everywhere resonate with this traditional Celtic blessing:

> "May the peace of the Lord Christ go with you,
> wherever he may send you.
> May he guide you through the wilderness,
> protect you through the storm.
> May he bring you home rejoicing
> at the wonders he has shown you.
> May he bring you home rejoicing
> once again into our doors."

Pilgrim House
Santiago de Compostela, Spain

Learn more about Pilgrim House at www.pilgrimhousesantiago.com.

Discussion Questions

1. One of Abbie's main issues is her need to control. What memories of the past help Abbie along her journey toward letting go? Have you had life circumstances that caused fear and a need to control? If so, how have you handled these?

2. I was writing these discussion questions during the Coronavirus pandemic. Discuss how the loss of control and the act of being confined for weeks on end affected you.

3. Abbie says, "How perfectly ironic, that what drove Bill away was me trying so hard to make sure he never ever left." Have you ever driven people you love the most away by trying to hold them too tightly?

4. Have you heard of spiritual direction? What is your response to spiritual disciplines that seem unorthodox? Have you ever tried Lectio Divina or breath prayers?

5. Diana, the spiritual director, tells Abbie that "So much

has a chance to get through to us when everything else is taken away." Do you agree or disagree, and why?

6. Which of the characters in the story can you most relate to and why? Whose faith journey can you most relate to and why?

Abbie   Swannee (Mary Swan)

Bill   Bastien

Bobby   Stephen

Caroline   Tracie

Rasa

7. Have you ever had someone who became a mentor to you, like Miss Abigail? Describe the relationship and the benefits of having a mentor. Do you have or have you ever had an accountability partner? If so, what was the experience like? How is this different from having a mentor? Discuss different ways that people overcome addictions.

8. Have you ever experienced something traumatic, as Caro, Rasa, and Bobby have, that destabilized you for years to come? Have you found help and healing? If so, how?

9. Caro says, "I'd heard it said that the Camino strips you bare, forces you to look at the junk inside, and then gives you a new start." Have you had any sort of experience that stripped you bare? Did it ultimately end up being a positive or negative thing?

10. Rasa says, "It is the first thing I see. The soul. Not the face or the color of the skin. Not the sound of the voice. First, it is the soul. I see it through the eyes some-

times. And I always, always want to see Isa in the face."
Have you ever met someone like Rasa? Does the way
she lives out her faith attract or repel you?

11. Discuss Bobby's passion to become a painter. Was
Abbie wrong to want him to do the next logical thing?
Discuss ways in which your passions/dreams as a young
person were encouraged or discouraged and the effect
that had on you.

12. Bobby says, "The idea of letting go of responsibility
that isn't really mine came from the therapist I saw after
Anna. But I've never done a very good job of putting it
into practice." How do you distinguish between responsibility that is or is not yours to take? Do you have a
hard time letting go of responsibility?

13. Bastien lies to Caro ultimately to protect her and others. Stephen withholds information from his sister for
the same reason. Is lying ever acceptable? Why or why
not? Give specific examples to support your position.

14. Discuss the metaphor of Abbie's perfect cross-stitch
contrasted with the metaphor of the underside of a tapestry being a tangled mess. What does the way Abbie
stitches the lighthouse emblem at the end of the novel
represent? Have you ever felt like you lost yourself? If
so, how did you get yourself back?

15. Abbie says "It's not like it's a new idea, what confession
does for the soul, but I haven't been practicing it in a
long time. Not true spit-out-the-worst-of-me confession. And I haven't really given anything over to the
Lord in a long time either." Do you regularly practice
confession in some form? What do you think of the
idea of giving things over to the Lord?

16. One of the main themes of the novel is pilgrimage. Had you heard of the Camino before reading *The Promised Land*? Does the idea of pilgrimage attract or repel you? Why? Have you ever done some sort of pilgrimage?

17. Characters from *The Swan House, The Dwelling Place,* and *The Long Highway Home* appear in this story. Do you like or dislike when an author brings in characters you have gotten to know in one of his or her previous works?

Acknowledgments

The Inspiration

Ten years ago, the president of One Collective, the faith-based organization we've been serving with for over thirty-five years, asked Paul and me to become "Pastors to Workers," providing pastoral care to our colleagues who serve in Europe and beyond. Quite a change from our work in French churches.

On one of the first pastoral care visits, we met a team of young people working hard to open a ministry center for pilgrims walking the Camino. Over the years we have visited these colleagues and watched with joy as Pilgrim House became a reality: a place at the end of the Camino in Santiago, Spain, where pilgrims can relax and process the journey they've been on with Christians who welcome them no matter their faith journey.

I give a big shout out to Pilgrim House directors, Nate and Faith Walter. I admire your faith, your perseverance, and your beautiful dream, which has become a reality.

A shout-out also to many other colleagues who have been involved in ministry to pilgrims over the years: Jeremiah and

Danielle Fox, Anne Hughes, Sarah Marshall, Mariano Pineda, Fanny Benitez, Gale Sherry, Michael and Carli Snyder.

Two years ago, with multiple ideas running around in my head for a novel about the Camino, I decided to walk a part of this pilgrimage myself. I started in Le Puy-en-Velay, and like dear Abbie, walked a few days alone. But of course, as every pilgrim learns, I was never alone on the Camino. Many of the scenes recorded in this novel were inspired by my time on the Camino as well as stories I heard from other pilgrims. If you'd like to see photos from my journey, please visit my Pinterest board for *The Promised Land*.

Another shout-out to our hardworking colleagues at The Oasis and the House of Hope, refugee ministry centers in Austria that we have had the privilege of visiting throughout the years. The true stories I've heard about how many refugees have found hope and redemption have inspired my stories.

At the same time as Paul and I began our new ministry of pastoral care, a mutual friend introduced us to John and Letha Kerl, who were living in Lyon and doing pastoral care for another organization. The Kerls became our informal mentors. Letha also became my spiritual director, a lovely practice that has gained popularity in recent years. I have found this practice and the spiritual disciplines incorporated within to be very life-giving for my soul, ever spurring me along in my walk with Jesus and helping me accept in deeper ways His extravagant love for me. A huge virtual hug to you, Letha!

And those Huguenots! They seem to find their way into many of my stories. One of the original 'ah-has' for this story came when dear friend and fellow Francophile, Ruth Ann Leduc, posted photos on Facebook from her visit to Fort Caroline. So I dragged hubby Paul to Ponte Vedra to visit another dear friend and Francophile, Margaret DeBorde, while

I researched Fort Caroline. A big *merci* to you both, Ruth Ann and Margaret.

During my thirty-plus years in France, I've heard many friends talk about the beautiful city of La Rochelle and its Huguenot history. So I grabbed hubby Paul again and we traipsed across France to the Atlantic Ocean and vacationed at Ile de Ré while researching La Rochelle. Yes, being a writer certainly has its perks—especially where research is concerned!

Finally, I knew that several of my beloved characters from other novels needed center stage in this one. I've always known there would be four novels in The Swan House Series, although each novel stands on its own and can be read without the others. (They've also been written during the course of twenty years!) *The Swan House* is Mary Swan's story, *The Dwelling Place* is her youngest daughter, Ellie's story, and now *The Promised Land*, is where oldest daughter, Abbie, gets the spotlight. Last, but not least, *The Wren's Nest,* a novel featuring Mary Swan's middle daughter, Nan, will hopefully find its wings sometime in the not-too-distant future.

Bobby, first introduced in *The Swan House* and *The Dwelling Place* has grown up and found his voice in this story. Caro is a brand-new friend, but Stephen, Tracie, and Rasa wandered into this story from a few years back in *The Long Highway Home*. Finally, both Mary Swan (Swannee) and Miss Abigail had their part to play, with Robbie Bartholomew (Granddad) and Rachel Abrams giving winks in the story too.

Special thanks:

To my agent and friend, Chip MacGregor. *Enfin les pommes de terre sont cuites!* Always thankful for your wise counsel, good humor, and unfailing support.

To Dave Horton, VP at Bethany House Publishers. My publishing journey began with you twenty-five years ago. I and all the other authors and staff at Bethany House will certainly miss you! But you've earned your retirement, so please enjoy some Clairette de Die with Jennifer. I can never say it enough: *Merci!*

To the wonderful team at Bethany House Publishers, I am thrilled to be working with you again. A big shout-out to Noelle Chew, Kate Deppe, Elizabeth Frazier, Amy Lokkesmoe, Serena Hanson, and Brooke Vikla. *Merci* for all you do behind the scenes. Your expertise is invaluable and reassuring, and I've enjoyed spending time with several of you in person.

To my editor *par excellence* and dear friend, LB Norton, I told you not to retire, but alas, as so often happens with the characters in my novels, you are not obeying! I'll miss you. It's been a great ride together and so glad we got to work on this novel together.

To Jori Hanna, so thankful to have you on board as my marketing assistant. You are delightful, savvy, and young, all of which are invaluable to me!

To David Durham and David Parks, both gifted musicians whose music has blessed my soul, starting during my college days and continuing to the present, thank you for giving me permission to use the lyrics from your songs, "Like a Beacon" and "Be Still," respectively.

To Jere W. Goldsmith IV, my precious and over-the-top generous daddy, and Doris Ann Musser, my energetic and lovely mother-in-law, you continue to model resilience, good humor, optimism, and courage in the face of aging and all the craziness that 2020 has thrown at us. To you and to all the others in the Goldsmith and Musser families, thank you for your support throughout all our years on the mission field and my years writing.

To my many friends on both sides of the Atlantic and around the world who pray for the work of my hands, I can't begin to name you all, so I won't try, but please be reminded that your prayers have been answered each time I birth a book.

To my family at One Collective, thank you for receiving what Paul and I have to offer with grace and for allowing me to pen my stories too.

To my sons, Andrew and Chris, one of life's greatest gifts is to watch the children I cared for become loving, responsible young adults who use their passion, gifting, professional skills, and faith to care for others. I remain in awe of the young men you have become. Thank you for the lovely way you care for me too. To Lacy, I am constantly in awe of your equanimity amidst the happy bedlam of four kids, a wild husband, numerous chickens and rabbits, a dog, a cat, a garden, and a forest.

To Jesse, Nadja'Lyn, Quinn, and Baby Lena Sky, your Mamie loves you and likes you over and over and over again!

To Paul, always to you, thanks for tagging along with me on this writing journey and also for encouraging me to fly on my own. Thank you for helping me let go of control and trust more and more in our great big and generous God. Thank you for loving me so much and so well. *Je t'aime tant.*

To my dear readers, your make my day over and over again with your comments and photos on social media and your heartfelt emails. And what a joy to get to meet some of you in person.

And finally, to Jesus, my Savior and Lord, thank You for calling me onto this pilgrimage when I was a child and guarding my going out and my coming in for all these decades. I owe everything to You—my life, my love, my all.

Elizabeth Musser writes "entertainment with a soul" from her writing chalet—tool shed—outside Lyon, France. Elizabeth's highly acclaimed, bestselling novel *The Swan House* was named one of Amazon's Top Christian Books of the Year in 2001 and one of Georgia's Top Ten Novels of the Past 100 Years. All of Elizabeth's novels have been translated into multiple languages and have been international bestsellers.

For over thirty years, Elizabeth and her husband, Paul, have been involved in missions work in Europe with One Collective, formerly International Teams. The Mussers have two sons, a daughter-in-law, and four grandchildren.

Find out more about Elizabeth and her novels at www .elizabethmusser.com.

Sign Up for Elizabeth's Newsletter

Keep up to date with Elizabeth's news on book releases and events by signing up for her email list at elizabethmusser.com.

More from Elizabeth Musser

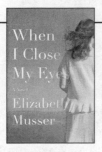

Famous author Josephine Bourdillon is in a coma, her memories surfacing as her body fights to survive. But those around her are facing their own battles: Henry Hughes, who agreed to kill her for hire out of desperation, is uncertain how to finish the job now, and her teenage daughter, Paige, is overwhelmed by fear. Can grace bring them all into the light?

When I Close My Eyes

You May Also Like . . .

Mary has always taken for granted the advantages of her family's wealth, but when a tragedy that touches all of Atlanta sends her reeling in grief, she's challenged to reach out to the less fortunate as a way to ease her pain. When she meets Carl, everything changes and together they endeavor to uncover a mystery, learning more than they could have imagined.

The Swan House by Elizabeth Musser
elizabethmusser.com

Forced to sell his family farm after sacrificing everything, 63-year-old Gerrit Laninga no longer knows what to do with himself. 15-year-old Rae Walters has growing doubts about The Plan her parents set to help her follow in her father's footsteps. When their paths cross just as they need a friend the most, Gerrit's and Rae's lives change in unexpected ways.

The Sowing Season by Katie Powner
katiepowner.com

After a life-altering car accident, one night changes everything for three women. As their lives intersect, they can no longer dwell in the memory of who they've been. Can they rise from the wreck of the worst moments of their lives to become who they were meant to be?

More Than We Remember by Christina Suzann Nelson
christinasuzannnelson.com

⬥ BETHANY HOUSE